Dreams of My Heart

"Oh my, an Irish marriage of convenience in the wilds of the West? Be still my heart! Fortunately, the heart never stills while immersed in this tender love story of a shotgun marriage gone a-right. This is a tale that sweeps you from heartbreak to hope with every turn of the page. Without question, *Dreams of My Heart* is a dream come true for lovers of historical romance."

Julie Lessman, award-winning author of Irish family sagas including The Daughters of Boston, Heart of San Francisco, and Isle of Hope series.

"With her typical humor-laced warmth, Barbara Scott delights readers with a beautiful historical romance that melts the heart and makes one pine for the faith, strength and tenacity of the old West. A true five-star read from beginning to end."

Award-winning, bestselling author **Ruth Logan Herne**

Take one feisty heroine, add a fine hero, dump them into an impossible situation, add plenty of twists and turns and you have a winner of a novel you can't wait to share with your friends.

Lauraine Snelling, best-selling author of the Historical Red River (Blessing) series

Dreams of My Heart

Dreams of My Heart

Reluctant Brides series
Book one

BY BARBARA J. SCOTT

Dreams of My Heart
Published by Mountain Brook Ink
White Salmon, WA U.S.A.

The website addresses shown in this book are not intended in any way to be or imply an endorsement on the part of Mountain Brook Ink, nor do we vouch for their content.

This story is a work of fiction. All characters and events are the product of the author's imagination. Any resemblance to any person, living or dead, is coincidental.

The author is represented by and this book is published in association with the literary agency of WordServe Literary Group, Ltd., www.wordserveliterary.com

Scripture quotations are taken from the King James Version of the Bible. Public domain.
ISBN 978-1-943959-40-2

The Team: Miralee Ferrell, Nikki Wright, Cindy Jackson
Cover Design: Indie Cover Design, Lynnette Bonner Designer

Mountain Brook Ink is an inspirational publisher offering fiction you can believe in.
Printed in the United States of America

Dedicated to the son of my heart,
David M. Scott

ACKNOWLEDGMENTS

My deepest appreciation goes to my forever BFF Gwen Ellis who for years regaled me with her stories of growing up in Deer Lodge, Montana. When the idea for *Dreams of My Heart* first captured my imagination, I knew the story had to be set in Deer Lodge to honor her and the men and women who had the courage and fortitude to weave their legacies into the fabric of our nation. If you would like to know more about Montana and Gwen's childhood, her book *Montana's Child: A Memoir of Life in Big Sky Country*, was published in 2015 and is available at Amazon.com. Thank you for reading my manuscript, Gwen, and for spotting any errors in the setting and history of the area. Any mistakes are my own.

I'd also like to thank my dear friend and agent Greg Johnson, the founder of WordServe Literary Group, who believed in my story from the beginning and suggested Mountain Brook Ink as its home. The team there comprised of Miralee Ferrell, Nikki Wright, Lynnette Bonner, and Cindy Jackson have taken *Dreams of My Heart* under their wing and nurtured it through the publishing process.

My deepest love and appreciation is given to my husband Mike, who has always believed in me, even when I didn't believe in myself.

Thank you, sweet Jesus, for your enduring love and for sending your Holy Spirit to help me in telling this story. I couldn't have done it without you. Lord God, Master Creator, may you be glorified in every word.

Chapter One

Deer Lodge
Montana Territory, 1875

"THAT'S AS FAR AS YE'LL BE comin' onto my land, mister." Kate O'Brien trained her shotgun dead center at the man riding toward her. "You can turn your horse around and head back where you came from. Tell Rafe Hamilton I'll never marry him, and he'll have to kill me to take my land."

Standing on the top step of her porch, close enough to make out the stranger's scruffy dark beard and the gun strapped to his side, fear gripped Kate's belly. For the first time since her brother died, she found herself a woman alone in Montana Territory, facing down who knew what. A hired gun? A dangerous drifter? Or a decent man? No one would even hear her if she screamed. She gritted her teeth, willing her hands to stop shaking. Patrick's black-and-white sheepdog Riley stood next to her, growling deep in his throat.

Making no move to get off his horse, the man slowly raised his leather-gloved hands, snowflakes sticking to his dark-brown Stetson and the sheepskin coat pulled up around his face. He had the gall to grin at her.

"I'd do that, ma'am, but I don't know any Rafe Hamilton," the stranger drawled. "Bill Stricklin, the owner of the mercantile—"

"I know who he is." Kate's words came out clipped as she gripped the gun stock and sighted down the double barrels.

"I'm not lookin' for trouble, Miss O'Brien—only a place to buy. Mr. Stricklin told me you might be wanting to sell your homestead."

"I'll not be sellin' this land and certainly not to the likes of you."

As though he was sizing up the worth of a cow, the man's gaze traveled quickly from her face, down past her grimy, denim britches, to the toes of the too-large boots. The shotgun weighed down her arms, but she held on tight.

"I hear your ranch hands quit on you, ma'am. I haven't had much luck finding a place to buy, and it's too late in the season to claim a homestead and start building from scratch." He paused and looked up at the softly falling snow. "My men and I need a place to light for the winter. If you're not selling, then maybe you need help?"

"Why should I even believe you know Mr. Stricklin?" She hated the tremble in her voice.

The stranger lowered one hand and reached inside his coat pocket. He stopped midway when she cocked the shotgun.

"I've got a letter of introduction from him, ma'am."

She studied the man's serious face for a moment. At least he'd dropped that silly grin. He seemed to have gained a healthy respect for the shotgun.

"Pull out the letter nice and slow and stick it on the chicken wire. Then back up your horse."

The stranger withdrew a folded piece of paper and walked his horse forward. Aiming the gun at his belly, her eyes narrowed as he followed her command, she then motioned with the shotgun for him to raise his hands again.

With only the pressure of his knees, the stranger backed the buckskin away from the log cabin behind her.

"I don't mean you no harm, ma'am."

"Ye'll forgive me if I don't take your word for it."

Stepping off the porch in her brother's boots, she winced at the pain of the blisters on her heels, rubbed raw by the ill-fitting footwear. Her whole body ached from doing chores by herself. But she had enough strength to pull the trigger if warranted.

The letter flapped in the breeze while she stared at the man's rugged, bronzed face. The stranger didn't move a muscle and stared at her with deep-brown, watchful eyes.

Snatching and unfolding the page, she quickly recognized Bill Stricklin's signature at the bottom. The words gave this unkempt cowboy the highest of praise. Buck McKean is a good and honest man, he wrote. Had cash money to buy her homestead. Advised her to sell out to him and move into Deer Lodge where she'd be safe.

In her opinion, with his scruffy face and dusty clothes, he looked more like some outlaw who should be locked up behind the tall stone walls of the territorial prison on the edge of town. She hesitated and worried her lower lip with her teeth. A cold September wind blew straight through her too-large shirt, causing her to shiver. Could the man be the answer to her fervent prayers for help? He looked dangerous, but if Mr. Stricklin recommended him... The owner of the mercantile had always been honest in his dealings with her. Bill and his wife, Abigail, were members of her church. But what was he thinking to send some strange man out to her place this late in the day?

She studied the stranger's face and then looked at his worn leather gloves. She could tell he was a working man. "You know anything about cattle, Mr. McKean?"

He smiled wearily and seemed to relax a bit. "Yes, ma'am, I just drove five hundred head of the meanest longhorns you'll ever meet from Fort Worth, Texas, to the gold fields."

The longhorns bearing her brother Patrick's brand still needed to be rounded up out of the timber and off the open range in the high meadows. Kate didn't know the first thing about herding cattle, but she knew Patrick had needed the money from the sale of his animals to repay Rafe Hamilton's father at the bank.

"Winter's comin' on. Why not head home?"

He lowered his hands, leaned forward, and crossed his arms over the horn of his saddle, then tipped up his hat and blinked the snow out of his eyes. He was handsome in a scruffy kind of way. The man studied her for a long moment while his buckskin shifted its feet.

"Why don't I head back to Texas? Because I've spent almost eight years eatin' cattle dust to sell beef to miners and the army, and Deer Lodge Valley is about the prettiest country I've ever seen. I've been lookin' to buy or homestead around here for a long time. Set down roots. Raise my own herd of short-horned cattle. They've got a better disposition." He smiled at her. "You gonna shoot me or what?"

Finally, after another long moment, she lowered the shotgun, but kept a suspicious eye on him. Riley flopped at her feet and put his head on his paws as if he approved of the stranger.

"It's awful cold out here," he said. "If you don't need my help, I'll be heading on out to Deer Lodge."

Lord, what should I do? She stared at him without speaking. Finally, he tipped his hat at her and pulled on the reins to turn his horse around.

"Wait." Her heart nearly thudded out of her chest. "You hungry, Mr. McKean?"

He grinned. "Buck. Yes, ma'am, I reckon I'd eat just about anything that didn't walk off the plate right about now."

Kate studied his face for a moment. He looked friendly and harmless, but she'd made that mistake too many times. "I've got a pot of beef stew on the stove. If Bill Stricklin sent you, then I suppose I trust you...for now. You can stable your horse in the barn. There's feed and water. And you can sleep in the bunkhouse tonight. I don't know if there's any firewood in there, but there's a woodpile and an ax stacked behind it. Help yourself. When you're settled, we'll talk."

Kate turned on her heel and shut the door behind her, dropping the bar into place, and collapsed against it. She'd just made the best decision of her life...or the worst mistake.

After she slammed the door of her cabin, Buck chuckled and dismounted and then walked Applejack to the barn. Miss Kate O'Brien was a pretty little thing—a real fireball with that red hair escaping from her braid. Her Irish accent sounded like music. Yet he bet she couldn't hit the broad side of a barn with her hands shaking like that. Good bluffer though.

It was almost dark in the barn, but the familiar scent of leather, hay, dust, and manure smelled like perfume to him. Two bays, a mule, and a black-and-white cow stirred restlessly in their stalls.

As he unsaddled Applejack, he felt deep disappointment that Miss O'Brien didn't want to sell out after all. How'd Bill Stricklin get her intentions so wrong? The mercantile owner usually knew everything going on in this valley.

Maybe if he could convince her to hire him on for now, he could eventually persuade her to sell out to him. He'd love to buy this place and whip it into shape. It was clear the little gal was in way over her head.

After taking care of his horse, Buck pushed open the bunkhouse door and looked around in disgust. Heads would have rolled on his pa's ranch if the hands had left the sleeping quarters in this kind of shape. He picked up the corner of a filthy blanket and shook it out on the wood floor. No telling what kind of critters had made a nest in there for the winter. After tossing it on the lumpy mattress, he picked up a piece of firewood and laid it in the pot-bellied stove on top of a pile of dry kindling.

After he got the fire crackling and throwing out heat, he slipped his gloves on again and stepped out into the frigid night. He didn't tarry, taking long strides to the cabin and hopping onto the porch. He rapped on the rough wood, and a moment later he heard Miss O'Brien lift the bar on the other side.

When she partially opened the door and peeked out at him, he pulled off his Stetson. She held the shotgun in one hand and a plate of stew in the other, the fragrant smell of beef and onions causing his mouth to water.

"You can eat out on the porch." She shoved the plate toward him, her eyes wary, but he was a little afraid to take it. She might just shoot him. "Leave the plate by the door after you finish."

"Pardon?"

"We can talk in the morning." Her words were clipped.

Before she could close the door in his face, her dog snuck out and sniffed his britches, then jumped up on his leg, wagging its tail.

"Riley!"

"It's all right, ma'am. I like dogs." He knelt on one knee, laid his hat down on the crown, and scratched the animal behind its ears. A burst of wind blew snow under the porch roof. "Hi, boy. How ya doin'? You better git on inside now where it's warm. Gettin' colder out here by the minute."

"He doesna usually take to strangers." Out of the corner of his eye, he could tell she still hid behind the solid door, but she had a firm grip on that shotgun.

Buck ran his fingers through the dog's thick coat, massaging its back, keeping his voice soft and easy. "Dogs have a sixth sense about people. He knows I mean no harm. Don't you, boy?" He looked up at Miss O'Brien and smiled.

Indecision warred on her face. But finally, she lowered the weapon and opened the door a little wider. "It's freezin' out there. I suppose you can come in and sit at the table. But don't try anything."

He looked up at her worried face. "No, ma'am. I wouldn't take advantage of any woman, but I can eat out here if you're scared."

Her backbone straightened. "I'm not afraid of anything or anyone. Now I extended you an invitation. Are you coming in or not?"

"You sure?"

She hesitated. "No, but Riley and Bill Stricklin seem to trust you. Come on in before I change my mind."

"Thank you, ma'am. That's mighty nice of you."

Moving slowly so as not to scare her, he picked up his hat by the brim and juggled it in his hands as she backed away, her eyes watching him like a hawk. Not that he blamed her, a woman out here all alone.

When he stepped over the threshold into the toasty cabin, she closed the door behind him, the shotgun lowered. She set his plate on the table and nervously wiped a palm on her big white apron. While he'd taken care of Applejack, Miss O'Brien had washed her face and changed into a blue calico dress that reminded him of a field of Texas bluebonnets. She was a sight to behold without those britches.

Shuffling his worn boots, Buck stayed close to the door, not wanting to spook her. He scrubbed the back of his hand over his whiskers. He probably looked like some outlaw with a week's worth of dust and stubble on his face.

"You can wash up over there." She indicated the basin with a swing of the gun barrel.

"Yes, ma'am." The water in the wash pan was still warm and smelled of lavender soap. He wiped his hands and face with her homespun towel and looked over where she stood beside the cook stove, gripping the handle of a cast-iron skillet now too. If she didn't look so serious, it would be kinda humorous. But if Miss O'Brien took a notion to clonk him over the head with that thing, she could do some real damage. "That stew smells real good."

"It's not fancy fare, but it'll be hot and filling."

He eased a chair from under the table, screeching its legs on the pine floor, and remained standing...just in case. His eyes darted to the shotgun. Maybe he should head on out to the bunkhouse before she blew his head off.

"Sure, and you're makin' me nervous," she said. "Go ahead and sit."

"That shotgun you're holdin' is making me a mite nervous too."

"A woman can't be too careful, Mr. McKean. Now sit."

"Yes, ma'am." The small wooden chair squeaked when he sat on it.

Returning the skillet to the stovetop, she picked up a plate of fresh-baked bread and set it in front of him next to the plate of beef stew. Pretty much like throwing a raw steak in front of a mountain lion. But minding his manners, he smiled and waited for her to sit first.

When she finally came to rest on the edge of the chair across from him, he almost forgot all about his hunger. Dark circles smudged her cheeks below her green eyes shot with amber. The little lady looked plumb tuckered, definitely too young and fragile to run this spread all by herself. Nineteen...twenty? It was hard to tell as tiny as she was. He hoped she'd listen to reason sooner rather than later and sell out to him.

If she could ever trust him. He sighed in relief when she finally laid the shotgun across her lap and lifted her chin as if in challenge. "Would you like to bless our meal, Mr. McKean?"

He nearly choked. "Pardon me?"

"You heard what I said."

Maybe it was some kind of test. He hadn't said a blessing out loud since...well, since Virginia City ten years ago. He obediently bowed his head to pray, even though he doubted God really heard or cared about his prayers anymore. But *she* definitely cared.

"Father, please bless this food we are about to receive and bless the hands that prepared it. In Jesus' name, we pray. Amen."

A small smile lifted one corner of her mouth, and her shoulders relaxed a little. "Amen. You're a religious man then, Mr. McKean?"

He blew on a spoonful of stew before answering. "Ma and Pa raised me right, but I haven't been to church in a long time. Kind of tough when you're driving cattle through the middle of nowhere." *And your bride leaves you standing at the altar to run off with another man.* The familiar sour taste rose in his mouth.

Her brow furrowed in apparent disapproval. They ate in silence for a moment before she cleared her throat.

"How do ya know Mr. Stricklin?"

"I've been drivin' cattle up to Montana Territory for years. He and Reverend Russell have been keeping an eye out for a good piece of land for me. The best homesteads are taken, but a lot of people are looking to sell out and move on to Oregon. Can't take this hard life."

"Well, then, I hope you find a piece of land soon."

"I hoped I'd already found it. You sure you don't want to sell out?"

Her eyes narrowed. "No, Mr. McKean, I don't."

"That's a real shame, ma'am. I'd be willing to pay top dollar. This is an awful big place for a little thing like you to be running on her own."

The touchy Miss O'Brien slammed her spoon down on the red-checkered tablecloth and glared at him. He swallowed hard, realizing he'd stuck his foot in his mouth. He needed to tread lightly.

She laid the shotgun on the table, and that's when he noticed the blisters on her palms. Yep, he could tell she was plumb wore out and overworked, doin' a man's job.

"I told you, Mr. McKean, I'll not be sellin' my land."

He stuffed another bite in his mouth and chewed slowly, wondering how he could put a pleasant look back on her face. He decided to use his horse-breakin' voice—real nice and gentle like.

"I meant no disrespect, ma'am."

She lifted her chin and gazed into his eyes as if trying to read his mind. "You are right about one thing though. I canna run this place on my own. I do need a foreman."

"Are you offering me the job?" He wiped his mouth with the flour-sack napkin.

"Aye, if it suits you. I canna pay you much...at least until we round up my brother's cattle and sell them at market, but I can offer you room and board and a small amount each week for necessities."

"Foreman." Better than he'd hoped for. He rubbed his neck. If he stuck around, surely she'd give in and sell out to him. As he saw it, she had no other choice. "That sounds fair, Miss O'Brien."

Her jaw relaxed. "Good. It's settled then."

A small, unexpected smile lit up her face and almost knocked him off his chair. *Whoa, boy.* He quickly reined in his emotions. As far as he was concerned, you could round up every woman in the territory and put 'em all on a slow boat to China. He'd been burned once, and he wasn't about to fall for a pretty face again.

"If you don't mind me askin', Miss O'Brien, what happened to the palms of your hands?"

She looked down at her hands and winced. "Ach, the wood ran out yesterday. I spent the mornin' chopping enough to get me through till tomorrow. The trees are soft around here. They burn fast. The fireplace and cook stove eat a lot of wood."

He chewed another piece of tender beef and swallowed. "Try carbolic salve. That should fix you right up. You better let me do the wood chopping from now on."

"I'm quite capable—"

"Yes, ma'am, I can see that. But you've got a hired hand now. Let me do the heavy lifting." He smiled to soften his words.

She opened her mouth as though to give him an argument, and then closed it before lifting her chin. "Perhaps that would be best. Thank you, Mr. McKean."

He swallowed his chuckle and tried to keep a straight face. He could tell it was hard for her to admit defeat and accept help.

"Call me Buck."

"Buck. I suppose since we'll be workin' together, you can call me Miss Kate."

He took a sip of coffee, restraining his smile. "Yes, ma'am."

Pretending as if nothing had passed between them, she bent her head and spooned a bite of potato into her mouth.

They ate in silence for the rest of the meal, the shotgun resting between them. After he cleaned up his plate with a piece of bread and swallowed it down, Buck pushed back from the table, stood up, and patted Riley's head.

"I best be turning in now, Miss Kate. Thank you for supper. It was real good." Shrugging into his sheepskin coat, he combed his fingers through his wayward hair before settling his Stetson on his head.

He reached for the door latch and flashed a smile over his shoulder. "I'll see you in the mornin'."

Hesitating, she finally nodded at him. He tipped his hat to her from the open doorway.

"Night, Miss Kate."

"G'night...Buck."

She hurried to close the door behind him, and he could hear the bar drop into place with a *thunk*. Buck looked up at the clear skies, the air smelling of pine trees and so crisp and clean it was like balm to a man's soul. An almost full moon shone down on the path, lighting his way to the barn and bunkhouse. The light snow had given way to a star-studded night. Pulling up his coat collar around his bare neck, he buried his hands deep into his pockets.

When he reached the bunkhouse, he opened the door into a warmer, but no cleaner, place to sleep. Once he fed the fire a few more sticks of wood, he crawled under a blanket fully clothed and still wearing his jacket. He didn't even pull off his boots, just set the crown of his hat on the floor along with his gun belt. He was almost asleep before his head hit the grimy pillow.

Chapter Two

Gunfire woke Buck from a dead sleep. Still a little groggy, he tore his gun from its leather holster as he rolled off the bunk. Slamming the door open, he ran and dove behind the stock tank. Five riders rode around the cabin, shooting their firearms in the air, whooping and hollering. A bottle smashed against the front door. A bullet shattered one of the front windows.

He peered around the trough and got off a couple of shots. The outlaws returned fire, but he was certain he might have grazed one of them. The coward turned tail and rode away. Miss Kate fired a rifle out of the broken window. Another member of the gang ducked down in his saddle and hightailed it into the trees near the river. Then she quickly fired a second round. Buck grinned. A Henry repeater.

Caught in a crossfire now, the rest of the gang retreated to the tree line, firing at both him and the cabin. Bullets whizzed over his head. Most of Miss Kate's rounds went wild. Yep, no doubt about it. She needed to sell this place to him before she got hurt. Alone out here, she was a sittin' duck. With Buck's next round, a rider lost his hat, whirled his mount, and galloped off. Three down. Two to go. Miss Kate continued to fire the repeater, but it was little more than a noisemaker in her hands. Riley barked his head off inside the cabin.

Then her rifle fell silent. Out of ammunition. One of the men must have reloaded because he still fired at the cabin. Buck only had one bullet left in the chamber. Right as he took aim, Miss Kate stepped out of the door with her shotgun and fired the first barrel. His heart slammed in his chest. What would make her do a fool thing like that?

The kick almost knocked her on her backside. But it was enough to scare the varmints off. The last two men split up and galloped toward town. Even with the outlaws in retreat, she fired her second shell and shot off the branch of a pine tree.

"You all right, Miss Kate?" He peered around the building and hollered. She swung his way with the shotgun. He was pretty sure she hadn't reloaded, but he ducked anyway. He pulled out his white handkerchief and waved it in the air above the stock tank. "It's me—Buck."

When he popped his head up, she lowered the gun, and he heard her groan. Taking off in a sprint, he cleared the porch steps in one leap, crunching broken glass under his boots.

He grabbed her shoulders. "Are you shot?"

"Nay."

Clad only in a white, flannel nightgown, she stood almost stock-still, biting her lower lip. A mite concerned despite her denial, he inspected her as best he could in the moonlight. That's when he spotted the blood seeping from under one foot. Gently, he took the shotgun away from her and set it inside the cabin door and then picked her up in his arms.

"At least you scared off those polecats. Let's get you inside and see how bad you're hurt."

After carrying her into the two-room cabin, he kicked the door closed. Now it was pitch dark except for the glow of coals from the fireplace. Stumbling against a kitchen chair, he figured he best set her down now.

"Lantern?" he asked.

"In the bedroom."

"Matches?"

"Above the stove."

"Hang on." Stumbling with his hands in front of him, he finally found the open doorway exactly where he remembered. Once he groped around and found the lantern on top of a bureau, he carried it to the kitchen table and searched for matches.

"On the shelf...to the right."

When his hand bumped the box, he quickly slid the lid open and struck a match. Once the lantern's wick glowed, he replaced the clear glass chimney. Now he could see the pain etched on her face.

"How're you doing?"

She bit her lower lip and lifted her bare foot without saying a word.

He knelt beside her and took her tiny foot in his hand, examining the large shard of glass stuck in her heel. Most women would have fainted by now.

"Got any whiskey in the house?"

"Patrick kept a bottle under the dry sink for medicinal purposes."

Poking his head through the curtain that covered the shelves under the sink, he found the half-empty bottle and then grabbed the wash basin off the small chest.

Kneeling in front of her, he looked up to see a single tear slide down her cheek. She quickly dashed it away with the back of her hand. Add brave to stubborn and hotheaded. Buck gritted his teeth, wanting to pound those low-down skunks.

"This is going to hurt."

Miss Kate nodded her head, but he could tell by her knitted brow she was in a lot of pain. Gently, he placed her foot in the basin and poured whiskey over her deep wound before slowly pulling out the glass, trying not to hurt her any worse.

She hissed in a breath and reached out to clutch his shoulder, squeezing hard with her fingertips. "Are ye trying to torture me, man? Pull it out and be done with it."

"Yes, ma'am." He yanked the glass out of her foot while she dug her fingers deeper into his shoulder muscle. "You can let go now."

She released the hold that had nearly paralyzed his arm and gripped her ankle with both hands, gritting her jaw in pain.

"You're doing fine." He poured more whiskey on her foot.

She winced and grabbed his shoulder again, glaring at him.

Buck pulled out the handkerchief he'd stuffed into his jacket pocket and held it to the bleeding cut. "Hold that for me."

He'd doctored longhorns that were more cooperative.

With a huff, she crossed her foot over her knee and pulled her gown down to her ankle.

Buck stood and rummaged through her shelves.

"Now what d'ya think ye're doin'?"

"I'm looking for somethin' to wrap your foot with."

"My sewing basket...next to my chair."

He snatched up the straw basket filled with what looked like a bunch of scraps and dug through the material to find a piece big enough to bind her wound.

"You're getting blood all over my quilt pieces."

He stopped and looked at her, clenching his jaw. "Would you rather bleed to death?"

She huffed and mumbled something under her breath. Likely, he didn't want to know what she'd said.

After using his teeth to rip off a few strips of a colorful flour sack, he pulled his blood-soaked handkerchief out of her hand, dropped it into the basin, and wrapped her foot, quickly tying off the bandage. Not much different than roping a calf. He stood up, resting his hands on his hips.

"There. I'm no doctor, but I think that'll hold until we can get you to town in the mornin'. It's deep enough you might need a few stitches." He picked up the basin and threw the bloody whiskey and his ruined handkerchief into the yard. "Who were those lowdown scum anyway? Did you recognize any of 'em?"

Shivering, Miss Kate crossed her arms over her chest and held her elbows as if she'd fly apart otherwise. "No, but I can guess who sent them. Rafe Hamilton."

Fire blazed from her green eyes at the mention of Hamilton, the same man she had accused him of working for when he first rode up. She hugged herself tighter.

"You cold?"

"Are ya daft, man?" she said in a sarcasm-laced tone. "Of course, I'm cold. The window's broken, and you left the door wide open."

Oh yeah. Pink rose in her cheeks. What kind of dunce was he? Dressed in nothing but her nightgown, she had to be embarrassed too. Suddenly nervous, he looked around for something to cover her with. She started to stand but winced when she put weight on her foot. She sank down again onto the squeaky chair.

"Do you need a—" He lifted his hands in near panic and felt the red creep up the back of his neck.

"There's a quilt on my—"

Swallowing hard, Buck edged toward the other room. "In the

bedroom?"

She nodded, and he fetched a quilt faster than a coyote can catch a jackrabbit, dragging it across the floor. He slung the colorful fabric around her shoulders and backed up.

"Better?"

"Aye. Thank you." Her teeth chattered. "Can you close the door and nail a board over that window?"

"Sure." He slammed the door closed and then stuffed his hands into his back pockets. "You need anything before I fix the window? Coffee—"

"Tea would be nice. It's on the shelf over the cook stove."

When Buck picked up the dainty handle of the fine China teapot, the top rattled. Carefully, he filled the rose-painted teapot with hot water from the water well in the cook stove, snatched up the tin of tea, and then looked at her in question.

"How much?"

"I can do it." At least she sounded like she'd calmed down a might.

Wrapping the quilt tighter around her shoulders, Miss Kate stuck out her hand. He passed her the tin, and she spooned dry tea leaves into the teapot. While she did that, he fetched the matching cup and saucer and set it on the table in front of her with a clatter.

"Don't break it!"

"Sorry," he mumbled, edging toward the door. Touchy little thing. He hoped he wouldn't be walking on eggs the whole time he worked for her. "I need to fetch something to cover that window, Miss Kate. Otherwise, you're liable to freeze to death tonight." He reached for the door latch.

She released her breath in a loud sigh, and he turned. "I didn't mean to speak so sharply."

When she glanced up at him with those eyes framed by long lashes, he felt a flutter in his chest. Everything in him wanted to take her in his arms and comfort her. That scared him near to death. Instead, he shuffled toward the door again and opened it. "I'll be back lickety-split." With that, he closed the door behind him and lengthened his long strides toward the barn, welcoming the cold air that cleared his head.

What were you thinkin'?

For a minute there, his mind had turned to mush. No pretty face was going to make a fool out of him again. If he ever married, which he doubted, he'd look for a widow woman with kids—somebody who'd be grateful for a husband—not some prickly Irish gal with a sharp tongue.

After he rummaged around in the barn for nails and a hammer, he finally found a leftover board under the work bench. When he returned to the house, it didn't take him long to patch the window.

"There. That should hold until I can replace the glass." He opened the door again. "I'll see you in the morning."

"Please, sit down," Miss Kate said.

Uh oh. His brows knitted. Now what. "Why?"

"Because I want to say something."

Since she asked nice, he reluctantly pulled out a chair and sat down, trying not to get lost in those Irish eyes. She cleared her throat but didn't say anything. He waited and wiped his palms on his pant legs.

If he were being truthful, he had to admit this little bit of a woman was different than anyone he'd ever met...even if she was pretty. While under attack from a gang of outlaws, she had kept her head and managed to cock a repeating rifle, hold a shotgun, and get off a last round with an injured foot, and yet here she was sipping tea as if nothing had happened.

He broke the silence. "Does your foot hurt bad?"

She nodded. "Aye, but it's nothing I canna stand. I've had worse."

"I'll hitch up the horses and drive you into town tonight if you want." Not that he wanted to. He was dead on his feet.

"No need. It's not bleeding like it was," she said in a soft voice.

"What did you want to say?"

"I'm...well...I'm really grateful you were here."

She looked at him with the wide eyes of a scared puppy. Now that the danger had passed, he could tell how frightened she was. Those eyes of hers begged him to stay. Or maybe he wanted to stay—stay to protect her. Maybe she'd feel better if they talked awhile.

Buck leaned his elbows on the table and clasped his callused hands together. "Tell me about this Rafe Hamilton."

She sighed and poured another cup of tea. "His father, Henry Hamilton, is president of the bank, and Rafe owns the land to the west of here."

"Why would he send out men to shoot up your place?"

"This ranch belonged to my brother Patrick. He escaped Ireland ten years ago and homesteaded this land."

"Escaped?"

"My stepfather was a cruel man." Her words sounded harsh and bitter. "Anyway, when Mam died, Patrick borrowed money from Mr. Hamilton's bank and sent for me. I only arrived in May. Patrick . . . died in August."

"I'm sorry." Her story chipped at the wall he had erected around his heart. She really was alone. All the more reason to sell out to him and move into town.

"Patrick promised to repay the loan by mid-September after he sold his cattle."

"You've still got a little time."

"I can't do it without your help, and you can't do it alone." Her jaw tightened in anger. "Rafe drove off my hired hands. Before Patrick was killed, Rafe wanted to— He said if I'd marry him, he'd pay off Patrick's loan."

Buck stared into her pain-filled eyes, his heart thumping with righteous anger. "What kinda man—"

"One who serves the devil," she growled. "I don't care what I have to do to save this ranch, Mr. McKean, but I sure willna marry Rafe Hamilton. I think he caused the stampede that killed my brother. The man is evil. His father's bank will foreclose on this land if I canna pay back the loan."

In the light of the flickering lantern, her eyes flashing with anger, Buck thought she was the most beautiful woman he'd ever seen. And the bravest. He leaned forward. "First thing in the mornin', I'll drive you into town, and I'll go talk to Sheriff Granger. Maybe he can pay Hamilton a visit—get to the bottom of your brother's death."

"The Hamiltons practically own Deer Lodge. Money has a way of covering up their sins. Besides, I canna prove anything. Not even attest those men tonight work for Rafe. But this isn't the first time they've paid me a visit, and I doubt it will be the last."

Buck leaned back, almost knocking over the chair, and ran his hands through his hair. "Are you sayin' this isn't the first time they've ridden out to threaten you? And you stayed out here all alone? Don't you know what they could have done to you?"

"Aye, I know full well."

"You should have gone to the sheriff, or Stricklin, or the preacher."

Her voice rose to match his. "And what could they do? Guard my land day and night? If I vacate this property, Mr. Hamilton will call in the loan. Nay, the Hamiltons will have to drag me out of this house. It was built with my own brother's sweat and blood. I've been bullied enough in my life. I'll not go quietly." Her breath came fast and heavy.

Buck's hands gripped the table edges as he stared at her, worry for her turning his gut inside out. For a woman he'd only met today, he'd never felt so protective of anyone in his life. He hadn't picked this fight, but he sure as shootin' wouldn't walk away from it. If he had anything to do with it, nobody was running Kate O'Brien off her ranch.

Chapter Three

KATE LOOKED UP AT THE TALL, muscular Texan, hoping against hope he could help her. She only had two weeks before the loan payment was due. But could she trust him, or would he turn on her like every other man in her past? She had no choice...now.

"Will ya help me, Mr. McKean?"

"Buck." He leaned forward, his forearms resting on the table. "Of course, I'll help you. I'm not of a mind to let you be run off your ranch by some pasty-faced banker and his rotten son."

Her heart felt lighter than it had since Patrick's passing—almost hopeful. "Do ya think then we can round up the cattle and sell them in the next two weeks?"

"I've got a few men who decided to stick with me. They're over in Deer Lodge celebratin' the end of a long cattle drive. Do you have a buyer yet?"

"I don't know what Patrick had planned. I can ask Mr. Stricklin. I know nothing about raising cattle."

"Then why didn't you just sell the land to Hamilton and move into town?"

Her temper flared again. "Didn't ya hear a thing I said, Mr. McKean? I willna give up Patrick's land. He gave his life and every cent he had or could borrow to rescue me."

At least her new foreman had the decency to look guilty. When he met her gaze, her heart beat faster. He was no doubt handsome with his deep-brown eyes, wavy hair the color of chestnuts, and a firm, square jaw. He hadn't shaved in several days, and he needed a bath and a haircut. But when he had smiled at supper, two dimples had appeared in his cheeks. He had no doubt broken the hearts of many a woman. Well, she wouldn't be one of them. She'd never trust another man. Mr. McKean would have to understand this was only a business arrangement.

She lifted her chin. "You're staring at me."

He ran his hands down his face. "You're right. I don't know what you and your brother went through. I was raised on one of the richest cattle ranches in Texas. I'd still be there if Pa hadn't remarried, and I hadn't been so stubborn. I ran away and hired on to drive cattle to Montana Territory. I can teach you what you need to know."

His eyes looked weary. She was still awake when those hooligans rode in, and Buck couldn't have gotten much sleep either before the shooting started.

Kate tried to stand, but pain shot through her foot and up her leg. She groaned, and he popped out of his chair to catch her before she fell. His broad hands spanned her waist, causing a hot flush through her whole body. She pushed him away.

He dropped his hands. "Maybe you should turn in for the night, ma'am. I'll stand watch till mornin'. Those varmints might decide to sneak onto your property again and finish what they started."

"You can return to the bunkhouse...Buck. You needna worry. I'll be fine now."

"We did some damage. They might be inclined to seek a little revenge tonight."

"Oh." She hadn't thought of that. "Well, I suppose you can drag one of the chairs over to the other window. I'll just sit here with you till morning." She tightly wrapped the quilt around her, stifling a yawn.

The Texan gave her an easy smile. "No need, Miss Kate. I'm used to standing night watch with little to no sleep. You go climb into bed."

Was the man an *idjit*? She had known him only a few hours, and she was supposed to sleep peacefully while he prowled around her cabin?

"I canna do that. It wouldna be proper." She straightened up in her chair.

"No, it's probably not, ma'am, but it makes good common sense. You can trust me. I could have taken a bullet for you." His eyes twinkled with kindness in the light of the lantern.

She stared at his rugged face. He *had* been a perfect gentleman, and he *had* bound her wounds. He seemed like a good man.

She sighed. "I trust Mr. Stricklin. He's a good judge of character, but I'll be latchin' my door behind me."

"I would expect no less, Miss Kate."

When she tried to stand, he swept her up into his arms and headed for the bedroom. "What do ya think you're doing, you fool man?" She struggled against his muscular chest.

He stopped and looked at her face. "Can you walk on that foot?"

No, she couldn't, but that didn't mean he should be carrying her to bed. Her whole body felt aflame with emotions she couldn't understand. He must have read the indecision on her face.

"That's what I thought." Buck carried her into the dark bedroom and set her gently on the bed, pulled the quilt up around her neck, then turned toward the kitchen. His broad shoulders were outlined in the doorway from the light of the lantern. "I'll be out here if you need me. All right?"

"Aye."

He shut the bedroom door behind him with a click of the latch, and she hopped over on one foot to lock it before snuggling under the covers.

Kate awoke the next morning needing to make a trip to the privy, but the thought of asking her new foreman to carry her outside in the dawn light was more than she could bear. Her face flushed at the very thought. She slid her feet to the cold floor and winced in pain, but she vowed to crawl all the way there before she asked him for help.

A thought cheered her. Perhaps he had fallen asleep during the night, and she could sneak past him. That's when she smelled fresh brewed coffee and sighed.

After she struggled into her undergarments and her serviceable, brown-wool dress, she undid her braid, brushed her curly, copper-colored locks, and pulled her hair into an unruly bun at the back of her head. Then she slid her feet into Patrick's boots and slipped her arms into his sheepskin coat. They'd never gotten around to buying her something warm to wear. The weather was still hot when she'd lost Patrick.

Thinking about losing her mother and now her big brother was like touching a sore tooth with her tongue. She almost couldn't stand the pain in her heart.

No use delaying. Lifting her chin, she opened the door and hobbled into the kitchen, a warm fire crackling in the hearth. Buck, still wearing his coat and gloves, held the coffeepot, pouring himself a cup.

"Good mornin'." Buck smiled at her, his cheeks dimpling.

Unexpectedly, her heart skipped a beat. Never had she thought she would ever meet anyone as handsome as Buck McKean in this wild country. Irishmen were known for their dark, good looks, but this Texan stood head and shoulders above them all.

"Something wrong?" His smile faded.

"Nay." Pushing away the thought, she limped forward, clutching at the wall. She was embarrassed and infuriated with her own thoughts.

At some point, he must have made a trip to the bunkhouse, because he had shaved and wore a clean shirt under his jacket. Truth be told, she felt small as a wee fairy next to him. He was tall—tall as she pictured her guardian angel.

"Miss Kate? Are you feeling all right? You look a mite pale."

"Aye, I'm fine."

"You shouldn't be walkin' on that foot until the doc takes a look at it."

He set down his cup and strode toward her as if he would lift her into his arms again, but in wide-eyed panic, she put up both hands to stop him.

"I'm feeling better this mornin'. Really, I'm fine." She wobbled across the floor slowly, pain shooting up her leg with every tiptoed step. She bit her lower lip.

A frown pulled down the corners of his mouth. "You don't look fine." He pulled out a chair and motioned her to sit.

Instead, she walked past him on the other side of the table and reached for her ragged scarf. "Nay, I need to be about my chores. I'll be gathering the eggs now."

"I can gather the eggs. I've already milked the cow for you, though it's been a month of Sundays since I've done that. Just don't tell anyone."

He chuckled. "You stay here, and I'll fix us breakfast before we leave. We need to get on the road early, so we can get back by this afternoon. Coffee?"

She held his gaze a moment before acquiescing. "Aye, thank you." Not that she cared for coffee. She tiptoed to a chair and sat down.

"Anything else I can get you now?"

"Nay. I'll be sittin' here drinking my coffee till you return."

"Yes, ma'am."

He flashed a smile at her as bright as the Montana sun, now peeking over Sugarloaf Mountain in shades of pink and lavender. Settling his hat on his head, he stepped out the door and latched it behind him.

As soon as she heard him step off the porch, Kate stood and limped to the door, opening it as quietly as possible, and bit back her pain as she made her way to the privy. Stumbling over rocks in Patrick's oversized boots, she gritted her teeth with every step.

When she had finished and pushed open the creaking door, her new foreman leaned against the cabin with his arms crossed. She couldn't look him in the eye. With her cheeks flushed bright pink, she stared at the rough ground and gingerly hobbled toward him.

"You could have asked for help," he drawled.

Sighing, he leapt off the porch and swept her into his arms. She could do nothing other than let him carry her like a helpless babe.

Kicking open the cabin door, he sat her down on a chair and tossed her lukewarm coffee out into the yard before refilling her cup. As he set down the mug, he looked at her and shook his head without saying a word.

Humiliated, she mutely watched him lay a few slices of smoked, cured bacon on the hot, cast-iron skillet. He turned around, a smile crinkling the corners of his eyes. He cocked one dark brow.

"How many eggs do you want?"

"One should suffice."

He turned back to the stove and cracked four eggs next to the sizzling bacon and scooted them apart with the spatula as they fried.

Taking a sip of the bitter coffee, Kate grimaced and glanced up at him, studying his broad shoulders. He still wore his coat. As he turned the bacon with a fork, she considered his wavy, chestnut hair curling over his collar. She tried not to stare, but Buck was a large presence in the small room. It was hard to ignore him.

"I don't know how to make biscuits," he said, "but I sliced the rest of your loaf of bread. This should hold us till we get to town."

Her new foreman turned around and caught her staring. His mouth curved in a knowing smile as he set a plate in front of her.

"Thank you." She swallowed hard and looked down.

Why did he make her feel so jittery? He had been a perfect gentleman, but still she felt nervous around him. As she took a bite of egg, her mind wandered again like it had the night before. Buck fit the role of a rancher. It would take a man like him to tame this land. But she had vowed to stay single the rest of her life after what her stepfather had done to her and what Rafe Hamilton had tried to do.

He sat across from her. "Would you like me to say a blessing again?"

A quiet peace filled her heart. It gave her comfort to know he knew the Lord.

"Aye...please."

"Heavenly Father, we thank you for this new day and thank you for protecting us during the night. Please bless this food you have provided for us to nourish our bodies. In Jesus' name, we pray. Amen."

"Amen."

Kate peeked at this giant of a man as he dug into his breakfast. How would she ever take on the role of his employer? Could she do it and keep him at arm's length? She didn't know, but she had no choice.

Mid-morning, the empty buckboard clattered down Main Street into Deer Lodge. The weather had warmed a bit. Kate's color rose in her cheeks when all heads turned toward them as they drove by. Most of the people in town knew who she was and that she was a single woman living alone now. With speculation in their eyes, they all stared at the tall cowboy by her side. What must they be thinking? She hoped they'd assume he was another brother or maybe a cousin come to help.

Kate lifted her chin. She clutched her hands in her lap and felt her face flood with color. Acting as though this were an everyday trip to town, she nodded and smiled at the women from church as they passed.

Buck pulled the horses to a halt in front of Dr. Mitchell's office right as the owner of the mercantile walked out of his store.

"Well, I see you found the place." Mr. Stricklin smiled as he ambled over.

Buck hopped down off the buckboard and shook the man's hand. "I did, but we had a little trouble last night."

"Oh?"

Kate started to step down out of the buckboard, but instead her new foreman reached up and plucked her right off the wagon seat and swung her into his arms.

"Honestly, Mr. McKean, I can walk." She pushed against his hard chest.

"No, you can't."

Mr. Stricklin's brows furrowed. "What's wrong with her?"

Buck stepped onto the boardwalk at the entrance to the doctor's office, and Mr. Stricklin hurried to open the door. He carried her into the toasty waiting room heated by a pot-bellied stove. Wooden chairs lined the white-washed walls.

She squirmed in his arms. "You can set me on my feet now."

Ignoring her, he spoke to Mr. Stricklin as if she wasn't there. "A gang shot up the place last night and broke a whiskey bottle against Miss Kate's front door. She stepped on a piece of glass when she ran out to shoot at the varmints."

A gray-haired Doc Mitchell walked out of the back room, wiping his hands on a white towel, followed by his plump wife Martha.

"She did what?"

"I'm right here," she said. "You needna talk over me."

"Bring her back here and set her on my examination table." Doc gestured toward the narrow, waist-high oak bench. "Martha, bring me a pan of hot water. Let's take a look at that foot."

His wife bustled to do his bidding as Buck set Kate down on the hard surface.

"Now what's this about a shooting?" Mr. Stricklin turned to Buck.

Frustrated, Kate answered in a loud voice before Buck could open his mouth. "Rafe Hamilton sent out a group of his men to scare me off my land, but it didna work."

"I'm headed over to Sheriff Granger's office next," Buck said, resting his hands on his hips.

"How do you know Hamilton sent them?" the mercantile owner asked her.

"I don't know for sure, but who else could it have been?" She gritted her teeth as the doctor slipped off her boots and started to unwind the calico bandage from her foot. "He's the only one tryin' to scare me into marrying him."

"Now, Miss Kate, everyone in town knows you live out there alone." Mr. Stricklin said. "Liquored up, it could have been miners or a few drovers, riding out there to raise a little Cain, although Rafe Hamilton is mean enough to have sent over a few of his men to scare you."

"Wounded two of 'em." Buck pulled off his gloves and stretched his hands toward another pot-bellied stove. "Did you patch up anybody last night, Doc?"

"I was out delivering Mrs. Crawley's baby. Didn't get home till dawn. Martha?"

"Nobody stopped by." His wife set the pan of water on a small table next to her husband. Martha looked at her with concern. "You poor dear. It must have been terrifying."

"Aye, but Mr. McKean and I were able to drive them off my land."

"And that's how you cut your foot," Doc said, "stepping out on your porch...barefoot...while you were being attacked by a bunch of drunks." He said it like she didn't have the sense of a goose. Inside, she sizzled, but pressed her lips tight. "It's going to take a few stitches. You men skedaddle."

Buck and Mr. Stricklin stepped toward the door to the waiting room.

"I would have been scared to death to stay out there after that," Martha said. "Why didn't you come on into town, Kate?"

"It's all right, ma'am." Buck glanced over his shoulder. "I spent the rest of the night with her in the cabin."

Everyone froze, and all eyes in the room turned toward Buck. He hadn't just said that. *Please, Lord, no.*

His face flushed red. "No, I didn't mean—"

"What did you mean, son?" Bill Stricklin asked in a firm voice. "Did you or did you not spend the night with Kate in her cabin?"

"Well, yes, but I was awake the whole time—"

"He was afraid they would attack again." Kate's face burned.

"The reason don't matter," Stricklin said to Kate. "It's what everyone will be thinkin'. Word'll get out, especially if Rafe Hamilton had something to do with that raid. He probably had a man watching the cabin all night after Buck came out shooting." He turned and glared at her new foreman. "Son, you've compromised this young lady."

"But I—"

"I'll go get the preacher. You'll have to marry her today." Mr. Stricklin wasted no time buttoning his coat and pulling on his gloves.

"But nothing happened." Buck had a look of stark fear on his face.

"I don't want to get married!" Kate protested. "I don't even know the man!"

"Even worse." Martha tsked.

"Bill, you know I wouldn't harm Miss O'Brien...Miss Kate. You were the one who sent me out to talk to her in the first place. You told me there was another offer, and I best hurry."

"I didn't tell you to spend the night with her, Buck. That was all your doin'." The hefty, gray-haired merchant huffed and shook his head. "The whole town will be talkin' about how you rode into town together, and you carried her into the doc's office. Now they'll know for sure she's been compromised."

Kate watched as her life spun out of control. Fear lodged in the back of her throat. She couldn't marry a stranger, even if that stranger was as handsome as Buck. She had vowed never again to live under a man's thumb and be subject to unspeakable abuse. Never!

"It's all right, Buck." She waved her hand toward the door, hoping she could be the voice of reason. "You don't need to marry me. You go on back to Texas, and I'll figure out another way to repay Patrick's loan. No need to round up my brother's cattle."

Buck's eyes were as wide as hers, looking toward the door again as if to make his escape. She would do the same thing if she could walk. Bill Stricklin reached over and gripped Buck's shoulder.

"I've been talking and corresponding with Buck here for years," Mr. Stricklin said. "He's got plenty saved up to pay off your loan, don't you, son?"

"Uh...I planned on homesteading or buying a ranch around here with that money and building up a herd."

"So? If you marry Kate it will solve both of your problems. Her reputation won't be ruined, and you'll own a ranch together. You afraid of a little hard work, boy?"

"No, sir, but—"

Kate thought he looked like a fox in a trap ready to chew its foot off.

"Then what's the problem?" Mr. Stricklin raised his gray brows.

"The problem is I willna marry him just to save Patrick's land." Kate's voice rose in angry protest. "If I willna marry Rafe Hamilton to pay off the loan, then I'll not be forcin' another man to do the same thing."

Mr. Stricklin looked at Buck with sad eyes and shook his head as if disappointed in the Texan. "She needs you, Buck, and you know it. You already told me you wanted to settle here in Deer Lodge—get married someday and have a family."

"Someday. Not today!" Buck pulled off his hat and wiped the sweat off his forehead with his sleeve.

Kate's dread increased. She started to hop off the table, but Doc put a restraining hand on her shoulder.

Terrified, she stared into Buck's deep-brown eyes and saw the same trapped expression on his face. No one spoke for a long moment. He looked first at Mr. Stricklin, then at Doc Mitchell, and finally at Martha, who shook her head, tsking again.

"She'll be marked for life," Martha said. "A life filled with shame."

Martha's words pricked her heart. What would she do now? How would she ever face the women at church? She looked up at Buck in desperation. He sighed deeply, and his shoulders slumped. Resignation settled over his face. He spoke in a quiet voice to all of them but looked straight at her.

"I'd like a moment alone with my bride."

Oh, dear Lord, no. He can't be serious!

Kate forgot all about her injured foot. All she could feel was her heart pounding in her chest as the others left the room and closed the door behind them. Buck walked toward her until he stood in front of her. Like a rabbit cornered by a dog, she looked up at his grim face.

"Buck, I canna marry you. Ya don't have to—"

"I know I don't, but I won't let your reputation be ruined because of me. You'd never be able to hold up your head in this town again. Then what? Go back to Ireland? And what will you do if you can't pay off the loan? Would you rather marry Hamilton?"

"No, but—"

Suddenly, Buck dropped to one knee and held out his hand for hers. She stared at him a moment—a long moment—and then not knowing what else to do, she placed her small hand in his large, callused one.

"Kate, will you do me the honor of becoming my wife? I promise to take care of you for the rest of my days."

The days and nights of worry finally overwhelmed her. Tears choked her throat and spilled down her cheeks. He was right. What would she do if Hamilton took her land? She had no money to leave town, and she'd never, ever return to Ireland. With the help of her brother Patrick, she had finally escaped her stepfather's control. Her future looked bleak, but what choice did she have?

Buck stood up and sat down beside her, putting a reassuring arm around her shoulders. She leaned her head against him, her tears soaking his coat. She had escaped only to run into another snare. As she cried, he made awkward soothing noises and tucked her head under his chin.

"I bet Mr. Stricklin has a pretty white dress over in his store," Buck said. "And I'm sure we can find some flowers...somewhere."

She looked up at him, and his serious face was full of kindness.

Without any forethought, she had ruined this man's life, and yet he was still willing to stay in town and marry her. She was such a dimwit, letting him stay with her last night. She faced a fork in the road, and now she had to choose—marriage to this man or an uncertain future.

Buck took a handkerchief out of his back pocket and gently wiped away her tears. She took a shuddering breath and blew her nose.

"We're stuck between a rock and a hard place, Miss Kate, and that's the truth of the matter. I won't force you to marry me, but I'm hoping you'll say yes. I need a ranch, and you need a husband. With the good Lord's help, we'll make this wor...somehow. I don't drink, or smoke, or chase after women any more. I'd never hurt you or make you do anything you didn't want."

With a flicker of hope, she looked up at his eyes. Did he mean that? "Ever?"

His expression turned firm. "Ever." He paused and cleared his throat. "There's just one thing..."

"Aye?" Somehow, she already knew what he would say. Her stomach tightened.

"Yes, ma'am." He cleared his throat again. "If we're gonna be stuck with each other for life...I want this to be a real marriage. I want a passel of kids to carry on my name." He hesitated, his cheeks bright red.

Her eyes widened in alarm. "But you said—"

"Not tomorrow or anything. Maybe six months or a year? When you're ready to receive me as a husband. I won't force myself on you."

She breathed a deep, inward sigh, but she still wasn't sure she could trust him. "Don't make the mistake of underestimating me, Mr. McKean. It will be my decision when or *if* I invite you into my bed. I will be no man's slave."

"No, ma'am. I'd never ask it of you. I'll need a partner to run the ranch, not a slave. Do we have ourselves a deal?"

Obviously, he didn't want this anymore than she did, but what choice did they have? Her head drooped as she tried to think of another way out. Then finally, she sighed. "Aye, I'll marry you."

He lifted her chin with his hand and wiped the remnants of tears from her cheeks. An electrical charge sparked between them, and she started in surprise.

How had this happened? She was getting married today to a man she barely knew. A man she'd only met last night. A man who might beat her...or worse. She supposed she should be grateful to him for coming to her rescue, but right now she felt as if she had fallen into a bottomless black bog.

Chapter Four

After Buck stopped by the sheriff's office and reported the attack on Kate, he went looking for his men. The Red Rock Cafe was his first stop where he spotted Grizzly Joe, shoveling flapjacks into his mouth. Two other hung-over cowpokes who had followed him to Deer Lodge sat beside Joe, nursing their headaches and drinking coffee.

Explaining his sudden marriage would prompt questions, but he hoped they'd mind their own business. Expelling a deep breath, he pushed open the door into the warm, moist air, a bell tinkling overhead. Joe looked up with a smile and waved him over with a gnarled hand.

"There you are," Joe said in a loud, gravelly voice. "I looked all over for you this mornin', but somebody said they saw you ride out north of town yesterday. I thought you'd deserted us."

Buck pulled off his gloves and stuffed them in his coat pockets before straddling a scarred, mismatched chair. He nodded at Josh and Billy before answering Joe. "You knew I was looking for a place."

"I thought you'd hang around town a few days to have a little fun and rest up before you went out lookin' for land. Don't seem neighborly to just up and run off without telling us where you were going."

The old man scratched his thick, gray whiskers and slurped a sip of coal-black coffee.

"You know I wouldn't run off without you," Buck said.

He glanced over at the shaggy blond Billy. The sixteen-year-old needed a haircut, but he supposed that was the last thing on the boy's mind when he hit Deer Lodge. The kid couldn't even grow a beard yet, but he supposed he'd spent the evening blowing off steam. The rest of his men had already skedaddled back to Texas and warmer weather. Josh, a seasoned drover, sat beside the kid, dark circles under his eyes. Fightin' the war in his dreams again, he supposed. Sometimes he forgot Josh was about the same age as him. The battlefield had aged him—put a sad look in his eyes. Billy took a loud slurp of coffee and looked at him with bloodshot eyes.

"So did ya find some land?" Joe asked.

Buck rubbed the back of his neck and delayed answering. "Sort of...well...yeah."

"What's that supposed to mean? Either you did or you didn't." Joe swirled a forkful of flapjacks in syrup and stuffed the bite into his mouth

Buck didn't exactly know how to answer. Stalling for time, he studied Billy, who looked a little green around the gills, testimony to the night spent drinking. No doubt he'd spent all his pay after his first trail drive. That's what he'd done when he was a kid. It had taken him a while to grow any sense, but he hadn't darkened the doors of a saloon since he was eighteen. Too much temptation inside.

Josh, his straight, coal-black hair hanging in one eye, looked plum wore out. Men didn't last many years riding herd. Too hard on the body, sitting in a saddle all day and sleeping on the hard ground at night. At twenty-five, that's why he wanted to stay put on his own land. That's why Josh had rode into Deer Lodge with him.

And Joe, well, he was past his prime and stove up with rheumatiz. "Buck!"

"Huh?" He looked at Joe. "I didn't find a place to buy, but I can provide room and board for all of you if you're willin' to stay the winter and help me run a ranch. Plus, some pay. We need to round up cattle over the next couple of weeks."

"Cows," Billy said, groaning. "I'm sick of cows. Why don't you raise horses instead? The army always needs more horses." He grimaced and slurped more coffee.

Joe rolled his eyes, and Buck chuckled. When Joe offered the boy a biscuit, Billy pushed it away, turning greener by the minute.

"I've had my fill of pushing cows too," Josh said, leaning his elbows on the table. "But like I said, Montana Territory's pretty country, and I'll give it a try. In the spring, I might head on to Oregon with one of the wagon trains."

"You gotta stop runnin' sometime." Buck smiled and patted Josh's shoulder, pleased the men would stick with him. He motioned for the waitress to bring him coffee and then gave the boys detailed instructions on how to find the ranch.

"I don't know when I'll get back tomorrow, but it might be late. I'll need you to milk the cow, Billy, and the animals will need feed and the stalls mucked out. Josh, you'll need to chop wood for the cabin and bunkhouse, and Joe you can start cleanin' up that pigsty."

"They got pigs? I ain't no pig wrangler."

"No, the bunkhouse. Looks like pigs wallowed in it."

"What're you gonna do?" Joe asked.

Buck grinned sheepishly and rubbed the back of his neck again. "I'm gettin' married. I need to make a stop at the mercantile for some weddin' duds, and then head on over to the bathhouse for a shave and a dunk."

All three men's jaws dropped.

"Married!" Joe said. "That how you got hold of a ranch? You gonna marry a widder woman with a bunch of kids? Sounds like trouble to me."

"No, I'm marryin' a little fireball of a woman who's been trying to run the place all by herself since her brother was killed. Her name's Kate O'Brien."

"Irish." He shook his head. "Why you got to marry her? Can't you just work for her?"

Buck looked down at the worn plank floor and then back up at Joe. "It's a long story. I'll tell you about it later. All you need to know is you'll have a roof over your head and food in your belly for as long as you want to stay."

"How much pay? A man's gotta blow off steam every once in a while," Billy said.

Buck pointed his finger at the boy. "I told you to stay out of saloons, kid. I made your pa a promise I'd look out for you."

"I hope you know what yer doin'." Joe shook his head while he stroked his beard. "Irish. You're signing up for a world of trouble."

He hoped he knew what he was doing, too, but he wasn't about to tell his men that. He didn't even have it figured out himself. Buck finished off his coffee, leaving the dregs, and unfolded his tall frame from the scarred chair.

"I know what I'm doin'. I'll see you boys sometime before tomorrow evening."

"Ain't you gonna invite us to the weddin'?" Joe asked.

"Sorry, but somebody's gotta take care of the livestock."

Joe guffawed. "Have a nice weddin' night then. I hope she's purty. I'd hate to think you'd have to look at an ugly woman the rest of your life."

Buck slapped the old codger's back and grinned.

"Oh, she's pretty all right." He pulled up his coat collar around his neck and quickly headed for the door, drawing on his gloves. Pretty, but stubborn, and not exactly a willing bride. Then he strode across the street and down the block toward the two-story McBurney House—the most expensive hotel in Deer Lodge—to book a room for the night. His wedding night.

Even though the water was hot, Kate shivered in the hip bath set in front of Martha's cook stove above Doc's office. Her bandaged foot hung outside the tub. The stitches hurt, but she had more important things on her mind. With still blistered hands, she poured a pitcher of water over her head, washing out all the soap until her hair felt clean. The strands hung heavy down her back as she swiped water out of her eyes.

Swallowing hard, she stepped out of the bath on her good foot and dried off with one towel while wrapping her hair with another—a real luxury.

Martha bustled out of the bedroom with a wide-tooth comb. "You just sit in that chair by the stove to dry your hair, sweetheart. As thick as it is, it'll probably take a while, but those men can wait. A bride needs time to get ready for her wedding. I sure am glad you're marrying Buck. He's a fine man. For the last five years, after every cattle drive, he's stayed for a while in Deer Lodge, sometimes until the next spring, looking for a place to homestead. According to my husband, he's got a bit of a past, and he's a little rough around the edges, but you can civilize him. He's been on the trail far too long, and I know he wants to settle down and raise a family. You could do a lot worse."

Kate scrubbed out as much water as she could with the towel on her head, then Martha gently ran the comb through her hair, starting at the very ends.

Kate sighed. If only Patrick were still alive, none of this would have happened. But there was no use wishing. She tried and failed to stiffen her resolve, realizing her life was totally out of her control.

Lord, help me! If there's any other way, take this cup from me, but nevertheless, not my will, but thine be done.

"That surely is a beautiful dress Abigail Stricklin brought over, isn't it?" Martha broke into her thoughts. "It might be a tad long, but with that foot, you won't be walking in it anyway. He'll have to carry you down the aisle."

Kate nodded, giving in to the older woman's ministrations, knowing she needed to be gracious despite the knot in her stomach. "Thank you for everything, Martha."

"You're welcome, child. I didn't have any children of my own, you know, so this is a dream come true for me. It's almost like helping my own daughter get ready for her wedding day."

Thoughts of her stepfather churned through Kate's mind. So charming and kind before he married her mother. Then the beatings. The whiskey on his breath. His razor strop connecting with her back.

The memories flew out of the box where she had stuffed them, and the fear nearly paralyzed her. Grabbing the towel close, she jerked away, the comb stuck in her hair. "I can't do this! I can sell the homestead to Mr. McKean. Patrick wouldna blame me. Then I'll have enough money to pay off the loan and move on to Oregon in the spring."

"Calm down, Kate, it's going to be all right." Martha placed her hands on Kate's shaking shoulders. "Even if you wanted to leave Deer Lodge, there's not a wagon master who would take you on as a single woman. You can't stay here alone. Every man in town will see you as fair game, especially Rafe Hamilton. You think he's gonna leave you alone? You think just because you sell your homestead to Buck he's going to back off? The man's been after you since you first stepped foot in this town."

"But what if Mr. McKean is even worse. What if..." She couldn't breathe.

Marsha hugged her to her bosom, patting her like a child. "Shh. Buck McKean is not Rafe Hamilton. He's a good man, a kind man, and there aren't many of those around these days. If he had time to court you, that would be one thing, but I'm sure your brother would have approved of him. Buck's a hard worker, and he'll build that ranch into a home you'll be proud of. You're not marrying a poor man, you know."

Kate stepped away and hugged herself to keep from flying into tiny pieces. "I don't care about his money. I don't want to marry him. I wish Patrick were here."

Martha smiled sadly. "I know you do. He would have been proud of his little sister." She hugged Kate again and tucked a wet strand of hair behind her ear. "I know you're scared of your wedding night, but you don't need to be frightened of Buck."

Martha gently lifted her chin and looked into her eyes. "Loving a man is the way God made us and the way we bring children into the world. It's the natural way of things. Buck will keep you safe, and in time, you'll come to love each other."

But who would keep her safe from him? Goosebumps rose on her arms. He said he didn't drink strong spirits, but did he have a bad temper? Had he fooled everyone in town? He seemed kind enough, but how could she know for sure? He said coming together as man and wife would be a time of her choosing. There would *be* no wedding night.

"What's done is done, Kate." Martha patted her cheeks. "I believe our prayers have been answered that the good Lord would send someone to help you. Trust Him to know what's best."

The comb fell to the floor. Numbly, she stooped to pick it up and gripped it in her hand, leaving marks on her palm. In the darkness of her soul, she suddenly heard her Da's laughter as he swung her into the air. If only he had lived . . . When she was a wee girl, she would dream about her Da walking her down the aisle, a wreath of flowers on her head.

Straightening her spine, Kate lifted her chin and nodded.

Martha kissed her on the cheek. "Good. You'll see. Marrying Buck is God's will. Now I need to press the wrinkles from your dress. You're going to make a beautiful bride."

Kate looked down at the tiny gold ring on her right hand in the shape of two hands clasping a heart and topped with a crown. The bottom of the heart pointed toward her fingertips.

"That's an unusual ring." Martha picked up her hand for a closer look. "I guess I've never noticed it before."

"It's a *Claddagh* ring. It was my mother's wedding ring and her mother's before her into generations past."

"I've never seen anything like it." Martha traced the heart with the tip of her finger. "It looks well worn."

"Aye. It was first worn by my great-great-great grandmother. The heart symbolizes love, the hands represent friendship, and the crown is for loyalty. When I marry, I will transfer it to my left hand with the bottom of the heart pointed toward my heart."

"We should let Buck know so he doesn't spend his money on a wedding ring. He asked Bill whether he had any in the store he could buy. You need to tell that young man what it means to you."

"It doesna matter." Kate swallowed her tears. "Those were the old ways of Ireland. I'm in this country now."

"Just because you live in Montana Territory doesn't mean you need to throw away the best things about your tradition. Every marriage needs love, friendship, and loyalty."

"But we don't love each other. I don't know if we ever will."

Martha straightened up and hurried for the stairs, her heels clicking across the pine floor. "Love will come, honey, hopefully sooner than later. I'll let your groom know how important that ring is to you."

Before Kate could protest, Martha's shoes clattered on the stairs, descending to the office below. Sighing, she twisted the ring on her finger and transferred it to her left hand with the bottom of the heart pointed toward her fingertips. She supposed she was engaged now...for a few hours anyway. Upon their marriage, a stranger would turn the point toward her heart, symbolizing the joining of their two lives. No matter how much she might wish it away, no matter how terrified she was, she was destined to become Buck McKean's wife...unless God intervened and sent her a miracle.

Buck paced at the back of the clapboard church, pulling out his silver pocket watch to check the time again. How long did it take to get ready anyhow? He ran his finger around the inside of his white shirt collar and straightened the sleeves of his black jacket. It was a little tight across the shoulders. Hopefully, the seams would hold until this was over. Now that he had accepted the fact he was getting married, it couldn't come soon enough. He was like that. Once he made a decision, he stuck with it.

"Settle down, son." Bill Stricklin grinned and slapped Buck on the back. "She'll be here soon enough."

Buck nodded and took a deep breath to still his racing heart. Was this what he wanted? He had been convinced of it when he looked into her panic-stricken eyes at Doc's office. No doubt, she was the finest looking woman he'd ever met. The woman who broke his heart and left him dangling at the altar turned out to be nothing but a con artist. She never had any intention of marrying him. Instead, she ran off with the big diamond ring he'd bought her in Virginia City and left him a lot poorer and a whole lot wiser. He swore no woman would ever trick him like that again.

Yet here he was about to ford another unpredictable river. Kate was different...he hoped. She was pure and innocent. She deserved better than the likes of him, but he'd made her a promise. He never thought he'd get married in a shotgun wedding though.

A voice niggled at the back of his mind. *You don't have to marry her. You can walk out that door right now. You've been roped and hog-tied like a steer headed for the slaughterhouse.*

He shook his head to clear it and thought of the alternative. Driving cattle the rest of his life? Settling down in Texas on his pa's ranch? He'd never be able to show his face again in Deer Lodge, and this was where he wanted to settle. And truth be told, he'd never be able to look at his face in the mirror again.

Just then, the door of the church opened, and Kate hopped over the threshold on one foot braced by Doc and Mrs. Mitchell. Buck swallowed hard to clear the buzzing in his ears. A shaft of sunlight lit her copper hair that had been intricately braided around her face. Curls trailed over her right shoulder, and dried **sprigs of baby's breath were** tucked into the silky strands. She wore a white gown made from a shiny material trimmed in delicate lace. Her cheeks were pale, and her eyes looked like a hunted deer.

They both stood motionless, staring into each other's eyes as if they were joined as one already. At that moment, he knew in his gut this was what he wanted, as strange as their getting hitched might seem. He'd never thought much about whether he was following God's will. He'd always made his own way in the world. He sure didn't think God was pleased about how he'd lived his life for so many years. Hopefully though, the Lord would smile down on him now and bless this marriage.

Unexpectedly, a picture of his mother flashed through his mind, a smile on her lips. She would approve of Kate. He knew it. The little sprite continued to stare at him with those wide, green eyes as though he was her executioner.

"You look beautiful."

She dropped her gaze, her long lashes fanned across her cheeks, and then she raised her eyes to his.

"You look nice too." Her voice sounded breathy. Was her heart beating as fast as his?

"Help the girl in the door, son," Mr. Stricklin said. "You're letting in all the cold air."

Buck stepped forward and swept up his tiny bride. Her arms twined around his neck, and she continued to stare at him with that haunted look. Somehow, he would prove to her she needn't fear him.

Doc Mitchell chuckled, turning to Bill, and Buck saw the two men exchange a wink. He didn't care what they thought. He only had eyes for his bride at this moment.

The two older couples walked down the aisle and took their places at the front of the church as witnesses. Reverend Russell, the Presbyterian minister, motioned Buck forward. He wasted no time carrying Kate to the altar in his strong arms.

The pastor looked at them with all seriousness.

"You two are in agreement that you will be married until death do you part?"

"Yes, sir," Buck said.

Kate hesitated for a long time, and he thought she might say no after all. Then she nodded with resignation.

"You've got to say it out loud so we can hear you, Kate," the preacher said.

"Aye...I'm in agreement."

It wasn't until they began to exchange their vows that either of them knew the other's full name: Lucas Daniel "Buck" McKean and Kathleen Rachel O'Brien. Kathleen. Kate. Katie McKean. He liked it.

As Mrs. Mitchell had instructed him, Buck turned Kate's ring around with the point toward her heart. Love, friendship, loyalty—the kind of marriage his ma and pa had.

He smiled at Kate when the pastor said, "You may now kiss your bride."

Buck leaned forward filled with wonder at the thought that this incredibly beautiful woman was now his wife. With his lips only inches from hers, he heard the sharp intake of her breath. He pulled back, cocking one dark brow, and smiled at her. Would she let him kiss her? Finally, she gave a slight nod, and he planted a quick, sweet kiss on her rosy lips.

He sure couldn't help looking forward to their wedding night.

Chapter Five

STALLING, KATE PICKED AT HER MASHED potatoes, swirling brown gravy through the fluffy white mound. Finally, she laid down her silver fork and looked up at Buck who had finished long ago. He had been drumming his fingers on the table for the last half hour.

"You finished?"

She nodded, took another sip of water, and dabbed her mouth with the snowy-white napkin embroidered with the name McBurney House. The few bites of meatloaf she'd eaten now lay heavy in her stomach.

Buck hopped up and gallantly scooted back her chair, draping the new green wool travel cape over her shoulders. After throwing a few coins on the table, he swept her into his arms and carried her toward the lobby of the hotel instead of the entrance door.

"Where are ya takin' me?"

"I got us a room here for the night."

Alarm bells went off in her head when he looked down at her and smiled, his long legs striding into the hotel lobby.

"A room?" she stuttered. Her face drained of all color. "But what about the livestock? We need to milk the cow and feed the horses and chickens and..."

"Don't worry your pretty little head, Katie girl. I hired on three of the boys who rode the trail with me. I gave them directions to the ranch."

Sudden anger rose in her. It was something about the way he told her not to worry her "pretty little head." She pulled away from him to look him square in the face. "You hired men without talking to me first?"

He looked down at her with a puzzled look. "I told you last night I'd try to hire on a few of the men I rode with. I need their help to round up the cattle and keep the ranch running this winter."

Feeling deflated, she remembered he had said something like that, but it felt as though he had taken all control out of her hands.

"I suppose I forgot. But I think we should agree on any decisions from here on out. Marriage is a partnership."

"With the husband as the head of the household. That's what Pastor Russell said." He continued walking through the lobby as if the matter was settled.

Her temper flared again, and it was preferable to the fear that had gripped her since this whole farce began. She had been managing the ranch all by herself ever since Patrick died.

Not very well, the voice in her head said.

As he carried her across the lobby filled with overstuffed sofas and chairs, her breath caught, growing shallow and rapid. She swallowed to clear the lump of fear in her throat, her heart racing uncontrollably. It was really happening. Tonight, she would become this man's wife in every sense of the word. A shiver ran up her spine, causing her teeth to chatter.

"You cold?"

He pulled her closer to his chest, setting off unfamiliar feelings in her body. She remembered his sweet kiss at the altar—her first. Her stepfather, the rogue on the boat, Rafe Hamilton. They had all forced their kisses on her, but it was far from sweet. She had felt dirty and violated. Now she had promised a man she would sleep with him. But not *tonight*! Looking down the long road of her life, she was terrified of what marriage to a stranger would bring.

Oh, Lord, deliver me!

"I said, are you cold?" he repeated.

She shook her head. "Nay, I'm...just tired, and my foot hurts."

"I imagine it does. I've had a few stitches in my life. Doc gave me a dose of laudanum for you just in case. You won't need it, will you?" His brow furrowed, and he looked at her with concern in those dark-brown eyes that seemed to swallow her whole. "We'll get to bed early so we can get up first thing in the morning. We need to stop by the bank and pay off your brother's loan before heading home."

Get to bed early?

She gulped. Her shiver turned into full-blown trembling, her mind reeling at the thought of what Buck now seemed to expect of her. He had made her a promise. She had been perfectly clear.

Then she caught the last part of what he said, and her hands stilled. "Put me down."

"You can't walk on that foot." He continued his forward progress.

Her voice rose in volume. "I said put me down."

He set her on one of the brown, horsehair sofas and loomed over her, resting his hands on his hips. She looked up at the sharp planes of his face—that face that occupied her every thought now. His brows knitted in a look of puzzlement.

"I thought we were going to pay off the loan after we sold the cattle."

"Is that what you're worried about? I have the money now, and that way we don't have to worry about missin' the bank deadline." The set of his square jaw suggested he wouldn't be changing his mind any time soon. But she didn't want to be beholden to him.

"Sit down," she snapped. "I'm getting a cramp in my neck looking up at you."

He settled down next to her on the sofa, still a little too close for comfort, but she needed to make her opinion known.

"That's very kind of you," she said in a prim voice, folding her hands in her lap and staring up at him, "but not necessary. After the cattle are rounded up and sold, I can pay off the loan with my own money."

"With your *own* money?" People stared as he raised his voice. His mouth tightened when he pulled back from her. "We're married now, darlin', for better or worse, for richer or poorer, in sickness and in health, till death do us part. And what's mine is yours and what's yours is mine. *Our* money will pay off the loan. I'm paying *our* debt to the bank."

He shook his head in seeming exasperation and stood up, lifting her into his arms. She had married a stubborn, prideful man, that was for sure. But they were wedded now, and there was nothing she could do about it. She needed to accept her circumstances. She had made promises to him at the altar, and an O'Brien never broke a promise. She licked her cold, dry lips.

When Buck pulled her to his muscled chest, her breath caught, and her arms snaked around his neck of their own volition. She didn't want to be in debt to this man. With every step he took, her fear of the coming night increased. She could feel the tension in his arms, and somehow, she knew he felt as nervous as she did even though his stride was confident.

Turning her face away from him, she caught the clerk's expression as he nodded at Buck and smiled.

"I'd appreciate it if your boy could take my buckboard across the street to the livery stable like we discussed, Mr. Clark."

"Of course, Mr. McKean. Don't you worry about a thing. You and your bride have a nice night."

Another guest, a man carrying a black traveling case, smiled at her and tipped his hat. Kate's face felt so hot she thought it would burst into flames at any moment. She hid her embarrassment against Buck's shoulder as he swept by the desk to carry her up the carpeted stairs. Her new husband seemed winded by the time they reached the top, his breathing heavy. Was she that heavy? He didn't seem to have a problem carrying her down the aisle of the church.

Buck stopped at a hotel door and set her down, and then reached into his pocket and pulled out a key. When he inserted the key into the lock and turned the knob, she realized they had reached their destination. The bed was the first thing she saw in the light from a lantern that was already lit. Her heart nearly leapt from her throat.

Chapter Six

Kate watched Buck's large, capable hands handle the reins of the horses, the bays' harness jingling as they rode in the buckboard toward the bank.

Shame rose in her, thinking about the night before. She had refused her husband his due rights. But she couldn't give him what he wanted yet, no matter how good-looking he was. She had feared he would force himself on her, maybe even hit her. Instead, he had turned his back and ignored her. Still, she had felt the heat radiating from his body. She hadn't slept much, and she suspected neither had he.

Now she glanced at the strong planes of his face, his deep-brown eyes, his firm lips. He had not been happy when she had pushed him away, but he had honored her wishes.

After she woke up to an empty bed, she had dressed hurriedly in her brown, wool dress and limped downstairs, finding him in the dining room, eating a large breakfast of steak, eggs, biscuits and gravy, and a stack of pancakes dripping with maple syrup. Where did the man put all that food? Wiping his mouth on his white-cloth napkin, he smiled, stood up, and pulled out her chair like a gentleman, never once mentioning the night before. They had eaten in near silence like the two strangers they were.

Buck glanced over at her now and a sad smile lit his expressive eyes. He rubbed the stubble on his face with his gloved hand. "I didn't take time to shave this morning."

She ducked her head. "I dinna mind."

He took her gloved hand in his and squeezed it, then put his arm around her and pulled her close against him. "You know what?"

Tense, she tried to relax against him, but it was impossible. "What?"

He leaned down and whispered in her ear. "You don't need to be afraid of me." Then he hugged her tighter and kissed her forehead. "I won't hurt you."

"I... know."

"I don't think you do, darlin'. We'll take it slow until you get to know me better." He smiled down at her.

She pulled away and nibbled on her lower lip, relieved that he had given her a reprieve. Maybe she could overcome her fear. And maybe the sky wasn't blue. She saw Samantha Eggers carrying her newborn baby girl down the boardwalk and waved. That could be her someday.

"All of Deer Lodge is probably gossiping about us," she said in a small voice.

Somehow that struck him funny, and he threw back his head and laughed. "Yep, I think we've already forded that river."

Buck pulled back on the reins in front of the First National Bank. He set the hand brake, threw his saddle bags over one shoulder, and leapt down to the street, lifting his arms to her.

"I'd like to walk inside."

She wanted to march into that bank and stare Henry Hamilton right in the eye as she—they—paid off Patrick's loan against the ranch. She felt guilty enough that Buck was using his own money to pay the debt.

"Are you sure you can make it that far?"

"With your help, aye."

He lifted his hands and encircled her waist, sweeping her down next to him. Her foot hurt, but not as badly as it had yesterday. Maybe if she had taken the laudanum she would have slept better.

Her tall husband tucked her hand in the crook of his right arm as she hobbled beside him.

"It would be much easier if I carried you."

Gritting her teeth against the pain, Kate lifted her chin and straightened her spine. "I can do this."

Finally, they stepped up on the boardwalk, and Buck turned the brass knob on the front door of the bank. He allowed her to enter first. She stood as tall as her five-foot-one frame would allow, wishing she hadn't pulled the ribbons on her corset so tightly.

Henry Hamilton, the gray-haired, corpulent banker and father of Rafe Hamilton, stood up at his desk and smiled a greeting, rushing forward to take Kate's hand. She pulled back, and Buck stepped forward, putting a possessive arm around her shoulders. Mr. Hamilton stopped dead in his tracks, a frown on his face. His shrewd eyes darted between her and her new husband.

"Miss O'Brien. What a pleasure to see you."

"Her name is Mrs. McKean now." Buck pulled her to his broad chest. "We've come to pay off her brother Patrick's loan."

Kate leaned against Buck's muscled torso, grateful for his presence. After a long moment of perusal, Mr. Hamilton stepped away from them, the man's piggy eyes making her skin crawl. Tugging on his gray vest, he looked up at Buck with wary eyes. She schooled her features to that of a woman ready to do business.

"*Mrs.* McKean. Then the rumors are true." A snide expression crossed the odious man's face. "You married this cowboy yesterday, spurning my son's courtship."

Kate's jaw tightened. "Patrick never gave Rafe permission to court me, Mr. Hamilton, as you well know. And besides, my private business is no concern of yours."

Every fiber of her being wanted to slap the sneer right off his face. But she held her temper in check. After today, she wouldn't need to talk to the bank's owner ever again. Acid rose in her throat at the thought that she might have been forced to marry Rafe to save Patrick's ranch. She swallowed hard.

Buck squeezed her shoulder. "She's my wife now, and I suggest you step back. We're only here to complete our transaction. We don't owe you any explanations."

Mr. Hamilton looked Buck up and down as though her husband was dirt under his feet, then beckoned to them and turned toward his large, quarter-sawn oak desk. "Come this way." He marched toward his chair in his impeccably tailored gray suit and polished black shoes.

Kate leaned heavily on Buck's arm as she limped to the rear of the bank, and then he gently helped her sit down in one of the wooden chairs across from the desk. Still standing, he slapped his scarred saddle bags on top of Mr. Hamilton's desk, untying a leather strap.

"How much do we owe you?"

"I need to calculate the amount with interest."

She looked at Buck's tightened jaw, his apparent anger held in check...for now. At that moment, she was glad he stood beside her.

Buck nodded at Mr. Hamilton. "We'd like to conclude our business as soon as possible. We need to pick up supplies at the mercantile, so we can get on the road for home."

Home. Kate's smile quivered as she looked up at her new husband. Someday, Buck would expect her to make a real home. Now she thought of it as Patrick's home and probably always would.

"Very well." Mr. Hamilton frowned, pulling out his desk drawer. He rifled through his files and pulled out a sheet of paper. "Here it is. I'm assuming you are the one paying off Miss O'Brien's debt? The loan is due and payable by September 15."

"I'm aware of the deadline." Although they had only known each other a short time, she detected a lethal undertone to Buck's voice. "Mrs. McKean and I are paying it off early."

The officious banker lifted his chin and made calculations on a piece of paper with a sweep of his pencil. He flashed a tight smile at her.

"The total due is $35.25."

Kate bolted up from her chair, grimacing as pain shot through her foot. "My whole fare was only thirty dollars! Patrick had already saved half of that amount. You must be mistaken."

"He must have needed the rest of the money to make improvements to his homestead." Mr. Hamilton flashed an oily smile.

"I want to see that contract." Buck reached for the contract.

Mr. Hamilton pulled it back. "I'm afraid not, Mr. McKean. The note is in Mr. O'Brien's name, and as his heir, only Miss O'Brien—"

"Mrs. McKean."

Kate glanced at Buck and watched the red creep up his neck as he no doubt was having trouble holding his temper in check. She could almost see the steam boiling from his ears.

"Give it to me." Once the sneering banker handed the contract to her, she passed it into Buck's hands without even looking at it. She never broke her hard stare. She wouldn't humiliate her new husband in front of this man.

Buck read the agreement and dropped it onto the desk before

withdrawing the coins from his saddle bag—two ten-dollar gold eagles, fifteen silver dollars, and then he reached into his wedding pants and extracted a silver quarter. He slapped every coin in front of the banker. "Now you need to mark those loan papers as *paid* and give us a receipt."

Mr. Hamilton ignored Buck and turned to Kate. "You trust him to make business decisions for you? You can't have known him for long."

"I've entrusted my life to him. Please do as he says."

Kate realized she did trust Buck with her life. He had proved himself to be an honorable man, even though she'd reneged on the most important part of their agreement. Not reneged. Postponed. But she knew with certainty, he would have taken a bullet for her.

Slowly, his sneer firmly in place, Mr. Hamilton counted the money twice, stacked it neatly, and then reached into his top drawer for a bottle of red ink and a pen. He dipped his pen and wrote PAID IN FULL across the loan paper, signed his name with a flourish, and dated it September 7, 1875.

Kate felt as though a giant weight had lifted from her shoulders.

The banker wrote out a receipt for the money and handed the papers to Kate. Without even looking at them, she passed them on to Buck, who smirked at Mr. Hamilton.

"You know my son would have paid fair price for your brother's homestead, Miss O'Brien, or you could have married him. You needn't have wed this...person. He's only a cowboy—a stranger. He probably married you to get his hands on your property."

Buck leaned over the desk. Kate put a restraining hand on his arm, but he shook her off.

"I think we're finished here, Kate." Buck growled the words from deep in his throat.

She stood up. "G'day to ya, sir."

Mr. Hamilton leaned back in his chair and put his thumb in his watch pocket, a self-righteous look on his face. "Of course, I suppose you had to marry him after he compromised your reputation by spending the night with you. My son would have withdrawn his courtship anyway. No man wants another man's spoiled goods."

With wide eyes, she placed her gloved hand over her mouth. Mr.

Hamilton had insulted her loud enough that everyone in the bank had surely heard what he said. Turning her head toward the barred windows, she saw a few customers staring at her in shock, others in amusement. Her cheeks blazed with embarrassment, and tears threatened to fall. She had never felt so humiliated in her life.

Before she could think of a response, Buck grabbed the front of the banker's vest, pulling him halfway across the desk.

"If you *ever* insult my wife again," Buck said with a clenched jaw, "I'll sweep this bank floor with your carcass. And if I can prove your son sent those men out to scare Kate off her land, I'll haul you both into the sheriff's office myself."

"Take your hands off me."

"Gladly." Buck shoved the loathsome man back in his chair, tipping him onto the floor. Mr. Hamilton cried out in pain.

Kate looked at Buck, shocked by the rage on his face, and gasped. Before she could say a word, her new husband swept her into his arms and stomped out of the bank, brushing past Rafe Hamilton who unexpectedly walked in the door. When Rafe glared at her, she turned her face into Buck's shoulder, afraid—afraid they had not seen the last of the Hamiltons. She feared for Buck's life.

It had started to spit snow, and if Kate didn't know any better, she would say the flakes melted on contact with Buck's red face, it radiated so much heat. He didn't say a word as he carefully lifted her onto the buckboard seat and climbed in after her. She studied the rigid muscles in his jaw, and her hands worried in her lap as she remembered his reaction to Mr. Hamilton's insult.

"Thank you." She choked out the words, afraid of his rage—the kind of rage she had seen on the face of her stepfather in times past. He looked over at her, his look fierce.

"Now I know why you married me to save your property. I can't say I wouldn't have done the same thing if that man's son is anything like him." He turned the buckboard toward Mr. Stricklin's store.

His words pierced her heart like a knife, and her temper flashed. "That's a horrible thing to say. I didna force you to marry me. I told you to go back to Texas."

"You're right, darlin'. I walked into this with my eyes wide open." His words dripped with sarcasm as he gripped the reins.

"I didna marry you so you could save Patrick's ranch. I married you because I thought you were a kind, decent man who wanted to save my reputation. Maybe I was wrong."

Glaring at her, he barked, "It's not Patrick's ranch. It's our ranch now. Yours and mine. Not your brother's."

"That's right. You bought and paid for me like a sack of potatoes, along with the ranch. You've made that abundantly clear. Well, I'm your wife now unless you want to put me aside. I'd certainly not be opposed to that."

Buck looked over at her with blazing eyes. Her eyes spit fire right back at him, and his jaw clenched.

Then he turned away and ground out a reply. "You may be my wife in name only right now, but I'll hold up my side of the bargain. When you married me, you married me for life. I don't believe in divorce."

All the fight drained from her, and she slumped in her seat. Kate scooted away from him and stared straight ahead, brushing away the hot tears that escaped her eyes. She heard Buck take a deep, heavy sigh. He reached into his back pocket for a folded square of white cotton and held it out to her.

"I didn't mean to make you cry, Katie. I'm just frustrated and so dad-blamed mad at that overbearing little..." He sputtered out the curse word under his breath.

Kate blew her cold nose, but she couldn't seem to stop the tears that had been stored up since Patrick died. She felt guilty she'd trapped this man into a marriage he didn't want—that *she* didn't want. It wasn't his fault they were married. His kindness and honor had sealed his fate when he had insisted on staying with her when those hooligans attacked Patrick's cabin...her cabin...well, their cabin now. With one bad decision, she had ruined both of their lives.

Buck pulled her close and laid his head against hers. "Please don't cry, darlin'. I didn't mean to hurt your feelings."

She sniffed. "You were only speakin' the truth."

"No, I wasn't. Men get angry sometimes, and we say stupid things."

Yes. She knew that all too well.

She kept her face forward, her back rigid. The Bible said the words of your heart issue from your mouth. Of course, Buck meant what he said in anger.

"I'm sorry, Katie girl. Let's start fresh, all right?"

Kate turned and stared at him for a long moment, and he had the grace to look apologetic. Finally, she nodded yes, but she knew she wouldn't soon forget, and she would watch for signs of temper. Never again would she allow another man to mistreat her.

Buck pulled back on the reins in front of Mr. Stricklin's store. He looked down into Kate's woeful, sweet face, pale except for her reddened nose and eyes. He felt like a low-down polecat. He didn't deserve a fine woman like her. "Once we pick up our supplies, we'll head on home before this snow gets any worse. All right?"

Nodding, she looked up at him, her eyes dry now, but it would be obvious to everyone that she'd been crying. He didn't want people to think he was the cause of it...which he was. He could kick himself six ways to Sunday.

"I'll stay out here," she said, twisting his wet handkerchief in her gloved hands. "I don't want anyone to see me like this."

"Darlin', it's too cold for you to sit out here by yourself." He tucked an errant curl behind her ear. She pulled back. "Come on in with me and sit by the fire. Please? I want you to pick out material for new winter dresses."

"I dinna need a new dress." She raised her chin. "I dinna want you wasting any more of your money on me."

He groaned and studied the snow-laden clouds, wishing he could take back his words said in anger. Already he knew Katie was a proud, stubborn, bullheaded, but brave woman. She'd faced down that gang, yet last night when he'd reached for her, she acted scared to death—terrified even—like a dog that's been beaten half to death. Someone had hurt her. Someone had hurt her real bad. He'd need to be patient with her and watch his temper.

Lord, I've really messed up here. Show me how to make this better.

When he was a kid growing up, he had spent plenty of time in church with Ma and Pa. He knew what the Good Book said. He should have been slow to anger, but when Hamilton had insulted her, all he could see was red, and he wanted to pound on that little weasel. Then his anger had spilled out onto her.

Sighing, he pulled her to his side, but she was stiff as a board. "Remember what I said? It's our money now, and I want you to wear pretty things. You do know how to sew, right?"

"Of course, I know how to sew," she snapped.

Inside, he smiled, but kept his face neutral. The woman still had spirit. "Well, I need a few warm shirts too. You think you could pick out the flannel to make me a couple? I can't even sew on a button."

Katie looked up at him with a defiant tilt to her head. "How about red to match your mood?"

Buck laughed. "I think that would be fittin' right about now. You think I could have a blue one too?"

"I'm sure Mr. Stricklin has a good selection of scratchy wool."

"Cotton flannel will do just fine." He grinned at her, and the corners of her mouth turned up in a tiny smile. "Let's go, my sweet bride. We need to head home as soon as we can."

Slapping his saddle bags over his shoulder, he jumped down off the seat, his boots landing hard on the frozen dirt street. His heart skipped a beat as he lifted his calloused hands to help her down. She didn't deserve a cantankerous trail boss like him, treating her like he would a bunch of drovers. Katie needed to be gentled, not tamed.

Among all the other things Doc Mitchell had told him about marriage, he said Buck should court his wife since she didn't have the benefit of knowing him beforehand. And read the Song of Solomon to her at bedtime. He'd never read it himself and didn't know why it was so important. In fact, he'd never done much Bible reading. It was too hard to understand. And he sure didn't remember anybody preaching about that book of the Bible.

As he gazed into Katie's bright green eyes, her cheeks rosy and her nose red, he vowed to sweeten his temperament and treat her like that fine porcelain teapot she treasured. His ma had taught him how to treat a lady, and Kate was a lady.

"Have I told you how beautiful you are today?"

Under her new green cape, she had dressed in that old, worn-out, brown, wool dress. It was serviceable and warm, he supposed, but kinda ugly. He wanted to dress her in colors to match her eyes. She deserved better.

Instead of sweeping her into his arms, he slowly set her on the ground. Without thinking, he bent to brush a kiss on her full, rosy lips, but she turned her face away from him.

"Can't I at least *kiss* my pretty wife?" he teased, trying to leap over the fear he saw in her eyes. "We'll hold off on...you know...the married part until we know each other better."

Blushing, she pushed him away. "This is neither the time nor the place."

"Yes, ma'am." Buck took off his hat and raked his fingers through his hair, sighing inwardly. He set it back on his head and then swept her into his arms and mounted the wooden stairs in front of the mercantile.

For whatever reason, God had put an overpowering need in his heart to love this precious woman and become the best husband he knew how—to cherish her, to protect her, to heal her wounded heart. Did he have that much patience though? He'd never been a patient man, but he was gonna have to learn how to be one.

He stopped on the boardwalk and gazed into her eyes, making her a promise he hoped he could keep. "I never want to make you cry, darlin'. But I'm a man, and I'm not perfect. Far from it. We may get into arguments, but I'll do my best to make you happy so you'll never regret marryin' me."

Kate's eyes locked with his. He gazed at every sweet feature of his bride's face...until he heard the tinkling of a bell as the door opened. They both started and looked at Bill Stricklin.

"You gonna stand out here all day and freeze?" the store owner scolded, but his mouth looked like he was suppressing a grin. "Git that young thing in here and warm her up."

Chapter Seven

Kate let Buck carry her into Mr. Stricklin's store. Buck was a good man. Martha and Doc and Mr. Stricklin said so, and she trusted them. Shyly, she studied the deeply tanned, rugged planes of her new husband's face, shadowed with a day-old beard, his brown eyes warm.

When he set her down in a wooden captain's chair, she slipped off her gloves and held out her hands to the black, pot-bellied stove, the smell of burning pine wood mixing with the familiar scents of soap, leather, coffee, and spices.

Abigail Stricklin, dressed in a plaid, navy-blue and yellow dress, with her gray hair pulled back in a neat bun, bustled over to Kate and bent to give her a hug.

"How are you feeling this morning, dear? You look like you've been crying." The woman's worried brows lifted in an unspoken question.

Kate blushed under her scrutiny but was saved by Martha who rushed over and pressed a cheek against her cold one.

"I'm sure she's feeling just fine, aren't you, dear?"

If they only knew she was far from fine.

Buck had retreated to the other side of the store and leaned on the counter, laughing with Mr. Stricklin. What was so funny?

Martha glanced over her shoulder. "Your bridegroom looks happy this morning. I suppose he's here to load up on supplies with winter coming on. You two better hurry on home before the snow really starts coming down. We never know this time of year."

"If it comes down any faster, you might have to spend another night or two at the hotel." Abigail Stricklin spoke with a knowing smile.

Kate's face flamed with embarrassment, and she couldn't think of a thing to say.

Both these women undoubtedly thought she had willingly submitted to her wifely duties. Shame and guilt and stubborn rebellion warred in her emotions.

"Well, is he the only one shopping, or do you need a few things?" Abigail said.

Kate started to answer no when she realized Buck was staring at her from across the store.

"She needs to pick out warm material for a few dresses," he called out. "And, you know, maybe other material and fripperies women need. Oh, and she needs a good, warm pair of boots and a wool coat. Take your time. It'll take me a while to load up the supplies."

She shook her head in protest. "Buck, that's too much."

He pointed a gloved finger at her and grinned. "Don't argue."

Strolling over to a stack of colorful sacks, he slung a large bag of flour over his shoulder like it weighed next to nothing and stepped out into the cold.

"You've got a fine man there." Abigail Stricklin turned to Kate with a wide smile. "Big and strong as a bull. He'll whip that homestead into shape in no time, and you'll have all winter to get to know each other. Maybe by summer we'll be welcoming a new baby."

Did the woman have no limits? She knew her face flushed as scarlet as the bolt of wool stacked on a table in the corner. Her mouth gaped for a moment, and then she clamped it shut, not even knowing how to respond. Martha came to her rescue.

"Abigail!" Doc's wife scolded. She looked down at Kate. "Can you walk on that foot at all, honey? You need to hurry and pick out what you want, because if it keeps snowing, you might not get back into town for a while."

"Yes, ma'am." Kate sighed inwardly, relieved at the change of subject. "I'm limping a little, but I can walk."

Gripping a table nearby, she stood and shuffled over to the neatly stacked bolts of cloth. The scent of new fabric filled her senses. It had been a long time since she'd had a new dress.

"In a week or so, you'll need to come back into town to have those stitches taken out." Martha searched through the material with her. "That should give your foot time enough to heal. Is it painful?"

"A little."

By the time Buck was ready to leave, she had picked out enough flannel to make Buck two shirts, a red one and a blue one; a green-and-yellow plaid for a church dress; plus, a length of dark blue wool for an everyday dress. Mrs. Stricklin added enough soft white flannel and fine cotton for undergarments, plus needles, thread, and buttons. A pair of black children's boots fit her perfectly, as did a long, caped overcoat of fine, navy-blue wool. Matching braid embellished the collar. Surely, it was too fancy for the hard work of carving a homestead out of the wilderness, but the two women insisted she needed to look pretty for her new husband. She didn't want to make herself too pretty. She intended to keep him at arm's length for as long as she could until she knew him better.

Buck blew in through the front door, stomping snow off his boots, his sheepskin coat and hat covered in white flakes, and his face cherry-red from the cold. His expression was serious, and Kate wrinkled her brow. "You ready to go, Kate?"

"Aye."

Mr. Stricklin handed Buck three, brown-paper packages tied with twine. "Put that where it won't get wet. I wouldn't worry about this little snow squall. It won't last long. We'll have more warm weather before old man winter sets in for good."

Buck pulled off his gloves and blew warm air on his hands, then slipped them on again. "That's good to know. We still need to round up those cows."

"You need to bring them down out of the high meadows for sure. It snows earlier up there, but you've still got time."

"Don't you want to warm up by the fire?" Kate pulled on her gloves and wrapped a dark green wool scarf over her head and around her neck—another purchase for herself. She felt guilty she had spent so much of his money. Did that make her obligated to him? She straightened her spine. No more than it made him obligated to treat her right because he now owned half of her homestead.

Buck smacked his leg with his hat to knock off the snow and spoke to Kate. "Better get on the road. It's a fair piece to drive with a wagon load of supplies in this weather. We don't want to get stuck."

"You'll be fine." Mr. Stricklin stepped around the counter and shook

Buck's hand. "This doesn't look to be a bad snow. The sun will be shining on you before you get home. Pretty normal for September. Just wrap up and keep yourselves warm. The horses are used to it."

Catching her by surprise, Buck swept Kate into his arms again. A tingle shot up her spine at his touch. Even though it wasn't the first time she had reacted to him in that way, it still amazed her. Despite her reluctance to live with the man, she had to admit he was attractive. He had an effect on her like when she walked on a carpet with leather shoes and then touched a metal cooking pot—the bite of static electricity.

The mercantile proprietor rushed to open the door for them.

"Thanks for everything." Buck nodded, then strode out the door into the softly falling snow.

"Stay warm," Martha called.

"Hope to see you at church on Sunday," Mrs. Stricklin said. The two women waved at her and Buck through the steamy window after the door closed behind them.

Without a word, Buck set her on the buckboard seat, tucked her purchases at her feet, and wrapped wool blankets around her legs and shoulders. Then he stepped up into the wagon, threw the buffalo robe over their legs, and giddyupped to the matched pair of dark bay horses with black manes.

Smiling, he reached over and took her gloved hand in his.

"Let's go home, Katie girl."

Home. Did she dare make a home with him? What choice did she have?

The dry snow had stopped an hour ago and now blew across the wide-open valley as the wind chased white, puffy clouds across a brilliant blue sky. They hadn't talked much on the way home except about rounding up Patrick's cattle. It wasn't an awkward silence though. Kate had to admit he had acted civil given everything he'd been through. Maybe, just maybe, they could live together in peace, and he would respect her wishes.

Lord, please make it so.

Had it only been two nights ago that Buck McKean had ridden onto her land? It seemed like a lifetime. She glanced at him, and he looked over and gave her a small smile.

"D'ya think Mr. Stricklin planned all of this?" She looked at him with suspicion in her eyes.

"Planned what?" He held the reins loosely in his gloved hands.

"Did he know when he sent you out to my homestead so late in the day that we'd end up marryin'?"

He chuckled, his eyes twinkling. "Bill's a wily old fox. I wouldn't put it past him that he and the preacher have been scheming for a way to take care of you. They were all worried about you living out here alone so far from town."

"Everything happened so fast it's like a dream. I still canna believe we're married. Do ya not regret marryin' me? You didn't have to, you know."

He was silent for a moment. "No, I don't regret it. If I had my druthers we wouldn't be in this state of affairs, but what's done is done. No use crying over spilt milk."

"My da used to say that."

After what he had said to her after confronting the banker, she doubted Buck had no regrets about marrying her. He had plenty of regrets, and she had more. If they fought like cats and dogs, she might order him to leave. Better than fighting all the time, but surprisingly, her heart pricked at the thought. Truth be told, he made her feel safe. Since Patrick and then the hands had left her all alone, she hadn't slept well and had scanned her surroundings for danger every time she stepped out the door. Now she stared unseeing at the tall grass, waving in the wind, not worrying about whether somebody lay in wait to attack her.

"Well, it wasn't in my short-term plan to get married." He broke into her thoughts. "But I can't say I'm unhappy about the turn of events." He looked forward at the backs of the horses, their harnesses jingling in the crisp, cold air, the scent of fresh pine blowing in the breeze. Then he glanced at her with a furrowed brow. "You havin' second thoughts?

Would you rather I'd left you in the hands of Rafe Hamilton, about to lose your ranch to his father? Am I so hard to look at or be around?"

She glanced at him from under her lashes. He was very easy to look at...too much so.

"Nay, of course not." Her words made him smile. "I mean, ya have to admit everything happened so fast. I dinna think we gave our circumstances due consideration."

Kate felt her heart flutter a bit when she looked into his warm, brown eyes, staring down at her. Unexpectedly, he tugged her close to his side, and she stiffened a little.

"Lots of people out here get married in a hurry. Mail order brides do it all the time. If we're going to tame this land, we need each other."

She couldn't say he wasn't a practical man. "But that shouldna be a reason to marry."

"We've been over this, Katie. We can't undo what's been done." His brow furrowed with a frown.

"Come spring, you might decide you've made a terrible mistake and leave."

His voice grew louder. "Is that the kind of man you think you married?" His breath came out in a huff. "What if you decide you don't want a husband? Will you up and kick me out? A deal's a deal."

She realized in surprise that she'd hurt his feelings, like he had hurt hers this morning. Maybe he needed reassurance as much as she did. Did men have feelings like that? Even her da and her brothers were stubborn and prideful. Her stepfather was a different kettle of fish though. Mean. Brutal. Evil like Rafe Hamilton. They were cut from the same black cloth. She rubbed the gooseflesh that rose on her arms.

The silence between them stretched out, drawing them farther apart. He deserved an answer—the truth as she saw it.

"No, I think you're a decent man, but I'm...well, what if I dinna please you? Men are known to beat their wives for burning a roast or speaking their mind or..." Her words trailed off, not wanting to even mention his desire for a family.

His exasperated glance sliced over at her. "Now that's plain silly, woman. I'm not going to beat you because you burn my biscuits. My pa taught me never to hit a woman. Ever. And I never have. You must think I'm the lowest kind of varmint." A thoughtful expression crossed his face. "What's this really about, Katie girl? Are you afraid of me?"

Yes, she was afraid. What woman wouldn't be? She examined the scary thoughts that whirled through her mind, throwing her into that dark hole in the past. She hung her head.

"Yes."

He stopped the wagon and pulled the brake, then lifted her chin with his gloved hand. "You don't have to be afraid of me, darlin'. I won't force you to do anything you don't want to do. God created woman to be a helpmeet, not a slave."

She wished she could be comforted by his words, but she feared living in close quarters with him. Not to mention she might have put him in danger. "What if Rafe Hamilton—"

"I swear you are the worryingest little woman I've ever met. You can't live your life afraid about tomorrow. Where's that little fireball who met me on her porch with a shotgun?"

A smile tilted up the corners of her mouth. "I come from a long line of worriers."

"I know how to cure that." He grinned. "Ma used to say that God has a plan for us...a future and a hope. And that He would never leave us nor forsake us. I promised before God that I would always take care of you. I meant every word, and I always keep my word."

She sighed and knew he meant what he said at this moment. She needed to trust him...and Mr. Stricklin's judgment. She smiled inwardly. Wily old fox, indeed. She suspected the church elder knew what he was doing all along. He had sent Buck out to her late in the day, knowing he'd spend the night on her homestead. The Stricklins, the Mitchells, and Pastor Russell had decided that marriage was best for her. She suspected neither she nor Buck had stood a chance against their meddling.

Buck spotted the smoke rising from the bunkhouse and smelled it in the air before they were close enough to see the ranch. The horses seemed to sense they were close to home and picked up their pace. Before long, he saw Joe standing in front of the log cabin, Riley at his side, wagging his tail. After the dog barked a couple of times, it took out lickety-split down the road for the wagon.

Katie's laughter bubbled over and soothed his soul. He vowed he would court her and prove to her he wouldn't hurt her or abandon her or make her afraid of him—not ever. Dogged patience, determination, and sheer grit had gotten him through the last ten years of hard work—first in the gold fields where he made enough to start his own cattle company, then driving up his herds from Texas—and he'd apply that same hard work to proving himself worthy.

The longing for a permanent home in Deer Lodge Valley was what drove him through the trials and obstacles he'd faced through the years—the fifteen-hour days he'd spent in the saddle; the men he'd lost or who'd up and quit, leaving him short-handed; fighting off renegades or bandits who'd wanted to steal his herd.

It hadn't been easy as a sixteen-year-old kid to stick with panning gold in an icy river, saving every bit of dust or nugget he found. Oh, he had spent his fair share on whiskey and women, blowing off steam and sowing his wild oats. He wasn't proud of it.

In the beginning, plenty of claim jumpers had tried to run him off, thinking he was only a kid, but he'd stuck with the hard life. Not many men wanted to take him on after he bested the first man who tried. Joe was the one who'd finally knocked some sense into him. When others quit their claims in discouragement, Joe advised him to stop spending all his gold in the saloons and buy them out. Then he saved enough to build a sluice box.

That's when his mining operation had turned profitable and given him his stake to buy his first herd. It was a lot easier to drive cattle than pan for gold all day in an icy river. At the price beef sold for in the camps, he had soon realized he'd make more money supplying beef to the men hungry enough to pay top dollar than busting his back mining for gold. Once he had quit drinking, gambling, and playing cards, he prospered.

When the buckboard bumped over a few rocks into the yard, it broke his reverie.

Joe walked over to his side of the wagon. "You coulda warned us about that dawg before you sent us out here."

"He didn't give you too much trouble, did he?" Buck said, laughing. He jumped down off the wagon and ruffled Riley's ears, running his fingers through the long black-and-white hair on the sheep dog's wriggling body.

"The heck he didn't. Why, it was nigh onto an hour before he let us set foot on the ground. He kept nipping at the horses' legs, trying to herd 'em. I thought we'd all end up with broken necks. Finally, Billy came up with the idea of feeding him the rest of his jerky. The dawg finally settled down, but I was shore we were all gonna get bit."

Buck looked at Kate who seemed amused by Joe's story.

"Riley is a good guard dog." Her voice held a lilt. "I dinna wonder you weren't run off the place. He must have sensed you meant no harm."

"Yes, ma'am." Joe whipped off his hat. "You must be the new Mrs. McKean. Why, she's a beaut, Buck." He slapped his boss on the back.

A grin split Buck's face, and he reached up to lift Kate into his arms. "She is indeed. Joe, meet the former Miss Kate O'Brien. She's a McKean now."

"Right nice to meet ya, Mrs. McKean. I've ridden with Buck since he was a kid in the gold fields and taught him everything he knows."

"I've saved your hide a few times too," Buck said. "Don't believe everything he says, Katie. The first words out of his mouth are usually a tall tale."

Kate giggled and put her hands around Buck's neck as he lifted her down. His heart warmed when she let him pull her close.

"Now that hurts me, Buck." The old man frowned, then grinned through cracked, dry lips. "But I reckon there's a bit of truth to that."

"Go get the boys and help me unload the wagon. We won't starve this winter. Let me carry Mrs. McKean into the house, and then I'll help."

"Whatsa matter with yer legs?" Joe asked. Instead of heading for the bunkhouse, he trailed behind Buck as he strode toward the cabin, carrying Kate.

Before she could answer, Buck tossed an answer over his shoulder. "Cut her foot."

"Josh cleaned up that broken bottle from the porch. Smelled like a whiskey still. What happened?"

Buck stopped and turned around. "I'll tell you later. Go get Josh and Billy to help with the supplies."

"Yes, boss." Joe turned toward the bunkhouse and limped away.

Buck sighed inwardly. It was hard watching Joe grow old. His rheumatiz was probably acting up in this cold weather. Truth be told, he didn't know how much help Joe would be rounding up the herd. He'd rather have him stay close to home to watch over Katie anyway.

"He seems nice." She spoke near his ear, her warm breath sending a pleasant shiver down his spine. He pushed open the cabin door.

"He's a hoot, that's for sure. But don't believe half of what he says. He has a way of embellishing his stories."

She laughed. He loved the sound of her laugh. Better than tears and sharp words, that's for sure.

He stepped into the frigid cabin and set Katie on a kitchen chair. "The least he could have done was start a fire to warm up the place. But I guess we should be grateful he didn't burn down the cabin."

"I noticed someone split a lot of wood and stacked it by the house. That's a blessing." Katie shivered and hugged herself.

"Josh's doing. He's a good man. I'll have a fire going in no time."

Buck stepped out to the side of the cabin and loaded his arms with seasoned pine wood and kindling, then stepped back inside, closing the door with his foot, and knelt by the stone fireplace. He turned to look at Katie, but she had disappeared.

"Katie?"

"In here." A muffled voice came from the bedroom. She hobbled into the front room still dressed in her cape overcoat with a quilt wrapped around her shoulders.

"You don't need to be walkin' on that foot yet," Buck scolded.

"It doesna hurt like it did yesterday. You canna be carrying me around the house all day like an invalid. I need to be about fixin' dinner."

Buck stood and before he could answer, there was a knock on the door. Instead of waiting on the porch, Joe and Billy barged in, while Josh waited on the other side of the threshold. At least he had a smidgen of Boston manners.

"You boys better get used to waitin' for one of us to open the door." Buck spoke firmly. "We've got a lady in the house now."

Billy whipped off his hat and shuffled his feet. "Sorry, boss." The kid stared at his wife with wide blue eyes.

"Kate, this is Billy Thompson and Josh Carpenter," Buck said. "And you met Joe—Joe Burnett."

"Tis a pleasure to meet all of you. Welcome."

"Ma'am," they all said in unison, twisting their battered, dusty hats in their hands.

"Miss Kate will do," Buck said in a dry tone.

All his men towered over his petite wife, but he had no doubt they'd all be fetchin' and carryin' for her before long. They looked smitten, and he felt a little jealous. He pushed aside his feelings and staked his claim by putting his arm around his wife and kissing her on the cheek. He felt her stiffen, her normal reaction to affection. It was troublesome.

"We'll put away the supplies." Billy sounded eager already. "Just point us to your root cellar."

"In the back." She smiled at Buck. "I've got a beef roast in brine down there. I've already got potatoes, carrots, and onions in the house to make dinner."

"I'll run and get it." Billy whipped out the door and left it standing wide open.

"You'd think that boy was born in a barn." Joe hustled to the door. "He even let that dawg sleep with him last night. Probably got fleas."

"Daylight's wasting." Buck pulled his leather gloves on. "We've got work to do so we best get to it."

Silent, Josh leapt off the front porch, and Joe hustled out the open door, followed by Buck who looked over his shoulder and winked at Kate. She blushed. He loved it when she did that.

After supper when the men had finally gone back to the bunkhouse, Kate piled the dirty plates in front of her. Buck picked them up and carried them to the sink, filling a pan with hot water from the cook stove.

"You sit there," he said. "Your foot must be hurting somethin' fierce. I'll wash the dishes."

She stood, leaning her hands on the table. "Nay, I'm fine. That's very kind of you, but this is my job."

"You sure? It's no problem."

"Go. Sit down." She waved him toward a chair.

While Buck sat by the crackling fire reading a new-looking Bible, she washed the dishes. When she had dried and put them away, she sat beside him in her chair, relieved to give her foot some rest, and picked up the sock she had been knitting. Too small for Buck. Since her new husband would be the one out in the winter weather most of the time, she decided to cast off her stitches and start a pair for him.

She glanced over at the boot crossed over his knee for an idea of how large to knit a sock. The man surely had big feet. His foot jiggled like a drop of water sizzling in a hot skillet.

"What are you reading?" she asked.

He looked at her and a red flush crept up his neck. She'd never seen that reaction from someone reading the Bible.

"The Bible."

"Sure'n I know you're readin' the Bible. What book?"

"Um, I started reading the Song of Solomon. Doc Mitchell suggested it." Her husband ducked his head and looked down at the page in front of him.

"I thought he suggested we read it together," Kate said. "Why don't ya read it aloud to me? What with all the chores, I havna had time to read the Scriptures since I've been alone."

Buck looked startled but covered his reaction with a stretch and a yawn. Strange. He closed the Bible and then flipped the pages to another section.

"Maybe we can save it for another night. How about I read a short Psalm before we go to bed? Ma always said you can find help for whatever ails ya in the Psalms. The boys and I will need to get up early in the morning to ride out and round up those cattle."

She studied him with furrowed brows. "Is something wrong?"

"No...no. I'm just tired." He yawned again. "It's been a long day."

After staring at his bent head for a moment, she finally cast on what she thought would be enough stitches for his sock, letting her knitting needles fly as her mind wandered. Never once since she'd arrived at Patrick's ranch did she think she would be sittin' in front of a fire with a strapping husband this winter. She'd never planned on a lot of things that had happened in her life.

Looking down at her mother's wedding ring, she wondered if she would ever love this man as much as her mam had loved Da. Mam said she had fallen in love with Da the first time he came a striding up to her door with a bouquet of wildflowers, the sun glinting off his raven-black hair. Mam had only been sixteen, and he wasn't much older. They had courted for a year before they were married and settled into a little croft of their own as tenant farmers.

Inwardly, she sighed, her heart aching for all the loved ones she had lost—her parents, a baby brother, Patrick. She was all alone in Montana Territory far from Ireland and married to a total stranger. Kate glanced at Buck and found him staring at her. Well, maybe not alone, but her life had certainly taken a peculiar turn.

Their eyes locked. A day-old beard darkened Buck's face, and his eyes held yearning. Her backbone turned into iron. She had hoped she wouldn't have to fight him off tonight but fight she would. He had promised her they would take things slow—become friends first. She had hoped she could hold him off forever, but she knew she had wished for something that could never be. Men never kept their promises.

Buck stood up and knelt in front of her, removing the knitting from her hands and dropping it into her basket of yarn. Her eyes widened, and she pressed back into the wooden chair.

He leaned in, and his warm lips touched hers, igniting a fire in her that she had to resist. He was still a stranger, no matter that they were married. Pushing his shoulders away, she stood up and stepped back from him, her heart slamming against her ribs. He dropped his head in defeat.

"You promised." Her voice trembled. "You can sleep on the trundle bed where I slept before Patrick was killed, but I'll not be sleepin' with you." She clasped her hands in front of her, twisting her ring, her eyes darting around the small room for a means of escape if need be.

"You sure that's far enough away?"

Was he being sarcastic or simply stating the truth?

"I suppose I could make you a pallet in front of the fire if you'd prefer."

After pushing up off his knees to his feet, he dragged both hands through his wavy, chestnut hair before planting his hands on his hips. He looked disappointed.

"I'd prefer to sleep in the same bed as my wife, but I don't suppose that's going to happen anytime soon."

He strode into the bedroom and yanked out the small trundle bed, scraping it across the pine floor.

She limped to the doorway, feeling guilty. He'd never fit on the tiny bed. "Since you're so much taller, you can have the bed, and I'll take the trundle. I'm used to sleeping on it."

Slanting a look at her for a long moment, his lips tightened. "That's mighty generous of you, *Mrs.* McKean." He turned away and stepped back into the main part of the cabin, striding toward the door where he grabbed his coat and hat.

"Where are you goin'?" she asked despite herself.

Closing the door hard behind him, he left without a word or a backward glance.

Anger flared in her chest, and she stamped her good foot. What an infuriating man! He was the one who said he would be patient with her, but he acted like he'd never made that promise. Now she wasn't sure she could trust him to keep his distance.

Fear of what he would do when he returned to the house replaced her anger. She chewed on her thumbnail. Did he imbibe spirits? She didn't think so, but she might have driven him to it. With quick hands, she took down her bun, brushed her hair a hundred times, and braided it over her right shoulder. Maybe she should sleep in her clothes tonight, but she couldn't do that forever. Still... Wearing her brown, wool dress, with her corset underneath, she took off her boots and crawled under the covers of the trundle bed, curling into a protective ball.

Chapter Eight

FRUSTRATION MADE HIM WANT TO BLOW off steam. Buck kicked at a few loose rocks and headed for the barn. If he stayed in the cabin, he didn't know if he could control himself and stay away from her, and he had always prided himself on his control. He'd never felt this way about a woman before—not even Angel who turned out to be anything but her namesake. All he wanted to do was pull Katie into his arms and kiss her until she kissed him back.

Jamming his hands into his coat pockets, he stopped and looked up at the expanse of brilliant sparkling stars above him in the Montana night sky, so close he could almost touch them. He breathed in the crisp, cold, pine-scented air.

Lord, help me. I'm only a man and a pretty sorry one at that. He didn't know if God was listening or not.

But Bill Stricklin said God heard his prayers, and his Ma had taught him who Jesus was. But he didn't know if God cared about him or not. He'd gotten to where he was today by the sweat of his own brow, not with any help from God. Plus, he'd done enough things that the good Lord would probably throw him into the flames when he met his Maker. His neck prickled at the thought.

By the time he opened the barn door and stepped into the dark, inhaling the familiar scent of hay, manure, dust, and leather, his desire had cooled. Instead of lighting a lamp, he kicked a bale of hay outside Applejack's stall and slumped down on it, dropping his forearms on his thighs. He was an idiot. Nearby, the mule and the other horses shuffled their feet in the hay.

Two nights in a row, he had scared her near to death. Big, dumb ox. Today he'd promised her he'd take things slow. He'd give her time. Friends, he'd said...they'd only be friends. He lifted his head and snorted. He didn't know the first thing about how to court her now, especially after he'd tasted her lips and touched her soft, ivory skin. He could drown in those green eyes shot with amber. And her hair...hair hanging to her waist. He shook those thoughts out of his head. He couldn't allow himself to go down that road if he wanted to stay sane.

Truth be told, he didn't deserve Kate. He'd proven that. The fact was, he couldn't even keep his hands off her for a single day. He'd spent the last ten years working, not socializing with women. How were they supposed to live in the same house together? A woman was made for a man. His feelings were natural, weren't they?

Who knew reading the Bible could ignite a desire in him for his wife? From now on, he'd stick to Proverbs and Psalms. The rest of it was hard to understand anyway. No wonder he'd never heard anybody preach on the Song of Solomon when he was a kid. He would have remembered.

How could he make this right? How could he live with Katie and keep his distance until she was ready to be a real wife? Like he'd promised, that's how. Buck gritted his teeth. He needed to make friends with her and court her like he would have if he'd been given time, because there was no doubt in his mind he would have wanted to court Kate if he'd met her at a church social. He wanted to be a good husband, but after the rugged way he'd lived for so many years, was he even husband material? Buck took off his hat and raked his fingers through his hair and scrubbed a hand over his face.

At least he'd be out of her hair for the next week while he and the boys rounded up the herd. He wouldn't rush the work either. If the cattle wanted to stop and graze, he'd let them graze. Maybe if he wore himself out every day, he'd be able to keep his promise when he got back to the ranch.

But what about this winter? They'd be trapped indoors together unless he stayed outside, finding chores to do and freezing to death. Once snow started piling up, he was a goner for sure.

His thoughts were interrupted by Applejack nickering.

"You smelled that dried apple, didn't you, boy?" He stood up, reached into his pocket, and offered his horse the treat with the palm of his hand. He patted the buckskin's neck. "Bought some at the mercantile for you. Got any advice for me? I'm in kind of a pickle."

While he brushed out his horse's mane, he poured out his troubles. "I don't dare go back to the house before she falls asleep. She might clonk me on the head with a cast-iron skillet. What do you think I should do? Sleep in the barn? You want me to keep you company?" Applejack snorted and shook his head.

Buck chuckled. He knew what he had to do. He needed to apologize and ask for her forgiveness and keep his hands to himself from now on. But how would he know when she was ready to be his wife? He hadn't really thought this marriage thing through. Of course, he had made it clear to her he wanted a real marriage—kids—before they walked down that aisle. Well, before he carried her down the aisle. Come to think of it, she hadn't had a chance to run away even if she'd had second thoughts.

Ma and Pa never seemed to have any problems living together. Buck smiled when he thought of how his pa would sneak up behind Ma, put his arms around her, and nuzzle her on the neck. She'd always squeal and pretend to hit him with a wooden spoon. But he knew they loved each other. He wanted that same kind of marriage. He wanted to laugh and tease his wife and hold her close at night.

After Ma died, Buck had never understood how Pa could turn around and court another woman. Oh, he'd waited a full year...barely...but then he found Amanda, a young widow who went to church with them, and married her and brought her two small boys into the house. He wasn't about to share his room with two little brothers. That was the day he moved into the bunkhouse, and it wasn't long after that he'd signed on for the trail drive up to gold country.

It wasn't that he didn't like his new ma. She just wasn't Ma. They got on well enough when he went back home to visit. Her boys were growing into fine young men. But he felt like a visitor in the house he had grown up in. He missed Ma somethin' fierce right now. If she were still alive, he could talk to her about this marriage thing.

Someday, he hoped Kate would lose her fear of him. He put his arms around Applejack's neck and leaned in to smell the warm familiar perfume of horse flesh. Horses he understood. Kate? He had a long way to go.

The door creaked open into the dark barn, a shaft of moonlight falling across the floor. Buck grabbed for his gun. That's when he realized he'd walked out without it.

"Who goes there?" he bluffed.

"Josh."

He let out the air he didn't know he'd been holding. "What're you still doing up?"

"Couldn't sleep."

The drover's face was in shadow, but Buck knew it was one of those nights. He'd gotten used to waking Josh from his nightmares on the trail. The man's boots scuffed across the dirt floor.

"Fightin' the war again?"

Josh leaned his arms on Applejack's stall, not looking at him. "Yeah."

"You wanna talk about it?"

"No."

All the years Josh pushed cattle beside him, he never wanted to talk about what he'd gone through in the War Between the States. Guessed he was trying to forget. But it sure caused the man a lot of sleepless nights. He could always count on Josh to volunteer to ride herd at night.

All he knew was his drover had been a soldier in the Union army—had a funny accent. Boston he'd said. Whenever they landed in a town, the women always gawked at the broad-shouldered giant with hair like a raven's wing and deep-blue eyes. The man was good-looking. He'd give him that. But Josh never paid any attention to those eligible females. Swore he'd never get married what with his nightmares and all.

Buck had been too young to fight in the war. So had Josh for that matter, but when he was a kid, he ran away from home and joined up with the army. Lied about his age. Buck's pa had supplied beef to the South. Josh had fought for the North. Guess it didn't matter anymore which side you were on. Out West a man could forget his past and start over. Josh did his job and did it without complaining. He didn't have to talk a mile a minute like Joe.

Buck rubbed Applejack's velvet nose one last time and patted the horse's neck before he left the stall.

"I'm goin' back to the house." He slapped Josh on the back. "Hope you get some sleep. We've got cattle to hunt down come morning."

When Josh didn't respond, Buck left him standing in the dark with his memories.

Near morning, Kate suddenly woke and sat up in bed, her heart racing. Something had awakened her. Then she heard Buck snoring. She clutched the quilt under her chin and looked up at the dark figure on the bed, sleeping on his stomach, the quilt twisted around his torso, with one arm hanging over the side. Even in the dark, she felt her cheeks blush.

When he hadn't returned to the house right away, she had finally fallen asleep, but not before lying awake and berating herself for failing him as a wife. It wasn't going to be easy living like this. He was a normal man after all.

What would Patrick say if he knew she'd married a man less than a full day after she'd met him? She wouldn't be in this mess if her brother were still alive. He would have sold off his cows and paid Henry Hamilton what he owed. She wouldn't have had to choose between Rafe Hamilton and Buck McKean. The thought chafed her soul.

Instead, her reputation was in tatters, and she was married to a stranger...a nice stranger, she grudgingly admitted. He didn't have to marry her. He could have ridden back to Texas like she told him. After last night, she wished he had.

Quietly slipping from beneath the covers, she smoothed down her dress and swung her stocking clad feet to the cold floor. She picked up her new boots and tiptoed on her bad foot to the bedroom door, closing it softly behind her. Riley, who lay in front of the banked fire, raised his head.

"Go back to sleep, boy," she whispered. She bent over and scratched behind his ears. With a big sigh, the dog laid his head down on his paws and closed his eyes. Then she stirred the coals and added a few more logs.

Kate yawned. What time was it anyway? Pushing aside the red-checked curtain made from flour sacks, she peeked out the window. Streaks of pink, gold, and lavender lit the gray, eastern sky over the mountain.

"Everything all right?"

She nearly jumped out of her skin. Whirling around, she saw Buck standing barefoot at the doorway to the bedroom clad only in his trousers over unbuttoned long johns. She realized she was staring at his bare chest.

He rubbed the sleep out of his eyes. "When I came in from the barn last night, you were already asleep. I wanted to apologize and talk a while."

Turning her back to him, she limped to the cook stove to pick up a few pieces of kindling that had been neatly stacked by its side.

"Oh?"

She stirred up the coals in the stove and threw in a few pieces of kindling, watching them catch fire. She refused to look at him—at his dark, mussed hair, his sleepy brown eyes, his chest. The man was almost naked! Her face grew hotter than the flame that flared up in the stove.

"Maybe we can talk over a cup of coffee before you start making breakfast," he said in a husky, sleepy voice.

"Um."

She was tongue-tied. What did the man want to talk about? Her thoughts raced. Would he issue her an ultimatum?

"I'll go get dressed."

Not able to tame her wandering eyes, she glanced over at him one last time. He yawned and rubbed the stubble on his face before he retreated into the bedroom. Oh, my. Her heart thumped clear up in her throat.

Without knowing what she was doing, her hands moved of their own accord to first stoke the fire and then pour water into the black-enameled pot and dump in a scoop of coffee grounds.

Buck soon came out of the bedroom, shrugging into a flannel shirt and carrying his boots. He dropped them on the floor and sank down in a squeaky chair.

With trembling hands, Kate rummaged through the cupboard for ingredients to make biscuits.

"What would you like for breakfast?" Her voice came out in a squeak.

"Anything you want to fix will be fine, darlin'. I'm not fussy."

She looked over at Buck's bent head as he pulled on his scuffed leather boots. The hair at his neck curled over the collar of his red shirt, and she remembered how soft it felt. Shaking that thought out of her head, she walked over to put on her cape overcoat while he buttoned his shirt.

She avoided looking at him. "I'll go milk the cow and gather the eggs. The coffee should be ready in a minute."

Before she could even lift the bar on the door, he was there in two steps and stayed her hand. Startled, she looked up at him with wide eyes.

"Don't look at me like I'm going to eat you up. I just want to talk first before we start our chores."

Her feet felt stuck to the floor as she gazed up at him. Her heart raced. He was so...tall...and muscular. She wouldn't stand a chance if he wanted to take her as his own. Numbly, she let him lead her to her chair in front of the fireplace. He knelt before her, and she thought he was going to kiss her again. She drew back.

"Please don't look at me like that, Katie. I'm sorry for last night. I apologize from the bottom of my heart. I didn't mean to scare you."

"Well, you did." Her voice quavered as she crossed her arms over her chest.

"I know, and I'm sorry." He bowed his head and then looked straight into her eyes. "I made you a promise, and I intend to keep it. I won't lie to you though. It's gonna be hard for me, and I can only do it with God's help."

"Praying and reading the Bible didn't help last night."

"I know, and I feel guilty about letting my actions get out of hand."

At least he looked ashamed. But could she blame the man? She sighed.

"Forgive me?" he asked, his face serious.

"I guess, but I dinna want to fear you'll attack me every time you walk in the door."

Buck looked shocked and stood up to tower over her. She cringed as though he would strike her.

"You think I'd do that? That I'd take you against your will?"

"I dinna know what you'd do. We hardly know each other." She crossed her arms across her waist and gripped her elbows with her hands, craning her neck to look at him.

"I swear on God's holy name that will never happen. I've never hurt a woman in my life, and I've throttled a few men who have. You don't have to worry about that. I won't even try to kiss you from here on out. You'll have to kiss me first."

"Don't make promises you can't keep." She sighed.

"If I start feeling that way, I'll walk away, even if there's a blizzard outside."

She could see that...Buck wandering out in a blizzard to avoid kissing her. The corners of her mouth lifted in a small smile. He really was a nice man, and she hated that she couldn't be the wife he wanted.

Kate stood up, feeling reassured for the moment, and he stepped away from her, his hands raised. She smiled in relief.

"Sit down and let me do my chores. I'll fix breakfast when I get back."

Dropping his hands, the furrow between his brows smoothed out. He raked the kitchen chair legs on the pine floor and sat down. Swiftly, she turned her back and walked to unbar the door before she fell under the spell of one of his smiles.

"After I drink my coffee, I'll go wake the boys and load the mule."

She looked over her shoulder, smiling in relief. "You're leaving today then after all?"

He folded his arms over his chest. "You don't have to look so happy about it."

She ducked her head before slipping out the door into the cold dawn. Even though she would have a reprieve from his presence, unexpected fear niggled at the edge of her thoughts. She'd be alone while Buck was gone. What if Rafe's men attacked again?

Worrying her bottom lip, she hurried toward the barn, her breath fogging in the cold air. One thing at a time.

Buck double-checked the ropes that tied their supplies to the back of the mule. They were packing in their own grub, something to cook it in, and bedrolls—that's all. He wasn't looking forward to sleeping on the cold ground again, but they'd be roughing it until they rounded up the O'Brien cattle and herded them down to the valley. Next season, he'd use the McKean brand.

Buck glanced at the cabin and saw Kate standing at the one good window, watching them. Josh and Billy had already mounted, their horses stamping their feet and blowing steam. They waited for his order to move out. They were a small crew, but he didn't have time to hire on any more hands, not if they were going to beat the snow at the higher elevations.

A niggling fear ate at his gut. He hated leaving Kate out here with only Joe to guard the place and him sleepin' in the bunkhouse at that. Course she had Riley to protect her too. He'd rather not be riding out, but he knew he had to go. He couldn't let the herd freeze to death. He'd have too much time in the saddle to think about Kate, but at least he couldn't act on his imaginations while wrangling longhorns.

If Kate insisted on separate beds for very long, he might have to move into the bunkhouse to keep his promise to her. He gritted his teeth and squelched that thought. No way would he let his men know his wife wouldn't sleep with him. He'd never live it down.

Before he had walked out the door, Kate had reached up and given him a quick peck on the cheek before stepping back. So be it. It was a start. He sighed and tried to look at things from her perspective, but he didn't understand the woman. Why couldn't she accept what was and get on with their lives together? Maybe she'd miss him a little while he was gone and be more receptive when he dragged back in. But he knew different. Some man in her past had beat her.

Applejack bumped his shoulder, and Buck realized he had been staring at the cabin while his thoughts ran wild. He swung up on his shuffling horse, looked at Kate in the window one last time, and raised his gloved hand in farewell before turning to Joe.

"Keep that wife of mine safe, ya hear?"

Joe nodded his head, his jaw firm. "Don't worry, Buck. If anybody comes prowling around, I'll be waiting fer 'em."

"I don't think they'll try anything now that we're married, but—"

"I said I'd take care of her. Now you go on and do what you gotta do."

Buck nodded and turned Applejack toward the grass valley, looking over at Josh and Billy.

"Let's ride, boys. The sooner we round up those beeves, the sooner we'll be sleeping in our own beds again."

Turning on her boot heel, Kate hurried toward the bedroom to put on a pair of Patrick's britches and a flannel shirt. She wasn't about to spend every minute inside the confines of this cabin as Buck had ordered her to do before he left. The man was daft.

She wasn't some fragile doll who didn't know how to work hard. She needed to harvest the rest of the garden, dig potatoes, and store them in the root cellar where they wouldn't freeze and go to mush. She had already gathered her beets, carrots, turnips, rutabagas, beans, and made sauerkraut with most of the cabbage, but they'd need more than that to get through the winter. Of course, she had discovered Buck had bought a lot of canned goods too. They wouldn't starve, and he could hunt when they needed more meat. Patrick said there were a lot of elk and deer around.

After donning her brother's oversized shirt and britches, she rolled up the pant legs before slipping her feet back into her new boots. She tested her sore foot. Tolerable. Slipping her arms into Patrick's coat, she placed his hat on her head and stepped out onto the porch and breathed in the fresh, crisp air. It was warmer than yesterday.

She could just make out Buck and his men riding toward the foothills, a bright blue sky above them. Good. He wouldn't give her any grief about wearing britches. As if she'd let him tell her what to do. They might be married, but he didn't own her.

Chapter Nine

KATE'S FIRST TASK, AND THE HARDEST, was to dig the potatoes, but she had plenty of experience of that back home. After setting her empty feed sack at the end of a row, she took the spade and stabbed it into the ground with her boot and turned over the earth below the mature bushes. She smiled. Her shovel yielded a treasure trove.

Working quickly down the row, she continued to turn the earth, loosening the potatoes from their roots to lie in a neat line. Now sweating from her efforts, she took off Patrick's coat and rolled back the sleeves of his flannel shirt. His gloves were clumsy, but she'd learned her lesson after chopping wood and not wearing them, and besides, she didn't want to get her good ones dirty.

A voice startled her. "Miss Kate?"

She looked up at Joe leaning on the garden fence that kept out the deer and rabbits...well, most of the rabbits. He looked shocked when she stood up, the britches loose at her waist.

"Aye?"

"Buck would have a fit if he saw you dressed like that," he huffed. "It ain't ladylike."

Her jaw tightened. She bet he'd never tried to dig potatoes while dressed in a skirt and wearing a corset.

"Dinna you have chores to do?" She pitched her voice lower, hoping she sounded like his boss, which she was...sort of.

"I need to clean out the stalls and spread fresh hay, but I saw a man up here, sneakin' around the cabin."

That's when she noticed the rifle in his hand. She blew back a strand of hair that had fallen over her eyes. It was kind of sweet that Joe thought he was coming to her rescue.

She smiled. "As you can see, it was only me in dungarees. I need to finish harvesting the garden."

"Don't you have any work dresses?"

"What I wear is none of your concern, Mr. Burnett." She turned away, stuck her spade into the ground, and turned up more potatoes.

"I can give you a hand with that."

She glanced over her shoulder. "No need."

He opened the gate and set the rifle against a fence post before trying to take the shovel from her hand. "Buck would have my hide if I didn't."

Temper flaring, she pulled the handle toward her. "I said I didna need any help. I'm perfectly capable of digging potatoes by myself, thank you very much."

Joe wouldn't let go and tugged the handle toward him. This was ridiculous. They were fighting over a spade. Were all Texas men this stubborn? He needed to learn who was boss.

"Turn loose of that shovel," he said.

"You turn loose."

She glared into his faded gray eyes, determined he wasn't going to win this battle.

After tugging the handle back and forth a few times, Joe grumbled something under his breath and let go. It was so sudden, she fell on her backside and plopped in the freshly turned soil. Immediately, he stuck out his hand to help her up, but she ignored it and popped to her feet, breathing hard.

"Buck's gonna be plumb put out with you," he growled.

"That's none of your business. You can leave now. As you can see, I'm quite safe on my own." She swiped away a drop of sweat that threatened to run into her eye.

They locked gazes until he finally turned away, grabbing the rifle, and limping to the barn, muttering under his breath. Smug that she had bested Buck's hired hand, she finished digging the row even though her arms felt as though they would fall off by the end. She walked to her feed sack, knelt on the ground, and carefully rubbed the dirt off each potato before dropping it in the bag as she dragged it along behind her. Her back hurt, and she still had rows to go.

Pride goeth before a fall.

Kate shook the thought out of her head. Pride and hard work were what kept the O'Briens fed during the hard times. After arriving last spring, she had enlarged this garden with Patrick's help, then raked the rocks out herself, turning over the soil again and again. She was the one who used stakes and string to make her rows straight before she dug a trench to drop in her potato eyes. This was good land—rocky, but good. Because of her efforts, they would eat this winter. Buck would have to get used to her doing chores in britches. Otherwise, Patrick's ranch wouldn't survive.

After a few more hours in the garden, Kate looked up at the sun and decided it was about time to eat. Dragging the full sack behind her, she struggled toward the root cellar. That's when she heard hoof beats and looked up. Rafe Hamilton. She dropped the sack and ran toward the cabin to fetch her shotgun. She didn't make it, though, before he pulled up his snorting black stallion and swung to the ground.

"Miss Kate." He tipped his hat, a smirk on his face.

Like Buck, Rafe towered over her. "Mr. Hamilton."

"I heard you got married. Your man around? I've got business to discuss." He gave her a lazy grin. She felt fury rise in her belly.

"Whatever ya need to say, you can say it to me. Now that Patrick's gone, I'm still the owner of this place." She wiped the sweat from her forehead with the back of her glove covered in rich loam.

Rafe, his blond hair covered by his hat, raked his blue eyes up and down her body, slowly perusing her. His ogling made her feel dirtier inside than she was on the outside. It didn't matter what she wore, he had always looked at her like that. Well, maybe not at first. At first, he had acted all nice and sweet—a real gentleman—and then he turned into a monster. When she finally accepted his invitation to picnic down by the river, he showed his true colors when he tried to force himself on her.

"Maybe we can sit in your cabin and talk over a cup of coffee." His smirking grin grew wider as though he had something else on his mind besides talking. "You look mighty fetching in those britches."

"We can talk right here. What do you want?" Her fingers itched for the bulk of the shotgun.

"I came to make your man an offer for your property."

"I'm not interested." Her jaw tightened.

"No? Well he might be."

"I said I'm not interested, and neither is he. Now I suggest you get off my land."

To emphasize her words, Riley shot out of the barn, barking as he raced toward her.

Rafe, a leer still on his face, took off his hat and smacked it against his leg, dust flying up in her face. As she choked, he slowly advanced toward her, so close now she could smell his stale-cigar breath. Riley skidded to a stop, snapping at Rafe and barking even louder, trying to herd the intruder toward his horse.

She glanced at the barn, wondering where Joe was now that she really needed him. The man must be deaf.

"I'll pay top dollar, sweetheart. You and that Texan might as well sell out now. You two will never make it through a winter out here. Anything could happen to him. Grizzlies, wolves, Indians."

"Is that a threat? I suggest you leave before my dog sinks his teeth into your leg."

Pretending shock, he started to take a step closer, but Riley stood between them growling deep in his throat, his head down, teeth bared.

"Of course not. I'm just saying Montana Territory's an unforgiving place for people who don't respect the land. You're both new to this territory. New homesteaders leave for Oregon all the time."

"This is my brother's land, and this is where I'll die. I told you to get off my land."

"No cause to get huffy." Chuckling, he settled his hat on his head, stepped away, and leapt into his saddle, drawing up the reins. His eyes roamed over her body as he smirked. "Better keep that dog close. Somebody's liable to shoot him."

The black stallion reared on his hind legs and stomped the ground. Kate suddenly feared for Riley's safety.

"Riley, come." She patted her leg, but it was as though the sheepdog couldn't hear her. He continued to snap and bark at the horse's legs.

"Hey!" Joe limped out of the barn, carrying his rifle.

"Old men don't live long out here either." Rafe tipped his hat, whirled around on his dancing stallion, and loped away. Riley tore out after them, continuing to bark, but finally turned around and trotted to her side. Panting hard, his tongue lolled out as he sat. She knelt and hugged his sturdy black-and-white body to her. Her heart beat almost as fast as his.

For the first time since she'd married Buck, she really missed him. Rafe had made it plain he hadn't given up on her yet. And she doubted Riley or Joe could protect her if the man really wanted to do her harm.

Thunder rumbled as dark clouds rolled in over the mountains. Buck reached behind him and untied his rain slicker from the cantle of his saddle, shrugging into it. Buck had spent the last three days, whooping and hollering and bullying cantankerous longhorns out of the tall, grass meadows toward the valley, but with only the three of them it had been a battle. Now they had a new enemy. The herd was spooked by the rumbling noise, and it was near dark.

"Keep 'em bunched together next to the river," he yelled at Josh and Billy as the heavens turned loose a downpour. "We don't want 'em running scared."

Whistling and using their lariats, they drove the cattle into a circle. He sure hoped they'd settle down for the night. The rain drenched his hat, and soon the deluge cut off the last of their light. Cold, hard rain, but no lightning. Thank God for that. It would be a miserable night. Finally, the small herd decided to bed down in the steady torrent that soon turned the ground into a soggy mess. Swiping the rain from his eyes, he peered into the darkness.

"Josh?"

"Here," he heard from the right flank.

"Billy?"

"Here, boss."

Billy had ridden behind the herd, using his cutting horse to chase after strays and any calves that lagged behind their mamas. It would take all of them to keep the cattle quiet tonight. They'd only found about eighty head, carrying the O'Brien brand. He'd never thought to ask Kate how many cows her brother had, but she probably wouldn't have known anyway. Especially if rustlers had made off with some of them.

Buck shrugged, trying to work out the kinks in the bunched muscles of his shoulders, and stood up in the saddle to relieve his backside. Rain beat down on him and ran down his slicker in torrents. He was bone tired, cold, and hungry. If he got any sleep tonight, it would be on the back of Applejack. He tried to ignore the growling hunger in his belly. If he never ate another piece of beef jerky in his life, that would be fine by him.

Montana weather acted like a fickle woman this time of year. Even in the high elevations, they'd had a few snow flurries, a couple of broiling hot days, and now rain. He'd be glad to sleep in a warm bed again with a roof over his head, even if he couldn't sleep with Kate. He could almost smell her biscuits, dripping with butter. His mouth watered.

As he rode around the herd, his mind drifted to his wife, the prettiest gal he'd ever laid eyes on. He let his imagination wander although he knew it wasn't a good idea. He remembered how she had felt in his arms, her head pressed against him, her long copper hair so thick he could get lost in it. The faint scent of lavender.

He let himself think about the day sometime in the future when she'd turn to him and love him back and want his children. What would they look like? He hoped the boys took after him, and the girls looked like her. Giggling kids, running through the grass valley. He'd teach them all how to fish. His heart swelled with his dreams of a home and a future together.

Would she turn to him by Christmas? Before, he hoped. That was months away. How was he supposed to court a woman he was already living with? If it was spring, he could bring her wildflowers and they could picnic on a quilt by the river, getting to know each other.

What did Katie think about anyway? Did she think about him? Did she miss him? Shoot, they'd only had a couple of days together before he'd ridden into the hills with the boys. His heart sank, and his head drooped. She was probably glad to be rid of him. While he sat on Applejack in the pouring rain, she was probably sittin' in a chair next to the fireplace, enjoying a cup of hot tea out of that rose china cup, her delicate fingers caressing the handle. Her hair glowing in the firelight.

Those green eyes soft and smiling.

Buck shook his head and flung cold water off his hat brim into his face. No use lettin' his mind wander down that path. Dreams. What were Katie's dreams? She'd talked about wanting a real wedding in the springtime. Maybe if he asked, the preacher would come out to the house in the spring, and he could give her the wedding she really wanted.

But he'd never heard of two people getting married twice. Once you were hitched, you were hitched. A honeymoon maybe? They couldn't be away from the ranch that long. Maybe another night at McBurney House. That had been a real fine place to stay. But that didn't solve the problem of courting her first. They lived in the same house for Pete's sake.

Maybe if he shaved every day and put on his good clothes for supper every night. His wedding shirt and his black twill trousers. Buck smiled and swiped at the rain dripping down his nose. That could work. Then they could talk about her dreams...his dreams...their dreams of a future together.

But the boys would be there eating too. He could kick 'em out as soon as they were done filling their faces, then he and Katie could dress up and have tea. A grimace crossed his face. Maybe not tea. He hated tea. Cookies. Soft, oatmeal cookies that melted in your mouth. He'd brush a crumb off her cheek, and...

Lucas Daniel McKean, get hold of yourself!

He sighed, and his shoulders slumped lower. He shifted in the saddle. It was going to be a long, miserable night.

With Joe fed breakfast and her chores finished, Kate had put on her faded church dress and sat in a chair on the porch in the warm sunshine, keeping her hands busy by hemming the long-sleeved nightshirt she'd made for Buck. The man didn't seem to own one.

Her stomach did flip-flops, thinking about him coming home. Part of her dreaded their reunion, and part of her yearned for his company — his kindness, his gentle humor. Truth be told, she'd been a bit lonely since he'd been gone. *Ach!*

After arguing with Joe over her wearing britches to dig potatoes, the old man's conversation at the table had been limited to grunts. He'd stare at her when he thought she wasn't looking and shake his head. He only stayed in the house long enough to eat. Not that she missed his presence and the look in his eyes that seemed to judge her. She lifted her chin. Maybe she'd even buy a pair of britches that fit her better to do chores in—and a hat like Buck wore. She didn't want to ruin the new dresses she still hadn't made.

Today was Sunday. She had donned her washed-out green dress with tiny pink flowers, hoping Buck would get home early enough to take them to church, but it was already noon. Worry pinched her brows. Did a roundup take this long? He'd already been gone almost a week. What if something had happened to him?

Her hands stilled in her lap as she looked out at the grassy horizon. An undulating line of longhorns suddenly flowed over the hill through the bunch grass. Her heart quickened. Buck was home. She whipped the last few stitches in the hem, tied off the white thread in a knot, and bit through it with her teeth. Rushing inside, she put away her needle and thread and laid out the nightshirt on the other side of the big bed. There. Now he'd be warm and sleep proper.

The men would be hungry. Back in the kitchen, she used a dish towel to open the oven door. Hoping Buck would make it back to the ranch that morning, she had made a large shepherd's pie. Patrick had killed their only lamb and put it down in brine a few weeks before he died. There wasn't much left.

Did Buck like shepherd's pie? Mam had taught her well. Even with only a few staples, she could set a hearty meal on the table.

Quickly assembling the lard and flour and other ingredients for biscuits, she mixed up a batch while listening to the bawling cattle, whistles, and the men's raised voices. With trembling hands, she oiled the biscuits in hot grease and arranged them in the iron skillet. Her heart raced when she identified Buck's voice giving orders.

Now what? How should she greet him? The men would expect her to act like a wife. She certainly didn't want to humiliate him in front of the hired help. She washed her hands and pushed a few unruly curls back from her face.

Nervously, she finished setting plates and forks on the table, then she heard heavy footsteps on the porch. She froze and looked at the door in expectation. Buck flung it open. A wide grin split the scruffy beard on his face as he took off his hat and hung it on the peg on the wall. He took a step toward her, but she unconsciously responded by backing up. His face fell, and her heart sank.

"Kate."

"Welcome home," she said, her smile tremulous. She turned her back on him and pulled the golden-brown shepherd's pie from the oven, setting the heavy iron skillet down with a bang.

"Kate—" he said again but was interrupted by the clatter of boots on the porch.

"Boy, that smells good." Billy barged in, dried cow manure falling off his boots. "I could eat the south end of a northbound steer. What's for dinner?"

Chapter Ten

KATE LOOKED AT BILLY'S FACE, BUT couldn't help wrinkling her nose when Josh and Joe walked in behind them, stomping their boots on the floor she had washed on her hands and knees the night before when she couldn't sleep. They all smelled like cow dung.

She reached for the bar of soap and a hand towel she had laid out fresh next to the basin. What they all needed was a good dunking in the river. It was warm enough today. But she'd settle for clean hands and faces.

"Here." She handed the soap and towel to Billy first. "You can wash up outside."

"Yes, ma'am."

Everyone but Buck hustled out the door. She stared into those warm, brown eyes and felt them drawing her to him.

"Don't I even get a kiss hello?" he said softly, his eyes warm.

Kate hesitated and then stepped forward, stood up on her tiptoes, and gave him a quick peck on the cheek. She wrinkled her nose.

"You smell like...cows."

Buck cocked one dark eyebrow and frowned. "You would, too, if you'd spent a week sleeping with those sorry critters. That's a fine way to welcome me home. What did you expect? Rosewater?"

She grimaced and wrung her hands. "No, of course not." She cast about for something nice to say. Then she noticed the dark shadows under his eyes. "You look tired."

"I am tired—bone tired—and I'm lookin' forward to a soft bed tonight...if you can stand the smell." He planted his hands on his hips, scowling at her.

Blushing, she ducked her head and picked off a piece of white thread from her dress, rolling it between her fingers. Turning her back to him, she used her dish towel to grasp the handle of the heavy skillet she'd baked the shepherd's pie in and set it down in the middle of the table with a thunk.

"Did you have any trouble finding Patrick's cattle?" she asked.

"You mean *our* cattle." He still stood near the doorway, filling the room with his broad shoulders.

She glanced at him quickly and then bustled around the table, straightening the silverware she had already straightened.

"Still, they carry Patrick's brand. I meant, did you find all the ones with his brand?"

She avoided Buck's eyes and turned around again to open the oven door to check on the biscuits. Rising nicely. A few more minutes for a nice, even brown.

Kate turned back to Buck and retied her apron, giving her hands something to do.

"We scoured the hills, plus we found several strays in the timber. Not as big a herd as I thought the way you talked about your sainted brother. Maybe that's a good thing though since there were only three of us to bring 'em in."

Her temper flared as she faced him from across the table. "What do you mean my *sainted* brother?"

"The way you talk about him you'd think the man walked on water," he growled at her. "In your head it's still Patrick's land, Patrick's cattle, Patrick's cabin."

"This *is* his land," she yelled. "He built this place with his own sweat and blood and no stranger is going to ride in here and insult his good name."

She was so mad, she could barely breathe. How dare he slight her brother. Her face felt as if it was on fire. All the good thoughts she'd had about Buck were forgotten. He'd haunted her nights and her daydreams the whole time he was gone. Now that he was back she felt safe from the danger Rafe Hamilton brought onto the property, but she felt afraid of him too. It was obvious now that all he'd married her for was this ranch.

"That's what I am to you. Some stranger who rode in to save you from the big, bad banker. I still don't know why you didn't marry Hamilton. I figured you'd have married the first man who didn't look like a frog and had enough money to pay off your debt."

"How dare you!" Before she could think about what she was doing, she picked up a white, stoneware plate from the table and threw it at his head. He ducked as it crashed against the door, and she reached for another one.

"You throw that at me, and you'll regret it," he shouted.

"Why? Will you ravage me like you've wanted to ever since you laid eyes on me? I can tell you this, you...you...thief, I'll never share your bed."

He pointed his finger at her and opened his mouth, but before he could say anything else, she threw the plate, smashing it against the wall where he had stood. He advanced toward her, a murderous look on his face. She was afraid—very afraid. He towered over her, and she knew he could snap her in two with those big, callused hands of his. She backed up, panting, the scent of burning biscuits filling the air.

"You *will* share my bed, Katie girl. You married me for better or worse. It may not be tonight, but sooner or later, you'll want me as your husband. You'll want me as bad as I want you. I don't know what you're so fired up about. I'm the one who got hornswoggled into this marriage."

She glared up into his bearded face, wanting to scratch out his eyes. "I didna force you into anything. I told you to turn around and go back to Texas. I dinna need you."

"Well, I don't need you either, woman, but we're stuck with each other, so you better get used to the idea."

His eyes were dark brown orbs, and he panted as hard as she did. Nobody had ever made her lose her temper like this. She'd seen her da unleash that side of him too often. Oh, he'd never hit any of them, but he had an Irish temper and had slammed his fist on the table often enough when he was tired. Then there was her stepfather.

Suddenly, Buck reached out for her and kissed her with the passion of a husband. At first, she pushed against his rock-hard chest, but he only deepened his kiss, enclosing her in his embrace. A sudden flame rushed through her veins and swept through every limb, and before she knew it, she was kissing him back, her breath ragged in her ears.

He was the one who broke away first, giving her a wicked, knowing smile. The insufferable man. He had done that on purpose. She slapped him—hard. But not hard enough to wipe that smile off his face. He grabbed his hat from the peg on the wall and looked at her over his shoulder.

"You liked it, Katie girl, no matter what you tell yourself," he drawled. "Well, don't worry your pretty little head about it. I won't kiss you again till you beg me to."

"It will be a cold day in—"

He winked at her, and she stomped her foot. He had awakened desires in her she couldn't explain, and it made her afraid. Never. She'd die an old, married maid before she gave in to him.

"I'll sleep in the bunkhouse tonight, so I don't offend your sensibilities with my smell. But don't get used to it. Tomorrow night I'll be sleeping in my own bed whether you like it or not. Go ahead and feed the boys and send them down to the barn when they're finished. I'm not hungry."

After he slammed the door, rattling the one good window glass, she plopped down in one of the kitchen chairs and buried her face in her hands. She was married. Married! Her wedding was a blur, but she knew it had been real. She looked down at her Claddagh ring and twisted it around her finger, wanting to tear it off.

Tears filled her eyes as her whole body shook with anger. She was his, bought and paid for, and there was nothing she could do about his desire for a real wife. It wasn't right to sleep with a man she didn't know or like. And what if he got her with child? She'd be trapped for sure then. The man was daft if he thought she would ever beg him for another kiss.

If only Patrick were here, he would—but Patrick wasn't here. She was alone in the world and at the mercy of this...this...cowboy. He had just shown his true colors. Bill Stricklin didn't know him at all.

She gritted her teeth and swiped the tears from her eyes. Well, Buck would soon find out what she was made of. She wouldn't go down without a fight.

Leaping off the porch, Buck untied their three mud-spattered horses from the hitching post and tugged them toward the barn. He had pictured his homecoming a thousand times, but Kate hadn't thrown herself in his arms like he'd pictured. And he'd lost his temper. He never lost his temper. Well, maybe sometimes, like with the banker, but that was justified. He wasn't some cowpoke who got drunk and broke saloon chairs over everybody's heads. His conscience pricked. And maybe he and Kate had words the night before he left.

He was disgusted with himself. When she'd thrown the first plate at his head, he was shocked, but the second one made him see red. All he'd thought about when he grabbed her was stopping her attack, but then he looked at those soft, rosy lips and took what was rightfully his. His pa had raised him better. No matter what a girl did, he'd been taught to walk away until she cooled down. Now Kate would never want a real husband. He had broken her trust. He was an idiot, plain and simple.

Suddenly, Doc's words rang in his ears. *Slow and gentle.* He snorted. Too late for that. He'd made his bed and he'd have to lie in it—alone. She'd never give him another chance now. They'd be like two strangers living in the same house for the rest of their days. He'd never have any children to carry on his name.

"Hey there, pard. Watch where you're goin'. I heard you two shoutin' at each other clear down here. We all heard you. What'd you do now?"

Buck looked up and realized he and the horses had almost run over Joe while he was woolgathering. River water dripped from the man's grizzled beard.

"Nothin'." With slumped shoulders, he walked on by his old friend.

"Wait up, son. What kinda burr you got under your saddle?"

"I said nothin'." He kept walking. He didn't want to share his feelings with the old man. It was none of his business what they were yelling about.

"Well, something sure as shootin' got you both all riled up. The little lady say something to hurt your feelings?" Joe chuckled.

"None of your business, old man." Buck's jaw tightened, remembering how mad he was at her. She didn't have to throw a plate at his head. What decent woman would do such a thing? Course, they always said redheads had more fire. Kate was a testament to that old saw.

"Well, you don't need to bark at me." Joe curled his hands into fists.

Buck bit his tongue. He stopped and looked at the man who'd kept him from starving after he'd staked his claim in gold country. Joe had showed him how to pan for gold and then how to build a sluice box. When he was hungry, he shared his beans.

He opened the barn door, and Joe followed him inside. The familiar smells of a barn soothed his anger. This was where he belonged. He'd been a fool to think he could settle down and take a wife.

"You all right, son?"

"Yeah, I'm fine. Just tired."

"That's not a surprise. What you need is some good, home cookin' and a soft bed to sleep in."

Buck didn't comment as he led each of the horses into separate clean stalls. Joe had done a good job of taking care of the place while he was gone. All the tack had been oiled and hung on nails in an orderly fashion. His old friend helped him unsaddle the horses and then fetched a bucket of grain for each of their tired mounts. Buck picked up the curry comb and started brushing the mud off Applejack.

"Anything go on while I was gone that I should know about?" Buck asked, steering away from their earlier conversation.

Joe scratched his grizzly beard and leaned forward, half whispering. "Did you know that gal of yours wears britches? That's all she wore while she did her chores. You might want to put a stop to that with the boys back home. They might get ideas."

Buck remembered how Kate had looked the first time he saw her. Stance wide, flyaway red hair, those green eyes. And the shotgun pointed at his chest. Yep, he knew what she looked like in a pair of britches. And he liked it.

"Buck!"

"Huh?"

"Did you hear what I said? Your wife wears britches!"

"I heard you." Buck cocked his brow and rubbed Applejack's nose.

"I'll have a talk with her. She was used to wearing britches when she was out here alone, trying to do the work of a man, but I don't want the boys forgetting she's a lady."

"Billy's not that much younger than her, you know, and he acts like he's smitten with her. You'll have to watch that boy and keep him in his place."

Jealousy rippled through Buck's belly, but he tamped it down and snorted. "Billy wouldn't know what to do with a woman. Besides, he was raised right. He might moon over Kate, but he'd never do anything untoward."

Joe leaned in closer and almost knocked Buck down with his breath. The old coot must have taken a swig from the bottle he kept for medicinal purposes. He didn't allow any drinking on the job, but Joe had told him it helped the pain from his rheumatiz some.

Billy. He had noticed how eager the kid was to fetch and carry for Kate, but he never thought about him lookin' at his wife in a way he shouldn't. He'd have to set the boy straight and put the fear of God in him.

"Anything else happen while I was gone?" Buck said. He continued to brush Applejack's flank.

"Some stranger rode in and cozied up to your wife."

Buck turned and nailed Joe with a hard stare. "Who? What did he want? Did he threaten her?"

"I'm not sure. When I walked out of the barn with my rifle, he looked my way, said somethin' to her, and took off. Tall fellow. Dirty blond hair. Black horse. Kate looked madder than a wet hen."

"Did she tell you what he wanted?" Buck rested his hand on his revolver.

"Said it was the banker's son—Rafe Hamilton. Said he was lookin' for you."

"Me? What for?"

"She said he wanted to buy you out. I don't know what else he wanted, but I didn't like the way he looked at Miss Kate. But he rode out before I could talk to him. It was those britches. Gives men the wrong ideas. You best tell her to stop wearin' 'em."

Tightening his jaw, Buck only brushed Applejack's coat harder. "We'll talk about it. You better go on to the house now and get something to eat before it's all gone."

"Ain't you comin'?"

"I'm not hungry." He kept his head down and wouldn't look Joe in the eye. His growling stomach betrayed him.

"Not hungry, huh. What'd she do, son? Sounded like it was a knock-down drag-out fight."

"Nothin'. Now go on. I'll eat later." He stroked Applejack's nose, and his horse tossed its head, sniffing at his pocket for a treat.

"I'll bring ya back a plate."

Buck mumbled and pulled out a dried apple. "I don't think she has that many left."

He'd have to replace the stoneware she broke with tin plates. At least they wouldn't break—dent maybe, but not break.

Chapter Eleven

KATE SAT PRIMLY BESIDE BUCK ON the hard, buckboard seat, and stared out at the tall, dry, buffalo grass, waving in the breeze of a south wind. Last night had been bitterly cold, but when the wind turned, it warmed up and promised to be a mild October day.

They hadn't spoken but a few words since she'd thrown those plates at his head and slapped his face a month ago, and despite her fear, he had steered clear of touching her, putting up his hands and scooting around the kitchen to avoid her if they got close.

At night, he changed into his white wedding shirt and black twill pants and sat by the fire reading the Bible to himself, never once looking her way. He was stone cold silent and never as much as offered to read to her. And she wasn't going to ask. She hadn't seen him smile since the day of their shouting match. Oh, he was polite. He said thank you when she plopped food down in front of him, but he always got up and served his own coffee. And he never looked at her directly. He never asked her for anything.

The first week she had lived in terror that he would make her sleep with him, but instead he never once followed her into the bedroom as she changed into her old flannel nightgown. She'd lay stiff as a board in the trundle bed, listening to him undress in the dark, dropping his boots to the floor, and then sliding under the covers. But she didn't dare fall asleep until she could hear his steady, even breathing.

Finally, she let her guard down and almost always fell asleep by the time he went to bed. He was always gone by the time she woke up. The only reason she knew he slept in the big bed was because the quilts were tossed back in the morning.

The new nightshirt she had made him had been hung on a peg, and that's where it stayed as unwrinkled as the day she had finished it. The man hadn't taken the hint that it was unseemly for him to sleep without one. Maybe when it got cold enough he'd be forced to wear it or freeze.

But it was obvious he was as stubborn as the day was long.

They were strangers living in the same house. She didn't know any more about him—his past, his thoughts, his dreams—than the day she'd married him. The silence was getting on her nerves. She'd rather fight than pretend they weren't living in the same house. But he wouldn't even argue with her, although she'd said a few things that made him tighten his jaw and walk away from her and out onto the porch. Like telling him he should wear that nightshirt.

With a guilty conscience, she thought back to those first few days. Looking back, she realized now how kind and sweet and thoughtful he had been. At first, he hadn't always kept his word about giving her time to get to know him, but she had to admit he gave her plenty of space now.

Was this how she was going to live the rest of her life? Alone even though she wasn't alone? He might as well move into the bunkhouse, but he didn't seem inclined to give up his bed in the cabin. Said he didn't want the men to know he wasn't sleeping with his wife. It was humiliating, he said.

Even the hired hands kept their mouths shut now when they came to the house to eat. At first, Billy had smiled a lot and chatted about his days on the trail, but that had only lasted a couple of days. Now he wouldn't even look at her. She knew Buck must have said something to him. Silence was her sole companion these days, and she thought she'd go stir crazy.

Kate stared at the back of the bays, the only sound in the crisp air the jingling of the harness. Under her lashes, she stole a glance at Buck's classic features. His face seemed carved out of stone. She had done that to him, and she felt terrible about losing her temper that day. But he had made her so mad. Talking about her *sainted* brother. He hadn't even known Patrick—known what a fine man he was. He didn't know about Patrick losing his wife and baby and the pain she could see in his eyes at times.

Still, she never should have thrown those plates or slapped Buck's face. She felt so humiliated and disgusted with herself. She had prayed for God to forgive her, prayed fervently on her knees, but lately her prayers seemed to hit the ceiling and go nowhere.

Scripture was clear about the sin of anger. Folding and unfolding her hands, she thought about apologizing to Buck. But what if he spurned her apology? And shouldn't he be the one to apologize first? He had said dreadful things to her.

Then a thought pricked her heart. She had started the fight, telling him he smelled like cow dung. She had seen how tired he was. Why did she say that? But he had never given her an opportunity to apologize. He had shut down any conversation and avoided her like she had the Black Death.

Grudgingly, she had to admit her comment must have hit its mark. Now before he entered the house for supper, he always washed up and shaved in the bunkhouse first. When she needed complete privacy to bathe or wash her hair, she always barred the door first, and when he bathed using the same bath water, she always left the cabin until he opened the door fully dressed. But he never darkened the cabin door during the day except for mealtime.

At least his absence had given her time to sew her new dresses. Today she was wearing her green-and-yellow wool plaid that brought out the green in her eyes. Not that she spent much time looking in the mirror, but it was so much nicer than her brown wool dress. It made her feel better about herself. Not that Buck ever noticed or commented about how she looked anymore. And she'd had time to make new curtains for the window he'd replaced.

She sighed with relief when the white clapboard church came into view. Her thoughts had only depressed her. She missed female companionship during the week and looked forward to seeing her friends on Sundays. She had started talking to Riley as if he were a real person, and that couldn't be a good thing.

When Buck stopped the buckboard, she scrambled down to the grass without waiting for his helping hand. She spotted Martha, standing with a group of other women, crowded around Samantha Eggers' wee baby girl. Without a look back at her husband, she hurried over to join the group.

"Oh, she's so beautiful," Kate said. "Can I hold her?"

"Of course." The young woman smiled and carefully laid the babe in Kate's arms. Cooing, Kate swayed from side to side. Desire for her own child filled her heart.

"It's good to see you at church again, Samantha," Kate said. "We've missed you. What did you name her?"

"Elise Anna Eggers after my mother."

"Such a pretty name." Martha peered over Kate's shoulder, stroking the baby's cheek with her finger. "So soft."

Kate reluctantly handed the baby back to the new mother, who swaddled her tighter. "I suppose we should go inside before Elise takes a chill."

The women walked together toward the church entrance.

"Good morning, ladies," Pastor Russell smiled at them. His wife Bernadette stood at his side in a navy-blue wool dress piped with white and hugged each of them.

"Good morning, Kate," Bernadette said. "How are things going for you and that new husband of yours?"

Kate could tell Bernadette's question wasn't just for the sake of civility. She gave the woman a polite but tight smile. "Fine."

"Well, if you two newlyweds ever need any advice, you know you can come to me."

Kate nodded her head. "Thank you, Bernadette." The woman was the last person she'd ask for advice. Even in the short time she'd been attending the church, she knew the pastor's wife was a notorious gossip.

Kate smiled over at Martha, and the older woman entwined her arm with hers. She hadn't realized how much she looked forward to human touch on Sundays. She was so lonely most of the time. Even arguing with Buck was better than his silence.

They walked down the middle aisle toward the third pew back from the pulpit and sat down. She and Buck always sat with Martha and Doc Mitchell and Bill and Abigail Stricklin. Buck always managed to claim the aisle seat so he could stick out his long legs that didn't fit well in the pew. Or maybe he wanted to avoid sitting too close to her. Probably the latter. He went out of his way not to touch her these days.

Martha leaned close to her ear and whispered. "Now tell me what's wrong between you and your young man. You barely look at each other these days let alone talk. Did you have an argument?"

Kate blushed in embarrassment. She didn't want the whole church to know about their problems. To avoid Martha's eyes, she concentrated on taking off her gloves and unbuttoning her cape.

"It's nothing."

Kate was forced to look at the older woman when Martha nudged her with an elbow and whispered near her ear. "I know better. I've been married long enough that I can tell the signs of a marriage in trouble. And you two have got trouble."

"I don't want to talk about it." Kate looked back down at her boots peeking from under her new wool dress, wringing her hands.

Martha leaned closer. "If you can't talk about it to me, then the two of you need to talk to Pastor."

Kate kept her head lowered, along with her voice, afraid people would hear their conversation. "Nay, I couldna,"

Her stomach flip-flopped at the thought of airing her dirty laundry to the pastor, of all people. She turned and searched the room over her shoulder. The room was filling up, but Buck was in deep conversation with Pastor Russell. They looked so serious. Her heart beat faster. Surely, Buck wouldn't tell Pastor what she'd done. How she'd thrown dishes at his head. She'd be humiliated.

"Honey, the whole church is worried about you two." Martha patted her hand. "I blame myself that we forced you into marriage, but your reputation would have been ruined otherwise. Maybe we made a big mistake though. He hasn't...well...hit you, has he?"

"Nay. He wouldna do that."

Martha looked relieved. "It wouldn't be the first time a man mistreated his wife. We see it all the time in Doc's office. Women forced to take beatings. It's a shame."

"Buck would never do that."

"I didn't think so, but you never know." Martha scowled in Buck's direction and continued whispering. "Well, he must have done something to cause this rift. It's always the man's fault. Husbands can be so dense sometimes. But honey, it's nothing that can't be fixed. I can have

Frederick talk to him."

"That's not necessary." Kate's voice rose a bit, stricken that Martha would even consider the possibility of having Doc talk to Buck. "I dinna want anyone else to know."

"Know what?" Abigail said loudly as she sat down on the other side of Martha.

Heads turned, and Kate wanted to crawl under the wooden pew. The woman's voice could wake the dead. She looked over at Buck, willing him to come sit down beside her and put a stop to this conversation, but he and Pastor had their heads bowed in prayer.

Kate sat up straighter, pasted a church smile on her face, and leaned around Martha to speak to Abigail. "Sure'n it's nothin'. Have you gotten in a new shipment of material lately? I want to make Buck a new shirt." It was the only thing she could think of quickly.

Martha drew her mouth into a straight line and leaned back.

Abigail looked at Martha and then at Kate, braying, "Are you having a baby? That's what you don't want anyone to know? Honey, that's wonderful! You can tell us."

Kate felt a hand touch her shoulder, and she looked up into Buck's face, wearing a smug grin. She wanted to strangle him. He was enjoying this! Tugging at her suddenly tight lace collar, Kate knew her cheeks flamed bright red. Everyone in the church was looking at them. She ducked her head.

"Good morning, Miz Stricklin," Buck said. "I'm afraid to say we haven't been so blessed yet, but we're praying for that happy occasion."

Buck sat down beside her and put his arm around her. She looked up at the twinkle in his eyes and planted a sharp elbow in his side. Now everyone would think the worst. That she and Buck... She sighed inwardly. They'd be thinkin' they were a normal, married couple, that's what.

"Aren't we, darlin'?" Buck said.

He squeezed her shoulder and chuckled as he kissed her cheek. She couldn't very well push him off the pew without making a scene. They'd been living together like strangers, and now he wanted to cozy up and make the whole congregation think they were a happy couple.

She bit her bottom lip. Maybe that wasn't a bad thing.

"Well, you keep tryin' and before you know it you'll have a houseful of children," Abigail said. Didn't the woman have any shame?

Bill Stricklin and Doc joined their wives in the pew right as Pastor stepped behind the pulpit.

Buck didn't drop his arm, but instead pulled her closer to his side. Before they left home this morning, he couldn't even be bothered to look at her. She glared at him, but he only smiled as though he were madly in love with her. She wanted to smack that grin right off his face. But maybe now the members of the church would stop gossiping about the troubles in their marriage. She could only pray so. Clutching her small black Bible, she bowed her head as Rev. Russell opened with prayer.

As Pastor's sermon on the prodigal son progressed, Buck acted like he had ants in his pants the way he wiggled in his seat. She'd seen four-year-olds better behaved. Finally, she gripped his knee to stop it from jiggling. Surprised, he looked over at her with a red flush on his face and then back at the pastor, but he settled down, folding his arms over his chest.

Kate smiled with glee. Evidently, the sermon had struck a nerve in him. He really hadn't talked much about their heavenly Father even though he read from the Bible every night. It was as though he was trying to squeeze into a shirt that didn't quite fit. She knew he prided himself on his self-sufficiency, but maybe Buck needed to depend on God more.

She suspected there was a tug-o-war going on between God and Buck, but as she had learned on her hard journey to America in steerage, depending on her faith and God's grace was all that got her through the trial. Finally, she had bowed her knee to Him and rededicated her life and her future to Him. Without the help of His Spirit, she couldn't have made it through these last several months. Even as hopeless as things looked between her and Buck, she realized the Lord would work it all out for good. That thought gave her comfort.

Kate prayed her husband would come to know the peace that passeth all understanding—sooner rather than later.

Buck hugged Kate to his side, enjoying the feel of her in his arms again. Lavender. She always smelled like lavender. When Pastor Russell talked about the prodigal son, it was as though he spoke directly to him. He was a prodigal son who had left behind his faith with his childhood. He was that son wallowing in a pigsty. His many sins weighed heavily on him, and he felt overwhelming guilt. In fact, he wanted to get up and run out the back of the church, but he knew it would only cause a scene.

When Kate had put her hand on his leg to still it, he had startled and tried to settle, but he felt as though he were walking on hot coals with bare feet. He could almost feel the flames of hell licking at his boots.

After a while, his mind drifted to his conversation with the pastor, who had given him hope that he and Kate could work out their differences, but he would need to change. To accept God had every aspect of his life in His hands.

As much as it had galled him to confess he and Kate weren't living as man and wife, he still felt better for having unburdened his heart. He was at the end of his rope and willing to try anything—wanting her, but guarding his words and actions to keep from alarming her. He had meant what he said after she slapped him. If she wanted a kiss, she would have to make the first move. Freezing her out had been the only way to keep his sanity and hopefully make her trust him.

Pastor had advised patience and dependence on God's grace. He suggested he court his wife as though they were unmarried. Ask to court her. Give her small gifts. Restrict himself to occasionally holding her hand, asking first if it was all right.

Buck looked down at the woman beside him and knew she was worth the effort. He wanted her to love him, but he was afraid to tell her he was falling in love with her. He guessed that's what he felt. If she knew, she had the power to break his heart. Never, ever had he really loved a woman. What he felt for Angel was a tiny drop of what he felt for Kate. She filled his heart and mind every minute of the day.

Shifting in his seat, his arm started to go numb. He pulled it down into his lap. Tingling needles shot from his shoulder into his hand. Kate straightened, but did not pull away. It felt right to sit close beside her in church.

Heedless of where they were, he stared down at his wife, at her perfectly formed face—the soft curve of her cheek, eyes that glinted like emerald fire, rosy lips that he longed to kiss again, copper hair that glowed as though it was lit from within. Abruptly, he faced forward and tried to concentrate on what the parable of the prodigal son meant, but his mind wandered again.

It had been sheer torture sleeping in the same room and not being able to touch her. Sometimes at night he would sit alone in his chair by the fireplace, with the Bible in his lap unopened. For warmth, they left the bedroom door open now. He would watch her sleeping form curled up in the trundle bed as the flickering firelight from the kitchen hearth crept through the bedroom doorway and fell softly on her sweet face. He wanted to soothe her furrowed brow and assure her he didn't want to hurt her. He only wanted to love her as a man loves his wife. But she was so scared of him.

Am I wicked to feel this way, Lord?

He had hoped she would become accustomed to his presence in the last month, and he could prove to her he was an honorable man. He needed to apologize, but every time he started to open his mouth, his pride reared its ugly head. Most nights he read his Bible, searching out passages on anger and pride in the book of Proverbs. He knew he was at fault, but he didn't know how to tell her without her running away like a scared jackrabbit.

Lord, help me. I'm just a man, and you know how weak I am. Help me to love and honor Kate the way you want me to.

Suddenly, a Scripture he had memorized as a boy floated through his mind. It was a favorite of his ma's, and she often quoted it.

"Charity suffereth long and is kind; charity envieth not; charity vaunteth not itself, is not puffed up, Doth not behave itself unseemly, seeketh not her own, is not easily provoked, thinketh no evil; Rejoiceth not in iniquity, but rejoiceth in the truth; Beareth all things, believeth all things, hopeth all

things, endureth all things."

He'd heard enough sermons on First Corinthians, chapter thirteen, as a kid to know "charity" meant "love."

If he really loved Kate, he would suffer long and be kind, no matter how long it took to win her heart. With renewed hope, he smiled down at his wife who stared straight ahead at Pastor Russell. Today he would become a new man, putting a tight rein on his own hopes and desires to fulfill her dreams for the future.

Chapter Twelve

Kate dried her hands on a flour sack dish towel and looked out the window at the soft, gentle snow falling in near darkness. Still in his Sunday clothes, Buck sat quietly at the table, drinking another cup of coffee. She didn't know how he slept at night with as much as he drank after supper.

He had been silent on the way home from church, but somehow, he had changed. He no longer scowled, and his shoulders seemed relaxed. But he still hadn't said much to her. He had caught her by surprise at church when he'd put his arm around her. Even though she had been startled, she hoped his action had stilled the wagging tongues.

"Kate?" She startled and turned from the window toward Buck, who looked at her with a nervous expression. "Can we talk?"

She turned from his gaze and bustled to the sink to lay the wet dish towel over its edge. "About what?"

Behind her, she heard the scrape of his chair as he pushed back from the table. Her heart thumped, and her mind leapt to the conclusion that he was going to press her again about becoming a real wife.

"I want to ask you something."

She turned to stare at his face in the firelight. The warm glow of the flames turned his tanned skin to gold and warmed his deep brown eyes. Worrying her bottom lip, she sank into a chair, twisting the ring on her finger, a symbol of everlasting love. She faced him squarely, ready to listen to his arguments, but vowing not to give in to his demands.

"Aye?"

He cleared his throat and glanced down at the table before looking back up and staring into her eyes. "Uh, I had a talk with Pastor Russell today."

She knew immediately they had been talking about this sham marriage. Why couldn't everyone stay out of their business? Had he told the pastor about their fight? She gritted her teeth and waited for him to continue.

"You're not making this easy," he said. "You look ready to bite my head off."

"What do you expect after a month of total silence, and then your actions in church today?"

"I didn't mean to make you mad. I only wanted to stop the gossip."

She picked at a ragged fingernail but remained silent.

"I told Pastor Russell we weren't living as man and wife and—"

"Please tell me you didna." Her voice sounded shrill in her ears. "Now the whole church will know. His wife is one of the worst gossips in Deer Lodge. She'll no doubt tell tales to every other woman she knows, which is everyone in town."

"He promised to keep our secret. I trust him."

"He tells Bernadette everything. How do you think we find out who's expectin' a babe or who is ill in his congregation?"

"I didn't know what else to do." His voice held a pleading tone. "Please hear me out. I think you'll like his advice."

"I sincerely doubt it. He's a man and probably quoted Scripture about how the two should become one." She sat up straighter, her stomach tied in knots with embarrassment, and glared at him.

He smiled at her. "I think you'll be pleasantly surprised."

"I doubt it." She sounded petulant, even to her own ears.

"He advised me to start over as if we weren't married and court you."

"As you would say, I think we've already forded that river. We sleep in the same bedroom together. How do you propose we do that? Will ya move into the bunkhouse?"

His smile faded. "I told you I won't do that. What would the boys say? I'd be a laughingstock. They'd never take orders from somebody they don't respect."

"What's your plan then?" She stood up to put the tea kettle on the stove and crossed her arms, looking at him over her shoulder.

"Please hear me out, darlin'. I know it will be hard, but…" He cleared his throat again. "I've thought a lot about this. I'll make a pallet on the floor in here, and we'll pretend we're living in a…hotel or boarding house. I'll stay out of the cabin during the day except for meals—"

"You already work until after sundown. I think you've chopped enough wood to see us through two winters. I dinna see what will change."

"Did you miss the part about me sleeping on the hard floor?" His voice had a slight sarcastic bent.

"That's a start I suppose."

"I'll even wear the nightshirt you made me. You did some fine stitch work on it. Thank you for that."

She shrugged her shoulder and sat down, feeling somewhat relieved. "How will you court me? We still spend the evenings together. That's like having a beau come to live with you."

Tears started in her eyes at what she had missed with a real courtship, and he started to reach over to wipe them away, but she pulled back.

"I've proved I'm a decent man this last month, haven't I?"

"That's because you were so angry." She swiped at a tear that trickled down her cheek.

He sighed deeply and held up his hands in surrender. "You're absolutely right. I need to apologize for what I said and how I've treated you, shutting you out. I was angry and full of pride and disappointed—"

"I'm disappointed too. When I was a little girl I always dreamed about being courted by a man who loved me and about taking long walks and talking about building a home and a future. I always thought my mam and da would be there, and then when they died, I thought Patrick would be the one to approve of my choice. But then—"

"We didn't have the luxury of choosing, did we?" he said softly.

Kate looked into his eyes and saw compassion there. A few stones crumbled in the wall she'd built around herself to protect her from this man and sure heartache and pain.

"No, we didna."

"But that doesn't mean we can't build a life together." The pleading was back in his voice. "Am I so disgusting to you?"

She looked at the striking planes of his freshly shaved face. His strong jaw, straight nose, and gentle eyes. Most girls would be head over heels in love with him. They would think she was daft that she resisted marriage to him.

She sighed. "No, of course not. It's just the way we were forced to marry."

"Can you find it in your heart to start over again? To let me court you as I would have done had circumstances not taken over? I...I..."

"What?"

"Nothing."

He took a sip of coffee and wrapped his hands around the cup. The tea kettle whistled, and she spent the next few moments measuring the tea into the china tea pot decorated with hand painted roses. She carried it with her to the table along with the matching cup and saucer.

"This was my mam's." She sniffed back her tears. He pulled a white handkerchief out of his back pocket and handed it to her. She took it, blotted her face, and blew her nose. "I brought it all the way from Ireland. It's the only thing I have of hers except for my ring."

"I'm sorry you lost her."

"If she were here, she could tell me what to do."

"We can still build a life together, Kate."

"If you want to court me, you canna be kissin' me whenever you take a mind to. It's too much temptation for you."

"I know." He rubbed the back of his neck. "We'll start slow. We can sit at the table every night and read Scripture together and talk about our pasts and our dreams for the future. Maybe you'll let me hold your hand sometimes? I mean, when you feel comfortable. No rush."

Looking at him as if for the first time, she wondered if he could do it. Could he keep his promise this time? Could they really start over? If circumstances had not intervened, would she have chosen to let him court her? What if he had brought her a handful of wildflowers in the spring? Would she have seen him as a potential suitor? He did make the effort to attend church with her every Sunday. Yes, he was a good man. She knew that now.

She sighed again, knowing she would have been attracted to him if they had met properly. That was the problem. She was attracted to him now. "All right. I suppose we can try."

"And when you're ready for a kiss, you'll let me know?"

Reluctantly, she nodded yes.

"I'll even get on my knee again and ask you to be my wife."

Instead of commenting, Kate poured a cup of tea and took a sip, the liquid warming the cold spot that she had harbored in her heart. She had been so lonely since Patrick died. It *would* be nice to get to know Buck—to be his friend.

Buck laid his palms on the table and smiled big. "One more thing."

A niggle of fear ran up her spine, and she stiffened.

"What?" She furrowed her brow.

"Well...I think..." He drew out his thought.

"You think what?" When she set down her cup, it clattered on the saucer.

"What do *you* think about setting a date, like maybe Christmas? We could celebrate the season by becoming man and wife and start out the new year working toward a new life together."

"A time limit?"

"In a manner of speaking, but if you think that's too soon..."

"I dinna know." She wrapped her cold hands around the warm tea cup and stared into its depths, wondering if she should agree to a deadline. How long could the man wait? What about spring? "That's only two and a half months away. What about April or May?"

His face fell. "Don't you think we'll know each other well enough by Christmas? We'll be spending most of our time together, not like most courtin' couples who only see each other on Sunday afternoons."

"Well, in a normal courtship, we would have a chaperone and--"

"That's kind of difficult in our case, don't you think?" Buck leaned back in his chair and crossed his arms. "Do you want Joe or Josh or Billy here every evening?"

"No, of course not. I was simply stating that in a normal courtship, we wouldna be alone, and the...physical...temptations would not be there."

She paused. How to explain this to him without embarrassment. Her stomach did a flip-flop. "You're an attractive man."

He grinned and uncrossed his arms, folding his hands on the table. "That's nice to hear. I think you're really pretty too. In fact, you're the most beautiful woman I've ever met, bar none."

"I was taught that men have a hard time controlling their, uh..." She couldn't continue. She felt the flush start at her neck and engulf her face.

"I'm not sayin' it will be easy," he admitted, smiling at her. "But with God's help, I want to keep our courtship pure. I want to get to know you, and I want you to get to know me. But I'm just a man. When we're trapped indoors every day because of bad weather, it might be hard to... you know... That's why I suggested Christmas."

She nibbled at her thumbnail. "I suppose you have a point."

"If we were a regular couple, we could take a year, but we're not a regular couple."

"No, we're not."

Kate felt her walls crumbling. Sighing even deeper, she closed her eyes to think. Would it really matter whether it was Christmas or springtime? Eventually, she would become his forever wife. Down deep in her heart she desired a family. She desired to love him.

Either they lived a loveless, childless life, treating each other like strangers, or they both worked at making their marriage into what it should be. She *had* made a vow to him at the altar. She swallowed past the lump in her throat.

"All right. Christmas."

Buck smiled at her in apparent relief. Would she fall in love with him by then? *Lord, make it so.*

Buck woke up to Riley licking him in the ear. He swatted at the dog's head, but he knew he needed to let him outside. He groaned and rolled over onto his back. He'd slept on ground that was softer than this pallet on the floor. Every muscle—every bone—ached. He was stiff, sore, and felt like he hadn't slept at all. And it was only November 1. Could he endure another two months of this? If he thought the boys wouldn't catch on, he'd sleep under a buffalo robe in the hay loft.

Yawning and stretching, he threw off the bundle of quilts and shivered when the cold air hit his nightshirt. He wished Kate had sewn something warmer. He rolled to his knees and pushed off the floor. Coffee. He needed a mug of strong, hot coffee. Riley danced around his feet, his nails clicking on the floor, so the first thing he did was let the dog out into the frigid air. Good thing the sheep dog had a thick coat. The sky was beginning to lighten over the mountains to the east.

Stirring up the coals in the fireplace, he added a couple of large pine logs. When that cold front rolled in out of Canada yesterday, the temperature felt like it had dropped forty degrees. It had to be below zero out there.

After pulling on long johns, his denims, wool socks, and one of the cotton flannel shirts Kate had made him, he carried his boots to a chair in front of the fireplace and slipped them on. He yawned and rested his arms on his knees and prayed.

Lord, thank you for this new day. Help me to remain a man of honor and not grumble about sleeping on the floor. I pray you'll soften Kate's heart toward me so we can be truly united in the Holy Bonds of Matrimony. In Jesus name I pray, Amen.

Not bad for being so rusty at praying. He had depended on himself for a long time without God's help, but he knew Kate put a lot of store in praying and reading Scripture. And he had to admit, it was kind of comforting to think God was in control, although it was a difficult idea for a man to accept.

Riley scratched at the door to be let back in. When he opened the door, the dog rushed in and plopped down in front of the fireplace as close as he could.

"Smart dog," Buck muttered.

He tried not to clang too much as he stoked the fire in the cook stove, filled the coffee pot with water from the pitcher, and dumped in coffee grounds. While he waited for it to boil, he returned to the fireplace and toasted his hands and then his backside for a while before throwing on his coat and hat to make a trip to the privy. He envied the dog.

When he returned to the relative warmth of the cabin, he kept his coat on and poured a boiling hot mug of coffee, blowing on it to cool enough so he could take a sip. He closed his eyes as the warm liquid slid down his throat. Ah. He might live after all.

Buck glanced through the half open door and could barely make out Kate's red hair, peeking out of the covers. It was so cold, she had even hidden her face in the quilts. This weather wasn't fit for man nor beast. Smiling, he took another sip of coffee, warming his hands on the heavy, stone mug, enjoying the view. When she was awake, he tried not to stare at her too openly. It made her a mite nervous.

Yep, he was making progress in his courtship. He'd told her about his dreams of turning the ranch into one his pa would be proud of and stocking it with shorthorns. They were better suited to cold weather than Texas longhorns and produced a heartier stock. He needed to visit Conrad Kohrs and see if he'd be willing to sell him a bull and a few cows or point him toward his supplier. Bill Stricklin said the red cattle Kohrs had brought in three years ago were thriving, and the man was rapidly building his herd. Plus, their temperament was a sight better than longhorns.

Kate had finally made him a batch of oatmeal cookies last night. They were almost as good as Ma's. Big, hot, and chewy. That would sure help his coffee go down this morning. He rooted around in the cupboard until he found the plate she had covered. The cookie was a little hard, but when he broke it and dipped it in his coffee, it warmed up and slid down his throat quite nicely. It was going to be a good day.

Buck slid his hands into his gloves, pulled the sheepskin coat up around his neck, and poured himself another mug of coffee. That should hold him until breakfast. Before he could walk out the door, Kate appeared at the doorway to the bedroom in her dressing gown, her copper-colored braid hanging long over her shoulder. Yawning, she brushed stray curls back from her face, and her unusual gold wedding ring flashed in the light of the lamp.

He groaned inwardly. Now why did she have to go and do that. It was all he could do not to stride across the room and kiss that beautiful, sleepy face.

"Mornin'," he said. "You're up early."

He clasped his mug in both hands and anchored his boots to the floor. One wrong move could mess up everything.

"I smelled the coffee," she said, rubbing her eyes. "I need to milk the cow and gather the eggs before they go to freezin' right under the chickens."

"I'm headed out to the barn." He unglued his feet and walked to the door. He spilled coffee on his glove and shook it off. "Make sure you bundle up good before you do your chores. It's so cold out there it could freeze that pretty nose right off your face."

He grinned at her, and she actually smiled back at him. When his feet wanted to move toward her, he picked himself up by the scruff of the neck and shoved himself toward the door.

"I'll see you at breakfast." She pulled her dressing gown tightly around her.

Had she seen the desire on his face? He needed to keep a tight rein on his emotions. Every day he fell more and more in love with her. It had to be love. *Like* had never felt this way. Oh, he hadn't told her he loved her yet for fear she'd call the whole deal off.

His eyes never left her face as he fumbled to lift the bar across the door. "Whatever you fix will be fine, darlin'. You know how much I like your cookin'."

She continued to smile at him, and he wanted to kiss every square inch of that soft, sweet face.

Hurriedly, he opened the door, letting in a blast of frigid air. "I best get goin'. See you later."

Before he could change his mind, he stepped out onto the porch and hopped down on the ground not watching where he was going. He felt something squish under his boot and looked down. Riley.

Chapter Thirteen

"Buck, we've got trouble," Josh said as he entered the cold barn.

Curious, Kate looked up from her three-legged milking stool and patted the side of the brown-and-white cow. Buck stood at a workbench on the other side of the barn, fixing a harness, but he stopped and looked over at Josh. The man rarely talked in front of Kate unless it was something important.

"What?" Buck asked.

"One of the cows..." Josh paused and looked over at Kate as if he didn't want her to hear.

"Kate, maybe you best head on up to the house," Buck said.

Standing up with the bucket of milk, she set it down on the stool and brushed off her hands. "This is my ranch too. If there's somethin' wrong with the cattle, I need to know."

Josh looked between Buck and Kate, until Buck nodded and broke the silence.

"Let's hear it."

"Somebody slaughtered a cow last night."

"Indians?"

"Indians don't leave the meat behind. Her throat was slit. They left her where she dropped. Whoever did this didn't stick around long."

With apparent alarm, Kate moved closer to him and held onto his arm. "Why would someone do such a horrid thing?"

"To send a message." Buck growled and felt his neck cord with anger. "Rafe Hamilton has always had a hankering for this property. All I can figure is he wants free access to the river since he's landlocked. Your brother chose his homestead well, and he bought out other homesteaders along the river who gave up and moved on to Oregon."

"Aye," she said. "But he never stopped Rafe from crossing his land to water his cattle."

"Hamilton seems like the kind who doesn't like to ask for favors. He'd as soon you sold out to him."

"That's not gonna happen. Patrick poured ten long years into this property. Five he spent in a little shanty while he proved up the land, and it took five more to build the cabin, barn, and bunkhouse, not to mention his herd."

"What do you want me to do?" Josh stood inside the barn door, waiting for his orders.

Buck strode to Applejack and threw a blanket over his back, then followed it with his well-worn saddle.

"Get the boys to help you butcher the cow. We can't let the meat go to waste. I'm riding over to Hamilton's place for a little talk."

"Alone?" Kate clutched his forearm. He recognized the look of fear on her face. He had seen it before, only she had been afraid of him. "Take Josh with you."

"He's got a job to do, Katie. I can handle Hamilton." He pulled away from her to cinch the saddle. "Bill warned me that snake didn't fight fair and to watch my back."

"What do you mean?" she asked, moving between him and Applejack.

"Bill told me Patrick and Rafe spent a lot of nights at Ruby's, playing cards and drinkin'—until they got into a big fight over you."

Anger flashed in her eyes, and she poked a finger against his muscled chest. "Not Patrick. Not a brothel."

"Yes, Patrick." He ground out a reply. He had never wanted to tell her, but he'd gone and done it now. He laid his hands on her shoulders. "I know you want to believe the best of your brother, Katie, but Bill said he could slam back a few drinks with the best of 'em and was a little too fond of the cards and girls. That may be why he borrowed so much to start with. Maybe he had to pay off a few gambling debts. Either way, I figure Rafe Hamilton has wanted this land...and you...from the beginning."

"I dinna believe you." Her voice wavered. "Patrick wouldna jeopardize his land." The goodwill and growing affection between them seemed to be replaced by a need for her to defend her dead brother.

Buck didn't even look over when the barn door squeaked, knowing Josh wanted no part of their argument.

Planting his hands on his hips, Buck took a step back. "Why would Bill lie? He'd have no reason to. I suspect when your brother's wife and baby died, Patrick stuck his head in a bottle to forget."

Emotions warred on her face, and Buck knew it must be a struggle to admit her brother wasn't perfect. He wanted her to understand, but he didn't want to crush her memories.

He continued. "Bill said Patrick was depressed about losing his wife and baby boy in childbirth. I guess your brother felt responsible, and his grief and guilt drove him to ride into town at night, looking to drown his sorrows. Hamilton probably took advantage of him when they played cards, and Patrick had to borrow the money to pay off his gambling debts."

Buck moved away to slip the bridle on his restless buckskin, then he reached out and ran a reassuring hand down her arm. "Don't wait breakfast for me. You need to feed the men. They'll have to butcher that cow, and you'll have to help brine it. Save out a couple of roasts and some steaks. We can pack them in snow and freeze them for now. Hopefully, we won't get another warm spell."

Kate nodded and looked down. The tips of her black boots peeked out from her caped overcoat.

"Patrick had always been my hero—the one who would fight any dragon for me. If not for him, I wouldn't have escaped my stepfather."

Buck lifted her chin and saw tears welling in her eyes. "Your brother was a good, hard-working man, Katie. Always remember that. He loved you enough to go into debt for you. But he was a man—a man with a big hole in his heart after his wife died. I don't judge him."

Pulling her into an embrace, offering her solace, she rested her head against his chest. He stroked her hair.

"It'll be all right, darlin'."

It felt good to hold her in his arms. Warm honey seemed to flow through his veins as she snuggled against him. How he could love this woman so fiercely was beyond his understanding. Was this how his Ma and Pa loved each other?

Kate pulled away and leaned back to look into his face. "You've known about Patrick all along, haven't you?"

He couldn't deny it. Reluctantly, he nodded.

A tear trickled down her cheek, and he wiped it away with his gloved hand as she continued. "Rafe Hamilton is surely a blackguard, but why would he treat Patrick so? They were once friends until—"

"Until they fought over you. What happened?"

Her cheeks flamed, and he wasn't sure he wanted to know. "After I arrived in Deer Lodge, Patrick drove me into town a few days later to pick up supplies. That's when I met Rafe. He acted so nice. A real gentleman. After that he visited me almost every day, bringing me a bouquet of wildflowers. I was such a fool." She fisted her hands. "One day he drove over in a buggy with a packed lunch basket. He asked me to go on a picnic with him. Patrick didna want me to, but Rafe said we'd not go far. Just a wee bit down the river. It was my own fault. I persuaded Patrick to let me go. Rafe was charming, until he . . ." She dropped her head in apparent shame.

Thunder rumbled through his soul. Did he want to hear the rest? Hamilton had killed her brother, but what else had the man done to hurt her? Buck pulled her into a gentle, reassuring embrace, and coaxed her to continue. "He what?"

"He...kissed me, but then he..." She shivered in his arms. Closing his eyes, he stroked her back, dreading what she would say, fighting the impulse to seek out their murderous neighbor and end his life.

In the silence, he waited patiently until she was ready to speak. "I screamed, and Patrick heard me."

"Hamilton didn't—"

"Nay." Relief flooded through Buck. "Patrick didna trust Rafe with me and had followed us. When Rafe attacked me, they fought, and Patrick threw him off his land and forbade him from ever seeking me out. When we went into town in July for the Independence celebration, Rafe was there. All day he circled the crowd, staring at me and drinkin'. By evening, he was so drunk he could barely stand. He outbid everyone else to win my box supper. Patrick was so angry. They fought again, and Patrick bloodied his face. Some of the men in the crowd pulled my brother off Rafe and carried the rotter to Doc Mitchell's office. I thought Patrick had killed him."

"I wish he had." Bending to kiss her head, he struggled to tamp down his roiling emotions. Kate needed his love and reassurance now, not his anger.

Finally, she continued in a soft voice. "After Patrick died, Rafe's father approached me and told me about the loan and that I was now responsible for paying it off. He said if I married Rafe he would forgive the debt. When I told him I'd never marry his son, he said Patrick had agreed to it. They had shaken hands when he borrowed the money. I could either marry Rafe or face foreclosure."

"Your brother promised you to Hamilton?"

"Nay, he never would have done that. Rafe only knew I was Patrick's sister and that he was bringing me to America. Once Rafe met me, he started pursuing me. Since he acted so nice at first, I welcomed his attention—"

Buck growled deep in his throat. "Until you didn't."

She nodded against his chest. "Rafe kept after me, asking me to marry him."

Slowly, he pulled away and looked at her, awareness dawning. "So that's why Stricklin insisted I ride out here late that afternoon. He knew you weren't safe. I had planned on cleaning up and riding out the next morning, but he told me there was another offer on the table for your homestead, and I'd better get out here."

Kate shivered and rubbed her arms as he held her shoulders. "The man makes my skin crawl. Rafe knows that. Why would he still want to marry me?"

"I've known men like Hamilton, Katie. They're mean through and through. They never forget a grudge, and they don't like to lose. When you married me instead of him, he lost you for good. That had to stick in his craw."

Kate shivered. "The man is surely the devil incarnate."

Buck wrapped his arms around her again and held her tight, his heart beating like a blacksmith hammering a piece of iron. His breath caught in his throat. What if he hadn't shown up at the ranch on the night she was attacked? What if he'd ridden back to town? She would have been all alone and at the mercy of Hamilton's men.

Kate pulled back and reached up a hand to caress Buck's stubbled cheek. He kissed her palm. He had said she would have to kiss him first. Entwining her arms around his neck, her fingers played with the curls at the nape of his neck, and then she pulled his head down toward her. His lips were only a breath away when they heard the barn door squeak again. They startled apart.

Since they had stopped arguing, evidently Josh thought it was safe to stick his head back in the door. "You want me to ride with you, Buck? Billy and Joe can handle that cow."

"No, I want you to stay here and look after Kate."

Buck looked down at her as if she were the most precious thing in the world, then picked up Applejack's reins and led his buckskin gelding to the door. He turned and looked over his shoulder.

"Be careful." Her eyes were wide. "I'm afraid for you."

"I'll be back soon, Katie girl." He winked and smiled, hoping to reassure her. "Don't worry about me."

"Ya know he willna admit to anything."

"No, but I can put the fear of God into him."

Buck tipped his hat at her and turned his back, leading Applejack out the door. He mounted, his breath a frozen cloud, and rode away to confront Hamilton.

Please, dear God, protect Katie while I'm gone, and don't let me kill Hamilton for what he's done.

Buck slowed Applejack to a trot as he approached the Hamilton homestead, a white, stick-built house. It would have cost a small fortune to freight the lumber into the valley. The closest sawmill was near Helena over fifty miles away. Rafe Hamilton had money, but he doubted it came from honest work. Buck's jaw clenched as thoughts of the man touching his wife darkened his thoughts.

A ranch hand closed the gate to a corral that held a black stallion and walked over to meet him. He tucked his coat behind his gun. Buck held up his gloved hand in greeting and pulled back on the reins.

"Something I can do for you?" The man looked at Buck with suspicion.

"I'm looking for Rafe Hamilton. He around?"

"Who's asking?"

"Buck McKean. My wife and I own the spread north of his over on the Clark Fork."

"O'Brien's place?"

"That would be the one. Only now it's the McKean Ranch." Buck dismounted and held the reins loosely in his hand.

"So I heard. Anything I can do for you?"

Buck clenched his teeth, quickly growing irritated. He gripped the reins until his fingers almost cramped. "Nope. I need to talk to your boss face to face."

He started walking toward the house, but Hamilton's man stopped him with a hand on his chest. "He's busy. I'll let him know you stopped by."

Buck knocked the man's hand away. "I'm not leavin' until I talk to Hamilton."

The front door opened and a man who looked vaguely familiar swaggered out. Had to be Hamilton. The tall man wore a sneer on his face as he sauntered toward him. Physically, they were evenly matched, but the banker's son wore his holster low like a gunslinger. Buck widened his stance and flexed his right hand. He met the cold, blue-eyed stare without flinching.

"I've seen you in town," Rafe said, looking smug. "You're the one who was forced to marry Kate O'Brien."

"I wasn't *forced* to do anything." Buck wanted to slam his fist into Hamilton's arrogant face. It was all he could do to control himself, especially now that he knew what he had done to Kate.

"That's not what I heard."

"Don't believe everything you hear, Hamilton. Besides, I'm not here to talk about my wife. Someone slit the throat of one of my cows last night. You wouldn't know anything about that, would you?"

"Why would I know anything about your cattle?" Rafe said, rearing back and standing tall, acting insulted. "I've got my hands full here. Probably some renegade snuck up on your herd."

"The meat was left to rot. It wasn't Indians."

"Can't help you then." Rafe pulled a cigar out of his coat pocket, lighting it with a match he scraped on the bottom of his boot. He puffed on the cigar to get it going, and then blew smoke in the air before opening his mouth again. "I stopped by a while back to see you, but you weren't there. Wanted to make an offer for your place.

"Not interested in sellin'."

"Maybe you need to talk it over with your wife. She inherited the place." He blew smoke into Buck's face. "I suggest you take my offer. It's the best one you'll get."

Buck narrowed his eyes and glared at the man. He couldn't prove it was Hamilton or one of his men who had slaughtered his cow, but he knew deep in his gut it was him. He'd met his type before. His daddy was rich, so he thought he could break every law and not get caught. Before he made the mistake of grabbing the man around the throat, Buck mounted Applejack.

"If something else happens to any of my cattle, Hamilton, I'll track down the man who did it and make him pay."

Rafe grinned up at him, not commenting on Buck's implied threat. "Well, nice of you to stop by." He puffed on his cigar and pointed it at Buck. "You tell that pretty little wife of yours I said hello. Me and her brother were best friends, you know."

Buck held the reins so tight Applejack danced under him. "I told your pa and I'm telling you. Stay clear of my wife. If I ever catch either of you bothering her again, you'll answer to me."

"Now that's not very neighborly of you."

"I didn't intend it to be," Buck said through gritted teeth. "You've been warned. Stay off my land and stay away from my wife."

Buck turned Applejack and nudged him into an easy lope, his spine tingling the whole time. He wouldn't put it past Rafe Hamilton to shoot him in the back. After meeting the man, it wasn't a far stretch to believe he had started the stampede that killed Kate's brother. If he could ever prove it, he'd make sure Hamilton ended up swinging from a rope.

As he rode back to the ranch, he prayed for swift justice, but in the meantime, he'd be on his guard for what Rafe Hamilton had in store for him. The man wanted Kate. That was plain as day. Jealousy and rage warred in his gut. Hamilton would have to kill him to get to her, but Buck wouldn't be as easy to ambush as Kate's brother. He'd be watching for him.

Chapter Fourteen

"Miss Kate, I'd sure like more of those fried taters." Billy grinned and passed her his cleaned plate.

Kate smiled at the young ranch hand, took his tin plate, and stood up to refill it from the iron skillet on the stove. "Anything else?"

"A couple more biscuits and gravy should do it."

Kate laughed. "I dinna know where you put it all."

"In those hollow legs he's got." Joe sopped up the egg yolk on his plate with the last of his biscuit. "He's still a growing boy."

"I'm not a boy," Billy grumped. "I'm a full-grown man who puts in a full day of hard work like the rest of you. Besides, Ma says you need to eat more when it's cold."

Kate looked over at Buck's sober face. He'd hardly said a word after returning home yesterday. Whatever happened when he confronted Rafe Hamilton couldn't have been good. He had sat staring into the fire long after she went to bed.

Buck cleared his throat, pushed back his plate, and rested his arms on the table. Everyone stopped mid-bite and looked at him.

"Snow clouds are boiling over the mountain, boys. We had blue sky at dawn, but it looks like we'll need to scatter hay for the cattle by nightfall. Could turn into a blizzard. Better lay in a couple days grub for the bunkhouse."

Josh nodded. "We'll take care of it.

"Somethin' else on your mind, Boss?" Joe stroked his gray beard with a gnarled hand.

Buck didn't answer him right away.

Kate watched emotions flicker across Buck's face. His jaw looked tight like he was angry, but his eyes reflected worry. She sat down and put her hands in her lap.

"Somethin' else is wrong. You're not only worrying about a blizzard." It surprised her she could read her husband's face so well now.

He looked over at her for a moment before his gaze rested on each of the ranch hands in turn.

"I want every one of you to be looking over your shoulder from now on. Make sure your rifles are close by. Kate, I'll do your chores for the time being. I want you to stay in the house."

"What's wrong?"

"I don't trust Hamilton."

"I dinna trust him, either, but he's not likely to hurt me while I'm milking the cow." She laughed at his worry and picked up her plate to carry to the sink.

"I mean it, Kate."

She set down her dish and turned to him. "You can't be serious."

Joe pushed away from the table, scraping his chair on the pine floor. "Boys, we've got work to do. Let's get at it."

Billy swallowed a mouthful of gravy. "But I'm not finished."

"You are now."

Grumbling, Billy pushed back from the table along with Josh and snagged another biscuit, but he didn't argue. He held the biscuit in his teeth as he plucked his hat off a peg and donned his heavy coat.

"See ya at the barn," Joe said and shut the door behind him on the way out.

"What's this really about?" Kate asked.

"Like I said, I don't trust Hamilton." Buck leaned against the wooden kitchen chair and folded his arms over his chest.

"Neither do I, but there's nothin' new in that. He's a wolf in sheep's clothing. What happened yesterday? Did he threaten you?"

"Not in so many words, but I'm convinced he's the one who sent somebody to slit that cow's throat. He wanted to send a message that he doesn't take it kindly that you're married to me now."

She harrumphed and bustled around the table, stacking dirty plates. "There's nothing he can do about it."

Unfolding from the chair, Buck stood and stayed her hand. She looked up into his face, his worry now plainly written there. She set the dirty dishes on the table.

"Kate, please do this for me."

"I canna hide in the house for the rest of my life, Buck, just because Rafe Hamilton might ride over here." She searched his eyes. "What's the worst he could do with you and your men guarding me?"

"Shoot me in the back and maybe even kidnap you. I wouldn't put anything past him."

Kate startled, and her stomach clenched in fear. She searched his warm brown eyes that seemed to plead with her. He was sincere.

"I think he's mad enough at losing you and this place that he'll do anything to have you."

"No, surely he—"

He reached out and rubbed his hands up and down her arms.

She shivered. "You're as convinced as I am that he had something to do with Patrick's death."

He tucked an errant curl behind her ear. "My gut's telling me he's guilty, but I can't prove it."

"You really think he would..." She shivered, not able to say the words. Buck pulled her into an embrace, and she let him, resting her head above his heart, listening to its steady beat. She felt comforted.

"Will you please stay in the house until I can sort this out . . . for me? I couldn't stand it if anything—"

She reached up and put a hand over his mouth. "Don't say it. Sure'n nothing's going to happen to me. I'm more worried about you."

Buck took her hand and kissed her palm, lifting the corners of his mouth. "I'll be fine. I don't aim to give him a target to hit."

Stepping away, she wrapped her arms around her waist and furrowed her brow. "All right. I'll do as you ask, but I canna live the rest of my days hidden away in this cabin." She glanced out the window at the snow already blowing in the wind.

"I know, darlin'. I warned him to stay away from you and this property. I can only hope he heeds my warning, but I'm not taking any chances."

With his callused hand, he turned her face to his and smiled. She knew he wanted to kiss her, and Lord help her, she wanted to kiss him, but she hesitated, and the moment was lost. He trailed a finger down her jawline.

"Keep Riley with you at all times, you hear?"

She nodded her head and gave him a tiny smile. He tapped her nose.

"And keep that shotgun handy. I still need to give you lessons so you can hit what you aim at."

"If Rafe Hamilton comes ridin' up to my door, Buck, I know enough to drive him off my land."

"Our land," he corrected her.

"Our land."

Buck cupped her cheek in his hand and kissed her on the forehead. His lips felt soft and warm. "I'll ride out with Billy and Josh to check on the herd and take a look around. Joe will stay behind. If you need us, fire that shotgun in the air."

She looked at him with determination. "I won't be aimin' for the sky."

He grinned. "That's my girl."

Buck lay on the hard pine floor with his hands behind his head in the dead of night, the flickering fire casting shadows in the cabin. It had remained quiet on the ranch, and there hadn't been any other incidents, but they were all on the alert for trouble. He didn't reckon Hamilton would give up that easy.

Letting his eyes roam to the half open door of the bedroom, he longed for a soft bed and a good night's sleep. He was too old to sleep on the floor when there was a perfectly good mattress in the next room. But stuffed with horsehair and wool, the thing was too heavy to drag out every night, plus he couldn't afford to have one of the boys know where he slept if some emergency came up in the night. He gritted his teeth. He didn't know how much more of this he could take. Christmas was still three weeks away.

But a promise was a promise. Trying to take his mind off his aching body, he let himself imagine what it would feel like to finally love Kate as his wife. When he finally made her his own, he wanted it to be special for her.

Turning over on his side, he punched his pillow and tried to find a comfortable spot—a muscle that didn't ache—but he didn't have any left. It wasn't only the hard floor and thoughts of making Kate his wife that were keeping him awake. He was tired of looking over his shoulder every minute, wondering when Hamilton would make his move against them. If the man was smart, he'd stay on his own ranch and leave them alone.

Buck didn't put any stock in that hope. He'd seen the evil light in Hamilton's eyes when he'd told him to tell his "pretty little wife" hello. Anger and jealousy knotted in his stomach. And if he'd admit it, fear. Fear for Kate. Fear he'd die and leave her alone to fend for herself. She didn't stand a chance against their neighbor. The man wanted her, and Buck knew Kate's refusal only made him want her more. Her brother had paid a high price for turning Hamilton down. He was sure of it. But it seemed like accusations slid off the man's back. He had other men to do his dirty work.

He turned over to his other side, his shoulder and hip bones sore as a toothache. For the last week, Kate had been even more standoffish than usual and wouldn't look him in the eye. He racked his brain, but he couldn't think of anything he'd done to make her mad. She didn't seem angry—just sad. She had almost stopped talking to him and the boys. When he had asked what was wrong, she shrugged her shoulders.

In disgust, he finally threw back the covers, sat up, and ran his fingers through his hair. Pulling on his denim britches and a blue flannel shirt over his long johns, he grabbed his pillow and a quilt and tiptoed to the kitchen table to sit in a chair. It had to be more comfortable than the floor. Riley snuffled in his sleep before the fireplace.

Buck thought about heading for the barn. Longing for the soft hay loft filled him, and he almost gave in. But he couldn't leave Kate alone in the cabin, especially with an unbarred door.

Sighing, he yawned and tossed the pillow on the kitchen table. He fluffed it, sat on the hard wood chair, and leaned forward to put his head on the pillow. The chair bottom wasn't any more comfortable than the floor. He needed an extra pillow for his backside. Closing his eyes, Kate's face haunted him. His eyes popped open. He snugged the quilt tighter around his shoulders and stared into the flickering flames, listening to the crackle and pop of the fire. His head snapped up when he heard the bedroom door squeak. Kate walked toward him, still wearing her navy-blue day dress, a serious look on her face. Why was she up and dressed this early?

"I heard you get up."

"Floor's too hard. Thought I'd try a different position." He felt cranky as a two-year-old.

She sat across from him.

He rested his elbows on the table and raked his fingers through his hair again, staring into her green eyes ringed with worry. He wanted nothing more than to kiss her worries away. *Christmas.* Just three more weeks.

"What are you doing up?" He stifled a yawn.

"I...I...need to say something. I've come to a decision." She didn't look at him, and something told him he wasn't going to like what she had to say.

"What kind of decision, darlin'?" He threw the quilt off his shoulders and reached across the table to take her hands, but she withdrew and put them in her lap.

Despite all his best efforts to court her, the woman blew hot and cold, keeping him at arm's length at times. Mostly, she seemed to trust him now, but there were times she was as skittish as a new colt. Maybe this was how a decent woman was supposed to act. He wished he could come to her as pure as the driven snow, but he couldn't change his past. The simple fact was he'd known other women—not women like Kate though. Guilt racked his soul. Sometimes, he felt like a wolf ready to devour a kitten.

"Do ya want some coffee?" She was stalling.

"No, tell me what's on your mind. You've been acting standoffish lately. I thought we'd gotten past that."

"I'm..." Her spine straightened, and a resolute look settled on her features.

Whatever was wrong, she had made a decision. He didn't say a word or move toward her, afraid she would bolt.

But her gaze never wavered. "I'm sorry, Buck."

He didn't know what she meant, but her words scared him. He stretched out his hand toward her, but her hands stayed in her lap. He pulled away and crossed his arms as though he could protect himself from what she was about to say.

"Sorry about what?"

"I've tried. I really have, but..." Her voice broke, a slight waver in her voice. "I canna ever be a real wife to you."

"But you *are* my wife, Katie. We've talked about this. We can't change the fact that we got married too quick." His heart thumped, not liking where this conversation was headed.

"I know, but—"

"I've been patient like you asked, haven't I? And respectful?"

"Aye, you have—"

"And you seem to trust me now...and feel something for me."

"I do. It's nothing you've done."

"Christmas is coming, darlin'...isn't it?" He tried to smile, but instead had to swallow past the big lump in his throat.

She shook her head no and then buried her face in her hands.

He uncrossed his arms and reached across the table to pull down her hands, stroking her cheek.

"Are you sure I haven't done something wrong?"

"Nay...it's me." She inhaled a deep breath. "I canna give you children."

His heart stuttered. Something was wrong with her. "You can't have children? Maybe Doc—"

"No, I mean, I'll always be your wife in name only. I canna...I willna..."

He felt the color drain from his face. "You won't sleep with me." Even in his own ears, his voice sounded harsh.

"I'm afraid." There was a pleading look in her eyes. "Try to understand. My stepfather beat my mother and me half to death. Then when she died, he turned his eyes on me. I canna let any man touch me again. I'm...I'm not the pure bride you think you married."

His heart clenched. "I'm not your stepfather, sweetheart. If he were here, I'd—"

"I've thought a lot about this, Buck. It's not fair to stay married to you. You need a wife who will love you fully and give you a family. Not a wife whose memories and body and soul are tainted with sin."

His heart broke for her—for what she had endured at the hands of someone who should have protected her. He had suspected something terrible had happened to her in the past, but not this, never this. He couldn't imagine how she felt, but now at least he understood.

"Honey, I've not lived a pure life either, but it's my own fault. If any man has hurt you, has violated you, has dishonored you, he's the one who will burn in hell forever—not you. The Lord doesn't hold you responsible...and neither do I."

She lifted her head, unshed tears shining in her eyes. "Rafe Hamilton—"

"You told me he never—" She shook her head as though he were dense.

"Nay, but that doesn't mean he won't stop until he gets what he wants. Before the winter is out, I'm convinced he'll find a way to kill you, just like he murdered Patrick. Don't ya see? I'm not the one in danger. You are. Every time you walk out that door, he'll be watching and waiting for the right time."

Buck gritted his teeth. "Let him try. I'll—"

"You know I'm right, Buck." Her deep sigh broke his heart. "So in the morning, I'll drive into town and file for an annulment. It's the only way to save you from me and from dying at the hands of that blackguard."

He felt as though she'd socked him in the gut. Sucking in air, he stood up in a rush, knocking the chair over backward. Riley startled to his feet and walked over to his side. He reached down and ruffled the dog's head. Anger, hurt, frustration, despair, love—they all warred in his heart. He placed his hands on his hips and studied her for a moment. She was serious. Dead serious.

"You've made up your mind."

She stood up and faced him, her face hardened with purpose. "I have."

"And nothing I say will sway your stubborn Irish noggin' out of this."

"Nay. I've made up my mind. I'll not live like this anymore. I want you to leave. I want all of you to leave. I'm moving into town. Rafe can have this land. It's not worth dying for. In the spring, I'll leave this godforsaken place."

His heart sank clear to his gut. "Do what you want, but I'll never sign any papers."

"You'll have to—or move into the bunkhouse. But I'd rather you all left without—"

"How many times do I have to say it? I'm not letting the men—"

"I dinna care what they think," she yelled, and then a pleading look washed over her face. "Just let me go, Buck. It's the best for both of us."

"Seems like you're the one who's decided what's best for me. What if I don't want a divorce?"

"Annulment."

"Same thing."

Her jaw tightened. "It doesna matter what you want. It's what I want."

Studying her determined expression, Buck knew he couldn't win. Finally, she dropped her gaze, and he turned his back on her. Without a word, he sat down by the fire and jerked on his boots, and then he strode to the door, buttoning his blue flannel shirt. He grabbed his coat and hat off the peg, anger coiled like a rattler in the pit of his stomach. He plopped his Stetson on his head.

Maybe Kate would change her mind by morning, but he wasn't waitin' around tonight to find out. Ruby's offered what he needed right now—a drink. His conscience pricked, but his anger pushed aside all his reasoning power.

Kate had painted him with the same brush as her stepfather. Rafe Hamilton and his threats were only an excuse. She flat out didn't want to be married to him. He had been patient with her, had slept on the floor for her, had kept his hands to himself for her. And for what? It wasn't like she didn't know he wanted a real marriage from the beginning. Lifting the bar off the door, he let it clatter against the wall.

"Where are you going?"

He bit out his words over his shoulder. "I need a drink."

"If you're going to that brothel, don't bother coming back," she shouted. Red suffused her face.

"What do you care?" He buttoned his coat and pulled on his gloves. "It's not like we're really married. According to you, I'm just another hired hand. Don't wait up for me. I'll be back in the morning. Maybe by then, you'll have come to your senses."

Walking out the door, he slammed it hard behind him, but not before he heard her sob. He didn't look back, though all he wanted was to gather her into his arms and hold her, console her, wash away her bad memories. But she'd never let him...and never was too long for him to wait.

Crying, Kate ran to the door, picked up the bar, and slid it into place with a bang. Then she leaned her forehead against the hard wood, tears blinding her. Riley padded to her side and whined. Dropping to her knees, she threw her arms around the dog, yielding to the pain that threatened to tear out her heart. She had driven Buck to this. It was her fault he would seek pleasure in town tonight.

But she had no choice. She was falling in love with him, and it was increasingly hard to fight the temptation to allow him to kiss her and hold her. Once she let that happen, she would be lost. Even though he said he had a soiled past, too, even though he said it didn't make a difference how he felt about her, it would surely plague his thoughts forever. It was different for a man than a woman. Men were forgiven for their indiscretions. They were expected to sow wild oats. Women bore their sin for life. She knew Buck loved her now, but eventually it would be a stain she couldn't remove. It was better to let him go now while he still had a chance of falling in love with someone pure and unspoiled, not someone whose wounds were still raw and might never heal. He deserved a loving, giving wife and a happy home.

Riley whined and licked her face as though he wanted to comfort her. She didn't think she could ever be comforted. She took a hard look at the woman she had become. Damaged...broken. She had prayed for God to forgive her, to wipe away her memories, but she still felt dirty, unclean.

But she had sworn after she escaped Ireland that she would never let another man touch her. Even the smell of whiskey that Buck poured over the cut on her foot when they first met had made her want to wretch. She had sworn no man would ever control her again. Not Rafe Hamilton...not Buck McKean.

The memories she had tried to forget once she arrived in this new country poured out on her like scalding water tonight. She had found a measure of peace living with her brother...now the memories tormented her day and night.

Finally, her heart emptied of tears, she took a shuddering breath. Standing up, she shuffled into the bedroom and lay down on the rumpled covers of the trundle bed.

She never should have married Buck. She knew that now, but she had thought it would all work out, that she'd change. That she'd want a real marriage. Instead, she had ruined his life. She had brought nothing but trouble to him. She gathered the pillow to her chest and sobbed into its softness.

Maybe Buck could buy her out, and she could move into town. Her friends would protect her, but Buck would never be safe if he stayed in Deer Lodge Valley. Thoughts of him lying in a pool of blood tormented her.

She knew he was in love with her. Oh, he had never told her so, as she had never spoken of her feelings for him. She had kept her emotions bottled up inside, and now she had destroyed any love he might have held for her in his heart. But this was the only way to save him from the pain she would only cause him later. Even though her arms ached to hold a babe of her own—Buck's son or daughter—she wouldn't allow herself a future with him. This was for the best.

For whom? The words came unbidden to her mind. *Have you asked Me?*

Guilt pressed against her sternum and made it difficult to breathe. Hadn't she prayed for God to help her? But He had never given her an answer. What else could she do but take matters into her own hands? She groaned as the Scripture floated before her eyes as though she looked at the words in her Bible.

Trust in the LORD *with all thine heart; and lean not unto thine own understanding. In all thy ways acknowledge him, and he shall direct thy paths.*

It was the Scripture she had clung to in Ireland after her mother died and the troubles had grown worse. Kate didn't understand why God had allowed her mam to marry such a cruel man after her Da had passed. She didn't understand why her mother died bearing her stepfather's babe after he had beaten her in a drunken rage. She didn't understand why God had allowed the man to abuse her. All she knew was He had delivered her from the hands of Pharaoh exactly as He had done for the Israelites.

Patrick's letter, containing her ticket to America, seemed like an answer to her prayers, a way to leave the past behind. A way of escape. So, she had traveled the long way to Patrick's Montana Territory. Surely, here she could be happy. Her memories would fade. Her wounds would heal. Then Rafe Hamilton entered her life. The lust on his face when he attacked her down by the river. The man had killed her brother.

Was it God's will that she had lost her whole family at the hands of evil men? What kind of God would take away everyone she had ever loved?

I gave you Buck, but you sent him away.

A knife sliced through her heart. Had it been God's will that she marry Buck? Everyone seemed to think so at the time. She had come to think so too. Then how could she now put him out of her life? Her regret tore her heart in shreds. She fell to her knees on the cold, pine floor beside the trundle bed and clasped her hands under her chin, tears spilling down her cheeks.

Oh, Lord, forgive me. I've been such a fool. I havna trusted You. I've only trusted in myself. I've let guilt and fear rule my life. And now I've ruined Buck's life. Help me. I was wrong to tell him I wanted an annulment. Please protect him tonight, and don't let him do anything he'll regret. I couldna bear it if he sins against you. Guide us, Lord, in Your paths of righteousness. Show us Your will and help us untangle our knotted lives.

Kate didn't know how long she remained on her aching knees, interceding fervently for Buck and begging for forgiveness for her selfishness and willful disobedience. But finally, God's peace settled around her shoulders like a warm shawl, and sighing, she crawled into bed fully clothed, hoping the Lord would give her a second chance to make things right. Plucking the pins out of her bun, she tossed them on the floor, letting her hair spill down her back. She was too tired to braid it. Crawling under the covers, she pulled the quilts to her chin and fell into a deep sleep.

Chapter Fifteen

BUCK SLAMMED BACK ANOTHER WHISKEY AND slapped his hand on the sticky bar, signaling for another shot. He didn't remember how many he'd had to drink. He hadn't been counting. But finally, the pain that had gripped his chest since leaving Kate behind had slowly numbed.

His vision a little hazy, he looked in the mirror over the bar and surveyed the girls in their bawdy dresses. A little blonde stared at him with a lazy smile. She sashayed over and snuggled up against him. He had sworn never to have truck with a soiled dove again, but his conscience had been silenced in a sea of whiskey.

"Hi, cowboy, you lookin' for a little company?"

With his mind fogged, he pulled her closer and whispered in her ear. "You offering?"

"Why don't you come up to my room, and we'll have us our own little party?" She giggled and tugged on his hand, placing it around her tiny waist. For a moment, he shook his head no and tried to pull away.

But in his whiskey-fogged brain, he suddenly felt like a sixteen-year-old again, remembering what it felt like to take a woman for the first time. Memories rushed up from the pit of hell, making him forgot his vows to God, to Kate, and to himself.

"What's your name, cowboy? Mine's Pansy."

The soiled dove ran her hands up his chest and pulled his head down for a hungry kiss. He claimed her ruby-red lips that opened like a flower when she wrapped her arms around him. Somewhere in the back of his mind, he knew he had just committed adultery with a woman who was not his wife. Guilt threatened to overwhelm him and he broke away, wiping the back of his hand over his mouth.

But then a voice whispered in his ear. *Kate's not a* real *wife. You're a free man...a single man. You can do whatever you want.*

Before he knew what he was doing, he allowed Pansy to pull him toward the stairs. She giggled.

"You sure kiss good, cowboy. And you sure are handsome."

Buck grinned through the haze of alcohol and leaned against the woman when he stumbled. Another vision of Kate flashed like lightning in his mind, but he pushed it down into the darkness. Still, a prickle of shame and guilt shinnied up his spine.

Like a bull led to the slaughter, he followed Pansy up the stairs and into her room and then fell back on the soft mattress when she pushed him down. She started to unbutton his shirt, grinning.

Buck.

Startled, he looked for the source of the voice he heard. Then he shook his woozy head and let Pansy kiss his neck.

Please don't do this, Buck.

It sounded like Kate's voice, but that was impossible. She had made it clear he wasn't her husband.

Buck, please.

He groaned and pushed Pansy away. Kate had made it clear he wasn't her husband, but he knew in his heart, she was his wife, and he'd never love another woman. He rebuttoned his shirt as he stood up and swayed on his feet. The room spun around him.

"What's the matter, cowboy?" Looking puzzled, Pansy reached out for him.

He shrugged her off in disgust and turned around, catching his image in her long mirror. Was this the man he had become? A man reduced to seeking pleasure in a brothel? He thought he'd left that part of himself far behind. He pulled out a handkerchief from his back pocket and wiped off the red lip rouge smeared over his face and neck. He looked down at Pansy who had a confused look on her face.

"Did I do something wrong?" she asked.

"No, but I did." Swaying, he reached into his pants pocket and withdrew a couple of silver dollars, tossing them on the bureau.

Without looking back, Buck stumbled out of her room and down the stairs, gripping the railing to keep from falling. He wiped his hand across his mouth again. What had he done? He loved Kate. He would always love her, and a night spent with a saloon girl wouldn't satisfy his dreams for a home and family. Only Kate could do that.

His vision spun, and he closed his eyes for a moment, weaving and holding onto the railing. He had to get home. He had to convince Kate he loved her. Why hadn't he told her he loved her? He wasn't thinkin' straight, that's why. His anger had bested him again.

Pushing his way through the crowd, he staggered toward the pegs on the wall in search of his coat, but a tall, blond man stepped into his path, a sneer on his face—Rafe Hamilton.

"Well, well, well, if it isn't the high and mighty Buck McKean."

Buck sucked in his breath and swayed on his feet.

Rafe laughed. "Looks like you and Pansy had a little fun upstairs. I wonder what your new bride would think about that. Maybe I'll tell her."

Buck's fists doubled up, and his eyes narrowed. "It's none of your business, Hamilton." His tongue felt thick. "Get out of my way."

Rafe tucked his coat behind his low-slung gun. "What's the matter, McKean? Kate not enough for you? Need a little somethin' on the side? If you don't want your wife anymore, I'll take her off your hands."

Growling with rage, Buck drew back his fist and punched Hamilton in the face. Blood shot out of the man's nose, and Buck felt a measure of satisfaction...until the banker's son drew his gun.

Then he heard the click of a revolver cocked behind him.

"That's enough, you two," Ruby said.

Buck didn't take his eyes off Rafe to turn around and look at the madam.

"You've both had too much to drink tonight, and if you don't put that gun away, Rafe, I'll send somebody for the sheriff...and your father."

Rafe wiped his bloody nose on the back of his hand, but he holstered his gun, a threat still in his voice. "We'll settle this another time, McKean."

As if the hounds of hell were chasing him, Buck grabbed his coat and shrugged it on. Then he plopped his Stetson on his head and pushed open the saloon doors, stumbling toward Applejack. Untying the reins, he swung up on the horse's back. The cold air helped to clear his head some, but he was still drunk and disgusted with himself. He kicked his buckskin in the flanks, and snow flew up from the hooves into his face.

"Take me home, boy." He gave Applejack his head, and they loped out of Deer Lodge. Bile rose in his throat at the thought of what he had done—he had sinned. He thought he was a better man than that, but tonight proved he still had a long way to go.

Riley's sharp barking awoke Kate from a pleasant dream—a dream of walking arm and arm with Buck through a rainbow meadow of wildflowers. Still half asleep, she struggled to sit up and swiped her long, curly hair back from her face. Hoofbeats sounded outside the cabin. Her heart lightened. God had heard her prayers and brought Buck home to her tonight. Right as she reached the open bedroom door, a lighted torch smashed through the kitchen window, setting the curtains on fire before landing on the table.

Screaming, she ran toward the barred door, but the flames and smoke already blocked her way. She heard a thump on the roof. Stark fear seized her mind as Riley continued his frantic barking. Retreating into the bedroom with the dog, she slammed the bedroom door and tried to think of what to do. The window. Frantically, she searched the room with her hands in the dark while the deafening roar of flames filled her ears.

"Lord, help me!"

She coughed as smoke crept under the door. Groping in the darkness, her hand grazed her hair brush on the dresser, and she almost tripped over Riley. The ladder-back chair sat beside it. She grabbed her brush and dragged the chair to the window. If she couldn't open the sash, she'd have to smash the glass.

Outside, she could hear the men yelling her name and water splashing. A bucket brigade wouldn't save her. She'd have to save herself. Suddenly, she heard a pounding on the front door.

"Kate!" Buck yelled her name.

"In here," she screamed, but she didn't think he could hear her over the roar of the flames.

Stepping on the seat of the wobbly chair, she tried to pull up the window. It was frozen shut. Coughing, she turned her face away and smashed a glass pane. A cold wind swept into the room, and she filled her lungs with fresh air. She broke more window panes until there was room to crawl out. Throwing her shoulder against the thin grid of wood that had encased each piece of glass, it splintered. Relieved, she pushed again, and the frame fell to the ground.

Buck continued to call her name, his voice sounding closer.

Riley! She jumped to the floor in her stocking feet. The cabin crackled like dry kindling. She couldn't leave him behind to burn alive. She wrapped her arms around his middle, coughing in the smoke-filled room, and managed to lift his front feet to the chair. He seemed to understand what she wanted and leapt up, putting his paws on the window sill, barking.

Buck's face appeared at the window, his face lit by the flames, then reached in the window and pulled Riley through the opening. "Kate!"

Kate scrambled to the seat of the chair, and Buck pulled her out of the window like a sack of grain. He swept her into his arms and pressed his face against her hair.

"Buck!"

His breath smelled like whiskey.

"It's all right, darlin'." He groaned and pulled her close to his chest. She wrapped her arms around his neck and held on tightly. "I love you, Katie girl."

Slipping and sliding in the snow, Buck stumbled toward the front of the cabin. She turned her face into his shoulder to escape the intense heat of the fire. Just as they reached the front, the wood-shingled roof collapsed, and flames shot high into the night sky. She screamed as Buck collapsed into the snow face down in the front yard.

As she rolled him off her, she felt the sticky wetness. She looked down at her hand in the light from the fire. Blood! The front of her dress was covered in blood. Josh pushed her away and turned her husband on his back. Blood soaked his shirt. Billy and Joe lifted her out of the snow.

"Do something!" she screamed. Her teeth chattered in the cold wind, her wool socks soaked through.

With anger in his eyes, Josh looked up at her, and she feared what he had to say.

"He's been shot. That's a bullet wound. If God is on his side, it went straight through him."

Kate's stomach knotted with fear. She couldn't lose him. She loved him. Dropping to her knees, she brushed his dark hair away from his face. He looked so pale.

Billy advanced toward Applejack who had been ground tied with the reins where Buck had flung himself out of the saddle.

"Whoa, boy." He patted Buck's horse on the neck. In the light of the fire, she saw the bloodstains on Applejack's coat and the trail of red through the snow.

"No telling how much blood he's lost," Josh said. "I can't believe he made it this far. We need to stop the bleeding and get him to Doc's office—fast."

"Blankets," Joe yelled. "Billy—the bunkhouse. Grab as many as you can. Towels too."

Kate crossed her arms, shivering in the wind. No one wore coats. The men must be freezing in their long johns and trousers.

"Miss Kate, move." Josh yelled at her as though he were commanding troops on the battlefield. Joe and Josh dragged Buck by the arms away from the flames. She looked at the cabin. The walls would collapse soon.

Pulling up her dress, she ripped the ruffles off her petticoat and dropped to her knees beside the man she loved.

Josh scooped up snow and packed it against Buck's bleeding shoulder. He grabbed the white cloth from her hand, folded it, and pressed it on the wound with both hands.

"What—"

"It'll slow down the bleeding."

Billy sprinted to the huddled group and handed the blankets to Joe, who wrapped one around Buck.

"You two hitch up the team to the buckboard," Joe directed Josh and Billy. "Grab our coats. We've got a cold ride ahead of us." He draped a scratchy wool blanket around Kate's shoulders.

"Please, God, don't let him die," Kate prayed.

Joe squeezed her arm. "He's strong, Miss Kate. If anybody can make it, Buck can."

She nodded and hoped he was right. Blood had already soaked through the makeshift bandage and stained the quilt that covered him.

The buckboard clattered out of the barn, Josh pushing the horses. He stopped the wagon steps from Buck. Kate hurried to lay a couple of blankets down on the wood floor while the three men lifted Buck up and quickly loaded him into the wagon bed. She scrambled up next to her husband and tucked a heavy wool quilt around him. Joe leapt into the wagon bed with her, and Riley followed.

"Get out, dawg." He pushed Riley away.

"No." She yelled over the roar of the fire. "He's coming with us." The dog laid down at Buck's head, licking his forehead.

"Move out!" Joe shouted.

Josh slapped the reins of the bays, the jerk knocking her down on top of Buck. She pressed against him to help keep him warm.

"Buck," she said into his ear. "Wake up, Buck."

No response.

The buckboard flew down the road toward town, throwing its passengers from side to side.

"Hold tight, Miss Kate." Joe looked over at her in the moonlight. "This is going to be a rough ride and that can't be good for him. Pray we get him there in time."

She nodded numbly and held onto Buck's blood-soaked left arm, while Joe held him on the other side. Looking behind them, the blazing cabin filled her vision. She and Riley could have died in that fire. Buck saved them. He was shot, but he saved them. The realization hit her hard. None of them knew how long they had before God called them home. She cupped her husband's cold cheek in her hand and kissed him, then whispered in his ear.

"I love you too, Buck. Please don't leave me."

Kate paced in the waiting room of Doc's office, sipping on a cup of bitter coffee Martha had pressed into her hands. She couldn't stop shivering, whether from the cold or her fear over Buck dying. Joe and Billy sat in silence, each lost in his own thoughts. Once they had unloaded Buck, Josh had driven the buckboard and horses to the livery.

Through the door, she heard Buck scream in agony. She felt his pain in every fiber of her being.

Martha opened the door and bustled out, closing it behind her. Kate looked at her with worried anticipation.

"Will he be all right?"

"Doc's still working on him, honey." Martha's face looked grim. "He's cleaning out the wound before he bandages him up. My husband will be out when he's finished to let you know how Buck's doing. He's fortunate you got him into town when you did. He lost a lot of blood."

Kate stared into Martha's eyes, wanting the older woman to reassure her Buck would recover, that he would be all right. But she knew his life rested in the hands of God who loved him far more than she ever could.

She worried about his soul. If he died, would he go to heaven? One night he had told her he had not thought much about his faith since he was a boy. There was such deep sadness in him. She knew her tough, self-reliant husband had depended on his own willpower and sheer grit as a man to make his way in the world. Not through God.

She heard Buck groaning through the paper-thin walls and wanted to go to him. Instead, she hugged herself and rubbed her hands up and down her arms. She edged closer to the pot-bellied stove where Riley lay watching her, whining, his head and ears alert.

Please, Lord, save him. Don't let him die.

"Anybody need more coffee?" Martha asked kindly. "I baked an apple pie today."

"A slice of pie sounds good." Billy looked up with serious, bright-blue eyes.

"How can you think of your belly at a time like this?" Joe growled.

"She asked, didn't she?"

Just then Josh blew in the door, bringing snow with him. "It's really coming down out there." He stamped his boots and pulled off his gloves, holding his red hands out to the fire. "Good thing this didn't start earlier. We might not have made it into town."

"I reckon Josh could use a mug of coffee too." Joe spoke politely to Martha.

"I'll fetch the pot," Martha said. "You'll all need a warmup. Now try to get comfortable. It may be a while."

When the door to the examination room closed behind her, Joe asked the question that had plagued Kate's mind all night. "Who coulda done this?"

She clenched her jaw and turned toward the grizzled old man. "I'd look no farther than Rafe Hamilton. He's the only one wicked enough to do such a thing."

"I can wake up the sheriff," Josh volunteered. "But I doubt he'd find a trail now. That snow will cover any tracks."

"Of course, it will." Her bitter words filled the room with anger. "Not to mention Rafe will have an alibi. He killed Patrick for standing in his way and got away with it. Why should I expect he would pay for shooting my husband?"

After her outburst, Kate prayed in silence, waiting. Another hour passed before Doc opened the door and stepped out, weariness stamped on his features.

"Kate, you can come on back and see him."

"Is he awake? Will he be all right?" She hurried toward him.

"We'll know in the next day or two. Thank goodness, the bullet went straight through him and missed any vital organs, but he's lost a lot of blood. He was shot in the back."

Kate looked up at Doc Mitchell, startled.

"Back shot?" Joe exclaimed, fisting his gnarled hands. "What low-down skunk—"

"I got the bleeding stopped, but we never stitch up a bullet wound in case of infection. It's a good thing you packed the wound with snow. Slowed down the bleeding. I got a dose of laudanum in him to help with the pain. He'll sleep for a while. Now we pray."

"Can we see him, Doc?" Joe started up from his chair.

"In a minute. Come on back, Kate."

She followed the doctor into his back room. A clean, white sheet covered Buck's body, and all evidence of his blood loss had been cleaned up. Bandages wrapped his shoulder and upper chest.

"I thought you'd want to see him first."

"Aye, thank you."

Hurrying to Buck's side, Kate looked down at his slack features. He looked so pale beneath his tanned skin. She brushed back his wavy, dark hair and traced the planes of the face that had become so dear to her tonight.

"Buck?"

"He'll sleep for the next several hours, Kate. We'll watch him through the night."

"He sounded like he was in so much pain." She looked in earnest at the doctor.

"The pain's bad." Doc's face softened. "He rambled a little bit, but nothing that made any sense. Mainly, he kept mumbling your name over and over."

Tears started from her eyes. "May I stay with him?"

"Of course. I'll get his men to transfer him to a bed, and then you can sit by him if you like. When you get sleepy though, come on upstairs. Martha's already got a bed made up for you. You'll need your rest."

Doc laid a comforting hand on her shoulder and squeezed. "I've done the best I know how, Kate. Now it's up to the Almighty."

She reached under the sheet and took Buck's callused hand in hers. He was as still as death. He didn't even know she was there. She wanted to tell him she had changed her mind about an annulment—that with God's help she would become the wife he wanted. Now she might never get the chance.

Chapter Sixteen

Buck felt as though he were on fire. He was walking across the desert. He looked down and saw flames licking up around his feet. He started running, and then he saw the burning cabin. Kate! He pounded on the door.

"Kate," he screamed over and over. "Kate!"

He felt so weak. Why was he so weak? He looked down at his hands. They were bloody from pounding on the door. He had to save her. He heard glass breaking. He tried to run toward the other side of the cabin, but it was as though his legs moved through thick molasses.

"Kate!"

Searing pain gripped his shoulder, but he ignored it and fought through the flames.

Suddenly, he felt a cool hand touch his forehead, and he started out of his dream, but why did he still feel so much pain? His eyes fluttered open, and he tried to focus. Her face swam before him.

He sighed in relief. "Kate."

"I'm here, Buck."

A cold cloth wiped his face, and he felt her hand, soothing his brow and stroking his hair. He closed his eyes and groaned. Pain. So much pain.

A hand lifted his head and pressed a glass against his lips. He was so thirsty. He drank deeply until there was no more, the cold liquid spilling out of his mouth onto his chest. It felt so good on his parched tongue. He laid his head back on the pillow and then fell into the dream again, flames licking at his boots. Kate was in the cabin. He had to save her.

"Kate!" he yelled, and then darkness descended once more.

Dawn had broken, and Kate's eyes felt gritty from lack of sleep. Buck had been restless all night. She heard Doc's steps and turned around, worry gripping her heart as she tucked blankets around her husband to keep him warm.

"He feels so cold and clammy, Doc. Earlier tonight he had a bit of a fever, but that went away. Now his breathing is a little uneven."

"How long's he been like this?"

"Not long. He woke up groaning and grabbing for his shoulder. I was afraid he'd rip off his bandages, so I gave him another dose of laudanum like you told me."

As she combed her fingers through Buck's damp hair with one hand, she tugged the blanket up around his neck with the other. He had thrashed so much, she thought for sure he would tear off the dressings. A spot of blood had soaked through his bandage.

Walking to the other side of the bed, Doc felt Buck's forehead and pulled up his eyelids. Then he checked his pulse. "At least he doesn't have a fever. That's a good sign. But a little bit of shock has set in." He hurried to the end of the bed and elevated Buck's feet. "Take the pillow from under his head and give it to me. Then find me a couple more."

Carefully, she lifted Buck's head and pulled out the pillow, then looked around for more pillows in his curtained room.

"Behind the curtain." Doc stuffed the pillow she gave him under Buck's feet.

Kate stuck her head through the screening draped between Buck's bed and the one next to his and grabbed the pillows, handing them to Doc. He stacked them on top of the one she'd already given him and gently let go of Buck's feet, tucking the blanket around him.

"That should do it. Now we just need to keep him warm and comfortable. The laudanum should relax his breathing, but it also might depress it. Elevating his feet should help."

Kate pulled in her bottom lip and raked it with her teeth. She felt so helpless.

Please, Lord, don't let him die.

"What can I do?"

Doc looked at her kindly. "Don't worry, Kate. He'll pull through. I saw a lot worse than this on the battlefield. Now let me change his bandage."

Kate watched Doc cut off Buck's bandage. He smelled the grievous wound, then he reached for a brown bottle and poured a sweet-smelling liquid onto a clean pad.

"Carbolic acid," Doc said before she could ask the question. "It acts as an antiseptic to keep the injury clean. But it can burn the skin if we use too much of it."

He dabbed the medicine directly on Buck's wound, which looked jagged, irritated and red, and then covered it with the soaked pad.

"Help me turn him. I'll take his shoulders, and you push on his hips."

She did as Doc asked, reaching under the sheet to shove against her husband's lower back and hips, feeling his bare skin. It was the first time she had ever touched a man so, but now wasn't the time for modesty. He was so much bigger than her, and she breathed heavily from the exertion.

The doctor redressed the wound in Buck's shoulder and then wound gauze around his shoulder to bind the entry and exit wounds.

"Let's turn him over again."

She helped Doc resettle Buck, pushing the pillows firmly under his feet, and tucked the blanket tightly around him. She straightened her spine, grimacing.

"That should do it," Doc said. "The wound looks clean, so hopefully, infection won't set in. I used Lister's methods to keep it sanitary. Keep him warm. When he wakes up thrashing, use a soothing voice and reassure him he'll be all right. He'll be in a lot of pain the next time he wakes up. I can stay with him if you'd like to go upstairs and sleep."

Kate shook her head. "Nay, I want to stay." So tired she could barely stand, she sank into the chair vacated by the doctor and stroked Buck's cheek.

"All right then. After I eat breakfast, I'll sit by him while you rest. We don't want you getting sick."

"I'll be fine."

Doc patted her shoulder. "You're a good nurse, but you need to eat and take care of yourself."

"Are you sure he'll be all right?" Worried, she turned hopeful eyes to the physician.

"I suspect he'll be just fine. He made it through the night, and that's a good sign. Buck's a strong, healthy man. He'll be laid up several weeks though."

"He won't like that."

Doc chuckled. "I expect not."

After the doctor left, she continued stroking her husband's face, murmuring words of encouragement. In a little while his color looked a wee bit better, and his chest now rose and fell in a normal rhythm. He didn't feel as clammy, but his skin remained cool to the touch.

She stole another blanket from the bed next to his and laid it over him. This was the first time she had ever really looked at Buck since they were married, and she let her eyes rove over his body covered with the blankets she had tucked around him. He was exceedingly handsome. She laid her head next to his on the mattress and closed her eyes.

Buck's eyes fluttered open. He turned his head and stared through his dark lashes at the copper-haired beauty who had fallen asleep next to him. Kate's delicate hand held his fast. He stroked her fingers with his thumb, tracing the design of her wedding ring, and she stirred, raising her sleepy eyes to his.

"You're awake." She started to withdraw her hand.

The pain in his shoulder was agonizing, but Buck held on tight. He started to say something, but his mouth felt like cotton. His tongue stuck to the roof of his mouth.

"Water," he croaked.

She retrieved her hand to lift the glass to his lips, but lying flat as he was on the bed, he couldn't raise his head. Where was his pillow? He felt so weak. Kate bent over him and lifted his head with an arm supporting him. Water dribbled out of his mouth, but he managed to drink his fill, then sighed and laid back.

"That tasted good."

She smiled at him. "How do you feel?"

"Like h—" He bit back what he wanted to say and grimaced as he tried to roll toward her on his good side. Burning pain shot through his left shoulder. He kicked impatiently at the pillows under his feet.

"What can I do?" She stood and readjusted the covers over him.

"I'm too blamed hot." Kate quickly whipped one of the blankets off him, and he felt better. Cooler. "I need a pillow for my head."

She removed the pillows from under his feet and fluffed up one before lifting his head and scooting it under him.

"Better?"

Nodding, he closed his eyes and tried to bite back the groan that escaped his lips. His shoulder throbbed. He turned his glance on her.

"What happened?"

"Do ya not remember?"

"Everything's fuzzy." He furrowed his brow and searched the images that danced just out of reach. His mind lit on one. "The cabin. It was burning."

"Aye, it was." She ran her fingers through his hair, the look on her face tender. "Do ya remember pulling Riley and me through the window?"

He thought for a moment, but the pain was so severe, he almost couldn't think. "No...wait...I remember carrying you. That's all."

His shoulder burned. He moved his hand to grip it, but she stopped him.

"No, ya canna do that. Ya canna touch it."

Irritated, he pulled the blanket down and saw the bandages. His eyes then roamed over his surroundings.

"Where am I?"

Kate brushed the hair back from his forehead, and he closed his eyes. Her hand felt so soft and cool, like his mother's. Ma had fine, long fingers that stroked his brow whenever he was sick.

"You're in Dr. Mitchell's office."

Images jumbled and twisted in his mind. He remembered leaving Ruby's, but it was kind of a blur from there. He was drunk. He remembered that much. Guilt nearly drowned him.

"You need to lie still." Kate pulled the blanket up and smoothed it over his shoulders. He uncovered his right arm and reached out to touch her face. She laid her cheek in his palm.

"You're safe." Sudden tears formed in his eyes, and he dropped his hand. He felt so weak and helpless.

She took his hand in both of hers. "Yes, I'm safe. You saved my life, Buck. And Riley's. I don't know if I could have crawled out that window by myself."

His voice broke. "I dreamed I couldn't get to you."

Kate rubbed his arm, and he felt soothed.

"As you can see, I'm perfectly fine." She smiled at him and squeezed his hand. He liked holding her hand. "You've been unconscious for the better part of three days. We've been giving you laudanum for the pain. Do you need more now?" She turned toward the brown bottle on the table.

"In a minute." The pain was almost unbearable. He wanted to look at her and touch her and talk to her. He didn't want to sleep. "You didn't answer me. What happened?"

"You were shot." Kate sighed. "We dinna know by who. It was snowing that night, and Sheriff Granger and his deputy had to wait until the next morning to ride out to our place. He didna find anything. The cabin burned to the ground."

A vague memory surfaced—punching Rafe Hamilton in the face. He groaned as he suddenly remembered the girl and stumbling up to her room. Shame overwhelmed him.

"Are you sure you dinna want something for the pain?" She sounded so concerned.

Agitated and self-disgusted, he squeezed her hand tighter. "I'm sorry, Kate—sorry I ever rode into town."

As she ran her fingers through his thick hair, he felt his spirit calm.

"Shh. It's all right, Buck. You couldna know someone would do this."

Tears welled up in his eyes again. He had almost... He squirmed away from the thought. He had stayed out of saloons and brothels for the better part of eight years, and if she would forgive him, he'd never step in one again. Then he remembered why he'd left that night.

"Do you..." His voice cracked again. "Do you still want a divorce?"

She leaned over and kissed him on the cheek, her smile warm. "Nay. God brought you back to me, and that's all I care about now. We'll work it out."

Buck sighed in relief, but the pain grew worse with each passing moment.

"I don't deserve you, you know." His face twisted in pain. "I think I'll take a dose of that medicine now."

She reached for the bottle on the table, poured a spoonful, and mixed it in a little water, then helped him lift his head again to drink.

"Doc said he wanted you to have a bit of broth when you woke up. Would you like me to bring you a bowl?"

He nodded yes, but when she left his bedside, he fell into a dreamless sleep with his last thought giving him hope.

She doesn't want a divorce.

Chapter Seventeen

SITTING AT MARTHA'S KITCHEN TABLE, THE older woman reached over and patted Kate's hand. "Honey, you need to rest. I'll sit with Buck this afternoon."

After nursing him for almost a week, Kate felt exhausted. "He's going to be all right, isn't he?"

Martha looked at her with concern. "Of course, he is. There's no infection. It's you I'm worried about. Now you march on in there and take a nap. You've got dark circles under your eyes, and I swear you've lost weight. You could wrap that dress around you twice."

Kate looked down at the blue calico dress Pastor Russell's wife Bernadette had brought by. Her day dress had too many blood stains to salvage, and she hadn't left Buck's side to see if Mr. Stricklin had any ready-mades in the mercantile. The last thing she wanted to think about was shopping or making a new dress.

She pulled the frock away from her. "'Tis a little roomy and not very warm."

"More than roomy." Martha chuckled, the laugh lines at the corners of her eyes deepening. She took a sip of tea. "Course you could wear a flour sack and that man of yours would still love you. He thinks you hung the moon and the stars."

That thought warmed Kate's heart. After nearly dying in the fire, she had promised God she would honor her marriage if He would only save Buck. She would be the wife her husband needed and wanted. But right now, she had more immediate things to worry about.

"I dinna know where we're going to live. Doc said Buck will be laid up for weeks. The last time Joe came to visit him, he said they're doing fine in the bunkhouse. It's warm, and they still have food in the root cellar. We won't be able to rebuild until spring though."

"Don't you go worrying about that right now. When Buck feels up to climbing stairs, the two of you can stay with us until you decide what to do." Martha reached over and took her ice-cold hand and squeezed it. "Now climb into bed. I'll take care of Buck."

Knowing Martha was right, Kate nodded in weary agreement. She pushed untamed curls out of her face and stood up in her stocking feet. Martha had loaned her a brush, but she couldn't remember the last time she'd sat down and fixed her hair properly. She didn't have anything to wear except what the ladies from church had supplied—even her undergarments. No one had an extra pair of shoes that fit.

Soon she'd need to talk to Buck about what they could afford to replace. She was afraid to put anything on his account at the mercantile. He'd never really shared with her how much money he had, but she didn't want to go into debt again.

In the spare bedroom, Kate slipped out of the oversized dress and climbed underneath the mountain of quilts, shivering. The sheets were cold, but she was too tired to care. She rolled into a ball, craving sleep. Her mind kept whirring, even though her eyes burned with exhaustion. She sighed and tried to relax. It was no use.

Her thoughts wouldn't stop. How would they make it through the winter? Spring was months away. She didn't even know if they had enough money to rent a place in town. Even though Martha had said they could live with them, she couldn't ask her and Doc to put them up until Buck recovered. It was too much. What would they do? She didn't want to burden Buck with their troubles until he felt better.

Rubbing her eyes, she yawned, and despite her churning thoughts, she finally fell asleep.

Buck fought the lumpy pillow and tried to push himself up in the bed with one hand. It was agony to lie around when he had so much to do. But he still felt so weak. Doc said he'd lost a lot of blood, and it would take some time to get his strength back, but he didn't have to like it. He heard footsteps on the stairs. Eagerly, he looked in that direction, but instead of Kate, it was Martha who carried a tray. He felt disappointed. He hadn't seen Kate since this morning.

The smell of solid food wafted his way, and his mouth salivated.

"I hope that's not more broth." He hoped he didn't sound ungrateful, but he was starving.

Martha chuckled. "You're in luck. I fixed you a nice beef stew."

He grinned at her. "You must have read my mind. If I'm going to climb out of this bed, I need real food."

"You must be feeling better." Her eyes twinkled. "An appetite is a good sign you're on the mend."

He reached for the bowl she sat on the table beside him. She smacked his hand.

"But you're not well enough to feed yourself yet. I'm not of a mind to wash your sheets if you spill on yourself."

He growled, but the corners of his mouth tipped up. She spooned in the first mouthful, and he groaned in pleasure when the taste of beef and brown gravy hit his tongue. He chewed quickly and swallowed.

"You're an angel from heaven."

"Not quite. But that wife of yours just might qualify for sainthood."

"Where is she?" he asked Martha before she fed him another spoonful.

"Sleeping. That poor girl has sat at your bedside night and day. I hope she sleeps straight through till morning."

Guilt pinched his conscience, and he furrowed his brow. "I guess she needs to rest, huh?"

"That's an understatement. She was practically falling asleep on her feet."

Martha continued to feed him until she scraped the bottom of the bowl.

"Can I have more?" He looked up at her with expectation.

She patted his hand. "Let's see how you do with what I've given you. You haven't had solid food for almost a week, and your stomach might rebel."

Sighing, he leaned back against his pillow. "I'm still hungry." He knew he sounded like a whiny little boy, but his stomach still felt half empty. How was a man supposed to get better?

"If you hold that down, I'll bring you more later...and a big slice of apple pie."

"Now you're talkin'." He grinned.

She smiled and shook her head. "I'll be upstairs if you need me." She stood and stacked his bowl on the tray.

"When Kate wakes up, would you send her down?"

"That's another good sign."

He cocked one dark brow. "What?"

"You're bored." She turned and walked toward the stairs, smiling at him over her shoulder. "If you need something to read, the Bible's lying on the table beside you."

Buck stared up at the white-washed ceiling, tapping the fingers of his right arm on his chest. He *was* bored. His stomach felt fine, and the only thing he had to look forward to was pie—unless Kate came to visit him. He missed her sitting by his bedside and stroking his brow and talking about rebuilding the cabin in the spring. Telling him she loved him.

His eyes searched the curtained room for his clothes, and then he pushed up on his right elbow, wincing. Where'd they put his pants? If he had to stay in this bed another minute, he was liable to go stir crazy. Nothin'. He flopped back in bed. When Kate came down he'd ask her to fetch him something to wear.

What day was it anyhow? He'd ridden into town on Saturday night, or was it Friday? The last several days were a blur because of the laudanum. He snorted. It didn't help that he got drunk either. He closed his eyes and was immediately swept back to Ruby's bar. The smell of stale beer, cigar smoke, and cheap perfume assailed his memory. He tried to focus and remember what had happened there.

Rafe Hamilton had drawn a gun on him. He remembered that much. Buck felt rage boil in his chest, and he struggled up on one elbow again. That's who followed him home and shot him in the back—the man who burned down the cabin and almost killed Kate in the process. He needed to talk to the sheriff.

One handed, he threw the covers back and realized he only wore a night shirt. He pounded his hand on the bed and collapsed down again, sweat beading on his forehead with the effort. He wanted justice. He wanted to make Hamilton pay for what he had done to them. No, he wanted revenge. It filled his belly and spilled over into his every thought. He'd make Hamilton pay if it was the last thing he ever did.

Then he remembered a Scripture Kate had read to him last night. *For it is written, vengeance is mine; I will repay, saith the Lord.*

He'd always taken care of his own problems. He didn't know if he could hand his anger and revenge over to God and trust the Lord to bring down Hamilton. His fist uncurled. He knew what Kate would say.

In Pansy's room, he had taken a good, hard look at himself and been disgusted with who he had become as a man. He was right back where he started when he was sixteen. A selfish fool only concerned with his own needs and wants.

Then Rafe Hamilton had confronted him in the bar. He thought he might die right then and there, shot in a saloon. He squirmed with guilt. On the ride home in his drunken haze, he remembered promising God that if He would restore his marriage, then he would give his life to the Lord. He'd become the man she wanted. He'd even move into the bunkhouse. He'd live every day in gratitude.

A memory of when he was nine years old transported him to his childhood. He had been sitting next to Pa, and the lady on the piano had played that song she played every Sunday, "Just As I Am." He could hear the melody, but the only words he remembered were, "I come."

His heart constricted in his chest as he recalled that moment. He didn't know how it had happened, but suddenly, he was walking down the aisle of the church to the front. He didn't even remember standing up or scooting out of the pew. The next thing he knew, he saw the preacher smiling and holding out his hand.

Lord, he wanted to be as clean as that little boy again. He looked over the years of his life and realized how rebellious he had been as a youth. Resenting his Pa for remarrying. Resenting his big brothers for their freedom as men. Only leaving a note for Pa to find. Not even having the guts to face him like the man he claimed to be.

But his worst sin had been shutting God out of his life in the gold fields, grubbing through sharp rocks in all kinds of weather to make his fortune. Greed. One of the seven deadly sins. He always thought he'd made all that money that sat in a Virginia City bank on his own. He never once gave God any credit.

But now, he saw God's hand on his life even when he was sinning and walking his own way. So many times he'd cheated death. Yet the Lord had never stopped loving him. He was the one who had stopped loving God. That's what hurt the most. He had not only disappointed Pa and the rest of his family, but he had disappointed his heavenly Father. He had turned his back on Him.

Tears welled up in his eyes and spilled down his cheeks onto the pillow. He wanted to feel like that nine-year-old boy again—clean and forgiven. A new man. But did he want that for himself, or because he wanted Kate? Was she an idol he worshipped, putting his dreams of a wife and children before God? Was he willing to give her up if that's what God wanted? She deserved a better husband, one who would cherish her and put her needs ahead of his own.

He thought about the many times he'd lain with a soiled dove. Maybe he already had children and didn't know it. He wanted to vomit out his memories. They pressed him down with guilt and shame for all he'd done. After Joe made him see the error of his ways, he'd tried to live a clean life, but he'd done it on his own terms. He'd never once asked God for help.

Lord, please forgive me. In his mind, he threw himself at the nail-scarred feet of Jesus. *Help me to be the man you want me to be. I want to feel clean again.*

His tears continued unabated, until finally, he felt peace enter his heart and he took a big, shuddering breath. Then he cried tears of joy. He was the prodigal son returning home.

When Kate padded down the stairs and peeked around the corner, Buck was lying in bed, staring at the ceiling. Her calico dress rustled, and he looked over at her, his face unmarred by the terrible pain that had held him in its grip. He was getting better.

"Good morning, darlin'." His smile lit up the room.

A warm glow flowed through her veins, and she gave him a smile as cheery as the sunshine outside. Her long sleep had done wonders for her, and her fear of him dying had fled.

"Good morning. How are you feeling today?"

He held out his good right arm and beckoned her to his side.

"Better now that you're here."

Her heart reveled in his open admiration and the love reflected in his eyes. When she slipped her hand into his large one, he squeezed it. Pulling her down on top of him, he pressed a quick kiss to her lips. She blushed and pushed up.

"It's so good to see you awake. You had us all scared for a while." She sat in the chair, and he pulled her hand to his lips, kissing her palm.

"I missed you." The warmth of his smile echoed in his voice. "I thought you'd bring my breakfast, but Martha brought me mush." He shivered in mock disgust.

She tilted her head and giggled. "Their hens have stopped laying in this freezing weather."

"I don't blame them." He chuckled deep in his chest, then grimaced. "Oh, don't make me laugh."

"Is the pain still bad?"

He shook his head, and his expression turned serious. "Bearable, but Doc said I'll be good for nothin' for the next several weeks. I'm worried about the ranch, but most of all I'm worried about you. I can't even protect you in the shape I'm in."

Kate held his hand between hers and lifted the corners of her mouth. "You don't have to worry about me. Somebody's always with me, and the boys are taking care of the ranch. Joe's been by to see you a couple of times, but you were asleep. Bill Stricklin, too, and Pastor Russell."

"I need to cut back on that laudanum. I don't reckon I need it anymore. I've had a few broken bones in my life, and they've always healed eventually. A little whiskey was all I had then to dull the pain."

"But I ken you've never been shot." She leaned her arms on his blanket. She was so relieved to see his progress she couldn't stop smiling. Buck would be a hard man to keep down.

"No, I guess not." He ran his thumb over the top of her hand. "I don't like it though, laying around with nothing to do. Even after I broke my arm when a bull kicked me, I was still able to ride Applejack and herd cattle. No time to baby yourself when you're on the trail."

"We need to talk about renting a house, so you'll be close to Doc and have time to recuperate."

He shook his head and put on a stubborn face. "I'm going back to the ranch."

She looked at him in dismay. "And who's going to take care of you out there? I canna live in the bunkhouse with the men."

"I know that. Joe can take care of me. He always has. I've already talked to Martha, and she said you can stay with her and Doc until I rebuild the cabin next spring. By then my shoulder will be healed."

Kate stood and planted her hands on her hips, struggling to curb her temper. "And what are ya goin' to eat? Beans? How will ya ever heal on a diet of beans and cornbread? You dinna even have a stove to cook a roast out there."

"No, but Joe fries up a mean steak." A boyish grin lit his face.

She raised her voice, irritated with his cowboy mulishness. "I don't understand why we canna live in town for the winter."

Determination crossed his features, and she knew he had already made up his mind without consulting her. The man was infuriating.

"Don't fight me on this, Kate...please. Whoever shot me and burned down the cabin could come back and try to finish the job. We've still got a barn and a bunkhouse to protect, not to mention a herd of cattle. The boys can't do it alone. They need my help."

"But that's just it. You canna help. Dr. Mitchell was very specific. You need to stay in bed a few more weeks. You're weak from loss of blood, and your shoulder needs time to heal before you can even move it."

"I can still fire a gun with my right hand." His jaw clenched, and then his face softened, looking at her with pleading eyes. "Please try to understand, Katie girl. If we lose everything, it will take us years to rebuild."

She gnawed on her lower lip and lowered her gaze, trying to see things from his perspective. It was hard. He was as stubborn as an old ram. "Give it two weeks before you leave. By then you can take charge and be of some help to your men instead of a weight on them. In your condition, they'll spend all their time taking care of you instead of the ranch. You don't want that, do ya?"

"Two weeks laying around here will drive me around the bend, Katie. I feel useless. A man needs to work."

The crux of your problem. Men. Irish or Texan, you all want to be in charge of everything.

"A man needs to follow doctor's orders until he's back on his feet." She stood and rearranged his covers.

"A man out here can't lay down. If he does, he might not get up again."

"Then at least give it a week…a week of solid food and rest…please." But by the stubborn set of his jaw, she could tell her arguments for common sense fell on deaf ears.

He said not a word, only looked at her with those warm brown eyes. She stared back at him, willing him to see reason. Then she knew without a doubt, he'd do what he wanted to do. Feeling defeated, she settled on the chair by his side. He took her hand and kissed it again, nuzzling his lips against her palm.

Her heart melted. "I'm afraid for you."

His smile was meant to reassure her, but it didn't. He squeezed her hand. "Don't be afraid."

"How can I not?"

"I'll be fine."

"Dinna you understand?" She raised her voice, hoping he would heed her warning, looking him square in the face. "Rafe Hamilton willna stop until you're dead. Just like Patrick."

"Let him try. I won't turn my back on him next time." His tone turned pleading. "And when he comes, Katie, I don't want you caught in the crossfire. You're safer in town with Doc and Martha and the sheriff nearby."

Her heart skipped a beat. At some point, she had fallen desperately in love with the man and couldn't bear the thought of losing him. What good was the land if she lost him?

"Let's give him what he wants then," she argued. "We'll sell him the ranch."

He stared at her in stony silence, his expression saying more than he could ever say in words. She knew he wouldn't give in. Finally, she looked down at the blanket, sighing.

"I'll stay until the day after Christmas." He squeezed her hand. "Then I'll have the boys drive me home in the buckboard."

"I'd forgotten that it's almost Christmas. We didna even get to put up a tree and decorate it."

"I know." He pulled her closer. "Not exactly the Christmas I planned on either."

When she sighed, he cupped her face with his warm hand, his deep-brown eyes capturing hers. She leaned into his touch. Brushing her lips with his thumb, the question in his eyes, she leaned forward, feeling the warmth of his breath mingle with hers before their mouths met in a tender kiss.

He tried to pull her closer, but when he groaned and stiffened, she knew he was in pain. Pulling away, she laid her head in the cleft of his right shoulder. She could hear his rapid heartbeat as she snuggled against him. Gently, he stroked her hair, and she tried not to think about their future. There was only this moment.

Chapter Eighteen

BUNDLED IN MARTHA'S OVERSIZED, BLACK WOOL coat and wearing shoes too big for her, Kate pushed open the door of the Stricklin Mercantile. Abigail looked up in greeting at the sound of the bell and hurried toward her.

"Kate!" The woman enfolded her in a quick embrace. "It's so good to see you. How's Buck?"

She smiled. "Better. Much better."

"I wondered when you'd finally leave his bedside to get a breath of fresh air."

"Your husband is visiting with him now, so I thought I'd see if you had any ready-made shirts and dungarees he could wear."

Abigail threaded her arm through Kate's. "Let's see what we can find. He's such a tall man." She drew her over to a table stacked with denim pants and rifled through them, pulling out a pair and letting the legs fall to the floor. "You may have to take a few pair with you to see if they fit. It's hard to know. How tall is he?"

"I'm not really sure." Was that something she should know? "Well over six feet I'd say."

"Come to think of it, he's about the same size as Rafe Hamilton, and I know what he always buys. Two pair be enough for now?"

Kate's stomach curdled at the sound of the man's name. "Yes, ma'am."

"Oh, and I've got cotton flannel shirts over here and chambray, but he's going to need something warm. Flannel will be better. Can you believe how cold it is today? At least we'll have a white Christmas."

Kate trailed after her. "I'm sure whatever you have will be fine. We lost everything in the fire."

"I know, honey." Abigail put an arm around her and squeezed her shoulder. "It must be hard."

She ducked her head. "I lost my mother's teapot."

"The pretty one with roses?"

"Aye. I brought it all the way from Ireland with me and didna even chip it. It was all I had left of her except for my ring."

"That's the most important thing, I imagine." Abigail looked at her in sympathy.

Kate stared at her wedding ring and twisted it. "I should be grateful."

"It could have been so much worse." Abigail hugged her again.

"Aye."

"Thank the good Lord your husband was there to pull you out." Still holding the denims in one hand, Abigail held her out at arm's length with the other and lifted her chin. "Let's not dwell on what might have been. You're both safe, and that's all that's important." Abigail dropped her hand and hunted through the shirts. "Looks like you need a few things too," she said over her shoulder. "Did any of the dresses Bernadette bring over fit?"

Kate unbuttoned the oversized coat and looked down at the blue calico that hung on her. "Not really."

Abigail laid the denim trousers on the table and pulled on the waistline of Kate's dress, tsking. "You're such a little bit of a thing." Like a fluttering bird who can't stand still, Abigail turned back to the shirts. "Here's a couple that may do for Buck. I'll lay these over on the counter while you look through the few dresses I have. It's a good thing we received our Christmas stock. Course, you may have to take something in or put a hem in it, but I know you're clever with a needle and thread."

Bill Stricklin's wife smiled and bustled over to the counter with her arms full.

As Kate rifled through the wool dresses on hangers, feeling the quality of the cloth, she heard the bell ding in the background but didn't turn around. She hoped it was no one she knew. The dress she wore was faded as a rag. So intent was she on testing the sizes, she didn't hear the footsteps behind her.

"Good morning, Miss Kate," a familiar voice said.

A chill raced down her spine, and she turned in surprise, a Kelly green wool dress in her hand. Rafe Hamilton stood there, a leer on his face.

He took the hanger out of her hand and held the dress up against her. "That would be a real pretty color on you."

She snatched the hanger out of his hand and held the dress close to her waist. "What do you want?"

He pushed up his hat with his finger, exposing his blond hair. Evidently, he was also growing a beard for the winter.

"Why, nothin', Miss Kate. Just being neighborly." He glanced around the store in mock surprise. "I don't see that husband of yours."

"You know perfectly well where he is since you shot him in the back."

Rafe frowned, then he gave her an evil grin. "Now that's a harsh charge, Miss Kate. The last I saw of your husband he was over at Ruby's. Kinda drunk too. Shocked to see a married man over there, acting like that. He even went upstairs with one of the girls."

Kate felt the red flush of anger shoot up her neck into her face. "You're lying!"

"That's enough, Rafe Hamilton." Abigail quickstepped from behind the counter to the corner of the store. "Leave that poor girl alone."

Rafe ignored the woman like an annoying fly buzzing around his head. He widened his eyes. "Oh...I see now. You didn't know he frequented places like that. I was having a drink and playing a few hands of cards when I saw him kiss that little gal at the bar, then they went up to her room. It's a shame you married him instead of me. I'd never step out on you."

Kate slapped at the hand that reached out to touch her face. "You're despicable. I don't believe you."

"You need to leave, Mr. Hamilton. You're not welcome here." Abigail took his arm to pull him away from Kate.

Rafe wouldn't budge. He only chuckled, a smug look on his face. "I wouldn't lie to you, Miss Kate. Ask him about Pansy the next time you see him."

"Pansy?" The faceless woman had a name.

"If I were you, I'd send that husband of yours packing."

Kate pushed Rafe out of the way, so angry and hurt she could barely breathe. "Abigail, if you'll put those things on Buck's account, I'll be back to get them later."

"Of course, honey." Abigail planted her hands on her hips. "See what you've done, Rafe. You should be ashamed of yourself."

Kate pushed through the door into the bitterly cold day, swallowing the lump in her throat. She'd known Buck had gone into town. He had as much as admitted he was going to Ruby's that night, but she'd never thought— she'd hoped—

She choked back the sob that threatened to break from her throat, but she wouldn't cry. What would he say when she asked him about *Pansy*. Was Rafe Hamilton telling the truth? Surely, he had to know she'd confront Buck. This time, she didn't think the scoundrel was lying. What kind of man had she married?

"If I don't get out of this bed soon, Bill, I'll go nutty as a squirrel." Buck slid his right arm under his head.

"Don't get yourself all riled up. Take it easy and do what Doc says." Bill resettled his considerable girth in the squeaky captain's chair and steepled his fingers. "Your men can take care of the place without your help for a few weeks."

"I don't have to like it." He knew he sounded like a petulant child.

Bill slapped his knee and laughed. "It's hard to keep a good man down. Kate been taking good care of you?"

"Can't complain." Buck grinned. "She's over at your mercantile buying me clothes right now. None of the stuff the pastor's wife brought fit me."

"Oh, that reminds me." Bill reached into his vest pocket and pulled out a small box wrapped in brown paper and string. He leaned over and set it on the blanket. "The Christmas present you ordered."

"As soon as I'm on my feet, I'll make a trip to the bank and pay off my account at the store."

"No hurry, son." Bill tapped him on the leg. "I know you're good for it." His face turned serious. "Any leads on who done this to you?"

Frustrated, Buck balled his fist. "No. Sheriff Granger and his deputy looked around, but they didn't find anything. I know who did it. I just can't prove it."

"Rafe Hamilton." Bill rested his arms on his thighs and looked at him. "I wouldn't go stirring up a hornet's nest until you can prove it. The Hamiltons have got a lot of clout in Deer Lodge."

"Who else woulda ambushed me from behind?"

"I'm not saying you're wrong. I'm only saying you need to have solid proof. If you didn't see who did it, and the sheriff can't point a finger at Hamilton, it'll only make things worse if you accuse him. Did he have an alibi for that night?"

Buck squirmed and avoided Bill's gaze. "Sort of."

"What's that supposed to mean?"

"He was still at Ruby's when I left. He drew down on me after I bloodied his nose."

"Ruby's! What in tarnation were you doing in a place like that?"

Ashamed, Buck cast about for an excuse, but he knew he didn't have a good one. He cleared his throat and told the truth. "Kate and I had a big fight that night. I rode into town and got drunk."

"I've never known you to be a drinker, Buck McKean. I don't care if she called you ugly, you shouldn't have walked through the doors of Ruby's. You know what kind of place that is."

Buck nodded his head in agreement and scratched at the whiskers he'd grown since lying in bed, finally meeting Bill's snapping blue eyes.

"I know. Don't you think I feel guilty about it? If I hadn't left our place that night, this never would've happened."

Bill shook his head. "I thought you'd left that life behind a long time ago."

"I haven't been in one of those places in years. Not after Joe's partner had his throat slit for a bag of gold after leaving a saloon."

"You mean a house of ill repute." Bill spat the words.

"Same thing." Buck picked at the blanket with his fingers, scratching at a piece of dried stew he'd spilled. "I'm not making excuses. It was a dumb thing to do." He hesitated and decided to tell Bill everything. "I slammed out of the cabin that night because she asked me for an annulment. We've made up since, but it made me mad as fire that night."

"You mean a divorce? What did you do for Pete's sake?"

"Nothin'."

"Well, you must have done something pretty terrible to that little gal. I thought I was placing her into the hands of an honorable man." Bill sat up straight and glared at him. "Does she know you went to Ruby's?"

"She knows I got drunk, but I didn't tell her where I was." Buck sighed. Now that he'd started down this road, he might as well finish and get some advice. "She doesn't want to be a wife. That's why she asked me for an annulment."

Bill snorted. "Every woman wants to be a wife."

"Not Kate." Buck swallowed the lump in his throat and stared at the stain on the blanket. "She talks about her stepfather like he was the devil incarnate. He beat her and her mother nearly every night, I guess. It's hard for her to trust a man."

His head lifted when he heard the door from the waiting room open and a woman's footsteps. Bill looked over his shoulder. "Well, hello, Miss Kate. You're back early."

Kate glared at Buck with red-rimmed eyes before acknowledging Bill. "Mr. Stricklin. If you'll excuse me I need to see Martha about an urgent matter."

She whirled in that ridiculous oversized coat and clumped up the stairs.

"Looks like you've got some serious fence mending to do," Bill said.

Quizzical, he looked at Bill. "She was fine this morning."

What had happened and where were his clothes? He couldn't even go after her to find out what was wrong.

"Well, she looks pretty upset now. I'll leave you two to work this out." He patted Buck's leg and stood, pointing his finger at him. "You do what Doc tells you. I'll drop by tomorrow for a few minutes."

Buck picked up the small box Stricklin had set on the bed and gripped it in his hand. "Thanks, Bill."

Buck's stomach knotted in worry. What was Kate so upset about?

Bill buttoned his coat. "I'll be praying for you two. Whatever's wrong, don't let this fester too long."

After Bill left, Buck lay in bed, staring at the ceiling, willing Kate to come down and talk to him. Every minute seemed like an hour. Doc had gone out on a call earlier. A sick old man. He hadn't even heard any footsteps upstairs after Kate rushed by him.

Finally, he reached over and picked up the Bible on the table next to him and sat it on his lap, flipping it open. It was too hard to hold one-handed, so he pulled up his legs and propped the book against them.

The first words he laid his eyes on sent chills running down his spine and put the fear of God into his heart. *But I say unto you, That whosoever looketh on a woman to lust after her hath committed adultery with her already in his heart.*

His face flamed. He *had* committed adultery. He knew he had sinned greatly, but he thought God had forgiven him. Reading the words in Scripture though weighed heavily on him. If the Lord had truly forgiven him, then why did he feel so sick in his gut? Why did he feel so guilty? Why did he feel so ashamed? Maybe God hadn't forgiven him. Was this too bad of a sin?

Another Scripture he had read last night rose in His mind, and he felt God's grace wash over him, relieving his heart. *If we confess our sins, he is faithful and just to forgive us our sins, and to cleanse us from all unrighteousness.*

His brow creased with worry. He had confessed to the Lord, but he hadn't told Kate yet. He was waiting for the right time. Squirming on the bed, he knew he delayed telling her because he didn't want to lose her. He'd tell her he had gone to Ruby's, but did she need to know everything—even about kissing Pansy and going up to her room?

Then he thought about how she'd looked as she'd stomped past them, and a knife stabbed him in the heart. He realized she looked like a woman betrayed. His heart sank.

Buck spent the rest of the morning in prayer, asking for a second chance.

Kate woke, tears still wet on her cheeks, her hand curled to her chest. Rafe's words flooded back.

When she had hurried upstairs, she had told Martha she had a headache and threw in her monthly pain for good measure. Her friend had been so concerned, she had tiptoed to a chair and picked up her knitting so she wouldn't make any noise to disturb her.

Kate felt guilty she had lied to the dear woman, but how could she tell Martha what Buck had done? She couldn't bear the humiliation.

She knew she bore part of the blame. Buck had turned to another woman because she had refused to be his wife. But did that give him license to commit adultery? Everyone in town would know what kind of man she had married before the end of the day. That he had deserved what he got. Undoubtedly, Rafe Hamilton had spread his unsavory story to every man in Deer Lodge. And they would be telling their wives.

Raising up on one arm, she slung her stocking feet onto the floor and pushed back the curls that had escaped her bun. She had to face Buck sometime and putting off the inevitable wouldn't make things any easier. Why should she feel embarrassed? She was the aggrieved wife.

Tightening her jaw, she smoothed the bodice of her wrinkled, oversized, blue calico dress and stood. She would march downstairs right now and confront him. Let him deny it. She glanced at herself in the looking glass and frowned at the shrew looking back.

Silently, she padded to the bedroom door and pulled it open, stepping into the parlor. Martha glanced at her with worried eyes and a wrinkled brow.

"Feeling better, dear? Would you like a cup of hot tea?"

"Nay. Thank you though."

"Well, dinner will be ready soon. I put a roast on, and I suspect Buck will be pleased. He seems to like his beef. You can take a plate down for him after it's ready. Oh, and his clothes." She pointed to the brown-paper wrapped package on the side table. "Abigail came by earlier. Said you'd run out of the store without them."

Kate stiffened her spine, but she couldn't even dredge up the hint of a smile. She heard the shuffle of Doc's footsteps on the stairs and turned his way.

"Buck's asking for you, Kate," he said as he rounded the corner. "He's as restless as a dog with a tick."

"I was about to go see him." She bit back what she really wanted to say. Her feelings were too raw.

Doc looked surprised at her harsh tone and glanced over at Martha, who shrugged.

Not wanting to explain, Kate abruptly left the kitchen and padded down the stairs, taking a deep breath to slow her racing heart. She didn't want him to see her cry. She had cried enough tears to last a lifetime. No, it was time to be strong, and she let anger fuel her steps.

When she approached the end of Buck's bed, he looked up in expectation and then his face clouded. She stood as tall and proud as possible, her hands clasping the package in front of her.

"What's wrong, darlin'?"

"Don't you darlin' me. Save it for Pansy."

His face flamed red, and he dropped his chin. Rafe had not lied this time. It was true. She could tell by the guilt written all over Buck's face.

"It's not what you think, Ka—"

"Did you or did you not kiss her at the bar?" she bit out.

"Yes, but—"

"And did you visit her room?"

"Kate, I didn't—"

"You didna visit her room then?"

"No, I mean yes, but I didn't—"

"Did you pay her for her...services?"

"Yes, but I didn't touch her."

She had gripped her hands together so hard, her nails had dug into her palms. She threw the package on the bed, hitting his leg. Clamping her jaw tight, she continued to glare at him.

"You've already admitted to kissing her. Do you expect me to believe you went to her room and didn't touch her?"

"Yes." He looked hopeful. "I mean I touched her, but I didn't...you know."

"You must think I'm dim-witted to believe that."

His guilty brown eyes wavered first, and he looked down in shame. "I'm sorry, Kate. I never should have—"

"No, you shouldna," she ground out. "This sham of a marriage is over. Do you understand? I'll see a lawyer in the morning to draw up annulment papers and you *will* sign them." Stiffening her spine, she ignored his pleading eyes.

"Kate, please..."

Fiercely, she shook her head. "Dinna Kate me. What you did was reprehensible. You can live in the bunkhouse for a while, and then I want you gone. You can shake the dust of this place off your feet and start over somewhere else. But I'll never live this down. I'm branded for life."

He didn't argue, only continued to look at her with sadness in his eyes. He sighed deeply. "All right, Katie girl. If that's what you want, I won't fight you. I'm sorry—"

"It's too late for apologies, Mr. McKean. I willna be speaking to you ever again. I'll have the lawyer bring the papers for you to sign. I'll expect you to pay his fee."

Turning on her heel, she escaped upstairs, her heart and her dreams shattered. The thought of him with a soiled dove made her sick to her stomach. What love she had for him had been snuffed out by his betrayal.

She ignored that niggling voice that continued to say she bore part of the responsibility for the problems in their marriage.

Chapter Nineteen

Buck lifted himself up on one elbow and pulled the brown paper package toward him, grimacing at the pain it caused his shoulder. He hoped she'd bought him clothes like she'd planned. He wouldn't stay where he wasn't wanted. As soon as he was healed, he'd either hit the trail for Texas or spend the winter in Virginia City. He'd need to liquidate his bank account there anyway. He wasn't sure whether to push on to Oregon or head back to Texas and take on his birthright. Pa wasn't getting any younger.

If he stayed here, he'd only be an embarrassment to Kate. For her sake, he would avoid church and any other social gathering she might attend. But he'd never stop loving her, not as long as he lived, and he didn't think he'd ever marry again. He'd meant his marriage vows when he'd said them.

But he supposed an annulment would be easier to conclude than a full-blown divorce. Course, everyone would know they had never lived together as man and wife. He could leave the area, but she would take the brunt of his sin. His heart ached so much, he had a physical pain in his chest and rubbed it with his palm.

One night of losing his temper had destroyed his dreams of a future with Kate. He only had himself to blame. He'd driven the nails into his own coffin. He should have stayed that night and talked to her, tried to persuade her to talk to him.

Frustrated, he finally worked the knot out of the string with his teeth and right hand and ripped open the brown paper wrapping. Kate had bought him one dark brown and one dark blue cotton flannel shirt and two pairs of britches. His heart sank. They all had buttons, and she hadn't bought him a new pair of long johns...or socks. It would be a cold ride home.

He swung his legs over the edge of the bed and threaded his bare feet into the legs of the pants, standing to pull the stiff dungarees over his hips. Nothing worse than new denims. Sweat beaded on his brow as he battled the pain. Exhausted, he finally sank down heavily on the bed.

Now the shirt. He growled deep in his chest. He'd need to unbutton the thing before he could even put it on. It took nearly all his energy to work the buttons through the tight buttonholes, but finally, he slid his bad arm into the left sleeve and reached around back to find the hole for the right. Then he had to stop and catch his breath.

He needed help, but he wasn't about to ask for it. Doc would throw a fit if he knew he'd be walking out the door as soon as he was dressed.

Buck almost had his shirt buttoned when he heard the heavy footsteps on the stairs. Doc. Rolling his eyes, he knew he'd have a fight on his hands now.

Doc walked to his curtained space and threw back the screen he had drawn shut.

"What in tarnation are you doing?"

Buck leveraged himself out of bed and held his pants up with one hand, gritting his jaw against the pain. He'd need help to button the fly, or take another half hour to do it on his own. This would have been a good time for Joe to visit.

"I'm leavin'."

"You get back in that bed, son. You're in no shape to go anywhere. That wife of yours is upstairs crying her eyes out and won't tell us what's wrong. What did you say to her?"

"Either you button my pants, Doc, or I'll walk out of here holding them up. But I'm not staying." Determination suffused his voice. He meant it.

"If you can't button your own pants, how are you going to mount a horse?"

"I figure Roberts over at the livery will give me a hand. He's bound to have a horse I can rent."

Doc shook his head at him as if he'd lost his mind, so he struggled to button his pants himself by using his bad arm to hold open the fly. He cut lose with a swear word and felt his conscience prick.

"There's no need to run out of here half-cocked." Doc glared at him. "Now tell me what's going on?"

Buck sat down hard on the edge of the bed and rubbed his left shoulder. "Ask Kate."

"I told you, Kate's not talkin'. Spit it out."

"She wants an annulment!"

Doc gave a sardonic laugh. "That's going to be a little hard since you've been living together all this time."

Buck dropped his chin and mumbled. "Not if we haven't slept together." It was embarrassing to admit.

"You mean—"

"That's exactly what I mean," he bit out, raising his voice. He swallowed the knot in his throat.

Doc sat down hard in the visitor's chair and stared at him in astonishment. "Nobody's going to believe it."

"They will if you certify it's true."

"And you think Kate is gonna let me examine her? She won't even tell us you two haven't consummated your marriage."

"If we both swear in an affidavit it's true, the judge will grant us an annulment. I've been thinking a lot about this."

"Well, can you at least tell me why you two haven't—?"

"She's afraid I'll beat her or somethin'," Buck said.

"That's plain crazy. Where'd she get a fool idea like that?" Doc scowled. "Did you hit her?"

Buck looked at Doc. "Of course not. But somebody hurt her real bad in the past."

"That still doesn't explain why you're so fired up to hightail it out of here. It seemed like you two were getting along pretty well."

Blood rushed to Buck's face, and he hesitated. No doubt Rafe Hamilton had spread it all over town and Doc would hear about it anyway.

"The night of the fire, Kate asked me for an annulment. I got so mad I rode to Ruby's place, and I almost slept with one of the girls."

"Almost."

"I got drunk. She kissed me, and I went up to her room, but I couldn't go through with it. I couldn't do that to Kate."

"I thought you had more sense, Buck McKean. No wonder she's so upset. She thinks you did the deed. Where'd she get that notion?"

"Probably Rafe Hamilton. He was there that night and saw me go upstairs." Buck fisted his right hand.

"Well, you're in a fine pickle and that's for sure. Did you try talking to her?"

"Yes, but she won't believe me. She never wants to see me again."

Doc shook his head. "That gal's so in love with you she sat by your bedside day and night for almost a week. Somehow, you need to work this out."

"Not today." Buck stood up again. "Please button my pants, Doc."

Sighing heavily, the doctor finally rose to help Buck and then tucked in his new shirt.

"Now where's my boots and coat?"

"In the cupboard. There's a box of clothes the church ladies brought over for you, and I imagine there's a pair of socks you can wear." He looked at Buck with piercing eyes. "I still don't recommend you leaving. You could open up that wound and start bleeding again. I'll send you home with several bandages. Make sure you have Joe check it every day. If you see any sign of infection, you hightail yourself back here. I'll be out to check on you sometime tomorrow—make sure you made it home all right."

Doc looked defeated, but Buck couldn't help that. He was antsy to strike out of here. Doc brought him socks, his bloody boots, hat, coat, and his gun belt. He needed the doc's help with it all.

"Let Kate know I'm gone." Buck's throat ached with unshed tears. "She doesn't need to worry about ever seeing me again. I appreciate you and Martha taking care of her. Once I'm able, I'll make a trip to the bank and set up her own account, but in the meantime, I want her to buy new clothes and material from Bill."

"As proud as she is, we'll have to force her to take your money."

"She has no choice." Buck straightened his hat, biting back the pain in his shoulder. "I'll pay the boys through the winter, so she doesn't have to worry about that either. If you and Martha need extra supplies to feed and take care of her, you put it on my account."

Doc squeezed his good shoulder. "I'm sorry, Buck."

He nodded, not trusting his voice. When he reached the waiting room door, he threw a good-bye over his shoulder. "See ya later, Doc."

He hoped he could make it as far as the livery. His knees felt like a wet dishrag.

"Mrs. McKean, to complete your paperwork for an annulment, I need to know the precise reason for granting the voidance of your marriage." Mr. Sauter pulled a sheet of paper toward him ready to take notes and dipped his pen into the inkwell, dabbing off the excess.

Kate wriggled in the leather chair in front of his massive desk and cleared her throat.

"As I indicated earlier, I wish to be granted an annulment because my marriage to Mr. McKean has never been..." She cleared her throat again. "Concluded."

"Yes, I understand that, Mrs. McKean," he said looking over his glasses, "but the court will want to know *why* the marriage was never consummated. Was Mr. McKean incapable of fulfilling his marriage obligations because of impotence?"

Kate felt her face flame. "That is a highly inappropriate question!"

"Not in a court of law, Mrs. McKean. Judge Pratt will want to know why he should grant an annulment. Grounds would include an incestuous relationship—"

"Nay!"

Mr. Sauter held up his fingers, ticking off the reasons. "Lack of parental consent. Are both you and Mr. McKean of legal age, meaning you are over the age of fifteen and he is over the age of eighteen?"

"Aye."

"Then we cannot file under that portion of the law. Were you defrauded in some way? Did Mr. McKean commit bigamy?"

"Nay, but I was defrauded. I thought my husband was an upstanding and honorable man."

Mr. Sauter smiled as if at a child, and Kate felt her temper rising. She hadn't thought she would undergo an inquisition when she stepped into the lawyer's office.

"Those are not grounds for an annulment unless he is a known felon and wanted for arrest and you did not know that fact when you exchanged your vows. Is that the case?"

Kate's jaw tightened, her teeth clamped together. "Nay."

"Again, I must ask you, is Mr. McKean either mentally or physically incapacitated, which would include feeblemindedness or impotence?"

"Nay, but I'm feebleminded for marryin' him in the first place!" Kate gripped the plain, black reticule in her lap.

Mr. Sauter leaned back in his chair and looked at her sternly. "You are the plaintiff, Mrs. McKean. We are looking for a way to annul your marriage under the eyes of the law. For instance, if Mr. McKean is impotent, and you as his wife attempted to help him consummate your marriage, but he was still incapable of doing so, we will use those grounds as the basis for your petition."

"Is this really necessary?" Kate's face felt as though it would burst into flames at any moment. She twisted the strings of her reticule around her hand until it almost cut off her circulation.

Mr. Sauter gave her that supercilious smile again. She wanted to slap it right off his face.

"Oh, indeed, it is. The judge will ask you the same questions, and as you will be under oath, you will have to answer truthfully. Did you attempt to help Mr. McKean consummate the marriage?"

"Nay, I—"

"We must have a valid reason. An annulment hearing is an intrusive and intimate proceeding. Judge Pratt will ask you these questions in open court."

Suddenly, his words cut through the fog of embarrassment. "Open court? I thought we could file papers and the judge would grant me an annulment. You mean other people might be there?"

"Oh yes. I imagine a reporter from the *Weekly Independent* will be in court as well. In fact, it might be well attended after your filing becomes public record. Your annulment hearing will be of interest to the community."

"Public record?" she croaked.

"Once I file your petition, it becomes public record and open to scrutiny by any interested party, including the newspaper."

"I didna know," she whispered, her hand going to her throat.

"Can you give me any other reason for your annulment that would be acceptable to the court?" Mr. Sauter placed his elbows on his desk and steepled his fingers, looking at her over his spectacles.

Kate summoned up her anger at Buck's betrayal. "He committed adultery."

"Now we're getting somewhere." He pulled the paper closer. He dipped his pen again, blotted the tip, and poised his hand to write. "You do not have grounds for an annulment, but you do have grounds for a divorce. It will take longer, usually a year, but you will need to detail for the court your knowledge of his perfidious act."

"Perfidious?"

"Deceitful."

"But I dinna want a divorce. I want an annulment. I want to rip up this sham of a marriage by the roots."

"You do not have cause, Mrs. McKean, as you could not answer any of my previous questions in the affirmative. However, Mr. McKean might have grounds to file for a petition of annulment if you failed to meet those requirements." Mr. Sauter cleaned the end of his pen on the blotter while the clock ticked loudly in the background.

Kate cast her eyes about the office in desperation, frantically searching her mind for a reason. It was simple.

"Yes, I refused to...sleep with him."

"And the reason would be?"

"The reason is mine, and you need not know of it."

"I see." Mr. Sauter frowned at her, a look of disapproval in his eyes. "Was Mr. McKean aware of your feelings when you married him?"

"Nay, but I have made it plain to him since."

"Then Mr. McKean does have grounds to annul your marriage on your mental incapacity. I assume it was mental and not physical?"

"Aye...nay...I'm not feebleminded!" Kate felt trapped, wound in the yarn of her own knitting. Why, why, *why*, had she ever agreed to marry Buck? Mr. Sauter spoke to her, but she was not paying attention.

"Mrs. McKean."

"Aye?"

"Did you hear me?"

"Nay," she stuttered.

"I said, you will need Mr. McKean to come by my office, and I'll consult with him on filing a petition of annulment." He straightened in his chair, laid down his pen, and jerked on the hem of his vest.

"But what about the adultery?" She felt as if her corset had been drawn too tight under her new navy-and-yellow plaid dress. She could hardly breathe.

"Yes, those are grounds for divorce. Let me ask you this question. Did he commit the adultery before or after your refusal to consummate the marriage?"

Kate closed her eyes. She knew what he would say once she told him. "After."

"In which case, the court will probably overlook his indiscretion and not even grant you a divorce unless you can prove he has an intemperate disposition and has repeatedly harmed you physically."

"Nay," she said, shaking her head. Tears burned at the back of her eyes, but she wasn't about to cry in front of this judgmental man.

Mr. Sauter stood up behind his desk and gave her a tight smile of dismissal. "If you would have Mr. McKean stop by my office, we can move forward with his petition for annulment."

She stood up as well and smoothed down the front of her skirt, not looking the man in the eye. "That might be some time."

"And why is that?" He glanced at the clock on the wall as though he had another appointment.

"He was shot and is still recovering."

"Oh my, I had heard something about someone being shot, but I didn't realize it was Mr. McKean. I'm afraid the court will look dimly on any petition you file at this time—a wife leaving her husband after he has been wounded and at death's door."

He tsked. The man actually tsked at her!

"Despite your claims to the contrary, Mr. McKean is the aggrieved party here in the eyes of the law."

"Then I've wasted your time." She lifted her chin. "G'day to you, sir."

"Good day, Mrs. McKean."

Kate grabbed her coat off the rack and fled out the door, not even pulling it on until she stood on the boardwalk. With trembling fingers, she buttoned it in the chill wind that blew beneath the wide, blue Montana sky.

That had been the most humiliating conversation she had ever had with another human being. Rubbing her throbbing temples, her heels clicking loudly on the boardwalk, she fled along the block toward Doc's place, her breath uneven.

She had sworn never to speak to Buck again. How could she now ask him to file a petition against her?

Chapter Twenty

"HURRY UP." A WEEK LATER ON Christmas Day, Buck stood near the privy, holding up his pants with his right hand. "I'm freezin'." His breath came out in a cloud.

Joe looked up at him and glared. "This ain't no picnic for me neither! I don't know why you didn't stay in town and let your wife take care of you."

The old man fumbled with the last of the buttons on his dungarees. He felt guilty, knowing Joe's fingers were stiff from the cold and his rheumatiz, but what else was a man to do? His shoulder still hurt too bad to wrestle with his pants, although he was getting faster buttoning his shirt one-handed.

Buck looked up at the cloudless blue sky above him, the sun shining so brightly on the snow it almost blinded him. He loved Montana, but he was hankering for warmer weather.

"Let's go warm our backsides by the stove," he said as Joe stood up. "I could stand another cup of that sludge you call coffee."

"I wouldn't be complainin' about my coffee if I were you. Next time I might leave you to fend for yerself."

Buck clapped him on the shoulder before Joe took off limping fast for the bunkhouse. He stared at the black char of the burned-out cabin covered with snow, a reminder of the ash heap of his own life.

Hearing the jingle of a harness, he turned and squinted into the glare off the snow and saw an approaching buggy. Doc, but somebody sat on the seat next to him. Surely, Martha wouldn't come out in this weather on Christmas morning.

As the buggy drew closer, he recognized Kate's copper-colored hair, shining red and gold in the sunshine, at the edge of a dark blue head scarf. His heart leapt at the sight of her, exactly as it had the first day he'd seen her standing on the porch in her britches, sighting down the barrel of that shotgun.

A smidgeon of hope flared to life. She had said she'd have her lawyer bring out the papers to sign. Had she changed her mind? He pasted a smile on his face as Doc pulled back on the reins to stop.

"Merry Christmas, Doc. Kate. I didn't expect to see you today."

"If I hadn't brought her out, your wife planned on renting a buggy at the livery and making the trip on her own. Couldn't let her make that outing alone. Besides, I need to look at your shoulder."

Ignoring Doc, Buck looked into Kate's green eyes glimmering in the bright sunlight, hoping for some sign she had changed her mind. But the eyes that stared back at him were hard as emeralds.

"We best get your horse out of the cold, Doc."

"I'll meet you at the barn." Doc laid a light rein on the horse's back to drive his rig toward the red-painted building, stark against the brilliant snow blowing across the valley.

Buck turned his back on the ruins of the cabin and followed, every step feeling as though he were walking to the gallows.

Kate hadn't said a word—not even a hello. She wanted something, but he knew without a doubt it wasn't him. She hadn't changed her mind. Hope flew away on tattered wings.

By the time he joined them at the barn, Doc had already helped Kate down and opened the doors. He stepped up into the buggy.

"You two need to stop staring at each other and talk," Doc grumped. He drove the rig out of the weather and jumped down. "As soon as you're through here, I'll meet you in the bunkhouse where it's warm."

Doc closed the barn doors on them, shutting out the light. Buck walked over and fumbled with the lantern to light it.

"Here, let me do that." Her words were sharp as she took the match out of his hand. He could smell the faint scent of lavender and damp wool as he stood close to her. She had bundled herself in a new navy wool coat. Evidently, Doc had persuaded her to put it on his account. After the first of the year, he needed to make a trip to the bank and pay Bill.

"Did you bring the papers to sign?" Buck wanted to reach out and touch her, but he figured that'd earn him a slap in the face.

Kate took a step back, shaking her head. "Nay."

His heart leapt into his throat. Had she changed her mind after all?

"I've missed you." He let his eyes reflect his love for her, but the words he wanted to say stuck in his throat.

She took another step back and cleared her throat, not meeting his eyes. "I met with my lawyer."

"And?"

"And he said you would need to file the petition for annulment."

Buck furrowed his brow. "Why?"

She hugged herself, cupping her elbows in her gloved hands. An errant curl had escaped from the bun at the back of her head and fell across her cheek, but he didn't dare reach out and tuck it behind her ear.

Kate stared at the hay-strewn floor for a moment before raising her eyes to him. A blush colored her cheeks. Despite telling himself it was over, his heart thumped in his chest. She looked even prettier than when they first married.

"It's a little hard to explain."

"I've got all day," he drawled.

She turned her back on him and paced in front of Applejack's stall. Reaching out to stroke his horse's nose, she spoke but he could barely hear her.

"I didn't catch that." He stepped closer.

"I *said*, he needs to meet with you because it seems you are the aggrieved party." She turned and glared at him.

He frowned. "And why is that? I thought this was a simple annulment."

"It seems there's nothing simple about it," she huffed. "I could only file for annulment if I could attest that one, it was an incestuous relationship—"

Her color heightened.

"Two, that we were underage when we entered the marriage contract."

"Leaves that one out." He leaned against the barn post, embarrassment burning up his neck like fire.

"Three, if you had defrauded me in some way, such as being a bigamist, or four..." Her words trailed off, and she looked at the floor again like she hoped it would swallow her whole.

"Four..." He tried to help her along.

"Four, if you were mentally or physically incapacitated and couldna... you know..."

"What do you mean 'physically incapacitated'?"

Fisting her gloved hands, she planted them on her hips. "You canna be that dense."

Light dawned, and he dropped down on a hay bale, shocked. "Well, I'll be. That is a conundrum."

"More like a tangled ball of yarn."

"I don't suppose you could lie." He raised an eyebrow.

"What do ya think? I would be committing perjury."

"I suppose you would." A tiny flicker of hope ignited in his heart that maybe they would remain husband and wife. "What—"

"You need to file a petition, saying I..." She swallowed hard. "Defrauded you. That I never told you before we were married that I didna want a husband."

"You want me to tell the town that—"

"I'm a failure as a wife. Aye." She paced in front of him as her voice rose. "Then we must appear in front of a judge in open court, and he'll put us on the stand and he'll ask us questions—humiliating, embarrassing, *stupid* questions—in front of the whole town!"

"The whole town? So why can't you file for divorce? You can charge me with adultery. Wouldn't that be simpler?"

"Divorce takes at least a year. An annulment is quicker and simpler."

He pulled off his hat and raked his fingers through his hair, swallowing hard. "There's nothing simple about any of this."

Tears swam in her eyes as her shoulders slumped. "Nay. I thought it would be easy to—"

"Easy to end a marriage that never got started?"

She caught a tear with the back of her glove before it fell. "It doesna matter. You are the injured party and need to file the petition."

"And that's what you really want?" He stepped closer and lifted her chin with one finger, their breath mingling in the cold barn. "Why can't you find it in your heart to forgive me, Katie? I love you, and you said you loved me. Please, darlin', I don't want to lose you."

She stepped away from him. "You lost me when you decided to walk into Ruby's. I can't trust you, Buck. I'll never trust you."

His shoulders slumped, his hope now a cold lump of coal in his belly. "You don't know how much I regret what I did that night. I wish I'd stayed and talked to you. I wish I'd never walked through the doors of that saloon. I wish I'd never gotten drunk and lusted after Pansy. or committed adultery, even if I didn't take it all the way. You have every right to hate me." He paused. "Is there anything I can say or do to make this right? Do...do you think you can ever forgive me?"

"No. You betrayed me, Buck. Too many people in my life have betrayed me. I... I can't forgive you." Then she turned and walked out of his life.

Kate sat on the wooden pew next to Martha, trying to concentrate on Pastor Russell's New Year's sermon. It was hard. It was a new year—a time for new beginnings. A time to forget the past and look forward to the future. A time to renew her faith.

Dropping her head in despair, she stared at her folded hands. Faith? Her faith wasna even as big as a mustard seed. Her life was such a mess. She'd lost everyone she had ever loved, including Buck. Aye, she still loved him, but love wasn't enough to save what they had lost. A marriage without trust would be a sham in the eyes of God—*was* a sham. Not that she laid all the blame on Buck. If she hadn't told him she wanted to end their marriage, he never would have stormed out that dreadful night. Now she didn't know how to forgive him...or herself.

Surreptitiously, she glanced to the right side of the church where Rafe Hamilton sat, his hat resting on his knee, acting all holy. She had been shocked when he sat down in a pew. With his new haircut and fresh shave, he reminded her of the man who had first come calling, but she wouldn't let his appearance fool her this time. A frisson of fear raced up her spine, and she shivered remembering how he had tried to force himself on her.

If Buck didn't leave Deer Lodge soon, she feared for his life. There was no doubt in her mind that Rafe had shot Buck in the back. Something told her he would never give her up.

Finally, the congregation stood to sing the closing hymn, and after Pastor Russell's benediction, the service concluded. Martha took her elbow.

"You seem distracted this morning, dear." The older woman's voice was but a whisper in her ear. "Thinking about Buck?"

Kate's mouth quivered, attempting to smile. "Nay, I'm fine."

"I don't know how you could be." Sadness and empathy laced Martha's voice.

Before she could say another word, Rafe smiled at her and stepped into the aisle, twirling the brim of his hat in his hand. "Miss Kate."

"I'm surprised to see you in church this morning, Mr. Hamilton." Martha moved in front of Kate.

"I'll be here every Sunday from now on, ma'am. It's time I got right with the Lord and settled down." He pierced Kate with a smoldering look, and she knew his mind wasn't on God or making amends for his sins.

"I'm glad to hear it," Martha said. "I hope you'll feel welcome here."

"Thank you, I already do." Grinning at Kate, he covered his blond hair with his black Stetson, a new one from the looks of it. Color tinged her cheeks. A man shouldn't look at a married woman that way...or any woman for that matter.

Of course, he probably knew she had talked to an attorney about dissolving her marriage to Buck. Since Mr. Sauter was supposedly the best lawyer in town, she assumed he knew the Hamiltons well, and she could imagine him discussing her over a snifter of brandy. Word seemed to travel fast in Deer Lodge.

There was only one way to rid herself of his attention. Sell him Patrick's land sooner than later. She didn't need to wait for spring. The sooner Buck left town, the sooner he would be out of danger. If she lived in town, she could avoid Rafe. She hoped. At least she wouldn't be living by herself in the middle of nowhere. Did she have the legal right to sell the land? Probably not now that she was married to Buck. But the land was not Buck's. It was Patrick's. She would not ask Buck for permission to sell what was not his. Surely, an annulment would restore her inheritance.

"I didn't see your husband this morning." Rafe looked around in mock concern. "Is he still feeling poorly?"

How could a man with such an evil heart act so innocent?

"Aye, he is. Thank you for asking, Mr. Hamilton."

"Mr. Hamilton?" he said, chuckling. "That's my father."

Doc finally exited the pew and stood next to his wife. "Rafe."

"Good to see you, Doc. Would you all do me the honor of joining me at the McBurney for Sunday dinner?"

Aye! It would be the perfect time to bring up the sale of her land.

"Maybe some other time." Doc gave him a tight smile as his wife slid her hand into the crook of his arm. "I believe Martha has a roast in the oven. Don't you, dear?"

"Yes, thank you for the invitation, but I'm afraid today is not an opportune time. Perhaps next Sunday."

Martha pulled Kate up the aisle away from Rafe. Kate looked over her shoulder and saw him staring after her. He hadn't moved.

"Martha, I need to talk to Rafe," she whispered.

Martha looked shocked. "What on earth do you need to talk to that vile man for?"

She hoped Martha and Doc would understand. "If he'll still buy me out, I want to sell him the property. I was foolish to think I could make a go of it by myself."

Once they exited the church, Kate took a deep breath of the fresh air, smelling of pine trees. A Chinook wind had blown in this morning from across the mountains, and the temperature had warmed by at least forty degrees. It had been below freezing last night, but now the snow was melting in the unexpected January thaw.

Doc leaned over Martha's head to pierce her with a look of disappointment. "Your husband might have something to say about selling that land."

Kate ignored his remark to smile at Bernadette and the pastor and to shake their hands. Rafe brushed by the crowd to catch up with her. He touched her elbow, and she shivered as she turned to him. The McBurney would be the safest place.

"Are you sure you won't have dinner with me, Miss Kate?" He ignored her friends.

"I hardly think it's appropriate for Kate to dine with you alone, Hamilton." Doc gritted his teeth. "She's a married woman."

"Not for long from what I hear." Rafe's gaze never left her face, and she felt as if she stared at the dead eyes of a serpent.

"That's irrelevant," Doc said.

Kate touched Doc's arm and looked up at her protector, hoping he would understand. "This would be an excellent time to discuss business with Mr. Hamilton. If you'd be kind enough to drive me to the McBurney, it's but a short walk back to your home. I willna be long."

Frowning, his brows knitted together, his lips tight, Doc finally nodded. "If that's what you want."

"Excellent, Miss Kate, I'll meet you there. It was a pleasure seeing you Doc, Martha."

Rafe tipped his hat and walked through the slushy snow in his shiny leather boots to untie his black stallion. As he mounted, the high-strung horse danced in the mud. Grinning in triumph at Kate, he turned his horse's head and loped toward town without a backward glance.

"You can't honestly be serious about having dinner alone with that man." Martha blocked Kate's way, her hands on her hips.

Kate reached out to touch Martha's shoulder. "If you came along, I wouldna be alone. It's better to discuss business with him in a public place than to meet him at his ranch."

Martha twisted the strings of her reticule as though she were wringing her hands and looked at her husband, a grimace on her face. Doc's forehead puckered. Obviously, neither of them were happy about the situation.

Doc sighed heavily. "All right. But I would think twice about selling that property to Hamilton. Buck is legally your husband and entitled to make decisions about that land."

She lifted her chin. "He willna fight me on this."

"I wouldn't be too sure. He'll have to sign those papers too." Doc helped his wife into the buggy before taking Kate's arm. "Let's go take that roast out of the oven. I'll not let you face Rafe alone."

Chapter Twenty-one

KATE, FLANKED BY DOC AND MARTHA, entered the opulent dining room of the McBurney House. Rafe sat at a table for two. When he spotted them, anger flashed across his face, but he quickly covered his feelings with a smile of greeting. Oh, the man was a good actor, she would give him that. He waved over the hostess dressed in a black dress and starched white apron.

"We need a table for four, please."

"Of course, Mr. Hamilton."

After they had all been seated at a larger table covered with a pristine white tablecloth, she clasped her hands in her lap and glanced between Doc and Martha. She was so glad they had agreed to accompany her on this mission.

"I'm pleased you could all join me for Sunday dinner." Rafe lifted a glass of water to his lips. "Now that I'm joining the church, I'd like to become better acquainted. I hope your roast won't be too dry, Miss Martha."

Kate glimpsed Martha's tight smile.

"Not at all, Mr. Hamilton."

Before the conversation could dwindle into niceties for the sake of propriety, Kate decided to come right to the point. "I agreed to have dinner with you for one reason—to discuss a business proposition."

Rafe's blond eyebrows rose in mock surprise. "Really?"

"Are you still interested in buying Patrick's land?"

He paused for a moment before answering, pushing his chest out and smiling in triumph.

"So, you're interested in selling now. I think that's a wise decision." He picked up his snowy white napkin and laid it across his lap. "Of course, without the cabin, the value has depreciated somewhat, but I'm sure we can come to an equitable agreement. It's rather an inconvenient time to buy it though."

Doc opened his mouth slightly, ready to jump in, but Martha laid a restraining hand on his arm.

"I thought you might wait until spring," he continued, "seeing as how Mr. McKean is living on the property."

"Circumstances have changed." Kate shot daggers with her eyes.

"As I've heard. In his condition, your husband is hardly capable of running a ranch."

Doc leapt into the conversation. "I expect her *husband* to make a complete recovery, despite his grievous wound. By roundup in the spring, he should be fully able to rebuild the cabin that was burned down by some nefarious person."

"Such a heinous crime." Rafe shook his head. "I can't imagine who would have done such a terrible thing. Renegades or an outlaw gang I suppose."

"How much are you willing to offer?" Kate tightened her jaw before she could spew out any accusations against him. She couldn't afford to charge him with wrongdoing now, or he might not buy the property just to spite her. "I still own a sizable herd, along with the outbuildings—a barn, bunkhouse, corrals. And its location on the river makes it more valuable than other homesteads."

Rafe shrugged. "No doubt, it would make a nice addition to my ranch. Your brother had a good eye when he staked his claim."

"Well?"

Rafe pretended to look thoughtful, but she could see by the gleam in his eye he wanted Patrick's land. He would buy her out, but he would make her squirm first. The man had no conscience.

He sat back in his chair and picked up his menu to read the selections, a heavy gold ring flashing on his right finger. "Yes, I'm interested." Rafe paused. "Have you decided what you want?"

She fumed. "I want to sell my property."

He chuckled. "No, Miss Kate, have you decided what you'd like to order. I'll need a few days to consider a fair offer for your ranch in its present state."

"We're agreed then?"

"Of course."

She wanted to smack him in the face with her menu. He had her over a barrel, and he knew it. No doubt he already knew what he would offer. He didn't need a few days to think it over or inspect the property, nor would he. Since his men were the ones who burned the cabin, he already knew the homestead's condition. No, he only wanted to control her—to make her wait on him and dance in the wind for a while. Well, if he wanted the land as badly as she knew he did, then she'd stipulate he couldn't take possession until spring so Buck and his men would have someplace to live for the winter.

The waitress walked up to their table, holding a slate in her hand, a smile of expectation on her face. Kate realized she might soon stand at tables like this waitress, taking their orders from sunrise to late in the evening. It was hard work, but respectable. Now that she was selling the ranch, she'd need a job to support herself. Hopefully, the McBurney would give her one. She would wash dishes if she had to.

"Are you ready to order, Mr. Hamilton?"

Rafe grinned with familiarity at the attractive server and touched her arm. "Hello, Molly. I believe I know what I want." He deferred to Kate and tilted his head. "And you, Miss Kate? Do you know what you want?"

His words seemed to hold a double meaning. A shiver of fear ran down her spine. In the end, Rafe always got what he wanted. And he wanted her and her land.

Restless at his forced inactivity, Buck walked out into the freezing cold and tapped the thermometer hanging on the outside wall of the bunkhouse—twenty below. Their January thaw had only lasted a couple of days, melting the snow on the ground, and then a blizzard moved through followed by this frigid air. It had stuck around for weeks. How could it be this cold when the sun blinded you it was so bright?

He burrowed his neck inside his scarf and pulled up the collar of his new, long, black wool coat. It was either continue to wear his jacket with bullet holes and blood stains or send Joe into town to buy him warmer clothes at the mercantile. The sleeves were a little too short, but it was the biggest one Stricklin had.

Looking down at Riley, wriggling next to him, he stroked the black-and-white dog's head and smiled. "I've still got you, don't I, boy?" The sheepdog leapt up on his hind legs, wagging his tail. Buck pushed him down, only feeling a slight twinge in his shoulder, and patted his side. "Let's go check on Applejack, all right?"

As he opened the barn door, Riley stayed right at his heels. The familiar scent of the barn was a balm to his soul. After his last visit from Kate at Christmastime, he had been forced to acknowledge the death of their marriage, even though he still hadn't ridden into town to talk to a lawyer about an annulment. But he couldn't put off the inevitable forever no matter how much he loved her. Did she realize how much her reputation would be damaged? If he cut and ran, she would be left at the mercy of Hamilton and the rest of the town.

Opening the stall, Buck stroked Applejack's velvety nose in the dim light and laid his forehead against the horse, drinking in his musky scent. Then he gave him a scoop of grain, threw another blanket over his back, and tied it on.

"What are you doing out in this cold?" Joe's voice snapped him out of his reverie. He hadn't heard the old man come in. "It's dinnertime. You'll freeze your patootie off out here."

"I needed some air. I couldn't stand Billy's bellyachin' anymore."

Buck patted Applejack's neck, and the horse snuffled at his pocket. He pulled out the piece of dried apple and let his horse nibble it out of his gloved hand. He liked Joe and the boys, but he was sick and tired of being cooped up with them in the bunkhouse all day and night.

Joe walked over and rested his foot on the bottom rail of Applejack's stall. "Ain't that the truth? That kid's about to drive me 'round the bend. I think come spring that boy will be headin' back to Texas. He's not tough enough to survive a Montana winter." He cleared his throat. "What about you? You headed back to Texas come spring?"

Buck looked over at his friend for a moment and then back at

Applejack. "No. I've dreamed of owning a ranch in this valley for years. I can't leave Kate by herself to face what's coming."

"Gossip's all over town, you know."

"I figured."

"Most everybody knows the details, or think they do."

"Spit it out. What're they saying?"

"They're split down the middle. Most of the women are taking Kate's side from what I hear, saying you got what you deserved, and the men think you're either a saint or a fool for not bedding your wife right after you got married. Can't understand a man not taking what's rightfully his."

Joe stroked his grizzled beard and chewed on the tip of his moustache, but he didn't add anything. His old friend had never told him he was a fool for marrying Kate, but he knew that's what he thought. Joe was like a second father to him.

Buck's pride stung. It would be tough to stay in Deer Lodge now, but surely people would find something else to gossip about after a while and forget about Kate and him. He could hope anyway.

One of the things he missed most, other than Kate, was attending church. He read his Bible every day, searching for answers on how to fix his marriage, but he hadn't found one yet. Pastor Russell had visited once. He had reminded Buck to love Kate like Christ loved the church and be patient.

Last night, he'd finally laid it all down at the Lord's feet. If God wanted him to leave Kate behind, he'd do it for her sake. But he couldn't get any peace about that. Nowhere in the Bible could he find that he was supposed to leave his wife when things got tough.

His hand stilled on Applejack's neck when he heard the thunder of horses' hooves. Buck looked over at Joe. "Where's your rifle?"

"Left it in the bunkhouse. Didn't think I'd need it."

Buck growled, and the muscles in his jaw clenched. He looked around for a weapon. If it was Hamilton and his men, a pitchfork wouldn't stop a bullet.

"McKean!" He'd know that voice anywhere.

"You stay here," he told Joe. "No sense both of us gettin' shot."

"I'm not hiding out in the barn."

Buck pointed a finger in his face. "If you hear shots, lay low. Josh and Billy know how to take care of themselves."

"And I don't?" Joe said with indignation.

"McKean...you in there?"

Buck strode to the barn door and slipped out into the open. Five riders, led by Hamilton on his black stallion, waited for him, the horses tossing their heads and blowing steam in the frigid air.

He stood tall and stared Hamilton in the eye. "Get off my land."

Rafe sneered. "Not your land anymore. I bought it. Signed the papers today."

Buck felt as if he'd been gut punched. Kate wouldn't do that, would she? She'd fought tooth and nail to hang on to her brother's homestead.

Hamilton leaned down to shove a piece of paper toward him.

"What's that?"

"An eviction notice. You've got till the end of the day to clear out."

Buck grabbed the paper out of Rafe's hands and read through it. The heat of anger raced from the top of his head to the soles of his feet. "I don't care what it says. Kate didn't get permission from me to sell our land."

Rafe laughed and leaned back in his saddle, a gloating expression on his face. "You'll have to take that up with your wife, though from what I hear, you won't be married for long. Money has already changed hands. Clear out by nightfall, or I'll bring Sheriff Granger back tomorrow to throw you off my property."

Enraged and feeling impotent, Buck crushed the paper in his hands, wishing he had strapped on his gun, although it wouldn't be a fair fight. Rafe's men all carried rifles, and they were pointed straight at him. He knew when to back down.

"We'll go," he ground out, "but don't get too comfortable. This isn't legal. I'll be back."

Rafe sat high and mighty in his black leather saddle backed up by his hired hands. "I wouldn't advise that if I were you. It'd be a shame if Miss Kate had to bury you next to her brother. Face it, McKean. You've lost. You've lost this land, and you've lost Kate. You might as well pull up stakes and head back where you came from. You're not wanted here."

"I'm not goin' anywhere except to Deer Lodge. You may have won this hand, but I still hold a few cards."

Rafe smirked and pulled back on the reins, making his horse dance. "Nightfall, McKean." He looked at the man beside him. "Harding, you stay here and make sure they clear out." He turned the stallion around, and his men followed behind as he rode away.

Now that the immediate threat was over, Buck slumped against the barn, feeling defeated. Kate might as well have cut out his heart and handed it to him on a silver platter. He felt just as dead.

Kate stared at the ice-coated window, her hands lying still in her lap, her embroidery forgotten. She dreaded telling Buck she had sold the property. It was for the best, but she didn't think he'd see it that way. Rafe would have threatened her until he got what he wanted. As long as Buck lived on that property, his life was in danger. Now he had no reason to stay in Montana. She had made sure of that.

Martha walked into the parlor from the kitchen, carrying two cups of tea. She set one beside her on the doily-covered table. "This should warm us up."

Kate held the cup between both of her hands, huddling under a quilt as close to the wood stove as she could get. "Is it always this cold in the winter?"

"Oh, honey, this is normal. I've known it to get almost fifty below." Martha took a sip of her tea. "They say up in the mountain passes, it can get down to sixty or sixty-five below. In Rogers Pass, north of Helena, they found a poor miner still frozen solid in April. Some tenderfoot who didn't know any better than to cross the mountains in the wintertime."

"Such a harsh land. So different than Ireland."

"That it is, but there's no place else like it. The fields of wildflowers in May are like a rainbow stretched out clear to those purple mountains.

You'll get used to the cold once you've been here a few years." Martha blew on her tea and then took a sip before setting it down to continue working on Doc's new wool sweater. "Now that you've sold your homestead, have you thought about what you'd like to do? What Buck will do?"

"I'll need to find work...maybe in one of the cafes. Or mayhap there's a need for another seamstress in town?"

Martha's hands stilled. "Deer Lodge is growing. Abigail might be better able to answer that question than me." She paused for a moment and leaned forward. "Are you sure you and Buck can't resolve your problems, Kate? He loves you so much."

She felt tears sting the back of her eyes. "I don't think I'll ever forgive him for going to that...place." Sticking her needle into the pillowcase, she pulled through a blue satin stitch.

"That's pride talking, Kate. The man has asked for your forgiveness. What more do you want from him? Yes, he committed adultery when he lusted after that woman and kissed her. That's bad enough, and I won't justify his actions, but Doc said he didn't sleep with her."

"Rafe Hamilton said—"

"You'd believe Rafe Hamilton over your own husband? That man has wanted you since the first time he laid eyes on you last spring. I wouldn't believe him if he told me the sky was blue if I couldn't see it for myself. He's a scoundrel of the highest order." Martha's needles clicked furiously. "What happened between you and Buck anyway? Why'd he go storming off to Ruby's that night?"

Color flooded her face. She hadna told anyone about that night—even Mr. Sauter.

"Kate?"

She stayed silent, nibbling at her lower lip.

"Something's eating you up inside, honey. If you don't let it out it will only get worse. You know I won't tell anyone."

"I know, it's just..." She sighed, then took another sip of tea to fortify her. "We had a fight, and he got mad."

"That much is apparent." Martha's hands stilled mid-stitch. She rolled her eyes and shook her head.

"I... I told him I wanted to end our marriage," she said in a soft voice.

"What on earth would ever possess you to do that? I thought the only reason you wanted a divorce was because of what he did at Ruby's."

Kate held the hot cup tightly in her hands, not wanting to admit her failure as a wife. She closed her eyes a moment and remembered how it had all started. How could she blame him for what he'd done?

"I canna say it."

Martha laid aside her knitting and stood up to walk over to her chair. With a caring hand, her friend slowly rubbed circles on her back. "Honey, whatever it is, I won't judge you...or Buck. What did he do that would make you ask him for a divorce?"

"Nothing. He never raised his hand in anger to me. But I could not find the trust in my heart until it was too late." She felt so ashamed. "I've never been a real wife."

Martha's hand stilled, and she bent down to look her square in the face. "Are you telling me you've never—"

Kate nodded her head yes.

"Well, I'll be. That man must have the patience of Job. Don't you know how rare he is?"

"Aye, I do now. But I'm still so afraid."

"Afraid of what?"

"My stepfather used to beat me somethin' fierce...and...I can't say the rest—the despicable things he did to me." She drooped her head in shame. "He beat my mother to death when she was carrying his child. Then when I came here, Rafe tried to force me—"

Martha put a finger under her chin and tilted her head up. She brushed wispy curls back from Kate's face. Her hand felt so soft—exactly like her mam's.

"Oh, honey. No wonder you don't trust men. Why didn't you say something before you got married?"

"Because I felt trapped. And you all thought so highly of Buck."

Martha pulled her to her feet, the pillowcase falling to the rug, and took Kate into her arms. It felt so good to sink into a mother's embrace.

"I'm so sorry, Kate. We did what we thought best for you. Living out there by yourself, trying to keep that place running."

"I don't blame you, Martha." The dam of tears she had held back burst open. She cried against her friend's shoulder, while Martha patted her back.

"Shh, it's all right."

Martha put her arm around her shoulders and led her to the sofa where they sat side-by-side. Kate felt better with the telling. Sighing, she leaned her head on Martha's shoulder, her tears finally spent.

"So, you see why I've made a mess of everything."

"I see a girl who has been wounded by evil men."

Kate sat up and wiped the last of her tears from her face. "I should never have married Buck, Martha, knowing the way I feel. But I wasna thinking straight that day."

Martha gave her a gentle smile. "Buck is not like Rafe or your stepfather. That man would never raise his hand against a woman."

"I know that now."

"Do you love him?"

Kate shook her head. "Aye."

"Then it's not too late."

"But what about Ruby's? His sin? Going to that woman's bed?"

The older woman squeezed her hand. "At some point, you've got to put your trust in the man. If he says he didn't lie with that woman, who are you going to believe? Him? Or Rafe Hamilton?"

"Buck admitted he kissed her. How can I forgive him for that?"

"Honey, the Lord has already forgiven him. What does the Bible say about unforgiveness? If you don't forgive others, how can your Father in heaven forgive you on that last day?"

"I've been such a fool."

"The Bible says call no man a fool. That includes ourselves. Now wash your face and let's figure out how to fix this."

Chapter Twenty-two

BUCK RODE INTO TOWN WITH RILEY trotting beside Applejack. Since Hamilton had left a man behind, he and the boys hadn't wasted any time throwing their things together and saddling their horses. Fury had driven him at first, but now it felt as though his heart had turned to stone. First Angel had left him at the altar alone and now Kate. He thought she was different.

Joe rode up beside him. "Where we gonna stay, Buck?"

"We'll try Mrs. Cramer's boarding house first. Hopefully, she's got room. If not, we'll stay at a hotel for the night and look for a house in the mornin'."

"You got that kind of money to take care of us over the winter? Maybe we should head back to Texas. Course, it'd be a hard ride this time of year. Likely freeze to death."

Buck looked over at his oldest friend and sighed. "Haven't I taken care of us all these years? I've got enough money in the bank to get us through a lotta years and more than enough to buy the biggest spread I want. If you and the boys want to leave in the spring, feel free, but I'm not goin' anywhere."

"You mean you'd stay after what that little gal did to you?" Joe huffed into his wool scarf. "I'd no sooner stay in this town than—"

"You're not me." Buck gritted his teeth and spoke with a tight jaw. "I'm not turning tail and running. I said I'd settle down in Deer Lodge Valley, and this is where I mean to stay. You can either stay or go. Suit yourself."

"You are the stubbornest man this side of the Rockies."

"Maybe so." He pulled up on Applejack's reins in front of Mabel Cramer's boarding house and dismounted. Riley trotted up beside him and sat down.

"That woman's not goin' to let no dawg stay in her house," Joe grumbled. "He's probably got fleas."

"He can sleep with me, can't you, boy?" Billy dismounted his sorrel, then stooped and rubbed Riley's ears. "It's too cold for him to sleep outside."

Josh didn't say a word—only dismounted. With his mouth turned down and eyes drooping with sadness, he tied his horse to the railing. Buck knocked on the door of the two-story white house. A moment later it was opened by a short, plump woman wiping her hands on a towel.

"Don't stand on my porch letting in all the cold air. Come on in."

Buck, Joe, Billy, and Josh all crowded into the foyer with Riley while Josh closed the door behind them. They all swept off their hats.

"We're looking for a couple of rooms for the winter, ma'am. I'm Buck McKean."

"I know who you are." Mabel threw the towel over her shoulder. "I've seen you sitting near the front of church with that pretty little wife of yours. Heard you'd had some trouble."

"Yes, ma'am."

"Well, you're in luck. A couple of my boarders left last fall before winter set in, so I welcome your business. The dog can sleep in the kitchen. Don't make me regret renting to four cowboys."

"No, ma'am, you won't regret it." Buck felt a major burden lift from his shoulders.

"I don't put up with any drinkin' or carousin'. I lock the door promptly at nine o'clock at night, and it stays locked until morning. I don't want you pounding on my door at midnight wanting to be let in. I expect rent to be paid every Saturday morning without fail. Otherwise, I'll boot you out."

"Yes, ma'am." Buck stood ramrod straight.

"I'll feed you three square meals a day, but from the looks of you four, you'll eat me out of house and home. You'll be responsible for feeding the dog."

"His name's Riley." The sheepdog wiggled his back end and wagged his tail at the sound of his name. Buck reached down and patted Riley on his side. "He won't cause you any trouble. He's a good guard dog."

Mabel finally smiled. "Then he'll be a comfort to me. I like dogs.

Now let me show you to your rooms. I've only got two available, so you'll have to double up."

"That's not a problem," Buck said.

"You got a stable, ma'am?" Josh backed up against the door.

"Behind the house."

"I'll take care of the horses, Buck." Josh put his hat back on, pulled up the collar of his sheepskin coat, and opened the door, leaving quietly.

The rest of them climbed the creaking stairs. Buck hated the thought of sleeping with Joe, but it beat the alternative. Having somebody cook for you was better than finding a house to rent where they'd have to fend for themselves. If they could even find one. He missed Kate's cooking. Shoot, who was he kidding? He missed Kate, but he didn't reckon she missed him, or she wouldn't have had him evicted. No, her actions spoke loud and clear.

At least the church was warmer than outside, but Kate still shivered in her coat, scarf, and gloves. She shuffled down the aisle in front of Martha, her eyes focused on the plank floor to avoid the stares of the congregation, before she looked at their pew. She stopped in her forward motion, and Martha ran into her. Turning around to flee, Martha and Doc blocked her path.

"You knew." Kate tightened her mouth and pointed at them.

"And he's coming to Sunday dinner," Martha said. "You have to face him sometime so it might as well be in church." The woman took her by the arm and dragged her down the aisle.

Buck looked up, but he didn't smile. Without a word, he stood up in the aisle and gestured at the pew. Kate could almost feel his breath on the top of her head. Every nerve in her body tingled, and she thought she might die of heart failure right there.

Dressed in new black wool pants, boots, a black leather vest, and a white collarless shirt, Buck motioned for her to follow Doc and Martha.

She couldn't sit by him! She sat down next to Martha and tried to scoot her friend over, but Martha only stared at her with a firm jaw and refused to move. She felt trapped. When she leaned against the hard pew, her shoulders were squeezed between Buck and Martha.

She narrowed her eyes and hissed out the corner of her mouth. "What are you doing here?"

"The same as you, darlin'." He scooched his arm from between them and rested it behind her on the pew.

Kate's eyes darted around the church, looking for a way out, but Buck's long legs blocked her exit. She was stuck. That's when her gaze lighted on the scowling face of Rafe Hamilton, who sat down in his usual place across the aisle.

She froze. *Merciful heavens!* She didn't want a brawl right here in church, but with these two men in the same room, knowing now that Rafe had evicted Buck and his men, anything could happen. Why had she ever believed Rafe? He bought the property without Buck's signature and filed the paperwork at the courthouse. No one questioned him about the unusual transaction. Then he told her he wouldn't take possession of the property until spring. He was only doing her a favor by buying it now. But he hadn't kept his word. Doc had been the one to break the news to her that Buck had moved into the boarding house after Rafe threw him off the homestead.

Kate's heart thumped in her chest. She started to stand up, but Buck put a restraining hand on her knee, and she reluctantly sank down, her heart beating double time and her leg burning where he had touched her. There wouldn't be any escape. With doe-wide eyes, she glanced at his firm jaw as he stared straight ahead at Pastor Russell.

The loud, buzzing voices behind her silenced when Pastor lifted his hands and then led them in a prayer, but she knew what they had all been gossiping about. There were no secrets in this town, and especially not in this church. They were waiting for the fireworks to start.

"Before I continue," Pastor Russell said, smiling, "I'd like to welcome Buck McKean to our midst. Buck, stand up and give everybody a wave."

It seemed like Buck hesitated and then rose slowly as if he was embarrassed by the attention. Kate felt her face burn. She hoped the pastor wouldn't mention her.

After Buck dropped down beside her, his arm returned to the pew behind her, but a quick glance showed he remained stone-faced.

"As you all know, Buck was ambushed on his way home one night and shot by some evildoer who wanted to kill him. We're fortunate he didn't succeed. Buck's a valued member of our community, and I know we're all glad he's sitting here with us today, thanks in large part to Doc Mitchell, but we give all the glory to God for saving his life."

The congregation clapped, some louder than others, and the buzzing voices started again. Kate ducked her head and didn't look around, not even at her estranged husband.

"If you have your Bibles this morning," Pastor continued, "I'd like you to turn to some of the most well-known verses in Scripture—First Corinthians Thirteen—the love chapter. I'll read verses four through eight. It's a long passage, but I think we all need to hear it again."

Kate glanced over at Buck as he thumbed his Bible and ran his finger down the page. She had forgotten hers this morning. He held the book closer to her so that she could read it too.

"Let me remind you that the word 'charity' in the passage could just as well be translated as 'love'.

"*Charity suffereth long and is kind; charity envieth not; charity vaunteth not itself, is not puffed up, Doth not behave itself unseemly, seeketh not her own, is not easily provoked, thinketh no evil; Rejoiceth not in iniquity, but rejoiceth in the truth; Beareth all things, believeth all things, hopeth all things, endureth all things. Charity never faileth.*"

Pastor stopped and looked out at the congregation. "How many of us can say we love like that?" He looked straight at her and Buck. "I can't. I daresay none of us can. Oh, we try. We try to love our neighbors as ourselves, but the truth is, your neighbor may be a cantankerous old coot who lets his hogs run wild all over your property."

The congregation laughed.

"I once knew two neighbors who didn't speak to each other for twenty years, and when I talked to them separately, neither of them could remember what they had argued about. Stubborn pride kept them locked in a jail of unforgiveness.

"Do you get puffed up with pride and gossip about other people? Do you believe the worst of someone without knowing the truth and pass it on to willing ears? Or do you give that person the benefit of the doubt and extend love and grace?

"Husbands and wives, are you easily provoked? Do you snap at each other over little things that don't mean a hill of beans? Do you bear with one another? Do you dredge up past sins and throw them in each other's faces? Some of you treat strangers better than you do your own families. You're kinder and more courteous to people at church than when you enter the doors of your home.

"Love bears all things. We're all guilty. Bernadette and I have our spats, but we try not to go to bed angry."

Kate's face flamed. Squirming in her seat, she leaned against Martha's shoulder.

"Then how do we love others when we're not even capable of truly loving the person sitting next to us today—loving them so much that we forgive? Jesus said we are to forgive our brother seventy times seven. That's because unforgiveness eats us up inside.

"We can try to climb to the highest peak of the Rocky Mountains, but we'll never do it alone. Jesus said when He rose into heaven to sit at the right hand of the Father that He would not leave us alone and without help. When you confessed Jesus Christ as your Lord and Savior, the Holy Spirit came to make His home in your heart. We can only love because Christ loved us first and gave Himself for us by dying on the cross to take all our sin and deserved punishment into His own body.

"We can only love with the help of the Holy Spirit loving through us. We are weak and helpless without Him.

"I challenge you this week to read this Scripture daily and meditate on it. Let it fill your minds so that when you act out of anger, you will know it immediately and ask for forgiveness. Don't let your heart be hardened. Jesus said you who are without sin cast the first stone.

"Lay down your stones and have compassion on one another.

Love without reservation."

Kate knew without a doubt the pastor had written his sermon just for her, to show her the depth of her unforgiveness toward Buck. Her husband had tried to love her, and she had pushed him away. She had wronged him in so many ways.

Lord, forgive me.

She wanted to be a better person, but she needed help. She couldn't do it alone. Suddenly, as though he had read her mind, Buck pulled his arm down, reached over and took her hand, squeezed it, and then withdrew. Looking up at him, she noticed his tense jaw had softened a little.

How would she ever make it through Sunday dinner? What would she say to him? She needed to apologize, but she didn't know if her pride would let her. Would he, could he, forgive her? And could she forgive him and put the past behind her?

After the service ended, Buck stood up in the aisle and reached out his hand to help her out of the pew. At the same time, Rafe Hamilton stepped into the aisle and bumped into Buck hard, causing him to stumble. Martha, Doc, and the Stricklins were blocked in behind her.

Rafe drew himself up and sneered, but he didn't apologize. "Haven't seen you since I evicted you from my property, McKean. I thought you would've hightailed it out of town by now." His voice was loud in the now silent church.

"What made you think that?" Buck bit out.

"Just figured you wouldn't want to hang around now that you and Kate are getting a divorce. Surprised to see you here."

"Not half as surprised as I am to see you in church. When did you get religion?"

"About the same time you stopped coming." When Rafe grinned at her, Buck pushed her behind him.

Kate looked around frantically for someone to intervene, but everyone in the congregation stood frozen. They were all waiting to see what would happen.

"If you'll excuse us" —Buck ground out— "Kate and I have plans for this afternoon. I'd appreciate it if you would let my *wife* and me pass. You're blocking the aisle."

"Am I?" Rafe raised his hands and looked around in mock apology. "Didn't mean to get in your way." Rafe stepped away, pushed back his coat, and planted his hands on his hips. He had worn his gun to church. Who wore a gun in church? "Like the pastor said, maybe you and I can let bygones be bygones. Have a drink together some time. You still frequent Ruby's place?"

When Buck let go of her arm, she grabbed his balled-up fist in both of her hands, stepping between the two men. "Let it go, Buck. He's only trying to bait you. You're the better man."

Kate held her breath as fury battled on her husband's classic features. His chin jutted forward, and his lips had whitened as his jaw remained clenched. She thought for sure he would shove her out of the way, but instead, he looked down at her, and she knew he had regained control.

Pulling her against him, he stepped aside to let Martha, Doc, and the Stricklins exit into the aisle. Without another word to Rafe, his jaw clamped tight, Buck turned away from the man and ushered her out with a warm hand in the small of her back.

Her heartbeat raced, and she thought her knees might buckle. She had meant what she said. Buck *was* the better man. Shame spread through her chest like wildfire. Why, oh why, had she ever listened to Rafe Hamilton in the first place? Listened to his lies? She had known what kind of man he was, yet she had taken his side rather than listen to her husband's explanation of that night and his plea for forgiveness.

The pastor's words rang like a bell in her head. Love and forgiveness. Could she and Buck forgive each other? A tiny flicker of hope fluttered in her stomach.

Chapter Twenty-three

Martha served another piece of apple pie to Buck and then sat down at her end of the table. Cutting a large bite with his fork, he shoveled the pie into his mouth to keep from staring at his wife. Doc and Martha had carried most of the conversation during their tense dinner. The only time he and Kate had spoken to each other was when he asked her to please pass the butter.

Sighing in satisfaction, Doc leaned back in his chair and patted his belly, while Buck finished scraping his plate clean. He'd eat off the painted flowers if he thought it would buy him more time to figure out what to say to her. He'd gone over this moment a thousand times in his head, but he still didn't know what to do. She had broken his heart. Would she ever forgive him?

"Did you get enough, Buck?" Martha smiled at him with a cherubic face. "Would you like another piece?"

"No, thank you, ma'am." He dabbed his mouth with his napkin. "I'm full. Everything was really delicious."

As he looked at Martha, she motioned her head toward Kate. But Kate stared at her plate, eating her pie as slowly as possible.

"Why don't you and Kate go sit in the parlor while I wash the dishes?" Martha motioned toward the room in question.

Kate's head popped up, her face pale—drained of all color. "I'll help you while the men adjourn to the parlor."

When she reached for Martha's plate, her friend playfully smacked her hand. "No, you won't. Now run along."

"But—"

"We have a guest, Kate, and you two need to spend time alone together. Doc will help me clear the table, won't you, dear?"

"You bet. I need to work off that meal." He stood up to carry his dish to the sink, kissing his wife on the cheek as he passed. "I'm stuffed."

Martha beamed at her husband, and Buck wished Kate would look at him like that.

Instead, she looked at him with trepidation, her green eyes wide. The thought crossed his mind that she might bolt down the stairs. Finally, she scooted her chair on the wood floor and stood, dragging her feet even more by brushing a non-existent crumb from her plaid skirt.

"Thank you for a lovely meal, Martha," she said.

"You're welcome, honey." Martha patted her shoulder. "Now you two run along."

Kate walked in front of him and perched on a red velvet chair, staring intently at her hands clasped in her lap. Buck walked over to a front window and stared out at the frozen landscape of Deer Lodge. She wasn't the only one who was nervous. With his hands behind him, he rocked in his boots from heel to toe, his breath fogging the window, the clock ticking the seconds as they passed.

Sighing inwardly, he finally sat across from her on the sofa with his leg propped on his knee, jiggling his foot. He stared at Kate, but she never looked up at him once. The silence wore on his nerves. He was the first to break it.

"Kate." She lifted her eyes to his, a look of what he hoped was regret on her face. "I won't bite."

She scraped her lower lip with her teeth, a sure sign she was nervous, too. When Doc and Martha first insisted he come to church and dinner, he wasn't sure it was such a good idea. He still wasn't, but they couldn't ignore each other forever, not if they were going to live in the same town.

"I... I'm sorry," she said, her eyes pleading. "I didna know Rafe would evict you from the property."

"What did you think would happen when you sold it to him?" He tried to keep any hurt or anger out of his voice.

"He said he didna plan on taking possession until spring. I...I never dreamed he would—"

"Tarnation, Kate, the snake's wanted that property since your brother died. Before that even. I thought you'd never sell out. Wasn't that what you told me?"

She nodded her head yes.

He crossed his arms. "And he's always wanted you. Why do you think he smeared my name all over town?"

She lowered her gaze and shrugged her shoulder.

"Because he counted on you believing every word he said, that's why. He was probably dancing on my grave already. The man has always wanted to marry you, long before I got here."

"I would never—"

"That's what you said about selling your homestead."

"I know, but I couldna live on your bounty forever." She sounded defeated.

He huffed, and her head snapped up, showing a little fire in her eyes. It was a start. At least she didn't look like a scared rabbit anymore.

"I was wrong, Buck. Is that what you want me to say? I was wrong about you. I was wrong to sell the land to Rafe. I was wrong to marry you. I've ruined your life, and I'm sorry."

Tears welled in her eyes, but he knew she wasn't about to let them fall. She had apologized. Now it was his turn.

Buck stood then knelt in front of his wife, taking one of her cold hands in his. He sighed. "I guess our road hasn't been paved with roses, has it?"

"Nay, but if it weren't for me, you'd have your own place by now, and you never would have gotten shot, and you wouldna be living in a boarding house and—"

"It's not so bad, darlin', except Joe makes a pretty terrible roommate. I swear the man takes his half out of the middle of the bed. Most nights I end up on the floor with a pillow over my head so I don't have to listen to him snore."

A tiny laugh bubbled from her throat.

"And Billy." He rolled his eyes. "That kid is a pain in my behind. He's eating Mabel Cramer out of house and home, and she threatened to raise our rent. So I sent him out when it was five below to bag a deer to help feed us. I sure don't remember eatin' that much when I was his age."

"You're only trying to make me feel better." She sniffed.

"Is it working?"

"A little."

He reached up and stroked her cheek. When she tried to duck her head again, he tilted her chin up with his hand.

"I want you to look at me. Come spring, I'm looking in Deer Lodge Valley for a place to buy or homestead. I'm not running back to Texas, and I won't divorce you. I'll keep coming to church. I'll see you on Sundays, and if you ever decide to be my wife, if you ever decide to forgive me, I'll be waiting."

"But, I thought—"

"That's your problem, Katie girl, you think too much."

He leaned forward and placed a gentle kiss on her lips. She looked stunned when he pulled away.

"I forgive you, darlin', like Pastor said, and I hope you forgive me too. I should have given you more time. I should have understood. Pastor Russell made me realize how much you've been hurting—your brother dying, running the place by yourself, threatened by the Hamiltons. It's enough to break anybody. But every time life knocked you down, you got back up and even had enough fight left in you to defend your land. And then you were forced to marry a stranger."

Fear had left her eyes. Buck stood and pulled her hand. "Come sit with me on the sofa. That floor's a little hard on the knees."

"Aye, I imagine it is. You've spent enough time on the floor I suppose." She gave him a small smile. When she sat down beside him, he put his arm around her and rested his head on her hair. This time she didn't flinch or pull away. He closed his eyes. It felt so right to hold her.

"Oh, Katie, this is a mess, and that's for sure, but I believe God has an answer. I believe He was speaking to us this morning, don't you? It scares me spitless to say this, because I'm putting my heart on the line, but I love you. I know a lot has happened that we both need to get over. I won't say it'll be easy. I betrayed you the night I went to Ruby's. I sinned against God and you, and I'll regret it with every bone in my body for the rest of my life. But someday, I hope you can forgive me and we can start over again."

With her brow furrowed, Kate pulled away from him to touch his face. "I forgive you, Buck. Pastor held up my unforgiveness, and I realized that unless I truly forgive you, the Lord can never forgive me my sins."

He sighed and pressed his forehead against hers. That lump of coal in his belly caught fire and flared in his chest. She forgave him.

Katie pulled away, and he smiled at her sweet, dear face. She frowned.

"What's wrong?"

She cupped his face in her soft hand. "I'm afraid for you, Buck. I'm afraid if you dinna leave town, Rafe Hamilton won't stop until you're dead. I sold him Patrick's place because I needed the money to live, aye, but mainly, I thought it would stop him and he'd leave both of us alone."

"I'm not afraid of him."

"But I am. He's still coming to church, and the way he looks at me..."

His voice turned hard. "As long as I'm around, he won't dare touch you. And I don't die easy, darlin'. I'll be ready for him next time."

Sighing, she laid her head in the crook of his shoulder of her own accord. "I've missed you."

"I've missed you too." He planted a kiss on her head, his heart more at peace than it had been for months. This felt right. She had forgiven him. But she still hadn't said the words he longed to hear.

"But do you..." He swallowed the lump in his throat. "Can you..."

She pushed back from him and stared him straight in the eye. "I love you, too, and I want to spend the rest of my days with you." She lifted her left hand. "I'm still wearing my ring. I've not taken it off."

"Katie," he whispered and pulled her to him, kissing her like a man kisses his wife, and she kissed him back in full measure. Finally, he lifted his head.

"Are you sure, Katie? This time there won't be any turning back.

My heart won't take it."

She smiled and palmed his cheek. "I'm sure."

He realized there was no longer any noise in the kitchen. At some point, Doc and Martha must have snuck downstairs to give them privacy. He'd have to thank them later. "It'll be spring before I can find a place and make us a home."

"Doc and Martha would let us stay with them through the winter."

He cocked an eyebrow and smiled. "Do you really want to start married life with Doc and Martha sleeping right next door?"

Her face turned a lovable shade of pink. "Oh."

"There's no room for us at the boarding house, and I'm not sure we can even find a place to rent this time of year—at least not a place where I'd want you to live."

"What then?"

As much as it pained him to say so, he knew what they might have to do. "We may have to live apart for a few months." He held her hands and kissed her fingers. "It won't be easy, I'll grant you that."

"But you'll try to find a house, won't you?" She actually sounded eager, and his heart swelled with joy.

"Yes, I'll try. If there's anything available, Bill Stricklin should know about it. You know people will be talking about us though."

That fiercely proud face—the one that had faced him down the first time he saw her—looked up at him. "Let them. I dinna care what they say. It couldna be any worse than what they've said already."

He threw back his head and chuckled. "That's my little Irish ball of fire." His heart soared that she wanted to make their marriage about more than signatures on a piece of paper. "That's the truth. I don't hear Doc and Martha. They're probably sittin' in those hard chairs down in his office."

"Aye, but I think they suspected we might need a while to talk."

Buck pulled his wife to her feet and bent to taste her sweetness one more time. "Let's go tell them their meddling worked."

Kate browsed through the mercantile, fingering the bolts of cloth, more for something to do than that she needed anything. The long, cold winter seemed endless. It was the end of March, but it had only warmed up to the low thirties and there was still snow on the ground.

Back home, the meadows would be blooming with violet speedwell, yellow dandelions, and tiny red hazel. Crocus and daffodils would decorate cottage gardens, and the sun would warm her face. At least the sun shone here in a wide blue sky almost every day. She didn't think she could stand it if the skies were dark and gray all winter long.

A bolt of Kelly green wool worked in a plaid with red and yellow thread caught her eye. She caressed its softness. It would make a beautiful church dress. Not that she needed anything. Buck had been more than generous with her. All she had to do was mention that she liked something, and he would insist on buying it. His Christmas present had been a gold locket that he had saved for her. She'd finally stopped shopping with him all together. She was afraid he was spending all his savings.

It was so frustrating to live like this, putting their lives on hold. Since he had not been able to find a house for them, they had to content themselves with holding hands in church or in Doc and Martha's parlor or staring into each other's eyes over a cup of coffee or tea at the Red Rock Cafe.

It was too cold for a buggy ride. And there had been no parties or dancing. No one even celebrated St. Patrick's Day here. The calendar might say Easter would arrive on April 17, but Martha had told her it would be May before the wildflowers bloomed and spring truly arrived.

Sighing, she strolled toward the front of the mercantile. She could always knit another pair of socks to pass the time. She picked up a half pound ball of gray wool that would surely last until spring.

"Can I help you find something?" Abigail said from behind the counter. Another customer entered the store, setting the bell to tinkling.

She smiled. "No, just this yarn."

"That'll be thirty-five cents."

Kate reached in her reticule for a few coins and laid them in Abigail's hand. Buck had insisted she never be without money of her own.

"Are you sure you don't need material for a new Easter dress?" Abigail asked, bustling over to the table stacked with material. "I thought of you when we received this bolt of heavy cotton. It's such a pretty spring green with sprigs of yellow flowers. It might still be a little chilly on Easter, but spring will be right around the corner."

Mumbling to herself, Abigail dug through the material, leaving Kate to look on helplessly. Should she make an Easter dress? If Buck were here, he would say yes.

"Ah, here it is." Abigail drew out the bolt of fabric and plopped it on top of the stack. "Now isn't that pretty?"

"Aye, it is." Kate ran her hand over the smooth fabric. It reminded her of spring.

"I can cut off a length for you in a jiffy."

Kate smiled and yielded to the woman's sales ability. "All right. I'll take enough to make a dress."

"And I have the perfect white cotton lace for the collar and cuffs." Abigail retrieved the lace from a nearby shelf and walked to the front of the store with Kate trailing behind. "I'll put this on your account."

The material was a splurge. Should she? Then she looked at the bright yellow flowers against the spring green as Abigail cut the polished cotton, and she could picture wearing it to church on Easter morning, walking in on Buck's arm.

Abigail wrapped her purchase in brown paper and tied it with twine. When Kate left the store, pulling her scarf over her head, she bumped into two older women she knew from church, although not well.

"Pardon me, Mrs. Kent, Mrs. Cardwell."

Their gazes held hers for a moment, their mouths turned down in pity. Kate had seen that look before when she and Buck had separated, and everyone was gossiping about them.

"Is something wrong?" she asked, her heart skipping a beat.

Mrs. Cardwell straightened her black hat, which needed no straightening. "It's not for me to say. If you want to know, ask your husband."

The woman swept by her into the warm store, the bell tinkling as she followed Mrs. Kent. She shut the door firmly behind her.

Kate's heart raced. What did Mrs. Cardwell mean? She had to trust Buck. She would never doubt him again.

Chapter Twenty-four

As Buck clomped down the stairs in his black wool trousers, pulling on the cuffs of his white shirt, Kate opened the boarding house door. He had dressed up to take her to the McBurney House for dinner and was supposed to come by Doc's to escort her there. Pausing on the stairs to look at his beautiful bride, his smile faded. He didn't like the look on her face.

"Hello, Katie girl, what are you doin' here?"

"Can we talk?" she said, shifting a brown paper package into her other arm.

He took her by the shoulders and gave her a quick kiss. "What's wrong?" He led her into the parlor to the worn, brown-horsehair sofa that faced the crackling fireplace.

She set her package beside her and turned to him. "We promised to always be honest with each other from now on."

"That's right." Something was up, and he didn't like it.

"Is there anything you'd like to tell me?"

Racking his brain for something he might have done, he came up empty. He wanted to kiss that little furrow between her brows and reassure her.

"No, can't think of anything. Why?"

"People are gossiping."

He snorted. "People are always gossiping."

"This is serious, Buck. I just saw two women from church, and they said I should ask you what was going on. They made it sound like it was something horrible."

Surprised and confused, he took her hand. "Honest, Katie, I have no idea what they were talking about." But a knot had formed in his belly.

Kate nibbled her lower lip and looked straight into his eyes. He could see her question.

"Darlin', if I knew what they were talking about, I would tell you. I promised we'd have no secrets, and I meant it."

She looked relieved and gave him a little smile, her lips tipping up at the corners. Reaching over, she squeezed his hand. "I'm sure it's nothing."

But Buck felt in his gut it was something, and he'd bank that if rumors were swirling around town again, Rafe Hamilton had something to do with it. Whatever it was, he needed to get to the bottom of it, but not right now. Nothing was going to ruin their dinner together.

Sunday morning threatened snow. Kate could sense it by the way the heavy gray clouds hung low. She yearned for spring and looked forward to wearing the new dress she had made with the polished cotton material she had purchased at the mercantile. Stitching the seams of the green fabric dotted with yellow flowers lifted her spirits.

Glancing over at Buck driving the buggy he had rented for the day so they could be alone, her heart warmed at the memory of his kiss last night. Every day she loved him more and more. When they finally came together as husband and wife, he would no longer be the stranger who had ridden into the yard last September.

He looked over at her and smiled. "What?"

"I'm just happy." She slipped her hand into the bend of his elbow.

As he steered over a deep rut, she bounced against him, and he grinned at her, his eyes crinkling at the corners. "Sorry about that."

"I'm not." She giggled and kissed him on the cheek.

"Aren't you afraid someone will see us?" He pulled the horse to a stop next to Doc's buggy in the church yard.

"I don't care."

He leaned over and kissed her on the lips, ignoring the people gathering in the church yard, then hopped to the ground. After tying the reins to the hitching post, he lifted her down to the frozen ground, his hands spanning her waist. She tightened the green wool scarf around her neck, and they both stood staring into each other's eyes until Doc slapped Buck on the shoulder.

"Come on, you two. You can't stand out here all day mooning at each other."

Martha giggled, and Kate looked around at all the faces staring at them. She didn't give a fig what they thought of her display of affection for her husband. Pastor Russell left his post at the door and walked over to welcome them. He had a serious expression on his face, and his mouth turned down at the corners.

"Buck, Kate, I need to talk to you before service," he said without a greeting. "You, too, Doc, if you don't mind."

"No problem," Doc said. "Martha, you go on in where it's warm."

"Don't be long, dear." Martha's eyebrows raised, and she shot a worried glance at Kate. Turning, she picked up the hem of her heavy black coat and climbed the wooden steps carefully.

"Let's walk a ways over by that big cottonwood tree," Pastor said. "I don't want anyone to overhear our conversation."

Kate slipped her hand into Buck's elbow, and he drew her close to his side as soft snowflakes began to drift out of the leaden sky. She shivered and furrowed her brow, wondering why Pastor wanted to talk to them in private. They stopped under the bare tree branches and stood in a circle.

"What's wrong, Pastor?" Buck placed his large, gloved hand over hers as she clutched his arm.

The pastor's gray eyes locked on her husband's face. "Buck, several people in the church have come to me with a disturbing rumor."

Kate's heart sank, remembering the women's words outside the mercantile. *Ask your husband.*

"This is a delicate subject, Miss Kate, and I hate to confront your husband in front of you, but you need to hear this too."

"Just tell us what's wrong, Pastor." Buck's hand squeezed hers.

Pastor sighed and looked over at Doc. "Did you treat one of

Ruby's girls a few weeks ago after she took a beating?"

Doc looked fit to be tied. "You know I did, or you wouldn't be asking. What's this got to do with Buck and Kate?"

Pastor clasped his Bible in his hands and looked at Buck. "People are saying you did it, son."

Kate drew closer to her husband. If she hadn't been hanging on to his arm, she was afraid her knees would have buckled. She looked at him to deny it.

"That's a bald-faced lie," Buck said. Kate looked around to see if anyone had heard, but the church yard had emptied. Too cold to stand outside. "I've never set foot in that place except for the one time I told you about."

Pastor looked over at Doc. "Can you tell me what happened?"

Doc rubbed the back of his neck. "Ruby came knocking on my back door about midnight a few days ago, which is not unusual. You know I treat those girls. It's my duty as a doctor."

Pastor nodded.

"Anyway, Ruby's bartender carried in Pansy wrapped in a blanket. She had been beaten badly. One eye was swollen shut. Whoever did it had twisted her wrist until it broke. And..." He looked over at her. "I'm sorry to talk about this in front of you, Miss Kate."

"It's all right." But it wasn't. She didn't want to hear what he had to say about that...woman.

"She miscarried," Doc said. "She wasn't far along."

Kate gasped, and she could feel the flush race up her cheeks. She looked up at her husband whose face had gone white.

"Doc, you don't think I—"

"Of course, I don't, Buck. Neither Pansy nor Ruby would tell me who did it though. I wanted to report it to the sheriff, but they said they couldn't afford to. Ruby was scared, and she's not afraid of anybody. That's one tough gal."

"You mean people in this church think I'd do such a thing?" Buck's voice barely contained his anger.

"I'm afraid so, son," Pastor said. "They're God-fearing people, but they're sinners, too, and a lot of them are prone to gossip."

Buck looked down at her. "I didn't do this, Kate. Please tell me you don't think I did."

She put a hand to her racing heart and searched his face. Was he capable of such a thing? He had gotten drunk that night. Maybe he had lain with Pansy and didn't remember it.

No, she wouldn't believe that. Lifting her chin, her jaw tightened, and she stared into those warm, brown eyes that beseeched her to have faith in him. "No, I dinna believe you could ever do such a thing. You're an honorable man."

Buck's eyes closed for a moment, and he let out the air he had been holding in a whoosh. When he opened them again, he looked down at her with relief. With every fiber of her being, she knew he was telling the truth. He hugged her tightly to his chest and turned to face the pastor.

"I can prove it wasn't me. Ask Mabel Cramer over at the boarding house. She locks the door every night at nine o'clock sharp, and she doesn't unlock it till we all come down for breakfast. She can tell you I haven't been out carousing. Joe can too."

Pastor smiled at them. "I didn't want to believe it, Buck, but I had to ask. We have a big problem though. Somebody has been spreading this foul rumor all over town."

"So that's why women have been looking at me with pity in their eyes." Kate's spine straightened in anger.

"I imagine so," Pastor said.

"Doc, did you know what they were saying?" she asked.

"People know you live with Martha and me. And they know I don't like gossip. I'm probably the last person they'd tell. Or they figured I already knew. This makes me so mad I could spit."

"How do you think I feel?" Buck released her arm and clenched his fists.

"Keep a tight rein on your temper, son," Pastor said. "We'll straighten this out. Rest in the assurance that God will fight this battle for you. He won't let the enemy win."

"That enemy has a name," Buck ground out. "Rafe Hamilton."

"Around when this happened was the last time I saw him in

church," Pastor said. "In fact, he hasn't been here since you came back."

"I thought he was out of our lives for good." Buck took off his hat and raked his fingers through his chestnut-brown hair. "I should have known better."

"What are we going to do?" Kate's brow furrowed. "He'll never stop. Maybe we need to move home to your family. I'm afraid for you...for us."

Buck's handsome, chiseled features hardened with determination as he rested his hands on her shoulders. "I'm not running away, Katie. Deer Lodge is our home, and this is where we'll stay. Hamilton isn't going to drive us out."

"It makes sense." Doc rubbed his chin. "I've doctored him up from more fights than I can count, but his daddy has always gotten him out of his scrapes. If Pansy told him she was carrying a child and claimed it was his, I can see him beating the tar out of her. I had hopes for him when he showed up in church, Pastor. I'd hoped he'd been reformed."

"So did I," Pastor said. "Maybe I can still reach him."

"Don't waste your breath," Buck huffed. "Won't do any good. That rattlesnake wants me dead or gone so he can have Kate."

She gripped her husband's arm, her knuckles turning white. Rafe terrified her. He would stop at nothing, including ruining Buck's reputation or shooting him in the back again if he failed to run him out of town.

Hearing the clatter of hoofbeats on frozen ground, they all turned toward the road and watched Sheriff Granger, wearing his silver star on his coat, lope into the church yard flanked by his deputy Glen Madison. They drew rein beside the small group and dismounted.

"Pastor. Doc." The sheriff tipped his hat.

"You finally decide to attend my church, Sheriff," Pastor said, smiling.

The expressions on the two lawmen's faces were serious. "I'm afraid not." Sheriff Granger looked at Buck. Kate felt her heart flutter as fear gripped her.

"Buck McKean, you're under arrest for the assault of Pansy Whitlow."

Kate moved in front of her shocked husband as if to protect him. "You're mistaken, Sheriff. My husband couldna have done such a thing."

"Now, Miss Kate, you'll need to step out of the way. Pansy swore out a complaint last night, but I waited until this morning to arrest your husband."

Buck pushed Kate behind him. "She's lying."

"That's for Judge Pratt to decide. She has two witnesses who will swear otherwise."

Pastor stepped forward and held up his hand, clutching his worn leather Bible. "You're making a big mistake, Paul. He has an alibi."

"Like I said, Pastor, that's for the judge to sort out. My job is to lock him up for now. If you promise to come peaceably, Buck, I won't have to restrain you."

Buck looked down at her, his eyes pleading. "I didn't do this, Kate. You gotta believe me. In the morning, go hire that lawyer you talked to."

"Mr. Sauter." She clutched his arm, unwilling to let him go. "This can't be happening."

He gave her a pained smile. "Don't worry, darlin'. We'll straighten this out in a day or two."

She turned to the sheriff in anger. "You had to do this on a Sunday morning?"

"I don't get to pick and choose the day." He looked at Buck. "Let's go."

"We rented a buggy. I need to drive my wife back to town."

"That's fine. Glen and I will give you an escort."

Doc stepped up beside Buck. "Don't worry about Kate. Martha and I will take good care of her. We'll talk to Sauter first thing in the morning. You don't have to face this alone."

"Thanks, Doc." Her husband reached out and shook their friend's hand. "It means a lot to me that you believe I'm telling the truth."

"I'll go get Martha, and we'll be right behind you." Doc struck out for the church doors.

"I'll come visit you after the service, Buck," Pastor Russell said. "We'll be praying for you."

As Buck nodded, Kate turned to look back at the white clapboard church. Many in the congregation now stood in the yard, watching Buck's arrest, a few of them smiling in satisfaction, others shocked.

With her head held high, staring down Buck's accusers, several of them had the grace to look down in shame. Kate took Buck's hand and let him help her into the buggy. Then he climbed up beside her and turned the rig around in the church yard as Sheriff Granger and Deputy Madison flanked them on either side.

It started to snow more. Fitting somehow. She closed her eyes as the old doubts slithered back into her mind—thoughts of their troubles over the last several months. Thoughts of Pansy. The rumors racing through town.

She opened her eyes with a start when Buck reached over and took her hand.

"Look at me, Katie. I can't fight this unless you believe in me." It was almost as if he'd read her mind.

Staring into his deep brown eyes, worry lines creasing his forehead, the voices in her head receded. She believed him. He was innocent. She had forgiven him, and he had forgiven her.

She squeezed his hand. "I believe in you, Buck."

Despite the bleakness of the landscape, this was the day the Lord had made, and she would be glad and rejoice in it. She didn't understand why God had let this happen, but she had to believe He would bring good out of their trials and resurrect their shattered lives.

But how would she and Buck survive until His hand drew them out of this miry clay? Her husband—yes, her husband forever—pulled her against his warm side and drove the buggy one handed.

Buck gripped the iron bars of his chilly jail cell and spoke to Sheriff Granger who clanged the door shut and turned the key to lock him in.

"At least tell me who these so-called witnesses are. They're lyin' through their teeth!"

The sheriff stared back at him with sympathetic gray eyes. "Maybe, son, but like I said, once a serious accusation like this has been made against you, the judge has to make that determination."

"Tell me who they are." Buck's knuckles turned white as he gripped the bars, while the sour smell of his cell overloaded his senses.

"I don't suppose it makes any difference whether I tell you or not. Ruby Mason and Rafe Hamilton. The judge might discount Ruby, her being a madam and all, but Hamilton's father is an upstanding banker."

"But his son is a weasel," Buck growled.

"Now that's a fact." Sheriff Granger looked like he felt sorry for him. "But he'll swear on a stack of Bibles you did it, and Judge Pratt will have to decide if he's lying. I'll have my deputy bring you something to eat later. After my wife gets home from church, she'll feed you good. Might as well get comfortable till then."

Without another word, Sheriff Granger walked back to his office, his boots thumping on the pine floor, and shut the door.

Buck's shoulders slumped as he let go of the bars and looked around at the rock-walled cell with a barred window. Miserable, he sat down on the hard cot. No telling how many drunks and thieves and murderers had spent the night in this cell.

He'd only been in jail once back when he was still a stupid kid and started a fight in a saloon. The next morning, when he had sobered up, they let him go. It was Joe who put him on the straight and narrow.

Closing his eyes, Buck rested his forearms on his thighs and cried out to God for help—help to clear his name, for the lies to be exposed, and most of all for Kate to have faith in him, no matter what she heard.

The Bible said the Lord would never leave him nor forsake him. He clung to God's promise.

Only a miracle could save him now.

Chapter Twenty-five

THE NEXT DAY, KATE MARCHED INTO the sheriff's office, tired and cranky. She hadn't slept at all the night before. Deputy Madison rose from behind the desk.

"Mrs. McKean."

"I'd like to see my husband, please." Her words came out clipped, her chin tilted up. Wearing a dark-blue wool dress covered with her warm overcoat, she clasped her black reticule in front of her.

"I don't know if that's a good idea, ma'am." He shifted his feet and looked unsure of himself. He couldn't be much older than she.

"I want to see my husband, Deputy Madison," she snapped. "What do you think I'm here to do? Break him out of jail?" She opened her arms wide. "Obviously, I'm unarmed."

Still looking uncertain, he picked up the ring of keys from the desk. "I suppose it won't hurt nothing."

As he walked toward the cells in the other room, Kate followed him, the heels of her shoes sounding loud on the wide-plank floor. Nothing had prepared her for the foul smell of the cell area. When Buck saw her, he sprang from his cot and stood at the bars, an expectant expression on his face.

"Kate."

The lawman started to walk away. Kate spoke in a firm voice, her lips pressed thin. "Deputy Madison."

He turned immediately. "Yes, ma'am?"

"Unlock this cell and allow me entry."

"I'm not supposed to let anybody but the preacher sit with a prisoner in his cell."

"If you lock me in with him, neither of us can escape. This is cruel and unusual punishment beyond the pale. Separating a wife from her husband."

He shuffled his feet and stammered. "There's rules, ma'am."

"I shall file a complaint with Sheriff Granger if you do not let me in this cell." She hoped her indignant stature and her clipped words would sway the deputy.

"She means what she says. This little wife of mine is pretty stubborn." Kate recognized the twinkle of mischief in her husband's eyes. It gave her courage to stand her ground.

The deputy rubbed the back of his neck and looked at the floor. "Well, I suppose it won't hurt nothin' if she's locked in there with you."

Reluctantly, the deputy unlocked the cell and swung the door open on creaking hinges, allowing her to enter, and then he locked the cell behind her. "I'll be back in a minute. I can't let you stay long. The sheriff would skin my hide if he knew I was doing this." Deputy Madison turned and hurried into the office but left the adjoining door open.

Buck grinned. "Darlin', you shouldn't be here, but I'm glad you came."

She threw herself into his arms, and they hugged each other as if they'd never let go. He kissed the top of her head. Leaning back, she reached up to smooth away the worry lines between his brows. "Doc and I have been to see Mr. Sauter."

"And?"

"I couldna understand half of what he said, but he promised if he couldna get the charges dropped, he would represent you at your trial." She hesitated to tell him what else Mr. Sauter had said.

"What aren't you telling me?"

Kate sighed. "Mostly, unless...Pansy...withdraws the complaint or Rafe changes his story, it's your word against three."

His mouth tightened. "What about Mabel Cramer? She can testify I never went out that night."

Remembering the conversation with the snooty lawyer, she wanted to kick something. "He said the prosecution will say you could have stolen the key, unlocked the door yourself, and snuck back in later."

"That's idiotic." He ran both hands through his hair.

"Well, of course, it is." Fisting her hands, her words barely held back her anger at the so-called lawyer. She would fire the man, but he was the only attorney in town. "He said he would put Mrs. Cramer on the stand along with Doc and Mr. Stricklin as character witnesses. It's possible Judge Pratt might dismiss the case since your accuser is...you know...who she is."

"A soiled dove."

"Aye, and evidently, getting beat up is a hazard of her profession." The idea made her sick at her stomach.

"And if he doesn't dismiss the case?"

Kate hated to say the rest in fear it might come to pass. "Then you might be sentenced to a year or more at the Montana Territorial Prison here in Deer Lodge."

Buck's eyes widened, and his mouth opened. The thought of it was almost too much to bear. But he needed to know the truth.

"Mr. Sauter will argue for leniency," she continued, "and since it will be an all-male jury, there's a good chance your sentence will be short."

"In other words"—he ground out through clenched teeth— "if we can't get Rafe Hamilton to retract his statement, I'll probably go to prison."

She hesitated, the words almost sticking in her throat. "Aye. Mr. Sauter will try to establish doubt by bringing in Rafe's previous bad behavior, but the judge might not allow it."

Buck sank down on the filthy cot, resting his forearms on his knees, and buried his face in his hands. Kate had never seen him look so defeated. She sat down beside him, rubbing his shoulder, feeling the tight muscles under her hand. He sat up and looked at her, anger radiating from his face.

"He couldn't drive me out of the territory, so he's doing the next best thing—sending me to prison. I'm afraid for you, Katie. He won't stop until you agree to marry him. He's counting on you divorcing me while I rot in jail."

Her temper flared at the injustice. "Then he'll be waitin' until Jesus comes, because I'll never divorce you!"

Buck almost smiled. "That's my girl."

"We have a weapon he doesna have." She put as much strength behind her words as she could. "The truth is on our side, and God is fighting this battle. That's what Pastor said. I'll be prayin' for you day and night till you're proven innocent."

Buck pulled her into his arms and kissed her as if it might be for the last time. She returned his kiss with the same fervor. Rafe Hamilton wouldn't win. God would help her find a way to reveal the truth, even if she had to march over to Ruby's and talk to Pansy herself.

A soft snow was falling when Kate stepped out of the sheriff's office. She hesitated, looking first north toward Doc's office, and then south. Did she dare? She shivered and wrapped her scarf to cover her mouth. If she stood here much longer she'd be frozen solid. She turned her feet toward Ruby's at the edge of town, but she remained undecided for a moment.

Finally, she brushed the snow from her eyes and turned south, marching down the boardwalk with determination. She'd go straight to the source of the lies and cut off the head of the serpent for she knew the very devil himself was behind this plot.

By the time she had stomped the three blocks to Ruby's place, she was out of breath. From here, she could see the high stone walls of the prison in the near distance.

She reached out her hand to turn the knob of the red door, and then pulled her fingers away as if they had been singed. What was she thinking? She turned toward town and then stopped, straightening her spine. No one had ever called an O'Brien a coward.

Kate gritted her teeth and opened the door, smacking into a swinging saloon door on the other side. After pushing it open, she stopped as though her shoes were nailed to the floor. She had walked straight into the bowels of the netherworld. The sour smell of whiskey and cheap perfume assailed her nose. Blue cigar smoke hung in the air.

A massive, round, red velvet settee sat in the middle of the room, and although it was only noon, a woman with a painted face lounged on it in a purple satin wrapper. Kate stared in shock, her mouth open, and almost turned and ran. The woman raised up on her elbow with a smirk on her face.

With a trembling hand, Kate pushed the hair out of her face and broke the woman's gaze. The muscular man who stood behind the bar in a white apron, wiping down glasses, seemed frozen in time as he stared at her. At a corner table, the four men playing cards, smoke rising from their cigars, ogled her, smiles spreading across their faces. She felt like a cow at auction.

"Can I help you, ma'am?" the bartender asked.

She welcomed the interruption and strode to the bar, clearing her throat. "Aye. Yes, you can. I need to speak with Pansy Whitlow, please. I understand she...works here."

The bartender, a man in his early thirties, leaned his elbow on the bar and let his eyes roam from the top of her head to the tips of her toes and back. He grinned.

"I'll get Ruby for you."

When he walked from behind the bar stocked with bottles of every shape and size, Kate watched him mount the stairs and then stared at the polished bar surface a moment before glancing in the mirror. The girl was still there, looking bored, but she could also see one of the men rise from the corner table and straighten his green brocade vest. Her heart thundered in her ears.

Lord, protect me and give me strength to see this through.

As the man cocked his hip against the bar next to her, a woman's voice called out from the top of the stairs.

"Jake, leave her alone and get back to your game."

The man pulled the smoldering cigar from his mouth, stroked his black moustache, and grinned at Kate. "Ah, Ruby, I was hoping she was a new piece of merchandise." He tipped his hat at her and sauntered over to his gaming table.

Kate released a breath she didn't know she had been holding and looked up at the blonde, full-figured woman sashaying down the stairs in a pair of high heels and a red satin dress. Kate felt her face flame and clutched her reticule to her chest as if to ward off evil. She had been naïve to come here, but it was too late now.

The painted woman strolled toward her, swaying her hips. "You lookin' for a job, honey?"

"Nay!"

The woman smiled at her. "Shame. You'd bring in some new customers. Pretty red hair. I don't have a redhead right now."

Kate tilted her chin. "My name is Mrs. Kate McKean. I'm here to see Pansy Whitlow about her scurrilous accusations against my husband."

Ruby grinned and leaned against the bar. "Scurrilous, huh? You sure about that, honey? That big man of yours did a real number on Pansy. Broke her arm." She turned toward the bartender. "Whiskey, Nick." He poured the amber liquid into a shot glass.

Kate hesitated a moment, not knowing what to say, but then her temper rose. "That's a lie! My husband wouldna do such a thing. He's a married man."

Ruby lifted her chin and laughed. "Married? Most of my customers are married." She took a sip of whiskey. "Frigid wives keep me in business."

"I'm not frigid." Kate ground the words out through her clenched jaw and felt a hot flush warm her cheeks.

"Really? I heard you were still pure as the driven snow."

Kate's eyes widened, and she took a step back.

"In fact, I heard you almost filed for divorce because he spent the night with Pansy."

"He didna spend the night!"

"He didn't have to." A woman's sultry voice spoke from the top of the stairs. Her arm was tied tightly to her chest in a sling as she slowly made her way down each step.

"I told you I could handle this, Pansy," Ruby snapped. "Now go upstairs to your room."

"Are ya afraid she'll tell the truth?" Kate growled, her chest heaving.

Ruby gave her a tight smile. "Not at all."

"So, you're both willing to stand up in a court of law and lie. No one will believe you."

"I wouldn't be too sure of that, sweetie. A lot of those men on the jury don't want their wives to know where they've been plantin' flower seeds."

"Sure, it's possible they might not believe me" Pansy came to a stop beside Ruby, the fading green and yellow bruises still visible on her face. "But they'll believe Rafe Hamilton. He'll swear Buck McKean is a mean drunk and beat me to a pulp."

Ruby put her arm around Pansy's shoulder.

"Poor thing," Ruby said, her lips in a pout. "Hasn't worked a day since then." The madam took a sip of whiskey.

"Rafe Hamilton is a liar too!" Kate straightened to her full height and gave the woman a steely glare. "I want you to withdraw your complaint."

The woman had the decency to look guilty.

"You know," Ruby said, "when your husband goes to prison, you won't have any way to support yourself. I might be able to help you."

"I don't need your help. I can get a job as a waitress."

"They might not be too eager to hire a woman whose husband is in prison." Ruby smirked. "Bad for business. Besides, you'd probably only make six dollars a week. Can't hardly rent a room for that. Come to work for me, and I'll pay you twenty-six. This is the best job in town for a woman. After the first few times, you'll relax and start to enjoy it."

"If she couldn't satisfy her husband, Ruby, I don't know how she'd keep the customers happy," Pansy said. "You're wasting your time here, Mrs. McKean. I'll see you in court."

Kate turned and fled from their vile words, her heart sinking. How would she ever prove Buck was innocent?

Chapter Twenty-six

THE NEXT DAY, STILL DRESSED IN his Sunday clothes, Buck scrubbed at the dark whiskers on his face and paced back and forth in the small cell. His breakfast of fried eggs and bacon had congealed on the tin plate. He had no appetite. How could he fight Rafe Hamilton when he was locked up? He pounded the stone wall with his fist. There had to be a way. There had to be a way to fight back. If he was locked up in the territorial prison, he couldn't protect Kate from that snake.

But the trial was tomorrow, and he still didn't have an answer. How had Hamilton gotten it scheduled so fast? Three days. He exhaled. Sauter had been no help. The man acted like he was afraid of the Hamilton name. He was being railroaded, and there wasn't anything he could do about it.

As he had done since he'd been locked up, he cried out for God's help. He didn't know how the Lord would fight this battle, but he knew it would take a miracle now to get him out of jail. But why should he hope for mercy? A lot of men in the Bible got locked up, some for years—Joseph and even Paul. He'd pert near read through the Bible now. He practically lived in the Psalms.

He heard the door to the sheriff's office open, and he hoped it was Kate. He stood at the bars, looking at the doorway expectantly. She had been to see him every day since he'd been arrested, though he hated for her to be subjected to these conditions. The only thing that kept him from going crazy was that she believed in him.

Sheriff Granger strode through the door followed by Joe who carried a wooden crate in his hands.

"You've got a visitor, McKean."

"I brought you clean clothes, Buck. I didn't figure you wanted to stand up in court with the duds you've been sleeping in."

"Thanks."

Joe swung on the sheriff. "Well, are you gonna open the cell or not?"

"Only his lawyer and the pastor get that privilege. You can hand the clothes through the bars. I'm standing right here till you're finished."

Joe huffed and set the box down on the floor. He pulled out a pair of dungarees and shoved them in to Buck. "That's all you had clean. You're already wearing your best clothes."

"These will do. You got a clean shirt in there too?"

"What do you think, I'm dense?" Joe reached into the box and pulled out a blue chambray shirt.

"Don't I have another white one?"

"Don't gripe. That's all I could find. You had dirty laundry piled up in the corner, but I'm a little short on cash, so I couldn't take it to that Chinese laundry."

Buck sighed. "Clean clothes won't change the verdict. It's three against one."

"I should go beat the truth out of Hamilton." The old man raised an arthritic fist.

"Don't be making threats," Sheriff Granger said. "That's witness tampering."

"He didn't mean it, Sheriff." Buck glared at Joe. "You stay out of this, you hear? If I get sent to prison, I'll send a note to the bank and have funds released so you and the boys can head on back to Texas when the mountain passes open."

"I don't wanna ride all the way to Texas."

"My pa would give you a job."

"I told you I'm not goin' nowhere. I can get a job at one of the ranches to feed myself. Course, Billy might like to hightail it on home, but he'd be ridin' through Indian troubles by himself. I imagine he'll stay put too. Not sure about Josh. Told me once he lost his pa and two brothers in the war. Got a sister back east though. Gettin' a word out of him is like prying up a rock."

"How are you all doing?"

"Mrs. Cramer feeds us good." He grinned. "I like sleepin' in that bed all by myself."

"I bet you do, you old coot. What about Riley? You making sure he's got food and water?"

"You don't have to worry about that dawg none. He follows Mrs. Cramer round like a pup, and she's always loving on him, talkin' baby talk." Joe pulled on his grizzled beard and grimaced. "I swear he eats better than we do. Gettin' kind of fat."

"Any clean drawers in there?" Buck asked.

"Oh yeah." Joe pulled out a clean pair of red long johns and pushed them through the bars. Then he reached into the crate and gingerly pulled out a covered plate, lifting the lid.

Buck inhaled, and his mouth watered. He smelled cinnamon and nutmeg and whatever else Mrs. Cramer put in her apple pie. A slow grin spread over his face.

"Our landlady sent over a batch of hot fried chicken and taters and a big slice of apple pie."

"Haven't had much of an appetite, but that pie might change my mind." He looked over at the sheriff and cocked a brow, a mischievous grin on his face. "You don't have a gun in that magic box of yours do ya, Joe, so I can bust out of here?"

"I've already looked, McKean," the sheriff said dryly. "Anybody tries to break you out of here, they'll have to go through me first."

"He's just joking, Sheriff." Joe glared at Granger.

"I'll stay and take my medicine," Buck said, "whatever it is. God's truth will come out."

"For your sake, I hope so, but it's not looking too good."

Buck heard the front door open again.

Sheriff Granger looked over his shoulder into the other room, then he pointed a finger at Joe. "You stay put and behave yourself."

"Now how's he supposed to get this chicken if you don't open the door?"

"Slide the plate under the bars. Just stay put."

The sheriff walked into the other room and closed the door. Buck could hear voices, but he couldn't make out what they were saying.

"Glad he's gone." Joe struggled to bend over and push the plate under the iron cage, then grimaced as he stood up slowly, pressing a hand to his lower back.

"You'd better go. Thanks for bringing me the clean clothes."

"And the apple pie."

"That too." Buck picked up the plate. "You've been a good friend."

"Now don't go actin' like I'll never see you again. If that wife of yours has anything to say about it, you'll be out of here in no time."

"What are you talking about?" Buck suddenly had a sinking feeling in the pit of his stomach. What had Kate gone and done now?

"Well, first she went to that brothel and tried to talk that fancy woman into dropping the charges and —"

"She what?" he bellowed, almost dropping the plate.

"Don't take it out on me. She's a feisty little thing when she gets her back up about somethin'."

Buck set the plate on the floor with a clatter and gripped the cell bars. "Did you go with her?"

"No, I heard about it over at the mercantile. I overheard Stricklin and Doc talking. They were both fit to be tied. She went and faced down Ruby and Pansy all by herself."

"At Ruby's?" He pounded his head against the bars. Maybe he could get the sheriff to lock her up with him. It was the only way to keep her safe.

Joe chuckled. "That gal of yours is so mad right now, I doubt if anybody wants to tangle with her. Probably shocked the socks off those women."

"So, she's back at Doc's." Buck felt relief flood through his body.

"How should I know?"

"What do you mean you don't know?"

"I haven't been keepin' track of her! That's Doc's job. But Billy said he saw her ride out of the livery on Applejack about an hour ago."

Buck's brow furrowed. "She can't ride a horse."

"I don't suspect there's anything that little gal can't do if she puts her mind to it. Wears britches, doesn't she?"

"Where was she going?"

"Headed out toward the ranch. That's all I know."

Buck pulled his hair until it stuck out in every direction. "You and the boys go find her. If she'd try to get Ruby and Pansy to change their stories, she's liable to face down Rafe Hamilton all by herself."

Joe scratched his whiskers. "Billy did say she had a rifle in the saddle boot."

Buck swore and grabbed the bars, his knuckles turning white. "What are you waiting for? Go after her!"

"Now settle down and think about that for a minute. It's Kate he wants. He's not gonna hurt her, but if me and the boys go ridin' into his place all lathered up, he'll shoot us all for trespassing."

"If I wasn't locked up—"

"You'd probably get yourself killed. Maybe she can talk him out of testifying."

Buck knew Joe was right. There was nothing he could do about it now. He swore and shook the iron bars. If that snake so much as laid a finger on Kate, he'd— what? Buck buried his face in his forearm.

Lord, please keep Kate from doing anything stupid. Please keep her safe from all evil, especially Rafe Hamilton, and bring her back to me.

Kate threw her leg over the saddle horn and slipped off Buck's horse, bracing herself with a deep breath of warmer air. She smoothed the skirt of her long coat to make sure she was decent. Patting Applejack's neck, she stared with trepidation at Rafe Hamilton's sprawling white house. She'd only been here once before with Patrick for supper when Rafe was still acting all nice to impress her.

Tying Applejack to the hitching post, she held up her skirts to mount the steps and then clacked the brass knocker against the blue door. She clasped her hands at her waist, so nervous she was afraid she'd lose her breakfast if she didn't get a hold of herself. This was far worse than confronting Pansy and Ruby. Anger would be her only defense against Rafe. Righteous anger. But she wouldn't scream at him like a fishwife. She took a deep breath.

A woman wearing a large white apron over a blue-flowered dress answered the door, smiling.

"Hello, I'm Kate O'Bri...McKean. I'm here to see Mr. Hamilton."

The woman opened the door wide. "I'm Mrs. Palmer, his housekeeper. I remember you. Please come in and make yourself comfortable in the parlor. Would you like some tea or—"

"Nay. Thank you though. I need to talk to Mr. Hamilton for a moment."

"Beautiful day, isn't it? I love the sunshine."

Kate smiled politely and nodded.

"Before we know it the pastures will be full of wildflowers. I can't wait for spring to arrive."

Must the woman be so friendly? Kate wanted to say her piece and ride back to town.

"I arrived in May last year, and the weather was lovely."

"From Ireland if my memory serves me right. You have the accent. That brother of yours was such a handsome man. It's a shame what happened. So tragic." Mrs. Palmer clucked and shook her head.

"Aye, it was. Mr. Hamilton, please?"

"Oh yes. He's in his office. I'll go let him know you're here and then I'll fetch a pot of tea and a plate of sugar cookies I pulled out of the oven a moment ago. I'm sure you prefer tea to coffee."

"You dinna have to bother. I willna be stayin' long." Kate moved quickly into the parlor and perched on the edge of a brown horsehair chair.

"No bother."

Kate sighed when the woman finally bustled away. Her footsteps were muted by the carpet runner in the hallway. Chewing on one of her fingernails, she looked around the richly decorated room. Every piece of furniture was brown, and the elk head hanging over the stone fireplace stared down at her with dead, glassy eyes. She shivered.

Hearing heavy footsteps in the hallway, she leapt to her feet and put the sofa between her and the doorway. Rafe sauntered in, wearing a pair of denims and a white, collarless shirt unbuttoned at the top. A slow grin of delight spread across his face.

"I wondered when you'd finally come calling. I heard you visited with Ruby yesterday. A little foolish for a lady, don't you think?"

Kate's heart beat double time. She felt like the proverbial fly trapped in a spider web, but she feigned confidence. "I came to ask you not to testify against my husband."

"Is that a fact?" He dropped into a chair, hiking his polished black boot over one knee. He gestured toward the sofa. "You look like a scared rabbit, Kate. Why don't you sit down, and we'll talk about it?"

"I'm fine where I am, thank you."

A frown crossed his mercurial face. "Sit. Down."

Mrs. Palmer bustled in with a tray holding the blue-flowered, porcelain teapot, two cups, and a plate of cookies. She placed them on a side table and poured a cup of tea.

"Here you go, dear." She handed the cup and saucer to Kate whose hand trembled. "Let me know if you need anything else."

"Thank you, Mrs. Palmer. You can go now. We don't want to be disturbed." Rafe pulled a cigar from his pocket and twirled it with his fingers, but he didn't light it.

Her tea threatened to spill on the brown-patterned rug as Kate rounded the sofa and perched on the edge at the far end.

"Now, let's talk," Rafe said.

Kate set the teacup down on a side table and clutched her hands in her lap. Her chin lifted. "You know Buck didn't hurt that woman."

"Really?" He gave her an evil smile. "What makes you so sure?"

"He's not that kind of man, and you know it. You're willing to perjure yourself just to get rid of him."

"Perjury is a serious crime, Miss Kate. Who do you think the jury will believe? Him or me—a fine, upstanding citizen of Deer Lodge?" He leaned toward her.

"You're no saint, Rafe." Her words held a growl, but she kept a tight rein on her temper.

"Maybe not, but McKean is a stranger in this town." He paused and relaxed in his chair, looking smug. He slid the cigar into his pocket. "Of course, I might be persuaded to forgive and forget."

Kate's heart leapt with hope, but she knew Rafe well enough that there would be a price to pay.

"What are you suggesting?" She looked at him with narrowed eyes. He wanted something.

"I might be willing to talk to Pansy and have her drop the charges if—" A slow, evil smile spread across his face.

"If what?"

"If your husband leaves Montana Territory and never steps foot in Deer Lodge again. He's been a thorn in my side since he first rode in."

She felt relief. "Agreed. He and I will leave at our first opportunity."

"Now hold on, sweetheart. That's not part of the bargain."

Her heart clutched. "What's not part of the bargain?"

"You leaving with McKean. No, you're going to divorce your husband for desertion, and after the decree is final, then you're going to marry me."

Kate quickly stood. "You're insane! That's blackmail. I'll report you to Sheriff Granger."

"And risk sending your husband to prison?" he said with a satisfied grin. "I don't think so." He stood up and walked toward her. She backed away from him. "After I testify about how he tortured Pansy, beat her senseless, and twisted her arm until it broke, I doubt Judge Pratt will show any mercy. No telling how long he'll get in the territorial prison. And anything can happen in there. I hear men get into fights and kill each other all the time."

Kate's hand flew to her throat. If she didn't agree to his demands, he would make sure Buck died in prison. He had enough money to pay off the guards to look the other way.

"Nay. I won't do it!"

Rafe reached out and took her by the shoulders and tried to kiss her. She pulled away from his grasp and slapped his face.

"That's what I've always liked about you, sweetheart." His breathing quickened. He advanced on her again. "You've got fire. Makes a man's blood boil."

"Stay away from me." In terror, she retreated until she hit the wall. He put a hand on either side of her head and leaned in to kiss her. She turned her head, but he grabbed her jaw and forced a kiss on her.

A sob rose in her throat as she pushed against the hard muscles of his chest. He wanted her. He'd always wanted her. And he'd kill Buck to have her.

Finally, he pulled away and stared at her with hard, glittering eyes. His breathing was rapid. "Who's it gonna be, Kate? Me or him? He can leave and live, or he can stay and die. Your choice. Either way, you're mine."

Tears streamed down her cheeks. He ran his forefinger down her jawline. She recoiled from his touch.

"Now don't cry, sweetheart. I'll take good care of you. I promise."

"All right," she choked out. "Please, don't hurt him." When she uttered those words, her heart shattered.

"I'll keep my end of the bargain," he said, stepping away. She covered her face with her hands, not wanting to see the look of triumph on his. "In fact, why don't we ride into town together, and I'll go talk to Pansy and persuade her to drop the charges today. McKean'll be out of jail by nightfall." His voice turned cruel. "Then I want him and his men to hit the trail by sundown tomorrow, or I might change my mind."

She dropped her hands, swiping at the tears on her face. "I hate you," she hissed, glaring at him. "I'll always hate you."

He tapped her nose with his finger and looked like a boy who'd gotten what he wanted for Christmas.

"We'll see how you feel after our honeymoon, sweetheart. You might change your mind."

God forgive her, she spat in his face, and he slapped her—hard— snapping her head to the side...just as her stepfather had slapped her so many times.

Chapter Twenty-seven

BUCK RACED UP THE STAIRS TWO at a time to Doc's apartment, his boots pounding on every step. He reached the kitchen with its smells of cinnamon and apples and skidded to a halt when he saw Martha, worry furrowing her brow.

"Where is she?" he said, breathless. Doc's wife hugged him quickly.

"In the parlor."

Rounding the table, he stopped in the doorway. Kate stared out the window at the melting snow.

"Katie."

She turned, tears running down her cheeks, and he saw the ugly bruise on the side of her face that Doc had described. He opened his arms wide, and she ran into them, hugging him tight around his waist. Drawing her closer into an embrace, he buried his face in her hair and smelled the faint scent of lavender. He felt whole again.

"I'm not leaving here without you," he assured her, caressing her shoulder, his heart racing.

Tears moistened his eyes as he held her sweet face in his hands and touched the bruise on her face, wanting to kill the man who put it there. Tenderly, he kissed her cheek and then her soft lips. His Katie. His life. His love.

Finally, he pulled away from her and pulled her down on the sofa beside him, holding her tightly to his side. With every fiber of his being he wanted to ride out to Hamilton's place right now and put a bullet through his brain for what he had done to his wife.

"I love you, Katie," he whispered in her ear. "I love you with all my heart."

"I love you, too, Buck."

He pulled away and stared into her moist eyes that looked at him with sadness and defeat. Then he touched the ugly purple bruise on her cheek and kissed it again gently. He couldn't imagine the terror she had been through.

"He didn't..." His eyes held the question.

She shook her head vigorously. "Nay, but you've got to leave the territory, Buck. He'll kill you if you stay."

"Darlin'," he said, holding her face in his hands, "he aims to kill me whether I stay or whether I go."

"But they dropped the charges against you. He said if you leave without me, he'll let you live."

"Katie, look at me." She raised her head, and he thumbed away her tears. "As soon as me and the boys put some distance between us and town, he and his men will ambush us and bury us in shallow graves."

"But he said if I divorced you—"

He gave her a solemn look. "I thought we'd put that nonsense behind us. You and I are going to live out our days together right here in Deer Lodge. I'm glad Doc told me what happened while I was still locked up, or you might be a widow by now. But he convinced me to talk to the sheriff before they unlocked the cell door. We've got a plan."

"What kind of plan?"

He gave her a crooked grin. "All that's important is we're together again, and Rafe Hamilton won't win this war. We can outsmart him."

She palmed his cheek and stroked his face with a feather-light touch of her thumb. "I'm so afraid for you. If I hadna agreed to his plan to publicly spurn you, he would have sent you to the territorial prison, and he would have made sure you died inside. He's a madman."

"Don't worry, darlin'." He gave her a quick kiss and leaned back. "We need to talk about how to handle this, but first I smell something really good in the kitchen." He tapped the tip of her nose. "I've got plenty of time tomorrow to pull all my money out of the bank, pay off my account at the mercantile, and buy supplies. Hamilton's got men watching me, and he needs to believe I've had enough of this town. But let's enjoy ourselves tonight. By tomorrow night, with God's help and the sheriff's plan, this will all be over, and Hamilton will be the one behind bars. I can promise you that."

Kate buried her face against his chambray shirt. "I hope so."

"I know so." He stroked the worry lines on her forehead, then stood, pulling her up with him. "Now let's eat. I've got my appetite back."

Katie laughed, and it was music to his ears. He was a free man.

Kate's heart raced as she scanned Main Street and saw several of Rafe's men, lounging against business fronts or strolling down the boardwalk. She knew they were there to make sure she played the part of an aggrieved wife. Most of the town folks lined the walkways, wanting to see Buck get his due...to be run out of town to confirm their suspicions. This had to be the performance of a lifetime. Rafe Hamilton hadn't bothered to hide. He thought he was the author of this farcical play, but Buck had rewritten the ending.

The sun was low in the sky behind her, shining its soft golden light on Buck's strong features, hidden under his scruffy, unshaven beard. Rafe had already made sure everyone in town heard that Buck had lost his temper and given her the bruise on her face. Everyone had turned their backs on him. She only hoped when this was over, people would know the truth.

She wanted to throw her arms around her husband, but she knew she couldn't. Instead, she schooled her face to look at him with anger. In turn, his features looked as though they'd been carved in stone, but when she gazed into his soft brown eyes, she saw his love there, and that gave her courage.

Please, Lord, let this work.

Josh, Billy, and Joe sat in their saddles, watching them with long faces, while Buck said his good-byes on the boardwalk in front of Doc's office. Billy held the reins of a pack horse, and Sheriff Granger and his deputy straddled their eager horses ready to escort Buck and his men out of town. All part of the plan.

Rafe leaned one shoulder against the front of Bill Stricklin's mercantile, smoking a cigar, and smirked in their direction. Trembling, she edged closer to Riley's solid body and stroked the dog's head. He sat whining at her feet. Crossing her arms, she glared at Buck, playing her role in this charade. Rafe had to believe Buck was headed back to Texas.

Doc and Bill Stricklin stood beside her, glaring at Buck.

Her husband stepped forward and looked her square in the face. "Sorry it didn't work out, darlin', but I value my hide a whole lot more than staying here with you and facing prison time."

"I want you out of my life for good, Buck McKean," she shouted, touching the bruise on her face. "You've caused me nothing but misery since you rode into Deer Lodge."

Rafe *wanted* the town to believe Buck had hit her, had beaten her, so that when her divorce was final, no one would blame her for marrying Rafe. Half of Deer Lodge thought Buck was guilty of his crimes anyway, but Rafe still insisted on this public display of rejection by her when Buck left town. It had been part of Rafe's bargain to save Buck's life from prison and death.

"I'm sorry you feel that way." Buck jumped off the boardwalk and mounted Applejack, then tipped his hat at her. "I don't imagine I'll ever come through this way again. So long, darlin'."

"Good riddance."

Buck turned Applejack toward the south, loping away without another word. Her heart slammed against her ribs.

What if something went wrong? What if this didn't work? How would she ever live without him now that she had given her heart fully to him?

Riley whined, but she patted his side.

"It's all right, boy. We're better off without him."

Rafe couldn't know the truth—the truth that Buck valued her more than his life, that her husband would never leave her nor forsake her. In Rafe's twisted mind, he thought of life in terms of winning and losing, like a game of chance. He had won, and Buck had lost. Buck had been shot, tossed off his land, falsely accused and thrown in jail, threatened with prison, and now rejected by the woman he loved. What man would give up his life for a woman—a second-class citizen, a plaything to be used and abused? But he had underestimated Buck...and her.

Kate smelled Rafe's cigar smoke and turned at the sound of his boot heels on the boardwalk. Straightening her spine, she faced him without fear. Riley growled deep in his throat.

"Satisfied?" she hissed.

"It's a shame things didn't work out for you and McKean, Miss Kate, but at least you came to your senses about that liar and con man," he said loudly.

People drifted away, now that the curtain had closed on the play. It was the same people who attended every hanging. They were no better than the spectators in the Roman Coliseum, who watched and cheered as Christians were slaughtered. Speaking softly, so that prying ears wouldn't hear, Rafe gave her a triumphant smile. "I believe this is a cause for celebration, don't you? I'd like you to accompany me to McBurney's for supper. We have a lot to talk about."

Kate's heart skipped a beat. After what he had done to her, she trembled at the thought of standing alone against the evil that abided in Rafe's soul. This wasn't part of the plan. Rafe had told her that when he was convinced Buck had left town for good, he would leave her alone until her divorce was final.

"We have nothing to talk about, Mr. Hamilton."

"Besides, it wouldn't look right for a married woman to have supper with another man," Doc bit out. "What are you thinking, Rafe?"

Rafe seized her upper arm and squeezed her to his side in possession. "This is between Miss Kate and me, Doc. We have business to discuss."

"You'll ruin her reputation," Bill snapped.

Kate held up her hand. She was afraid Rafe would do harm to her protectors. "It's all right, Mr. Stricklin. We'll be chaperoned by the other diners."

She glanced up at the face she had thought so handsome when

she had first come to live in Deer Lodge. But she had found out quickly that Rafe had no conscience when he tried to force himself on her a few short weeks later. If Patrick hadn't heard her scream... She shivered in remembrance. He was evil incarnate.

"I'll escort her back to your place, Doc," Rafe said, blowing cigar smoke into the air, "after we're through discussing our...business. Isn't that right, Miss Kate?"

Looking at Doc and then Bill, she pleaded with her eyes for them not to interfere. Right now, she was more afraid for these two dear gentlemen than she was for herself. Doc's hands had fisted at his sides, and she was afraid he might do something foolishly gallant. With the sheriff and his deputy gone, there'd be no one to stop Rafe from hurting them.

"I'll be fine," she said, with a tremulous smile at Doc. "It's only supper at McBurney House."

"That's right." Rafe smiled as he held his cigar in one hand. "It's only supper."

Doc finally relented. "I'll leave the office unlocked. Martha and I will be waiting for you, Kate. Don't be long."

"Of course. I'll be home soon." Riley started to follow her, but she put up her hand. "Stay." The dog obediently sat down next to Doc.

She let Rafe lead her down the boardwalk, his hand still gripping her arm.

When they were out of earshot, she barked at him. "You can let go now."

"Only if you put your arm in mine and paste a smile on that pretty little face of yours. I want to enjoy your company tonight."

He let her go and dropped his cigar to the boardwalk, crushing it under his boot exactly as he had crushed her. He offered his arm, and she reluctantly slipped her hand into the crook of his elbow, her skin crawling at the thought of touching him.

"This wasna part of the bargain," she spat. "I'll file for divorce tomorrow like you asked, but it will be at least a year before it's final. Then you can come courting."

Rafe chuckled. "And risk you running out on me? I don't think so.

I'm an impatient man, Kate. You should know that by now. I've already talked to Judge Pratt, and he'll bend a few rules to push your paperwork through. You'll be a free woman soon. The judge owes my father a lot of money."

"You're a blackguard," she hissed. "Why are you doing this? You know I'll never love you."

He leaned down to whisper in her ear, an intimate gesture that everyone still on the street would see. Her face flamed.

"Because you're mine, sweetheart. You'll always be mine. If you had only married me like I wanted, nobody would have gotten hurt."

She had known without a doubt that Rafe had killed Patrick, tried to murder her husband, and burned down their cabin, but that he had done it all just to possess her body and soul chilled her to the bone.

A quiet fury stiffened her spine. For now, she would play along and eat supper with him, but he wouldn't win. The derringer Buck had bought for her today felt heavy in her pocket and gave her a measure of comfort. If need be, she wouldn't hesitate to use it.

Now that it was dark, a half-moon and the stars their only light, Buck veered off the road into a stand of cottonwoods along the river. Joe, Josh, and Billy followed him. Several men on horseback waited for them under the canopy of trees.

"Granger?" Buck whispered.

"He's comin'," Deputy Madison whispered back, holding the butt of a rifle against his thigh. It was too dark to make out the faces of the rest of the men in the posse. "Probably took him a while to circle back through town and hightail it out here."

They waited in the gloom for what they all expected to happen next. A set of pounding hooves galloped down the dirt road and pulled up quickly, the horse blowing loudly. The sheriff joined them and patted the neck of his horse as it flipped its head, jangling the reins.

"Steady, boy," Granger said as he turned his horse in a circle.

"You ready for this, McKean?"

"More than ready."

In silence, they waited another fifteen minutes and were not disappointed. Finally, a group of riders rode hard toward them in the half-light.

"Wait till they pass before we show ourselves," the sheriff whispered. "If we can help it, I don't want any bloodshed tonight."

A group of six riders, with scarves tied over their faces, flew past them, the posse's sign to give chase. But the sheriff signaled them to stay back under the trees and rode out alone, discharging his gun into the air.

"Halt!"

The masked men reined in and rounded on the sheriff, guns drawn, ready to fire. It didn't look like they were giving up without a fight, and Buck sucked in his breath. Granger had ridden into a hornet's nest.

When one of the gang pointed his gun straight at the sheriff's badge, Granger dove off his horse and darted behind a tree, cursing under his breath. While the posse followed suit, Hamilton's men fired blindly into the trees and then spurred their horses to take off across the prairie through the tall buffalo grass.

"Guess we got us a gunfight," Buck said, not bothering to lower his voice.

"Anybody hurt?" the sheriff yelled.

"No," each one yelled out.

"Then let's get after 'em." Sheriff Granger remounted his horse. As they rode out from under the cover of the trees, Buck kept pace with the lawman who looked over at him. "You recognize anybody?

"Nah. You?"

"A couple, but Hamilton's not riding with them."

"I shoulda known he wouldn't get his hands dirty." Buck raised his voice over the sound of their horses racing through the blowing grasses.

"They're headed in the direction of the hot springs mound. They'll never make it that far. I guess they figure they can take cover there and hold us off. No place else to hide out here. Open fire," Granger yelled. Gun blasts went off around them, and one of the gang was knocked out of the saddle.

As they continued to chase the men farther away from town, something niggled inside of Buck's belly. It was like God was trying to tell him something. The farther he rode with the posse, the stronger he felt a sense of urgency to find Kate. Panic gripped his gut.

"Granger," he yelled. "I'm headin' back to town. Hamilton stayed for a reason. There's nobody left to protect Kate."

The sheriff cursed again. "I shoulda thought of that. The men can take care of this. Hamilton's liable to kill you and make it look like self-defense."

After letting his deputy know what they were doing, Buck and the sheriff veered off from the posse and turned their horses around in a wide circle. Then he rode Applejack like a man possessed, praying with every breath he took for God to keep Kate safe.

Kate didn't even pretend to eat the food on her plate. Instead, she sat there and watched Rafe drink champagne and eat a steak. Even the thought of food turned her stomach.

"Now, Kate, don't be like that. Smile." He sat back in his chair and downed another glass of champagne. He'd almost finished the bottle by himself.

When they had walked into McBurney's, there had only been a few people at the tables, but now the place was filled with the aromas of fine dining, the noise of conversation, and the sound of silverware clinking against china. No one looked at them. When they had seen her with Rafe, they had all acted as if she didn't exist.

Rafe had ruined her life and her reputation, and now he expected her to smile and play nice. She wouldn't give him the satisfaction.

"No?" He cocked a blond eyebrow, a smug look on his face.

She glared at him.

Standing up, he reached into his pocket and pulled out a generous amount of money and tossed it on the table. She felt relief. Soon, this night would be over.

Chapter Twenty-eight

Rafe gallantly pulled back her chair and helped her to her feet, then offered her his arm. She refused and turned her back on him to walk to the entrance. The next thing she knew, he slid his arm around her waist and pulled her tightly to his side. She tried to step away, but his grip was like iron.

"I'm in the mood for a stroll, sweetheart." His voice rose, loudly enough for everyone to hear. Her face flushed hot. "Such a nice evening."

Removing his hand from her waist, he opened the wide door for her to exit onto the dark street and escorted her outside. He stroked her back in full view of every window.

"Now take my arm like a good girl, Kate."

Gritting her teeth, Kate slid her hand into his outstretched elbow, and he turned south rather than north toward Doc's.

She stopped, but he pulled her along, gripping her arm to his side. Her heart raced with fear. The street turned darker the farther they walked.

Digging in her heels on the plank boardwalk, she struggled to escape. "Let go of me." He grabbed her hand and bent back her arm until she thought the bone would snap. A tiny yelp escaped her throat, but there was no one to hear.

"The night is still young, Kate." He inhaled deeply and jerked her tightly to his body, twisting her arm behind her back.

"No," she groaned. Her mind froze in terror.

Buck! Buck, help me! God help me! Someone help me!

"If you scream," he hissed in her ear, "I'll break your arm like I did Pansy's. Now smell the pine trees. There's nothing like the promise of spring in Montana Territory."

Without a doubt, Kate knew he would do what he threatened. The man was insane.

"When we're married," he went on, as if they were out for a leisurely stroll, "I'll let you redecorate the house any way you want. Would you like that? Maybe we'll take a trip to Virginia City for our honeymoon. No, somewhere back east where it's more civilized. Europe maybe. Nothing's too good for my bride."

She tried to pull her arm away again, but he only twisted it harder until tears flowed unchecked down her face. "Please, Rafe. Let me go."

He ignored her and kept spinning fairy tales as if they were a couple in love. "I'll buy you expensive dresses and take you to the finest restaurants in New York. We'll stay in the finest hotels."

Suddenly, she realized they were almost at Ruby's, and she dug in her heels again. Her heart banged against her ribs as they drew closer to the alley. "Take me home!"

No one was on the street, but she could hear the piano music and laughter coming from the brothel.

"Not yet, sweetheart. Tonight, you're all mine. McKean may have been a fool to wait on your favors, but I'm putting my brand on you tonight. Then you can't walk away." He chortled with glee and easily lifted her into his arms.

"Help!" she screamed as loudly as she could and tried to wrestle free.

He only laughed. "I told you not to scream, Kate. Now I may have to hurt you."

Her body shook as fearful images swept through her mind. Panic squeezed her heart as she pushed against him to escape.

Rafe stepped into the alley, but she continued to scream for help. Kate clawed at his face, but he quickly stood her on her feet and crushed her against the rough siding of Ruby's place. Then he claimed her lips with a cruel, hard kiss. Bile rose in her throat as she tasted his cigar and champagne. She tried to wrench her head away, but he gripped her face with a steel hand and forced another kiss on her.

Finally, he pulled back, panting.

She screamed. "Help! Somebody help me!"

His slap snapped her head to the left, leaving her dizzy, but she'd not go quietly. If she could only reach the gun in her pocket.

"Women scream around here all the time, Kate. They'll think you're having a good time."

Unexpectedly, he slung her over his broad shoulder and strode toward the back of Ruby's, opening the door into a hallway lighted by a candle in a wall sconce. He swiftly mounted a back stairway, as she once again tried to reach her gun. Slung over his shoulder like a slaughtered calf, the lower half of her body pressed tightly against him, it was impossible to slip her hand into her pocket.

Left with no access to her weapon, she pounded on his back. "Put me down! Help!" Her words had no effect on him.

She heard Ruby's foul laughter coming from the top of the stairs. "My room's all yours, Rafe. Be my guest."

Kate felt like such a fool. Why had she ever agreed to dine with him? She knew what kind of man he was, but she couldn't have ever conceived that he was evil enough to kidnap her.

"Stop squirming," he said, a smile still in his voice. "Relax and enjoy the beginning of our lives together."

"I'm still married to Buck McKean," she screamed at him. "And I always will be."

"Ah, but you're still pure, so it doesn't count. I'll be your first, exactly like I always knew I would be."

He kicked open a door and tossed her on the bed draped with a red brocade coverlet. Scrambling off the bed on the other side, she backed away from his hard, blue eyes, frantically searching the room for a means of escape.

The derringer. She pulled the gun from her pocket and held it out in front of her, her hands shaking violently. She would have only one chance. It only held a single bullet, but it was deadly at close range.

Her stark fear and the strong smell of perfume permeating the room made her nauseous. There was no one else to save her.

Lo, I am with you always, even unto the end of the world.

An evil grin slashed across Rafe's face. "Feisty. That's what I love about you, Kate."

"Stop or I'll shoot!"

He laughed at her again. "You haven't got it in you. Now hand me that toy pistol."

As he reached for the gun, she closed her eyes and squeezed the trigger.

WITH BUCK'S HEART THUNDERING IN RHYTHM with his lathered horse, he rode past the looming territorial prison at the outskirts of Deer Lodge, frantic to find Kate. The sheriff rode right behind. A dark figure ran into the main street, waving his arms and yelling "Buck!" Applejack almost ran the man down, before he could rein in his mount.

"Doc, where's Kate?"

The doctor planted his hands on his knees, panting, before he could answer. "Rafe's got her. He took her to supper at McBurney's, and she was supposed to come right home. But when I came looking for her, neither Kate nor Rafe was there. I talked to a couple on the boardwalk walking fast toward your office, Sheriff. They heard a woman scream and saw a man push her into the alley by Ruby's. I think it was Kate."

Buck leapt out of the saddle and dropped Applejack's reins on the ground, sprinting toward Ruby's, with Sheriff Granger on his heel. As he slammed open the swinging doors at a dead run, Buck heard a shot upstairs, followed by a woman's scream. His heart stopped. He shoved through the crowd at the smoke-filled bar and ran toward the stairs, but Ruby blocked his way. Her face looked pale under her paint.

"You can't go up there."

He growled and shoved her aside before he pounded up the stairs two at a time, the sheriff right behind him.

"Kate!"

Another scream issued from a room at the far end. Breaking glass. Like a wild man Buck tore down the hallway and reached for the doorknob. Locked. He kicked the door and splintered it wide open. Flames from a smashed lamp licked the wall and burned the red brocade curtains hanging at the window.

Rafe held Buck's wife, his fisted, bloody hand raised to hit her in the face. Buck launched himself through the air and knocked the other man to the floor before the blow found its mark. He landed on top of him, his fists pummeling Rafe's head. He felt a strong grip on his shoulder, pulling him back, but he jerked away and landed another punch.

The crackle of flames grew louder, but Buck didn't care. Pure rage drove his fist into Rafe's bloody face.

"McKean!" Granger shouted as he grabbed Buck's arm and dragged him off Rafe. "You'll kill him."

It gave Rafe enough time to pull the gun still belted at his waist. Buck wrenched free from the sheriff and seized the barrel, grappling the pistol toward the ceiling. The gun fired, singeing his fingers.

Rafe kneed him in the groin, and Buck fell against the sheriff, knocking them both to the floor. They were trapped in the small space between the bed and the armoire.

Scrambling to his feet, Rafe pointed the gun at Buck's head, but before the man could fire his weapon, a shot rang out. A bullet pierced Rafe's brain.

The sheriff dragged Buck to his feet and toward the door, flames now engulfing the bed. Buck resisted, frantically searching the room for Kate.

"Buck!"

He turned and saw her standing behind Pansy who still held the gun out in front of her, her face emotionless. Even with one of her arms in a sling, she had killed Rafe.

The sheriff grabbed his shirt and pulled him toward the doorway. Buck could feel the heat of the flames at his back.

"We've gotta get out of here," Granger yelled in his ear over the roar of the fire.

Pansy turned, the gun hanging loosely at her side, and shuffled toward the stairs like a sleepwalker.

Buck's eyes locked on Kate's, and she coughed, covering her nose with her hand. His eyes stung from the thick smoke. He had to get Kate out before the whole place went up in flames.

The sheriff shoved them both through the splintered doorway. "Get her outside!"

Buck wrapped Kate's hand in his and pulled her through the crowded hallway. Soiled doves screamed, running down the stairs, as their customers shoved ahead of them.

The hallway had filled with smoke, and it was hard to see. At some point, Kate had dropped his hand and now clung to his arm. Frantic, he pushed ahead.

Finally, they made it to the stairway. He looked back and saw the flames licking the flocked walls of the hallway. The sheriff protected Kate from behind. He spotted Pansy at the bottom of the stairs pushing through the crowd toward the entrance. A jury would never convict her of murder. He'd make sure of that.

As they scrambled down the staircase, Kate tripped behind him, but his solid back broke her fall. He reached behind him to steady her as they fled down the wooden stairs. When they reached the bottom, they were almost crushed by the mob escaping. Coughing, Buck pulled Kate by the hand and pushed toward the swinging doors. The upstairs was fully engulfed in flames. No bucket brigade would save Ruby's from the fires of hell that raged through the building.

Finally, he pushed out into the chilly night air, his hand still clinging to Kate's, and ran to the other side of the street. Coughing, he pulled her into his arms.

"Are you all right?" he cried. She nodded and continued to cough.

Suddenly, shattered glass showered down on them as the fire shot out of the windows. Realizing how close he had come to losing Kate, he held her tightly and kissed every inch of her sooty face. A cough rose in his throat, and he broke the sweet moment as his lungs spasmed.

He dropped his hands to his knees and coughed up more smoke, sucking in clean air, while Kate pounded on his back. With burning cinders raining down on them, he stood and pushed her farther along the street. The building could collapse at any time.

It was finished. Rafe was dead, and God help him, he couldn't find a single bit of remorse inside of him. If he hadn't nearly ridden Applejack into the ground...if Doc hadn't run into the street and yelled at him...if he hadn't gotten there in time...

He crushed Kate to his chest, smelling the smoke in her hair, and thanked God she was still alive. He heard a crash, and they both turned to watch the roof of the building collapse, sparks and burning embers flying out into the street.

Buck saw Ruby in her red satin dress, standing shoulder-to-shoulder with Sheriff Granger, passing buckets of water down the line as they tried to save the barber shop and bathhouse next door. A second line formed to throw water on the Chinese laundry. They'd be lucky to save either one.

Buck walked Kate farther down the block. "I need to help." He kissed her forehead.

"I know."

"Go on back to Doc's, and I'll be there when I can."

Buck saw that stubborn look cross her face and knew he would lose this battle, even though one of her sleeves hung by a thread.

"I can help." She ripped it off and pulled up the sleeve on her other arm.

Frustrating woman! "Kate, I won't let you—"

"You won't let me? I willna stand by and watch as businesses burn because of me."

"For Pete's sake, it wasn't your fault Hamilton dragged you into Ruby's and..." The words stuck in his throat.

Tears started to her eyes. "I knocked over the lamp."

"While you were defending yourself against that animal!"

He couldn't bear to think of what could have happened to her. He groaned and took her face in his hands, kissing her gently, hoping he could persuade her to leave. "Please go."

She stepped back and stroked his cheek with a delicate hand. "I'm not a china figurine knocked off a shelf. I'm not broken."

He sighed, knowing she wouldn't leave without a fight, so he might as well give in now.

"All right, but stay at the back of the line."

She smiled and kissed his cheek. "Go. I'll be fine."

He ran to grab a bucket and filled it with water from the trough.

By dawn, despite the best efforts of its citizens, Deer Lodge had lost the whole block, but at least they had prevented the fire from jumping across the street. Kate had spent more hours than she could count dousing embers that floated through the air and landed on other buildings. When she hadn't been able to lift her arms anymore, she had leaned against the wall of the blacksmith's shop, shivering in the cold night air. But she wouldn't leave.

The dawn, streaked with lavender, pink, and gold, promised a beautiful day. Kate stood on the boardwalk and watched Buck stumble to throw another bucket on the blaze even though only a few men were still able to stand. Even the sheriff had given up.

Her husband's hair and clothes were covered in ashes, and his face and hands were blackened with soot. But the man wouldn't quit.

Finally, she walked quickly to him and tugged on his arm. "Buck, you've done your best. It's time to stop."

His glazed, weary eyes looked down at her, and the wooden bucket slipped from his fingers. Hugging him close, she smelled the acrid smoke that clung to them both. He swayed against her.

"You're dead on your feet." Kate pulled his arm over her shoulders. "The fire will burn out on its own now. Let's go home."

"We don't have a home," he whispered in a hoarse voice.

She savored the feel of him against her. "Home is where you are."

He hugged her tightly. "I could have lost you, Katie. I should've stood up to Hamilton and stayed—"

Stepping back, she looked up at his red-rimmed eyes. "You would have gone to prison, Buck McKean, and that's the truth of it. Rafe Hamilton was a wicked, wicked man, and he got what he deserved."

Buck palmed her cheek and kissed her. "I'll take you back to Doc's and then head over to the boarding house to clean up."

"You'll do no such thing. We are man and wife."

He smiled at her. "As much as I'd like to share a bed with you, darlin', we've waited this long. We can wait a little longer."

If her face hadn't been so black with soot, he surely would have seen her blush. She dipped her head, but he tilted up her chin with his finger and kissed her.

Throwing his arm over her shoulders again, they turned away from the ruins of Ruby's and walked down the middle of the street toward Doc's place.

Chapter Twenty-nine

More than a month after the fire, Buck couldn't stop smiling as he drove the single seat buggy toward the little grove of trees he'd found along Cottonwood Creek. Kate's softness snuggled against his side filled him with contentment on this warm May morning, the sun shining in a cloudless blue sky, the perfect day for a picnic. Wildflowers bloomed on the prairie in a rainbow of colors to soothe the eyes—white columbines, yellow buttercups, blue lupines, pink shooting stars.

Looking down at her, his heart swelled with love. She sighed and leaned her head against his shoulder.

"Happy?"

"Aye, I couldna be happier."

He kissed the top of her head, her copper hair shot through with gold, glowing in the spring sunshine. Then he guided the buggy off the road and headed toward the stand of cottonwoods.

He helped her down and carried the quilt and picnic basket into the shade. Together, they spread the covering on the ground. He pulled off his hat and sat cross-legged on the quilt, leaning his head back to look at the wide, blue sky. "This makes the winter worth it."

"It surely is a beautiful land."

He loved the lilt in her voice. He loved her kind heart and her courage and her strength and her love of God.

Reaching over, he stroked her soft, ivory cheek with the tip of his finger and tucked a stray curl behind her ear. Her hair refused to stay put in the soft breeze. She smiled at him with love in her eyes, and he thought his heart would burst. As she laid out the food for their picnic, he couldn't take his eyes off her.

He stroked her arm. "Have I told you today how much I love you?"

She shivered when he took her hand and kissed each finger, then caressed her palm.

"Behave yourself." She swatted him playfully. "You said you were starving."

"I am...for you." He grinned widely.

"Well, I'm not on the menu today." She gave him an impertinent smile and smoothed her skirt.

Laughing, he picked up a cold chicken leg, took a bite, and chewed slowly. "I have a surprise. Well, actually two."

Reaching over to take her hand, he rubbed his thumb over her gold Claddagh ring. "I talked to Pastor Russell yesterday."

"Oh?" She raised her eyebrows.

"He's agreed to bless our marriage in a ceremony next Sunday. It won't be a wedding, but you can still wear a white dress and wildflowers in your hair like you always dreamed. And the whole church will be our witness. It'll be like a fresh start."

Her emerald-green eyes sparkled with teasing humor. "Do ya think we need a fresh start?"

"I want to make your dreams come true." He leaned over and kissed her. "This time we can walk down the aisle side-by-side."

"You're not going to carry me again?"

He had been thinking about this a lot. "I want you to be able to walk away if you want."

"And where would I be walkin' to?" Her tiny hand took his and shook it. "Buck, I'm not Angel. Nay, we've fought too hard for our marriage. I'll not be leaving you standing at the altar."

He searched her face and knew she was telling him true.

"Now eat your dinner before the ants carry it away." She brushed a large, black carpenter ant off the quilt. The corners of her mouth lifted, then she looked at him with curiosity. "You said you had two surprises. Have you found a place for us to live?"

"As a matter of fact, I have." He leaned back on his elbow and crossed his ankles.

"Really? Where exactly? Is it close to town?"

"Slow down." He laughed at the excitement on her face. "About as close as before."

He ripped a piece of chicken off the drumstick and chewed.

"Mighty fine chicken."

Swatting him on the arm again, she snatched the chicken leg from his hand before he could take another bite. "Tell me."

Grinning, he dragged out his surprise for her, chewing slowly. She looked like a little girl who couldn't wait to open her gift on Christmas morning.

"Well, we need to build a house, but it has a bunkhouse and a sturdy corral already. We can build a chicken coop for you. The root cellar looks solid."

"Can we graze a herd of sheep?"

He drew his brows together. "I'm a cattleman, not a sheepherder."

"I want a few sheep."

She smiled and ran a finger down his shirt sleeve. Did she know what she did to him? He cleared his throat.

"Okay, you can have a couple of lambs."

She clapped her hands. "And Riley can watch over them and keep them safe."

"I suppose so since he's a sheepdog. He's gotten kind of fat and lazy though, what with Miz Cramer treatin' him like a baby that needs to be fed every two hours."

She laughed. He loved her laugh. He loved everything about her.

"If it's an existing homestead, why do we have to build a house?"

"Well...the cabin burned down. We have to rebuild and..."

His food lay forgotten because he sure wasn't thinking about eating. He leaned forward to kiss his wife's sweet lips, but before he could, she squealed and threw herself into his arms. "Our place? You bought our place back?"

"That's the one, darlin'."

She smacked a kiss on him and gripped his shoulders with both hands. "Tell me everything! How? When? Mr. Hamilton sold it back to us? But what about the money? How can we afford it?"

He laughed at her excitement. "I checked with another lawyer in Virginia City. Not Sauter, the crook. The sales contract wasn't even valid because you were under twenty-one when you signed the papers."

She looked puzzled and drew back. "Why would that matter?"

"Because we were married, and you needed to be at least twenty-one to dispose of your inheritance."

She frowned, and Buck's heart skipped a beat. Now he'd stepped in a cow patty. "I thought you'd be happy."

"I am happy, but that doesna seem fair, does it? Women should have rights."

"Did they do it different back in Ireland?" His dark brows furrowed.

"No, as my husband, you would have owned all my property. I just thought it would be different in this free country."

"There's a do-gooder project for you. Maybe you can work to change the laws someday."

"Maybe I will. Women should have the right to vote too."

He pulled her into an embrace, her breath warm on his cheek. "If anyone can change the law, darlin', you can."

Oh my, it was like holding heaven in his arms. But he had to stop kissing her if he wanted to make their blessing day special. With great restraint, he gently pushed her away.

"Chicken," he croaked. After running his hands through his hair, he reached for another drumstick and bit off a huge chunk. If he was chewing, he couldn't kiss her again like he wanted to. He hoped she had a lot more food in that basket.

With pink shooting star flowers wound in her hair and wearing a white lace dress the ladies of the church had made for her, Kate felt like a new bride. She turned to face Buck out behind the church in a meadow dressed in all of God's glory, a bright blue blanket of heaven above them, and sun shining on his dear face. She had dreamt of this moment since she was a little girl, and now her dream was coming true with the man she loved. Their first wedding was a distant memory.

"You may now join hands," Pastor Russell said. "O Lord, you have so consecrated the covenant of marriage that in it is represented the spiritual unity between Christ and His Church. Send therefore your blessing upon these your servants that they may so love, honor, and cherish each other in faithfulness and patience, in wisdom and true godliness, that their home may be a haven of blessing and peace; through Jesus Christ our Lord, who lives and reigns with you and the Holy Spirit, one God, now and forever. Amen."

Kate broke her gaze with Buck and glanced over at Pastor Russell, smiling from ear-to-ear.

"Even though you were already married in the eyes of the church," Pastor continued, "you are now doubly blessed. Kate has asked me to read a traditional Irish wedding blessing for you." He pulled out a piece of paper from his Bible and read from it.

"May the road rise to meet you.

May the wind be always at your back.

May the sun shine warm upon your face,

and the rain fall soft upon your fields.

And until we meet again, my friend,

May God hold you in the hollow of his hand.

"You may now kiss your bride...again."

Grinning, Kate stood on tiptoes and Buck bent down to gently place a kiss on her ready lips, then picked her up and spun her in a circle. The congregation gathered around them clapped and laughed, even the women who had not believed in Buck's innocence at first. He set her down and kissed her again before they turned toward their church family. She thought her heart would burst with happiness.

Now and forever, their hearts were joined as one.

Buck inserted the key in the lock and swung open the door. His hands were damp, and he wiped them on his black twill trousers.

"It's the same room—number 210," he said. "I hope that's all right."

Kate looked up at him, smiling nervously. "Aye, it is."

They stood there in the hallway, lost in each other's eyes. He had forgotten almost all the advice Doc had given him so long ago for his wedding night. All he could remember were the words, "slow and gentle."

Slowly, gently, he bent down to lift his little Irish sprite into his arms. "Ready?"

She nodded and blushed, and he carried her across the threshold. He was more nervous now than he had been on his first wedding night. Tonight, they would finally become man and wife, joined as one. He wanted to cherish her and honor her and love her in a way that would be pleasing to God. With Christ at the center of their marriage, they were a three-strand cord that could not easily be broken.

Before setting her down, Buck caressed her lips with his, wanting her to love him as much as he loved her. Her arms entwined around his neck, and he kissed her thoroughly before he pulled back to search her face.

"I love you, Katie girl," he whispered, "as Christ loved the Church and gave His life for her."

"I love you, too, husband." Then she initiated their next kiss filled with promise.

EPILOGUE

AFTER SETTING A BOWL OF FRIED potatoes on the table outside, Kate shielded her eyes from the bright sunshine and watched her husband and the other men from church build a second bedroom onto their cabin.

Buck's muscled back strained against the wet chambray shirt as he pounded nails into the last of the wooden roof shingles, sweat dripping off his chin. The pleasant days of May and the memory of their wedding blessing had tumbled into a broiling summer, and now it was early September and still hot. Soon it would be winter again. The year had passed so quickly. When her husband drove the last nail, he and Josh slapped each other on the back.

Once she had gotten to know Josh, she held a deep respect for what he'd been through in the war. A lesser man would have given up on life. She hoped he would find a wife soon and settle down near them. She caressed her swelling belly.

She ignored the women who bustled around her, loading down the table with cold fried chicken, ham, roasted mutton, pickled beets, potatoes, and a variety of vegetable dishes and pies. It was enough food to feed an entire army, but the men would be hungry. They had started before dawn.

As she shaded her eyes, looking up at Buck, he glanced her way and wiped his face with his sleeve. Their eyes locked, and he grinned and winked at her. This was their home, their land, their future—the place where they would raise their children.

Someone rubbed her back gently, and she turned.

"He's a handsome man, and that's a fact." Martha stared up at Buck.

"Aye, I canna disagree with you."

"You deserve to be happy. You've both been through so much. I'm so glad you were able to rebuild here."

"It truly is a miracle, isn't it?"

As Buck climbed down the ladder, he looked so proud, and rightly should he be. They lived in a beautiful, sturdy home that would keep out the winter cold. It would be where all her wee babes were born. Aye, this was their home. Not Patrick's. Not hers. But theirs.

Pressing her hand to her aching back, she smiled. Tonight, she and Buck would snuggle together and talk about the wee one growing inside of her. Beaming, she praised the Lord for fulfilling every dream of her heart.

AUTHOR NOTE

Eric Liddell, a Scottish Olympic runner and missionary to China, once said, "I believe God made me for a purpose, but he also made me fast! And when I run I feel his pleasure."

Dreams of My Heart was conceived and written to rekindle the sheer joy of writing in me. God made me for a purpose. He gifted me with the abilities and skills not only to write, but from my first days as a newspaper reporter, He also taught me to edit.

While working as an editor at a Christian publishing house, I was faced with a decision one early morning in prayer. It was as though God whispered that He had many authors eager to serve Him and write books, but few who were willing to give up their writing dreams to encourage those authors, to acquire and edit their books, and to publish them.

Because of the way God knit me together in the womb, I could not be both a writer and an editor and survive my long, stressful days at work. He reminded me of another time in prayer many years ago when He said I was more like a thoroughbred, who had been made fast to run a short, mile-long track, but I had the heart of an Arabian horse bred to run long distances through the desert sands. Though my heart longed to continue writing *and* editing, I could no longer do both.

So I asked God to take away my desire to write. And He did. Instead, He gave me the desire to become an author's editor—one who loved her writers, encouraged them, talked them off the ledge when they despaired, assured them that yes, they had talent, and walked hand in hand with them through the mysterious world of publishing.

Then I retired. Surely now I would have the time to write and God would restore the desires of my heart. But I had nothing to say— nothing that people wanted to read. I continued to edit other authors' book manuscripts from home on a freelance basis. Like Abraham, I laid my child on the altar and lifted my knife to sacrifice my dreams for God if that was what He wanted.

Just as the Lord provided a ram in the thicket for Abraham to sacrifice instead of Isaac his beloved son, the desires of my heart flooded me with the story of Buck and Kate. Because my best friend Gwen Ellis grew up in Deer Lodge, Montana, she had told me the stories of her family and the small town—about her brothers who worked as cowboys on the Grant-Kohrs Ranch, about her parents who ice fished in the winter and hunted deer and elk to feed their family, about her dad who worked at the copper mines. I fell in love with the setting and wanted to know more about its history.

In my twenties, thinking I might move to Montana, I drove across the state to Glacier National Park. I loved the wide blue sky that seemed to go on forever, and the scent of pine trees and new fallen snow. But I didn't belong there. I was only a visitor. Little did I know, I would immerse myself in research to spin a story for you to visit as a reader. To fall in love with Montana. To fall in love with characters who lived in a real place and battled issues we still face today—rejection, fear, abuse, and the struggle to trust God and those who love us. Wounded people who find healing through the grace of God.

Thank you, Gwen, for reading the manuscript and pointing out any errors in my research. Who knew holly didn't grow in Montana? Gwen did.

When I research, I feel like a child blowing the dust off an old trunk in the attic and opening it to find what's inside, discovering a treasure trove of interesting bits of history. As I researched every aspect of the novel, including the annulment of a marriage, I thought it would be easy to dissolve a union in those days that was never consummated. I had no idea what I would discover. Annulment of a marriage in 1870s Montana Territory involved a lot more than having a judge sign a piece of paper. An annulment was only granted under specific circumstances. The whole novel is impacted by the difficulty of dissolving the marriage between my reluctant, Irish bride Kate and her Texas-born cattleman husband Buck McKean.

I didn't write this novel in the hope that it would be published, but rather for the sheer joy of writing again—to allow my imagination full rein. Even the music score from *Chariots of Fire*, the movie that tells the inspiring true story of Olympic runner Eric Liddell, often played in my head when I sat at the keyboard. God made me fast, Liddell said, and when I run, I feel His pleasure. In the same way, God made me a writer, and when I tell His stories, I feel His pleasure. I hope you felt the same way, too, as you read Kate and Buck's story.

BOOK CLUB QUESTIONS

1. When you read the title *Dreams of My Heart*, what's the first thing you thought of? Did Kate and Buck fulfill their dreams for the future, or by the end of the book had their dreams changed? Have you experienced a time when your dream changed to something you didn't expect?

2. In chapter 1, Kate is faced with a difficult decision. Put yourself in her boots. What would you have done differently? Did Kate have other choices?

3. Why is Kate a reluctant bride? Does her faith in God affect her decision to marry Buck? Have you ever faced a time when you did something you believed God was leading you to do, even though you didn't feel joy or excitement about doing it?

4. What happens to Buck to make him realize he needs to put his life in God's hands rather than depending on himself as a man? How is he changed after his encounter with Jesus Christ?

5. What emotional issues do both Kate and Buck need to overcome before they can love each other? Have you experienced a time in your life where God needed to heal your heart or your past, before you could fully move into the plan He had for your life?

6. Kate has experienced fear, pain, and abuse in her life at the hands of men. She has survived, but not without scars. How did her faith in God help her to finally trust Buck?

7. Do you think Rafe was insane, the product of his upbringing, or an evil man? Dig deep here—if evil, could he have changed? If the product of his upbringing, was he at fault?

8. Why did Kate believe Rafe's account of the terrible events at Ruby's and its aftermath rather than her husband Buck's account? Have you ever chosen to believe something a person told you that sounded right,

but didn't quite hit your spirit as truth? What is the best course to follow when you hear gossip and want to believe it?

9. What do you think happened to Pansy after she walked out of Ruby's? Is there redemption for a soiled dove like her?

10. How did good finally overcome evil in *Dreams of My Heart*?

A SNEAK PEEK AT BOOK TWO

Love of My Heart

Coming February 1, 2019

CHAPTER ONE

Boston, Massachusetts
May 1877

RAIN, AND NOT JUST ANY RAIN, pelted Beacon Hill with rare fury. A Nor'easter, a widow maker some said, when the waves, the rain, and the clouds churned together to turn the world into shifting shades of gray.

The kind of rain Joshua Carpenter knew as a boy, then as a young man before he left.

But he was back now, back home, such as it was. Such as *he* was. He paid the hansom cabbie, grabbed his seam-worn carpetbag, and dashed up the wide stone steps as a clap of thunder rolled down the South Slope. He banged on the door with his fist, ignoring the brass knocker.

No one answered.

He banged again with more purpose.

Still nothing.

He was about to crash through the door when it swung open, whining on creaking hinges. It didn't open quickly, either, but with a meek and measured pace, slower than he expected.

Joshua stepped forward, expectant, then stopped. "Reginald?"

He thought he breathed the name, but he wasn't sure.

The old man faced him as if he didn't know him. Then the clouded blue-gray eyes shot open wide, his mouth went loose, and he opened his arms like he'd done for so many years, long ago.

"Master Joshua!"

"Reginald." Joshua dropped his bag and stepped into the hug that felt older and weaker—frailer—because it was.

The old man stepped back, stared up into his face, then clasped his hands against Joshua's cheeks. "We'd given up hope long ago."

Anguish vied with joy on the old-timer's features, and Joshua understood both. "I've come home, Reginald." He thought he glimpsed hope in the elderly butler's eyes, but then a commotion drew his attention.

Four children, whom he presumed to be his nieces and nephews, stampeded to the front door and surrounded him, all talking at once. The youngest boy threw his arms around his waist and looked up in wonder.

"You came! Please don't let him take us away."

Puzzled, Joshua looked at Reginald for an answer, but the butler only stepped back from the fray, his face beaming, and closed the door.

Joshua crouched down in front of one whom he presumed was his nephew and clasped the boy's shoulders. "And who might you be?"

"He said you weren't coming." The tow-headed, seven-year-old boy hugged him around the neck. "He said we had to go live with him. I don't want to go."

Joshua's brow furrowed. "Who said I wasn't coming?"

The children all spoke at once, their voices colliding with the rain beating against the leaded-glass side windows.

At the sound of a quiet step on the stairs, his gaze turned to a tall woman dressed in black who had the warmest pair of light-brown eyes he had ever seen. She was dressed in a plain skirt and a high-necked shirtwaist, the black of mourning, with her slender hands clasped at her small waist. Her smile brought warmth to the chilly foyer.

"Mr. Carpenter. We're so glad you've come...and just in the nick of time. Children, please step back and let your Uncle Joshua take off his coat."

Reluctantly, the children quieted and looked at him with sheer joy on their faces, almost as if he were their savior.

Shrugging out of his dripping jacket, he took off his black Stetson and handed them both to Reginald, never breaking his gaze with the stunning woman. He pulled his soaked chambray blue shirt away from his chest and flicked water droplets from the fabric onto the marble floor.

"Reginald, would you please fetch us a tray of tea?" she said and then turned back to look at him. "Or would you rather change out of those wet clothes first, Mr. Carpenter? You're absolutely drenched."

Although normally a quiet man, he felt positively tongue-tied now.

"Mr. Carpenter?" she repeated.

"Yes, I'd like to change, but first...who are you?"

"Oh, how remiss of me. I'm the children's governess—Miss Emma—Miss Emma Stowell."

Governess. Of course, the children had a governess. "Joshua Carpenter."

"Yes, I know. That seems to be obvious." Her smile lit up the room. She looked at him as though he were a savior too.

Breaking his stare, he grinned at the eager children. "I think we should start with introductions, don't you?" He looked down at the overjoyed little boy who still clung to his side.

"I'm William, but you can call me Will. Are you a real cowboy?"

Josh chuckled. "I am indeed."

"I'm Lucy. I'm eight." The blue-eyed, raven-haired girl's face beamed. She looked so much like him, she could have been his daughter.

A pain pinched his heart when he stared into the pale face of the oldest boy. His features favored Josh's sister Sophia.

"Richard Covington, sir." The ten-year-old boy held out his hand to shake. He had a firm grip, much like his deceased father Henry.

"Ah, the man of the family now."

"Yes, sir."

Dressed in pink, golden blonde hair spilled over the shoulder of the blue-eyed girl nearing womanhood. "Then you must be Sarah," he said. "The last time I saw you...let's see...you were about four."

The girl giggled. "I've grown up since then. I'm fourteen."

"Yes. Yes, you have grown up." It seemed so strange how life had continued on a totally different course during his long absence. He had missed so much.

Glancing toward the governess, he allowed himself a moment to examine her soft, oval face. With her hair swept up into a bun on top of her head, the style emphasized her widow's peak and the long sweep of her neck. She was stunning.

Forcing himself to break his gaze, he turned to Reginald. "Will I be sleeping in my old room?"

"No, sir. That's Master Richard's room now. We've prepared the main suite for you." He struggled to pick up Josh's heavy carpetbag.

"Here, let me take that." Grabbing the handle, he looked at the children and Miss Emma, a rare smile on his face.

"I'll join you in the parlor shortly." He turned to the elderly butler. "A cup of hot coffee sounds better than tea, Reginald."

"Of course, sir. I'll tell Cook."

With his boot heels sounding loud on the Italian-marble floor, Josh maneuvered around the numerous stateroom trunks and carpetbags piled high in the foyer. He turned and raised a questioning eyebrow at the governess but decided to pursue the circumstances after he changed.

Mounting the polished mahogany staircase to the second floor, he strode down the carpeted hallway to his parents' room. Once his mother passed away, though, Sophia and Henry made it theirs. He still couldn't believe his fun-loving, older sister and her husband were gone.

After entering the silent room as though it were a sacred place, he sat down on the blue brocade coverlet and let the memories flood his mind. The sound of his mother's laughter. Chasing a squealing Sophia down the hall. Being tackled by his big brother Joe in the garden. He should have come home sooner. The last time he had seen them...the last time he had seen his father... His thoughts turned dark. He didn't want to think about the war, nor the months he spent after in the mourning house where he had been born.

The weight of his new responsibilities as guardian rested heavily on his shoulders. Before he escaped Boston, Sophia and Henry made him promise to take care of Sarah if anything should ever happen to them. Maybe it was their way of making him stay and fight his demons—to give him something to hold on to. Looking back, if he were Sophia, he would have been the last person he asked to care for a child. But to please his sister, he had signed the papers and never given his pledge another thought. He never dreamed she and her husband would pass before him.

Coming to himself, he stood and unbuttoned his wet shirt and then opened his carpetbag for a dry one. His gun belt lay on top. He had needed it on the range, but he doubted he'd ever have a reason to use it on the streets of Boston. Rummaging through his dirty clothes, he finally found a wrinkled white shirt that wasn't too bad and a pair of black trousers. His Sunday clothes.

After what the children had suffered, how would he ever tell them he was taking them back to Montana Territory with him? Or should he stay and raise them here? He'd thought a lot about it on the long, uncomfortable train ride slumped on a wooden bench to sleep. But he still didn't have an answer. All he knew was that Boston held too many painful memories for him.

Sighing, he pulled the shirt over his head.

Emma escorted the children into the parlor, rain still slashing against the bay window on this dark gray afternoon.

"Perhaps you should change as well, Will. You're quite damp after hugging your uncle."

Will looked down at his blue, long-sleeved shirt. "Do I have to?"

"I think it best. You don't want to catch a cold."

"I won't catch a cold. I can stand by the fireplace and dry out." He looked at her with pleading, dark-brown eyes. "Please, Miss Emma?"

Emma gave him a stern look, but her heart wasn't in it. "All right, but wrap an afghan around your shoulders and go stand by the fire. Not too close though."

Sitting down on one of the blue velvet sofas, the two girls sat down on either side of her and laid their heads on her shoulders.

Sarah sighed. "Everything will be all right now, won't it, Miss Emma? You won't go away now, will you?"

"Of course not." She put her arms around them both. "Your Uncle Joshua is here now, and he will need help." The moment the tall, sun-darkened man had swept through the door, the knot in her stomach had slowly untied itself. They needn't worry now.

She hugged the girls. They had been through so much, first losing their parents in that horrid train wreck at Christmastime, and then Mr. Covington's attempts to steal the estate and take the children back to his home in New York, not to mention her abrupt dismissal. Today had been her last day. They expected their father's cousin had arrived when they heard the banging on the door.

"Uncle Joshua came." Lucy snuggled closer, a sweet smile curving her lips. "He *does* want us. I'm so very glad."

"Me too." Emma kissed the top of the little girl's head. "Everything will be all right now."

Sarah sat up and turned to her in excitement. "And next year, I can have my coming-out party."

"Fifteen is still too young," Emma cautioned. "Perhaps when you're eighteen."

"Lots of girls come out at sixteen. Fifteen is only a year younger."

Emma tucked a wisp of blonde hair behind her young charge's ear. Sarah was so eager to grow up.

"Your mother and father wanted you to wait. Don't you think we should respect their wishes? You have lots of time to find a beau."

"Who's looking for a beau?" Mr. Carpenter said, striding into the room, filling it with his larger-than-life presence.

Mrs. Covington had talked about him and read some of his letters to her, but nothing could have prepared her for this bronze giant with hair like a raven's wing and deep-blue eyes. Broad in the shoulders, his rumpled shirt strained against his muscular frame. He wore black twill pants and the same pair of worn black boots. The dark circles under his eyes and his unshaven face testified to his long trip.

She smiled at him when he settled into a wing-back chair. "Sarah is already planning her debut into Boston society."

"But she's still a child."

Sarah frowned and crossed her arms. "I am not a child. I'll be fifteen in November."

"And too young for a husband," he said in a firm but gentle tone. "You're still a schoolgirl."

Emma smiled inwardly and thanked God again for their uncle's arrival.

He looked at Emma with a serious expression. "Now, what's this about someone coming to steal my wards?"

The children all started talking at once, and he held up his hand for silence.

"Miss Stowell?" He leaned forward and rested his arms on his knees, a furrow etched on his face between his black brows.

An angry blush warmed her cheeks. "Since it had been so long since the family attorney sent a letter, as well as a telegram to you, Gerald Covington laid claim to the children and the estate. He is the cousin of the children's father. When Mr. Morton—"

"Our family attorney..."

"Yes. When Mr. Morton received no word from you, he assumed you had decided not to exercise your rights as guardian of the children."

"I just received his letter a few weeks ago. Mail is slow, if not impossible, during the winter. The mountain passes have been closed for months this winter with snowdrifts as tall as a house. And we don't have a telegraph line in Deer Lodge yet. The nearest is in Virginia City."

Emma's face turned white. "Then it's truly a miracle you arrived today, Mr. Carpenter. Mr. Covington's train from New York should have arrived by now. He plans on coming straight here and taking the children home with him tomorrow morning."

"And you? Were you going to take care of the children for him?"

"No, I was dismissed. Everyone's been dismissed. I planned on moving back to Hingham to live with a great aunt. I haven't been able to find another position as a governess since I don't have a letter of recommendation. As soon as we've vacated the house, Mr. Covington plans on selling it."

Mr. Carpenter's jaw hardened. "He can't dismiss you, and he certainly can't sell the house. After my mother's death, I inherited it. I own my father's shipping company outright too. Henry only managed the business for me. Henry's cousin has no authority to dismiss you."

She believed him. He projected the qualities of strength and confidence—of a man not to be trifled with.

"Mr. Covington is contesting the will on the grounds that you have abandoned your birthright and have no intention of taking on the responsibilities of the children and their trust fund."

Unexpectedly, the children's uncle pounded his fist on the arm of the chair, a look of fury on his face. Startled, the girls clung to her, and Richard walked behind the sofa to lay a protective hand on her shoulder. William plopped down at his uncle's feet, an eager smile on his face.

"Are you going to shoot him?" William asked.

"Children, why don't you go up to the playroom while Mr. Carpenter and I unravel this."

"You won't leave, will you?" Lucy scooted off the sofa and ran to his chair.

The heir of his family's fortune pulled the girl onto his lap. "Of course, I won't leave you. I'll never leave you."

"What about Miss Emma?" She hugged him tight.

"Miss Emma isn't going anywhere either."

Emma's heart nearly burst with relief. He looked over Lucy's shoulder at her, the promise resonating in his determined eyes.

"Thank you, Mr. Carpenter." She breathed easier.

He smiled, and she felt an unfamiliar flutter in her stomach.

"Please, call me Josh. Out West we don't stand on ceremony. Tomorrow, I'll speak to Andrew Morton, and we'll sort out this mess."

A knock on the front door alarmed her, and fear swept across the children's faces. Lucy whimpered. Her uncle stroked her silky black hair that looked so much like his own and set her gently beside him before he stood.

"Covington?" Mr. Carpenter's blue eyes reflected his anger.

She could only nod, her heart in her throat, as both William and Richard crowded around her. When Reginald shuffled past the open drawing room doors to admit their unwanted visitor, the children's Uncle Joshua looked down at her. He must have sensed her fear.

"Don't worry. I'll handle this." He strode from the room and closed the sliding doors behind him.

"What took you so long?" A pompous popinjay pushed past Reginald, handing him a dripping black umbrella. "My bag is in the carriage. Fetch it."

"Reginald," Josh said, a lethal tone lacing his voice. "That won't be necessary. Mr. Covington won't be staying."

The blond, sour-faced man with a paunch, narrowed his eyes, raking him with a disdainful glance. "The prodigal brother, I assume."

"You assume correctly."

"You needn't have bothered making the trip. The court has already granted me temporary custody of Henry's children." He pulled a legal document from his inside pocket and offered it to Josh. "You're the one who won't be staying."

Reginald retreated behind Josh as he advanced to snatch the paper from Covington's outstretched hand. He scanned its contents.

"This order is signed by a New York judge. It's worthless in the State of Massachusetts. Sophia and Henry's will is irrevocable and states clearly that I am the children's guardian. They won't be going anywhere with you."

If he had any doubts about instant fatherhood, they dissipated the moment he entered the front door and was surrounded by his nieces and nephews. He itched to pick Covington up by the seat of his pants and toss him outside in the driving rain. But he was in Boston now, not Montana Territory. As difficult as it was, he restrained himself from pounding Henry's obnoxious cousin into the floor.

"Now I suggest you leave."

Covington sneered at him. "And what makes you think you can provide the care and oversight those children need. They don't even know you. You abandoned your mother and sister and disappeared. I'm surprised you're still alive."

Josh kept a firm grip on his temper, but his jaws ached with the effort. "As you can see, I'm very much alive. Now get out of my house before I throw you out." He swung the door wide.

"Your house? You're sadly mistaken."

Josh extended an arm to usher out the intruder. "I'm afraid you're mistaken. This is my house. You've overestimated your ability to steal the children's inheritance, Covington. My attorney will be in contact soon. Don't bother coming back."

He towered over the man in silence until Covington harrumphed and grabbed his dripping umbrella from the stand. "We shall see about that."

"Yes, we will."

When Covington retreated to the stoop in the driving rain, Josh slammed the front door in the man's face, the echo reverberating through the house. He turned as the drawing room doors opened and squeals of delight and applause greeted him.

"Well done, Master Joshua," Reginald said, smiling. "Well done. Welcome home."